To The Valley

By Kenneth Jewett

IP

ITHACA PRESS

NEW YORK

To The Valley

Ithaca Press
3 Kimberly Drive, Suite B
Dryden, New York 13053 USA
www.IthacaPress.com

Cover Design	Gary Hoffman
Cover Art	Original Oil Painting *Valley of Virginia* Paul McMillan
Book Design	Gary Hoffman
Edited by	Erika Cooper

Manufactured in the United States of America

9 8 7 6 5 4 3 2 1

Library of Congress Cataloging-in-Data Available

Jewett/Kenneth
Historical Fiction/American Fiction/Biographical

ISBN   978-0-9786211-9-3

www.KennethJewett.com

❧ *Author's Note* ❧

Every attempt has been made to depict events accurately using original historical documentation and reference books. In many cases, the documentations varied in the retelling of the same event. Often, individual accounts were vastly different and, in those cases, the author chose the description most useful for this story. The fictional characters' contain additional information that may not be verifiable. Actual historical figures grace the pages of this book. These characters were developed using information gleaned about their individual personalities from the writings they left behind and the observations written about them by their contemporaries

In addition, the author is grateful to the Rockbridge Regional Library, the Rockbridge Historical Society, The Colonial Williamsburg Foundation, and the Jewett Family of America.

❧ *Dedication* ❧

*T*his book is dedicated to the memory of Robert Wayne Jewett ("Sir Robert") and Mahala Elizabeth Jewett ("Aunt Bess"), two very special people who left an indelible mark on their extended family.

Preface

*E*ach time I visit Colonial Williamsburg, I send my nephew, who shares my love of history, particularly colonial history, a letter written as if I were visiting this city at some momentous point during our struggle for independence. This resulted in growing pressure from my family to expand this into a novel featuring family members and set in the Valley of Virginia, where I had property. My brother even went so far as to provide a list of characters as a way of encouraging me to move ahead with the writing. After retiring from the Air Force following 30 years of service, I ran out of excuses and sat down to write this novel.

Like with the letters my nephew received, I have placed family members in and around real events occurring during the years immediately prior to the opening of the French and Indian War. I have stayed very close to the personalities of several of my family members in writing this work, particularly those of my father, R. Wayne Jewett; his aunt, Mahala E. Jewett; my cousin, Esther Jewett; brother, Gregory L. Jewett; and his son, my nephew, Philip G. Jewett. For the other family members,

I stayed close to their personalities, where possible, but took more liberties where it would better fit the circumstances of the storyline. I am sure all of my family I have chosen to include will find things about their characters that do, in fact, match their personalities.

Where I have inserted a real historical character, I have tried to remain as close as possible to events they were known to have participated in. The main difference is the insertion of members of the family into the scenes. Edward Jewett, for example, is not based on any historical person though the events swirling around him are as accurate as I was able to make them.

Place names have changed over the years and I have strived to use those correct for the period by referring to the Frye/Jefferson Map of Virginia from 1751. So Staunton reverted to Beverly's Mill Place; Rockbridge County, the site of the Jewett family settlement and Bordon's Grant, reverted to being a part of Augusta County; the Maury River reverted to its original name of North River; Washington and Lee University at Lexington reverted to Augusta Academy located at Timber Ridge; and Natural Bridge reverted back to being called simply the rock bridge. I also saw enough 18th Century references to Richmond as "Richmond Town" to infer it was in common use before 1780 when it became the state capital.

Kenneth Jewett
2008

☙ *Chapter 1* ❧

*T*he Boston packet had barely touched the Rowley docks when the ship's Master and another man leaped
ashore and headed toward town. Mail was regular in a
town this close to Boston that was served by a good river
port but this was apparently something of some import.
By time his companion had directed the Master to the
store of merchant Robert Jewett, they had drawn quite a
following of townspeople, both the idle and the curious.
Seeing the crowd approaching, Robert met his visitors at
the stoop.

"Master Cole, is something amiss? Henry?" Rec-
ognizing his youngest son, Master Cole's companion and
normally too busy with his Boston carpenter's trade to
visit his father, Robert dreaded ill tidings.

"Mister Jewett, no, sorry to cause you concern. I
have a letter from Colonel Jewett, delivered into my hands
by the Captain of His Majesty's Frigate *Surprise* yesterday
morning. I sent a runner for Henry and brought him along
with all haste, knowing as I do how concerned your whole
family has been over the Colonel's safety since he went on
the King's business to the Mohammadans in Algiers."

Colonel Edward Jewett, oldest of Robert's three sons, had lived a rather charmed life since his father sent him to England to be properly educated, now 30 years ago. Having befriended James Russell and becoming a regular guest at that family's estate, James' father, the Fourth Duke of Bedford, had taken a liking to the young man and secured a commission for him in the Royal Army. From there he had proven his worth in successive campaigns and advanced in rank accordingly. This service, and his Colonial origins, resulted in his selection, not without Lord Bedford's influence, to command the Royal American Artillery during the siege and capture of the French Fortress at Louisburg, the entrance to the Saint Lawrence River. This made Edward a favored son of Rowley, which had contributed its share of men to the campaign and very little news of the Colonel was not eagerly passed around the town and surrounding villages.

The capture of Louisburg being the only high point of England's involvement in the War of Austrian Succession, called King George's War in the colonies, resulted in a colonelcy for Edward and presentation at court to His Majesty. Lord Bedford, now the Secretary of State for the Southern Department, employed his protégé in the aforementioned mission to try to curb the piracy of the Ottoman Empire states in Northern Africa against English shipping in the Western Mediterranean. While letters from Edward had never been frequent, mostly attributed to the distance and hard service, Robert had received no news since the troubling letter announcing Edward's most recent challenge and he was most anxious to tear open the now proffered packet then and there, but it was not his way.

"Thank you, Master Cole," said Robert and, ushering Henry into his small office off the store, he added "I know Aunt Bess made a fine roast for dinner and I'm sure you're hungry." Indicating to Master Cole the door to his adjacent house, he now sent his grandson, Philip, who was, as always, loitering near his grandfather, to fetch his middle son, Lewis, from his carriage shop. Lewis had become quite comfortable employing wheelwrights and carpenters making carriages, mostly riding chairs. Henry had chaffed in his brother's employ and sought his fortune in Boston, much to their father's dismay and not, as things turned out, to the betterment of Henry's fortune.

Though disappointed not to be invited to the reading of the letter, Master Cole was partial to Elizabeth's roasts. She was Robert's spinster aunt who had moved in following the death of Robert's wife and helped him raise his three sons and keep his household. While the family had arrived on these shores over a century earlier, and there were plenty of Jewett's both in Rowley and the surrounding towns and villages, Robert and his sons were the only family Elizabeth, known as Aunt Bess, had left in the world.

In very short order, Lewis arrived, breathless from having run to his father's store. He entered and took his normal seat near his father's desk, where his father was already seated. Henry had pulled a chair nearby and Philip slipped in to sit on a chest in the corner. Without looking up, Robert addressed Philip. "I know you're curious, but this is for your father, uncle, and me to read first. You will have your chance at its contents in due course. Now, please go keep your Aunt Bess and Master Cole company."

About to protest, Philip saw the look from his father and the barely perceptible shake of his head, indicating he could expect no support from that corner. Well used to keeping company with the adults, he reluctantly moved to the door, stopped to be sure there would be no recall, and then left the men to the letter.

Robert began by noting to his sons that the letter had been posted from London two months earlier. He then broke the seal and unfolded the heavy paper. Edward had thoughtfully included his good health and recent return to London in his opening lines, much quieting his father's fears. His mission to Algiers had been disappointing to him, but the King was satisfied by the reduced tribute he had managed to negotiate with the Dey of Algiers. Then came the big news. He had requested and been placed on the retired list and was returning to the Colonies.

Lewis took the paper from his father, whose emotions with this long awaited news made it too difficult to continue to read. Aside from the short visits both before and after the siege at Louisburg, he had seen little of his eldest son these 30 plus years and felt his absence daily. To him at this moment there was nothing more contained in the letter as important as this, or so he thought.

As Lewis continued, Robert quickly refocused his attention when he learned that George Montagu Dunk, Second Earl of Halifax and then serving as the first commissioner of the Lords Commissioners of Trade and Plantations, had arranged for a Royal Grant of 10,000 acres for Edward and had written a letter of introduction to the Governor of Virginia whose colony contained the grant. And Edward was proposing to share the grant, keeping half for himself and splitting the other half between his father and brothers.

"The rents alone," he wrote, "will provide a substantial income and comfortable circumstances for the entire family."

Lewis looked to Henry and Robert, seeing the same look of shock and amazement on both that he was feeling. They sat for several minutes, each lost in their own thoughts on what this would mean to them and their children. In addition to Philip, Lewis and his wife Marie had adopted the orphan Joseph Palmer into their household. Henry and his wife, Mary, had a son, Charles, and an older daughter, Sarah. Robert, in addition to providing for Elizabeth, still had an unmarried daughter, Esther, at home. Both Robert and Lewis were quite comfortable in their estates, though hardly Gentlemen, while Henry continued to struggle to provide for his family. Each knew this would make them landed and change their fortunes and those of their family forever.

Edward proposed meeting in Williamsburg, capitol of the Virginia Colony in the middle of May and repairing together to the grant, located in the newly formed Augusta County, west of the Blue Ridge and watered by the North River. Again looking at each other, all three realized just traveling to Williamsburg would consume the scant two weeks to the proposed meeting. The contents of the letter having thus been revealed, the three spent the next hour in serious discussion on how to respond to this generous and wholly unexpected offer.

By time they finished, it was dusk and the store was closed. Robert locked the door as they left and went to his adjoining house. Meeting them in the candlelit hall was Aunt Bess. Short and stout, she could intimidate any man that did not know it was mostly an act. Belying her 80 years, the hair that fell from under her cap was still mostly raven colored streaked with grey. She always attributed her good health and energy at such an advanced age to having avoided becoming entangled with men, even though she had raised two generations of men and was working on the third.

"Shame on you, Robert, and you, too, Lewis, for

keeping me waiting to hear the news of Edward," she squawked in feigned indignence. Then, grabbing Henry in one of her famous hugs, she welcomed him home. "My, you're so thin, Henry. Doesn't Mary feed you? Well, supper is ready so you sit down and eat. I hope you'll stay long enough for me to fatten you up before I have to send you back to Boston. Now, Robert, no more delays. What of Edward, is he well and when is he coming home?"

Between bites of cold roast, biscuit, and cheese, Robert passed along most of the news from Edward's letter, but withheld the part where he planned to share his Virginia grant with his family. Aunt Bess, Esther, Philip, and Joseph all listened intently, Philip even needing repeat reminders from Aunt Bess to eat while he listened.

"Well," observed Aunt Bess, "there will be many a young widow who will be crying into their pillow once it gets out that Edward won't be returning to live in Rowley. Remember how they flooded the store hoping to catch sight of him in his regimentals when he visited after Louisburg? There's many a comely young widow in town and he could do much worse. It would be good for him to marry again. He's been a widower now too long. But he's not going straight to Virginia, is he? Won't I get a chance to see my Edward again? It's been nearly seven years since I last saw him, and you, too, Robert, and that's too long."

"That's the part I was just coming to, Aunt Bess. Edward has proposed to share his good fortune with all of us, asking us to join him in Virginia. Lewis, Henry, and I have discussed it and we've decided to do just that..."

Robert was interrupted by a close impression an Indian war whoop as Philip jumped to his feet so fast he toppled his chair over. Joseph was only slightly less vocal in his approval of what both immediately saw as the grandest of adventures.

"Boys, remember yourselves!" Then, turning back to Aunt Bess, he continued. "We propose to hire Master Cole's packet to get Lewis and Henry to Williamsburg in time to meet Edward. I'll stay here and take care of settling our affairs and getting ready. Then, when Master Cole returns, the rest of us will embark for Williamsburg."

"And what do you propose to do with me, Robert Jewett? Leave me to the Town's charity? You know that in my four score years I've never been further than Ipswich, and not there since I was a girl! Am I to go traipsing through the wilderness at my age?"

"Now, Bess, no one is going to leave you to charity. If you choose to stay, Lewis has agreed to give you his house and Edward, though he hopes you'll come along, states he would leave the rents from his farms here to your support. Esther could, if she's a mind, remain to provide you comfort. If you do decide to join us, I'm to sell all and bring the proceeds along to help us as we establish ourselves beyond the Blue Ridge in Virginia."

"Choose, Robert, like I have a choice! Neither you nor Edward have a woman to run your households and, I'm sorry to say it Lewis, Henry, but Mary and Marie aren't much help, either. Mary fritters away her time and Marie spends hers at her father's stable, always riding her favorite horses while neglecting her household duties. No, I'm going. I'd rather spend what little time I have left surrounded by my family than to be left behind. Besides, Robert, you know how much you and Lewis like my mince pies. Who would make them for you if I stayed here? Esther is learning, but you said yourself hers are as yet not to your liking."

"And I suppose you've made my decision for me, Father, much as Lewis and Henry have spoken for Marie and Mary," injected Esther with mock irritation. "If I don't wish to finish out my days in the wilderness, what say you to that?"

"Well, Esther, you are of age, that's true, but as you have shown no interest in marrying and are now quite past the age when it would be probable, I had simply assumed you would join us in this project. I can hardly leave you here alone, now that Aunt Bess has stated her intention to join us."

"Of course, I'm going. It would just have been kind of you to have asked after my desires, that's all."

"Well, then, it's settled. Boys, you seem to have an uncommon amount of energy for this hour, what say you. Do you think you can find Master Cole and tell him I have need of him and will call on him first thing in the morning?" Robert had hardly finished when both boys dashed from the room, nearly knocking down Marie as she was entering, having returned from the stables to find her own house dark. From her countenance it was clear Lewis would have his work cut out for him this night as he relayed both the news and the decisions that were made without her.

Chapter 2

aster Cole set sail with the evening tide. His packet was old, but he kept her tight and trim. Small and old as she was, other than running the mail, Master Cole had been barely able to make enough to provide for himself and the crew. Being hired by Mister Jewett had saved him returning to Boston loaded only with a few pieces of mail, hardly a profitable undertaking. Now, however, he had three passengers to take all the way to Williamsburg, then to return to gather the rest of Robert Jewett's extended family, plus their goods, and take them to Virginia as well. This could make 1752 his best year since 1745 when the Crown hired him to run dispatches to and from the Army at Louisburg. He eyed his passengers at the rail and wondered if the others would be as sick as Henry had been on the run up from Boston yesterday.

Lewis was lost to his own thoughts at the moment. Marie had been surprisingly easy to convince of the benefits of this undertaking. She had always thought highly of Edward, even more so since he purchased the three farms around Rowley totaling nearly 200 acres and making him one of the largest of the local landowners. And the prospect of their becoming landed as well, to a level far above 200 acres, was very appealing, even if the removal from her parents to the frontier caused some reservations. No, the lure of becoming a lady of the manor had made Lewis' job very easy indeed.

Philip was another matter altogether. He was outright indignant when told he would not be accompanying his father this afternoon. Maybe he had indulged the boy too much, being an only child. Nearly all his time had been spent with either his father or grandfather, so he was more used to adult company than a boy of 12 should be. Adding Joseph to the household had helped. Philip and Joseph had been close friends even before the pox took Joseph's parents and he had moved in with Lewis and Marie. Now they were inseparable, meaning Joseph was also becoming a little too involved with the adults than was customary. No, Philip was smart, almost too smart, and could carry on a conversation with anyone. If only he wasn't so ready to express his opinions and expected to be included in everything his father or grandfather did. Perhaps Lewis needed to rein him in a little.

Henry and Esther conversed in hushed voices about the adventure ahead of them. Robert was not at all pleased when Esther announced her intention of going with her brothers, yet there was no denying her. Master Cole had been of no help when he offered his own cabin to her. Knowing Edward would not be expecting her and would likely not have lodging suitable for her, Robert had written a letter of introduction to Mister Prentiss, a Williamsburg merchant he had exchanged correspondence with over the years, both sharing the same London factor. Now, barely out of the river, both Henry and Esther were inwardly hoping their conversation would quell the first waves of seasickness they were already feeling but neither would admit to the other. No, for them it would be a long two weeks as they made their way down the coast.

While Lewis and Esther had packed for the journey, taking traveling clothes and little else other than Lewis bringing his fowler along, the one he kept for militia musters, Henry had not known what the letter contained or that he would be traveling. He therefore planned to gather his things during Master Cole's two hour stop in Boston to drop off the mail. That is also all the time he had to tell Mary of the significant change their lives were about to take. He knew Mary was not happy in Boston, nothing satisfied her these days, and it had been making life for him and the children tense and disagreeable. Their house was old and only provided the basics in comforts. She got along neither with the neighbors nor her family. This latter also made things difficult as Henry worked for her father. No, as he now confided to his sister, this move would likely meet with her wholehearted support, at least once she got used to the idea, and could not have come at a better time. If not for this, he knew he would have had to make a change for her sake and likely to their detriment in the long term. Still, telling her and then leaving again was not an idea he was relishing.

Seasickness was not long in sending Henry and Esther below decks, leaving Lewis alone at the rail. Master Cole, having full knowledge of the contents of Edward's letter by now, as did the rest of Rowley, left Lewis to his thoughts. If Master Cole knew how Lewis' mind was racing from one unknown to another, he might have intruded and distracted Lewis from his musings. Here Lewis was, poorly equipped to handle the wilderness himself, about to take his aging father, great aunt, sister, wife and children where they would be depending on his ability to handle whatever the wilderness sent their way. But weren't they all to be dependent on Edward?

Yes, Edward. He was well versed in the martial arts and in handling himself in the courtly halls of Europe. But what did he know of the frontier? And commanding troops was a lot different than husbanding a family across the wilds. Although few in the family would admit it, behind the façade, they really no longer knew him. He had left so long ago and his visits, out of necessity, were short and widely spaced. The entire family looked to Robert as the family patriarch, came to him with their issues. This change would, in effect, place Edward in the patriarch role. Would the rest, particularly the wives, accept this change? Lewis knew his father would never even consciously note the change in his status, any more than he acknowledged his position as the patriarch in the first place. Instead, he always looked for consensus without even realizing that most of the time that consensus was really the rest of the family taking his sage advice.

As for himself, he and Edward had been the closest of brothers growing up. But aside from the short visits, they had precious little time together these many years. He hoped they would be able to pick back up where they left off. Henry, on the other hand, had never really been close to Edward. He was proud of him and his accomplishments, yes, but not close. Their difference in ages had made their interests growing up too far apart for them to develop the really close relationship he and Edward had shared. Lewis often thought Henry jealous of them for this closeness. To be honest with himself, he and Henry weren't all that close either, not like he and Edward had been.

Master Cole's three passengers spent a restless night, Lewis because of his concerns over what the future would hold and his brother and sister due to the effects of their seasickness. They were all up early as the packet made its way into Boston Harbor. Despite her desire to go ashore, Lewis and Henry insisted Esther remain on board while they collected Henry's things, filled in Mary, and returned to make the scheduled sailing before the tide left them until evening.

"Do you think Mary can handle affairs here so as to be ready in a month's time?" Lewis asked as they walked briskly along.

"There's really not much to do. The house is a rental and our furnishings few. She'd be well advised to remove herself and the children to Rowley within the week where father can take care of any remaining details for her. I don't look for her father to be of any support or assistance. They are not exactly on agreeable terms right now. Ah, but here we are. If you would fill Mary in on the details of Edward's letter while I gather my things, it will speed us along our way. Don't make such a face, you needn't tell her of our current undertaking. I should be packed by time you've covered the other news from the letter and can then tell her myself, when there's little time left and we can hustle out the door. Ah, I can see that is more to your liking!"

As they approached the very small row house, really just two rooms, one over the other, and a garret above, Charles came bounding out the door and into his father's arms. Mary and Sarah both appeared at the door right behind Charles.

"Mother said you'd gone off to Rowley, and without even saying goodbye! Whatever was in that letter mother told Sarah and me about must be real important for you to be back so soon, and to bring Uncle Lewis with you. Well, aren't you going to tell me? I've been waiting nearly two whole days already and I'm about to bust. Well? What of

Uncle Edward? And how is grandfather. Did you tell him I miss him? Well?"

"You know, if you'd let me get a word in, you'd learn more. Right now I need to get some things together, so Uncle Lewis will give you, Sarah, and your mother all the news from Uncle Edward."

Henry quickly went above stairs to gather his things, ignoring the look Mary shot him as he hugged her on his way past. Lewis covered all of the main points from Edward's letter to a very eager group of listeners, each full of questions. Mary arose with a start when Henry reappeared with his ancient musket slung on his shoulder and a packet of clothes in his hand.

"What is the meaning of this? Obviously there is more in this letter than Lewis has told us, as I should have known when I saw that Lewis was with you. Out with it, what are you two up to?"

Now it was Henry's turn. He grinned in that shy way that told Mary immediately he wasn't exactly comfortable with the subject, a look she'd been seeing more of lately. Once he'd finished explaining Edward's generosity, the family's plan to accept, and their current mission, Mary jumped to her feet grinning and gave him a big hug.

"Finally we can get out of this place! I'm so tired of all the neighbors, watching everything we do, listening to everything we say. Sarah, quick, run and tell your grandfather we'll need one of his carts in the morning. That should hold our four chests plus the bed ticks. Then... And what is on your mind, Mister Henry Jewett?"

"I was just wondering if you liked the idea. And I had a silly question as to what you planned to do about the furniture. There isn't much, but it's more than will fit in a cart."

"Most of this furniture my father gave us, his cast

offs, and he'll just have to take care of it. There isn't a piece of it worth anything to anyone. Once we're in Virginia, you're just going to have to get us better furniture for our new house. You heard me, I'm going to insist on a new house. Now, don't you have to get back to the ship? I have a lot to do to be ready to load the cart in the morning. I hope you're father is expecting us as I'll not stay in this house one night longer than I have to."

Mary then started moving about the room, gathering items on the table and talking to herself about what goes and what would be left behind. Charles saw this as his opportunity.

"Father, why can't I go with you, now, instead of with mother to Rowley?"

"Someone has to accompany your mother and sister to your grandfather's. Besides, Uncle Lewis and I have to get back to the ship so we can meet Uncle Edward on time in Williamsburg. We don't have time to wait for you. After all, the King might be coming with your Uncle Edward and we can't keep the King waiting. I've told you how important your Uncle Edward is and how he and the King are such good friends. So, go help your mother and you can join us in about six weeks time. Now, Sarah, you've been awfully quiet, which is so unlike you."

"Well, father, I was just thinking about all my friends here in Boston and how you want me to go with you so I will never see them again."

"You weren't thinking about all your friends, if I read your blush correctly. You were thinking about Daniel. I've already told you that you're too young to be trifling with boys. There will be plenty of time for that later. Besides, aren't you the least curious as to the rich, young men in Virginia? Now, didn't your mother give you an errand to run? So, give me a hug and then off with you."

15

Once out of the house and on their way back to the quay, Lewis had to ask his little brother about what he had just heard.

"Henry, did you really tell Charles that Edward and the King were friends?"

"Well, aren't they? You told me yourself that that Lord Bedford had presented Edward to the King after Louisburg. And why else would he receive a royal land grant, especially one so large, when he already owns three farms around Rowley?"

Lewis just smiled, half to himself, and changed the subject. "Wherever did you get such an ancient musket?"

"Why, this was a gift of the King, you could say. They handed them out to us Boston militiamen that didn't have arms when they called us out for Louisburg, then let us keep them when we came home."

"Small wonder they let you keep them, such fine arms as that," Lewis retorted, grinning broadly. "Does it still shoot?"

"How would I know? I've never shot it! Edward knows about guns and such so he can look it over before we head for the frontier. It's not like either of us are much with a gun. Look, there's Esther waving her arms at us and it looks like our packet is about to cast off. We'd better run."

As they got within hearing, Master Cole called to them through his speaking trumpet to hurry and jump aboard or they'd miss the tide and not make it over the bar until after nightfall. He then ordered the lines let go. Esther got a good laugh as they ended up in a ball on the deck after leaping aboard the already slowly moving packet.

Turning to Henry while he rubbed a now sore shoulder, Lewis observed, dryly, "You know, we just may be getting too old for this."

∞ *Chapter 3* ∞

*R*obert was finding life's new pace a bit hectic as he hurried about getting all of his and his sons' affairs in order. Then there was the question of his accounts with his London Factor. He knew he would be quitting Rowley long before any reply to his letter could make its way back to the Colonies, possibly before it even reached London. So, once again, he had taken advantage of his acquaintance with Mister William Prentiss, who shared the same London Factor, and asked that his accounts be sent in care of Mister Prentiss. He had gone to great lengths to make it clear that Mister Prentiss would in no way be liable for his debts, being but a convenient address from whence Robert could collect the paperwork he would need to close out his accounts. He hoped he had not presumed too much on Mister Prentiss, though in their previous correspondence he had not impressed Robert as one prone to tempers.

And then there was Mary, Sarah, and Charles. They had arrived in Rowley less than a week after Lewis and Henry had departed, tired and foot sore from their trip up from Boston. Robert put up Mary and Sarah in Esther's

room while Charles stayed with Marie. Poor Marie saddled with three boys between the ages of 11 and 13. She
definitely had her hands full. But so did Robert trying to
get his youngest son's family properly outfitted for their
long journey. He knew Henry and Mary weren't prosper-
ing, that's true enough, he just hadn't realized how meager his youngest son's estate was until Mary answered
all of his questions the evening she arrived with not but
what barely filled a cart. That was just the way of things,
so Robert resolved to provide what they needed from his
warehouse, deducting the costs from whatever profits he
might make on the sale of the store and its contents. Selling Edward's farms had proven much easier than selling
the store and the contents of the warehouse, however, so
he was worried as he sat reviewing his account books.

"Robert," Aunt Bess' voice at his elbow breaking
his deep concentration over the store books, "you really
must eat something if you're to keep up your strength. We
can't have you getting sick, not now with everyone depending on you like we are."

"Oh, Aunt Bess, what time is it? Nine? I got so involved here that I completely lost track of time. I'll be
along as soon as I've locked up the store."

"Robert, may I ask you something?" Following his
nod, she continued, "My deciding to go along hasn't added to your worries, has it? I'm so torn, you see, between
not wanting to burden you with extra worries and wanting
to go along to be with all my dear boys, yourself included,
all together again for the first time in many a year." Wiping
her eyes, she continued, firmly, "If my going is to be too
much work on you, I'd rather stay behind than cause you
any of your sick headaches."

"Nonsense, Aunt Bess, you're the least of my
troubles at this moment. Why, here you have the house

already sorted into what's to go and what's to stay, a list of what needs purchased, and I wouldn't be surprised to find all your clothes already in those portmanteaus you purchased. And look at what you've done to help get Henry's household organized. If not for you, Mary would have little idea what she needed, let alone have gotten all those clothes they brought mended and ready to wear. No, Aunt Bess, you continue to take care of us all."

"Alright then, Robert, but the moment I become a burden on you I expect you to cut me loose to fend for myself. I've never been a burden to anyone and I'm too old to change my ways now." Then, softening, "You'll come home now for your supper?"

Though she never showed it and would never admit to it, Robert saw in her eyes how tired she was. Taking Aunt Bess' hand, kissing it softly and then patting it affectionately, Robert tossed the papers he had been studying into the desk, closed and locked the lid. Rising and putting his arm around her, they walked together out of the store, only pausing to lock the door behind them. The rest of the house having long since eaten and retired, the two of them sat in the kitchen near each other while they ate, lost in thought and enjoying the simple pleasure of being together. When they had finished, he kissed her on the forehead, she kissed him on his cheek, and they retired, he up the stairs to his room, she across the hall to hers, contented even though not another word had passed between them.

Another week passed and Robert continued to have difficulty disposing of all of the property, particularly his store and attached home. What was making it more difficult was the need for ready money, something perpetually in short supply in Massachusetts Bay Colony. He was making better progress accumulating the wares his extended family would need to remove first to Virginia and then to the frontier of that Colony. The one bright spot continued to be the excitement of his three grandsons. Even Charles, who had not originally shown much excitement, had caught the bug from Philip so that now all three were finding the wait extremely difficult to bear.

While the whole family was gathered around his table for dinner, a knock at the door interrupted Robert as he was finishing the prayer.

"Sam, is something wrong at the store?"

"No, Mister Jewett, everything is fine and I hate to interrupt you at your dinner. I have just received some news of my own and wanted to discuss it with you."

"Well, Sam, if you can talk in front of my family, you're welcome to pull up a chair and join us. No sense missing your dinner, or me either, for that matter."

Once Aunt Bess had Sam seated with plate and flatware, he introduced the nature of his business.

"Sir, I've been your clerk for 15 years this August and have learned a lot working for you. You have been very kind ensuring I understood the business so I could start my own store one day."

"Thank you, Sam, but it was only what I agreed with your father to do when I took you on."

"Yes, sir, I understand that. Do you think I'm ready now to run a store on my own?"

"Well, you've learned well and have a talent for the books. Yes, I believe you could. And with my departure, it is an opportune time to set yourself up as your own master."

"I'm glad to hear you say that, sir, which brings me to the heart of the matter. Would you sell me your store, warehouse, and house?"

Robert sat back in his chair, at first not able to comprehend what Sam had just offered while Philip let out one of the Indian whoops he was becoming especially fond of doing these days, much to his mother's annoyance. The pause seemed to cause Sam some embarrassment as he stole a glance around the table and proceeded to pick at his food. Robert took several bites of food, chewing slowly as he thought about the proposition just laid before him. It would solve his biggest problem and also resolve what was to become of his loyal employees should the store have to close.

"Have you given any thought as to how you would pay me, for I will be too far away to extend you credit?" Robert finally responded.

"That's just it, sir, why I haven't mentioned this earlier. I just this morning received confirmation from my uncle in Boston that he will provide a letter of credit drawn on his London account to cover the cost. As you also use Mister Hewitt as your London Factor, your ability to draw against this account should be much simplified. And my father and uncle both suggest to you, sir, that this is much preferable to carrying large sums with you."

Aunt Bess was studying Robert closely as he stared at his plate in thought. It only took a moment when she saw his countenance lighten as if a great weight had been lifted. At that she leaped to her feet, hurried around the table and gave Sam a big hug before darting into the kitchen so none would see her tears of joy. She had been very worried about Robert as time had passed without his being able to sell his estates. It was the last major detail before they could depart for Virginia.

Laughing as Aunt Bess left the room, Philip interjected "Sam, if Aunt Bess thinks you have a deal, no one here is foolish enough to argue with her, at least none who has experienced her bear hug when she's riled." Now all three boys broke into howls of laughter that were slow to respond to the remonstrances of Mary and Marie. The rest of the meal had a rather lighthearted feel as food was heaped at every course on poor, skinny Sam. After they finished, Sam and Robert retired to the store office to work out the details of the sale.

Now Robert turned his full attention to preparing those articles they needed to ship aboard the packet. This was not without its challenges. Mary, Sarah, and Charles had precious little, even after Robert had augmented their provisions, and Aunt Bess had Robert's household well sorted and prepared. Marie, Philip, and Joseph, on the other hand, had more than the little packet could possibly hold. After some, limited success in reducing what they had set aside to take, Robert unleashed his secret weapon, Aunt Bess. In fairly short order, the barn full of "necessities" had been reduced to a manageable level, though not without some drama and a few harsh words passing between Aunt Bess and Marie.

It was Philip and Joseph who unintentionally broke the ice that had developed between these two strong women. It seems as they "helped" they were taking much delight in setting the two against each other then watching the results. The ladies finally realized the cause of the boys' mirth and that they were the source of the amusement. Off they went to Marie's kitchen for tea and a laugh, emerging totally reconciled and ready to see the task through. Although they did not specifically address the boys, by the end of the day both realized they had been found out and were paying the price by being kept hard at work hauling items around. So successful were Marie and Aunt Bess that the boys barely ate supper before falling asleep from exhaustion.

A corner of Robert's warehouse, being convenient

to the dock, now became the repository for all of the crates and barrels ready for shipment. The family began living out of their portmanteaus and trunks at Lewis and Marie's house, Robert's store and house having been turned over to the new owner, Sam Brown, his father and uncle. After turning over his duties as Elder and Trustee of the Rowley Congregationalist Church, Robert suddenly found his days full of leisure and time to spend with his grandsons, who had not lost their excitement at all, if anything becoming more excited as each day passed until one day all three came running and shouting into the parlor where the adults were enjoying afternoon tea.

"The packet's here, in the river! Time to go to Virginia! Well, come on, what are you just sitting there for?" all three shouted in unison.

Crowds of townspeople came out as the entire Jewett family, less the three brothers and their sister already in Virginia, calmly walked down to the docks. The adults, at least, walked calmly, with the boys darting back and forth, unable to contain their excitement. They arrived just as Master Cole was warping the packet to the dock and making the final arrangements for tying off. As soon as this was done he greeted his passengers with a flourish of his hat from the deck.

"Master Cole, what news have you of my children?"

❧ *Chapter 4* ❧

They were three days out of Boston and Esther thought she heard a light tapping at the ship's cabin door, or was it just the creaks and groans of the ship? She was miserable, sicker than she had ever been in her life. So sick she had to stop herself from praying for death. No, that wouldn't do at all. She just needed off this ship. There it was again, a definite knock at the door. She called weakly for whoever it was to come in.

"Esther, I have Master Cole here with me," Lewis said in a voice full of concern. "We're worried that you haven't eaten and are as weak as a kitten. Master Cole would like you to try something that he thinks will help. Master Cole, if you please."

"Miss Esther, I want you to drink this, then try to eat this ship's biscuit."

"Master Cole, this smells vaguely of spirits and you know I don't take spirituous liquors."

"Aye, aye, you have me there, you do, for it is made of good dark rum that it is. I learned this from those Regular Navy folks back during the Siege and have found it to help. They call it grog, made of dark rum, water, and lime juice. They tell me lemons work as well, but I only had limes. It'll help settle you and keep the scurvy away at the same time."

"But it has rum in it," she protested weakly.

"Esther now's not the time to worry about that. It is medicinal pure and simple and you must drink it. Then we'll try to get this biscuit down you. Henry has already tried it and thus far it is working for him. If not, we'll have to put in to shore and let you off. With these on shore winds, Master Cole says it could be a week before we'd make sea again and you know Edward will be waiting for word from us. Now, here, I'll hold the mug for you while you drink. That's it, now a little more. Now sit back and let's see if that is going to stay down."

It did and Esther then nibbled on the dry ship's biscuit, washing it down with a little more of the grog. This drained her of all the energy she had, but it did stay down and seemed to settle her, so she drifted off to sleep.

"That's good that she now sleeps, the poor creature. She's having the worse of it, that's true enough. Now, Mister Lewis, if she's still able to eat when she awakes, give her a little more of the grog and another biscuit. Nothing but grog and biscuit today and we'll see if she and Mister Henry are strong enough for something else tomorrow. How is it the sea hasn't affected your own self like it does you brother and sister?"

"I don't know why that is, Master Cole, only that since we were children I'm the only one who could ride in a closed coach without the sickness. Even Edward suffered from it, though I don't think it bothers him much any more or he wouldn't have been able to sail to all those places with the Army like he has."

"Right you are about that. I've known many a boy, sick as a dog when they first sign on, become right smart sailors after getting used to the deck under their feet. Once they get the feel for it, most never want land under them again. It is a curiosity that I can't explain. Now, I'll be off to see to the ship in this wind. We have to watch close or it'll drive us onto the shore and bust us up quick as you please."

After checking on Henry and finding him still asleep also, Lewis sat down to read and started to doze off himself. His dreams were different now, not set in the dusty carriage shop or even the town. These were set in the country, with trees and grassy meadows around him. Philip and Joseph were playing about the meadow and into the fringes of the woods while he and Marie set out a picnic for them all. Marie was smiling at him like she hadn't smiled in years, happy and contented.

He awoke with a start to shouts and the sound of running feet on the deck above his head. The ship, which had been heeling to the starboard for most of the trip, was now leaning dangerously. He heard Esther calling for him but was having trouble making his way to the cabin with the deck under his feet tilting and bobbing as it was. He slipped and went crashing into the table and chair already against the hull. Before he could stand, there was a terrible snap followed by a crash and the ship suddenly came level before settling toward the stern.

Ignoring now the screams of Esther, Lewis made his way up the ship's ladder to the deck. What met his eyes was a scene of wreckage and ruin. The deck was littered with splintered spars and torn rigging. Master Cole stood among a knot of crewmen at the stern rail, plying axes at the railing, while more moved forward and the sound of chains soon added to the noise. The ship suddenly came level again and as the knot of crewmen came forward from the stern rail, Lewis caught Master Cole's arm.

"What has happened?" he asked anxiously.

"It was as I feared. This cursed wind drove us too close to shore and when we spied the land, we laid her over hard to avoid the rocks, too hard for the sail she was carrying, and we lost our topmast. It went astern and acted as a storm anchor, nearly swamping us. It was close for a few minutes, I'll grant you. But not to worry. We've cut away the debris and let the anchor go. We're in fairly shallow water and can ride here fine while we make our repairs. I have spare spars and rigging below that should fill the bill and we should be underway again in a few hours time. Shouldn't lose more than half a day, I figure. Now, unless you're good with a chisel I suggest you go below and see to your relations."

"I am actually quite good with a chisel and Henry is a carpenter's helper, so I think we can be of some good use to you, Master Cole."

Henry, though weak, was feeling better and he and Lewis set to work with the crew to make the necessary repairs. It was good they did for the small crew of the packet didn't contain a decent carpenter and, while Master Cole knew what needed to be done, he was not all that handy with carpenters tools either. They could have gotten the repairs made, though it would have taken them much longer than men familiar with the tools and techniques needed.

They had gotten lucky. Had it been the main mast instead of the topmast, there would have been nothing they could have done other than limp into the nearest port for repairs. As it was, one of the spars Master Cole had on board was fashioned into a new topmast, though a bit shorter than the original and two others replaced two splintered and lost when the topmast came down and went over the side.

Lewis found working with Henry to be very easy. Henry did the rough shaping quickly and efficiently, moving to the next piece while Lewis did the final shaping and fitting. Watching them work, the crew thought they were seeing men accustomed to working together, and in ways they were right. Although it had been years, Henry had gotten his start in Lewis' shop and the two brothers had worked together for several years before Henry moved on to Boston. Henry's skills had improved during his Boston stay and it took few words between them for each to know what the other needed. Lewis felt a renewed sense of pride in his brother and respect for his skills and abilities.

In just two hours the crew was hoisting the replacements into place and setting the rigging. It took them just an hour to be far enough along that Master Cole ordered the anchor hauled in and the ship underway. The final touches on the rigging continued on into the night, which was fine for the ship's master was being much more judicious in how much canvas he was willing to hoist under these conditions.

Henry was spent from his labors and, after two biscuits washed down by the grog, he returned to his bed. Lewis was able to get Esther to eat another biscuit and drink some more of the grog and she, too, seemed to be much improved. He then headed for his bunk for a much needed rest. Not having gotten the hang of entering the swinging ship's bunks, his first attempt landed him on the deck, resulting in what sounded like a chuckle out of Henry's bunk though he didn't answer when Lewis softly asked if he were awake.

The next day both Henry and Esther were much improved. So much so Master Cole ordered one of his laying hens boiled so they could have meat better suited to their situation than the ship's salt pork. Both responded well to the nourishment and the remainder of the voyage was uneventful, though Esther did occasionally have bouts of sickness when the seas were especially rough.

They were all on deck when Master Cole told them they were about to enter the great bay. He pointed out Cape Charles and Cape Henry, though neither was very visible from the deck and Esther had no desire to climb into the rigging to see them. The water was much calmer as they moved to what Master Cole called the Roads, and then they were clearly in a river, the James. Here Master Cole signaled for and received a pilot to guide them the rest of the way up river. They put in at Kingsmill, where they found a pilot to take them to the docks on College Creek. This pilot told Master Cole of an easier berthing on Queen's Creek that would get him closer to the city. It would mean going around the Roads and up the York River, so his passengers, now very anxious for their journey to be over, pushed them forward to College Creek.

As they entered the area the pilot called the "Thoroughfare" they saw one of His Majesty's brigs taking on provisions and water. The pilot told them the brig had arrived four days earlier from Bermuda bringing mail and official passengers, to include some important officer the pilot saw but was not introduced to. He knew this was someone important by how much deference the ship's captain had shown him and by his military bearing.

Lewis gathered his siblings to him and whispered that he believed this passenger was Edward. He reminded them how, when they saw Edward last, his squared shoulders and straight back fit the description just given. All three were now very impatient with the packet's progress up the creek and were ready to disembark as soon as Master Cole had her tied off. There was no need to tarry, Master Cole had his instructions and they had reviewed them before picking up the first pilot. He was to leave as soon as provisioned for Rowley and return straightaway with the rest of the family. Master Cole made one adjustment when he told Lewis to look for him to return to the Queen's Creek docks, as this would be much more convenient for all the possessions he would have on board.

Lewis hired two riding chairs, not without noting their inferior design and construction, and the three loaded their small bags and started for Williamsburg. Lewis and Esther saw a town not much larger than Rowley but with more grandeur and a more regular layout. Henry saw a village when he compared it to Boston and wondered how this could be the great capitol of His Majesty's largest and richest Colony, but as he was riding the second riding chair alone while Esther rode with Lewis, he had no one to make these observations to.

Inquiries resulted in their being directed to Mister Weatherburn's Tavern as the most likely place to gain information as to Edward's whereabouts. When Esther saw Mister Prentiss' store, she suggested they stop and deliver her letter of introduction, but Lewis thought it best to find Edward first.

Yes, Mister Weatherburn did know of the Colonel, had put him up for two nights, but he had taken lodging in a private tenement as he expected his extended family to arrive soon and he needed more room than Mister Weatherburn had available, even if his establishment was suitable for ladies, which it wasn't. He directed them to retrace their steps back to the market square. To their left they would see the Magazine and behind it, on Francis Street, stood a brick two story tenement owned by Mister Lightfoot and recently leased to Colonel Jewett. He said it was an impressive looking residence and they couldn't mistake it.

A tall man answered their knock on the Lightfoot Tenement's front door. He stared at the three weary travelers for a moment, then recognition flashed across his eyes and he smiled. "My dear sister, what in the world are you doing here with these two no-account brothers of yours? Isn't father with you to provide you some decent company and protection?" He then threw his arms out, embracing all three at once as tears flowed freely down all four faces.

Moving to the sparsely furnished parlor, Lewis and Henry related the family's excitement upon receiving the letter and the plans for these three to meet Edward while the rest made ready and followed, probably arriving in just over a month from now. Esther just sat quietly next to Edward with her hand on his arm, watching his face as he conversed and joked with his brothers.

Carefully studying his face, she thought he looked much older than she expected, and tired. While still fit and appearing overall much younger than his age, a common trait for the men in her family, there was some grey starting to streak his brown hair and the lines around his mouth and eyes were deeper. She had to agree with the pilot, he did have an air of authority to him, even now, dressed in fustian small clothes and a brown coat instead of his scarlet regimentals with their blue facings and ample gold braid. Oh, how the widows of Rowley had howled when they learned he would be retiring to Virginia and not there, and she could see why.

She remained quiet through supper and retired shortly thereafter to allow her brothers to continue their conversation. Saying very little, she knew there would now be plenty of time for her and Edward to talk, now that he did not have to rush back to some war somewhere. No, let the boys have their fun. She was well fed and on dry land for the first time in 16 days so all she intended to do the rest of this day was to sleep.

Chapter 5

sther woke after a peaceful, restful night, dressed and joined her brothers who were already at the breakfast table when she came down.

"Well, well, good morning little sister. I trust you rested well."

"Oh, Edward, it was so nice to sleep without the bed and in fact the whole room moving every which way. I swear I have taken my first and last ship's passage. If you're of a mind to send me back to Rowley, I'll just have to walk!"

With that, Sally, the hired girl Mrs. Weatherburn had loaned to Edward, entered and sat a brown bottle on the table right in front of Esther.

"Good morning, Miss, and here you are."

"Good morning, Sally, but what is this?"

"Why, it's good Jamaican rum, Miss, fresh from Mister Weatherburn's cellar it is."

"Rum?!? I'm sure I don't understand…"

"Why, Esther, after Henry explained the fondness for rum you acquired on your journey and how you just had to have it with every meal, I sent Sally to bring some, as rum was not something I thought to stock the house with. Good Madera, yes, but I had no idea you took rum."

As Esther puffed, not quite sure what to say, she saw a sly grin creep across Henry's face. As the youngest and only girl child, she had gotten used to more than her share of teasing growing up. It had never been malicious with these three, but she never knew when it would happen and she was usually caught off guard.

"Henry, you did this! Edward, if you must know, Master Cole gave me something he called grog to calm my seasickness, and to Henry as I'm sure he failed to tell you. It had rum in it, yes, but it was purely for medicinal purposes and not at all because I was fond of it. Lewis knows. Tell him, Lewis."

Edward turned to Lewis before he had a chance to speak and asked "Do you remember old Mister Kincaid from when we were growing up?"

Now Lewis was grinning as he realized where Edward was taking this. "I most certainly do remember him. He was sickly, as I recall, and had to take a lot of medicine on a daily basis."

"Medicine? Hardly! Now you both know as well as I do that Mister Kincaid was a scandalous drunkard who loved his rum more than...Lewis! So now you're in on this too?" she huffed as she realized she was being teased by all three of her brothers.

"Why my dear little sister, that is a lovely shade of red" offered Edward. "I do suggest you go right down to the milliner and see if they have any material in that shade for a gown. After all, you're in need of a gown if we're to call on the Governor this morning."

Caught a bit off guard by the sudden change in the course of the conversation, Esther sat blinking at Edward for a moment before she was able to ask what he meant.

"We, that is I, have an audience at 11 o'clock to-day so I may present Governor Dinwiddie with my letter of introduction from Lord Halifax, but I plan to take you all along. Even if I lacked the letter of introduction, it would have hardly been proper for me to come to Virginia with a Royal patent and not call on the King's Governor. I was joking, however, about the gown, as there won't be time to have one made."

"But, Edward, I haven't anything appropriate to wear to see the Governor! You should have told us in your letter and we'd have all brought our good clothes with us."

"Now Esther, you'll be fine. You, Lewis and Henry just dress in the best you brought. I, on the other hand, well, let's just say Henry gets his wish today as I must be in my regimentals. Did you see how disappointed he was last night when he found me simply dressed and not fully outfitted as a Royal Colonel? Now, I've hired a coach to ar-rive at quarter to, so plan your morning accordingly."

Lewis did not impress easily, though now he found himself very impressed with his older brother. His younger siblings were simply giddy throughout the rest of the meal in their excitement over meeting Virginia's Royal Gover-nor. As soon as the meal was over and Edward had moved to the parlor to see to some papers, the three younger sib-lings huddled with Sally around the table. Soon she was off on her errands while they returned to their rooms to look to their clothing.

Sally was able to find new stockings, white shirts, and neck stocks for Lewis and Henry at Mister Prentiss' store. Brushing their coats, breeches, and weskits helped but little though it was the best they could do. For Esther, she brought back some ribbon from the milliner's to dress up as best they could Esther's plan bodice. By time she and Sally had finished, Esther's plain clothes looked most presentable. They were all assembled on the front walk waiting for Edward when the coach arrived.

When the door opened and Edward came into the full sun, a small gasp of surprise and approval escaped from Esther and Henry grinned openly. It had been a long time since they had seen Edward in full uniform, seven years in fact. He was immaculate in his gold laced scarlet coat with the blue facings, black weskit, breeches, and stockings, and gleaming small sword, topped off by a black cocked hat trimmed in gold with white feathers. He had a very regal air, dressed as he was, with his upright posture and demeanor of one comfortable giving commands. After pausing for effect, Edward smiled broadly. Esther curtsied and her brothers bowed as Edward came near, then all followed him into the coach for the short ride to the Governor's Palace.

The Governor's secretary opened the door with a broad grin that quickly drooped as he looked past the elegant figure in front of him to the three behind. The officer quickly snapped the secretary's attention back to him and presented his letter of introduction. As befit someone bearing a letter of introduction from the First Commissioner of the Lords Commissioners of Trade and Plantations, they were ushered into the parlor to await the Governor's pleasure, though the secretary had obvious misgivings. It was Esther who broke the silence.

"This is what they call a palace? I'll admit it is larger than is common, but not what I would call a palace."

"And did you notice how shabby it appears, as if little maintenance has been done on it in years," added Henry in a hushed voice.

"Quite right you are, my boy," boomed a voice behind them. "I'm glad you see things as I do. This is hardly a fitting place for a Royal Governor to reside. I ask and ask the Burgess to provide money to make the appropriate repairs and they debate and argue and debate some more. And why? It's all because I've insisted on applying the law by charging patents on land with quitrents to the King. If I insist on applying the law, they're going to make me suffer by withholding funds for repairs and maintenance. But here, I forget myself. I am Robert Dinwiddie, Lieutenant Governor of His Majesty's Colony of Virginia, acting in the Governor's stead as he had the good sense to accept the appointment but to remain at Court instead of in this backwater colony. And you, sir, are Colonel Jewett. Sir George's letter speaks quite highly of you, quite highly indeed."

Edward executed a practiced bow, responding "Your Excellency and Lord Halifax are too kind. May I introduce my sister, Esther, and brothers, Lewis and Henry?"

Flashing a smile at her that caused Esther to blush, the Governor took her by the arm. "Come above stairs to my study where we will be more comfortable and, Colonel, you can tell me how His Lordship views the state of this colony." With that, the men followed Esther and the Governor down the hall to the grand staircase and up to the study above the entry hall. Lewis and Henry were very impressed with the display of arms arranged from the entrance all the way up the stairs while Edward, having seen many such displays over the years, was more taken by the obvious water damage and other signs of decay.

Esther, Lewis, and Henry sat to one side and let the Governor and Edward carry the conversation, though Esther was very conscious of the Governor's glances her way. By listening, they were able to learn a lot about what to expect on the frontier.

Edward passed along Lord Halifax's compliments to the Governor, and then expressed the general opinion in London that the French were going to push the two nations back into war. They were still embarrassed over the loss of Louisburg during the last war even though the Treaty of Aix-la-Chapelle had restored it to French control. The best way Lord Halifax believed the French could embarrass England would be in the Ohio Country, where both nations had overlapping claims. As these lands fell within Virginia's Royal Charter, Governor Dinwiddie would carry the burden of confrontation. Also as in the last war, Lord Halifax expected the New York frontier to see a lot of action, probably more from the regular troops than Virginia where it would be more irregular, the militia and Indian allies. What Governor Dinwiddie needed to protect against was primarily Indian atrocities, though there was the possibility of some regular troop action, the ground was not as easy to maintain a line of communications thus more limiting than in New York where the lakes north of Albany ran right to the Saint Lawrence.

"Hmm, well, Colonel, what I find most interesting is that His Lordship has such a clear view of things here. I tend to agree with him in almost every detail."

The Governor then went on to explain how tobacco was wearing out the land, causing increasing pressure to move further west. The used up land was frequently given as the entitlement when indentures expired. This resulted in a large plantation being divided into several smaller farms while the gentleman owner moved his main operations further to the west. The Valley of Virginia was as yet sparsely populated, but as this trend continued, the next big push would be over the mountains to the virginal lands beyond. For now, holding the Valley was his biggest concern. It was too far west to be properly supported from Williamsburg and had a population too scattered and small to see to their own defense. He had sent a militia Major to a crossroads called Chester to lay out a fort and see to the defense in that region, though Major Washington was more surveyor than soldier and his militiamen anxious to return to their homes east of the Blue Ridge.

The Governor, enjoying the conversation, had four extra places set for dinner for his guests. Over dinner the conversation turned more toward the Jewett's plans.

"You know, your grant is for an area south of the Borden's Grant, between the North and Fluvanna Rivers. Let me suggest you contact a man who has done a lot of surveying and one whom I trust to make good your patent. Peter Jefferson. He has a place called Shadwell on the Rivianna River east of the Blue Ridge and you'll most likely find him there, unless he's off with that partner of his, William Frye, or at Tuckahoe. Frye is always talking of making a map, but I have yet to see it. Now Jefferson, he is able to see in his head just about any property you ask him about, and he's done enough of the surveying to tell you if there are likely to be any competing claims on it. I'll write you a letter of introduction myself and have my secretary deliver it to your lodgings. You said you were at the Lightfoot house, did you not?"

"Yes, we are, and I thank you for your kindness."

"Yes, good. Now, you'll also want to discuss your plans with Colonel Byrd. I know he's in town and staying at the Raleigh Tavern. Do you know it? Good. He's had a lot of experience with his western plantations and should be able to steer you right on the best way to get to yours."

The meal concluded, the four made their way back to the coach and started down the Palace Green toward their lodgings.

"Esther, the Raleigh isn't a place for you, so we'll drop you at the house and we'll go on to see Colonel Byrd."

"Is he a real Colonel, as you, Edward?"

"I suspect not, Henry. Most likely he is Colonel of the local militia and holds his commission from the Governor and not the Crown. Just as the Prescotts have been Colonels of the militia in and around Rowley for generations. In any case, he is locally important and we shall treat him accordingly."

They found Colonel Byrd in the barroom at the Raleigh, having eaten his dinner and now sitting down to a bowl of punch. He greeted Edward warmly, scarcely glancing at his brothers, yet all three were invited to share the bowl with him. Lewis politely declined while Edward and Henry partook modestly from the bowl.

After explaining their mission in brief, couched terms, Colonel Byrd advised, "Your best bet is not even to unload here, just send your ship up to Richmond Town and unload there. Then you only need to freight them above the falls where you can hire flat boats to haul it up the Fluvanna. There are some rough sections of the river, but if you don't start too late the water should be high enough so you shouldn't need to off-load. Don't try to heavy load too few boats, more boats loaded lighter will serve you better. The shoals can really be bothersome above Bremo Bluffs, but they can be passed."

Edward ordered another bowl of punch for Colonel Byrd and left him to it while he and his brothers headed home to discuss this new advice. He was glad they had hired the coach so he did not have to walk through the streets in his regimentals. Just entering and lingering in the tavern had caused quite a stir and he really did not want to attract that much attention to himself. Arriving back at the house, Esther joined them in the parlor.

"What did you think of Colonel Byrd, Edward? I can't say I trust him too much. He is too fond of his punch and I suspect he has an interest in the river freight above Richmond Town," Henry began.

"If you noticed, I gave him only the vaguest of detail. It is not that I don't especially trust Colonel Byrd, but think of all the other ears in the tavern as we talked. You are likely right about Colonel Byrd's financial interest. That said it would be far easier to freight our goods up the river than to try to hire wagons. The roads, I've been given to believe, are quite difficult to non-existent above Richmond Town."

"I am with you there," chimed in Lewis, "and I think Aunt Bess and our wives will find the river much more pleasant, though still tiring, than bouncing along in a wagon or walking beside it. I can't speak for Mary, but Marie doesn't take much to walking."

"You bring up a good point, Lewis, though not the one I think you intended. We will need stock, riding as well as pulling, and aren't likely to find it the further out we travel. I'm starting to see this move being done in two groups. The women and children, father, and perhaps one of us, take the bulkier items in the boats up the river while two of us load a pack train. Packing horses would make us more mobile, less delayed by the roads and we would have the stock when we arrived in the Valley. It is the pack train that would stop by Shadwell to see Mister Jefferson, being less dependent on the river route."

"I can't speak as knowledgeable about Charles, Edward, but if you think Philip and Joseph will be content to ride the boats with the women, you seriously need to remember how you were at their ages," interrupted Esther. "I'll consent to another boat ride, this one being on a river, as I'm sure will the others. Just consider those boys when you're making all these plans. They will want to be where Edward is and, Edward, you're the one who'll have the letter of introduction from the Governor to Mister Jefferson, so you're with the pack horses if we choose to go this route."

"Taking young children on the trail? I think that's risky even though they are boys."

Lewis, Henry, and Esther all grinned widely at Edward, who was momentarily at a loss until Lewis filled him in on the laugh they were having at his expense. "Edward, you really should come home more often. Those young children aren't as young as you remember them. And wait until you see Sarah, all grown up and pretty to boot. Well, we've near a month to sort this out and it's been a long eventful day for me, so I suggest we all turn in. Little children, Edward? Are you in for a shock!"

ᗪ Chapter 6 ᗪ

Robert sat in the cabin of the packet reviewing his books. He knew Edward and Lewis would be quite pleased. He had driven hard bargains for Edward's farms and Lewis' coachworks and gotten better than a fair price for all. In fact, it had taken all three of Lewis' journeymen to combine resources to buy the coachworks. Robert smiled to himself when he thought of their surprise last evening when he delivered them the keys to the house. Why they thought the house wasn't included when it was in the contract and sat on the same lot as the barns making up the coachworks he couldn't understand. They seemed quite pleased with themselves when they realized they no longer would be sleeping in the shed.

And working with Sam Brown, his father and uncle at Robert's old store had also proved very beneficial. There wasn't enough coin in all of Rowley, even if he could carry it, to pay the price for all they had sold. No, taking £2,000 in coin was more than enough to carry with them. If they were going overland, even that would have been too hazardous to carry. Sam's offer to provide a letter of credit drawn on his London Factor had made perfect sense and, now that Robert looked back on it, was really the only way to do it. Everything was in order, the packet loaded, everyone on board, and they would leave with the evening tide. A quick check of his watch showed he had plenty of time for one final walk around the only town he had ever known.

The deck of the small packet was full of excitement. The boys were climbing the rigging and their mothers calling in vain for them to come down and to be careful. Their heads filled with stories of pirates and the excitement of getting underway was just too much for them. Master Cole was seeing to the final lashing of the cargo and final adjustments to the rigging. He had replaced the topmast and rigging in Norfolk, before the long haul back up the coast, but he was not completely satisfied with how they had configured the running rigging, so now was his last chance to set things to his liking.

Aunt Bess casually stood on the dock pretending not to be waiting for Robert. She knew, counted on, actually, that he would take one more stroll around the town and she wanted to go with him. They started off without a word passing between them, her arm through his.

"Now, where are those two going?" Mary asked Marie.

"To the cemetery, to say their goodbyes."

"But that isn't the way to the cemetery."

"No, but that's where they'll end up. You haven't had the chance to get to know them like I have. It's not the town they'll miss, it is all those buried in the cemetery. The town just contained the sights that triggered the memories. Lewis slipped out for his final visit, you know. Oh, he didn't tell me where he was going, nor did he tell me that's where he'd been, but I knew just by the look in his eye. They'll be back directly, and I doubt a word will have passed between them the whole time, yet they can each tell you what the other was thinking, what they were feeling."

"We've missed so much being in Boston, away from grandfather," Sarah interjected. A sharp look from her mother sent her back to the other side of the deck.

As the time approached, Robert and Aunt Bess were seen strolling back to the dock, still arm in arm. Mary and Marie had started to worry whether they would make it back in time for the tide, but did not need to. Once the decision to remove the family had been made, both were committed to it and would not look back.

Master Cole got the packet underway with the tide and they soon found themselves enjoying a star-filled night at sea. Robert sat on deck, leaning back against the stern rail. He could hear Master Cole below in the cabin, keeping the boys enthralled with tales of pirates. More than once he had made out the name "Captain Kidd" during these tales. Sarah came and joined him, sitting close. When she shivered in the night air, he put his arm around her and drew her close.

"Grandfather, do you think I'm pretty?"

"Why, yes, Sarah, I do. You look more like your grandmother every day and I always thought her the prettiest lady I'd ever seen."

After a pause while she collected her thoughts, Sarah continued. "Daniel thinks I'm pretty."

"Why, he does, does he? So you have a beau you haven't told me about?"

"Well, not a beau, actually, just a friend. Mother and father don't care for him much. They say I'm too young to be thinking about boys. Mother wouldn't even let me say goodbye to him as she hurried us out of Boston. She doesn't know it, but I sent him a note telling him goodbye and where he could find me, if he had an interest that way. It's been over a month and I haven't heard, so I don't suppose he's all that interested. Now, you won't tell mother I wrote Daniel, will you Grandfather? She'd be awfully upset with me."

"No, child, I won't tell her. That's for you to do. Don't look so surprised, you know you have to. And as for this Daniel, I quite agree with your parents, you're too young. It is nothing against the lad, for I don't know him at all, but at 14 you don't know your own mind yet. No, child, it's best you haven't heard from him just yet. It'll be a few years before we're ready to part with you and a lot can change, I dare say will change what with this grand adventure we've embarked on, before you're ready to take a husband."

Why was it, Sarah thought, that the same thing her parents had told her sounded so much better coming from grandfather? Perhaps it was not so much what he said as how he said it. It was his soft, comforting voice as he told her what she did not want to hear, how he pulled her closer to him at just the right moment. She now cuddled closer into his embrace. How she had missed him while they were in Boston. How good it was to be near him again.

The next morning dawned clear and warm. Everyone was up on deck right after breakfast, enjoying the sea breezes.

"Master Cole, what do you have those boys doing?" inquired Marie, looking aloft.

"Why, they're looking out for pirate ships, Ma'am, keeping us safe from the villains, as it were. I've given each a spy glass and told them to watch a different point of the horizon and to sing out if they see a sail, and if it is a black sail, then we've got a pirate ship sure as there's air. That should keep them occupied most of the day, I suspect."

"And later, when that gets old?" added Mary.

"Well, there's always practice with the swivels. I've assigned each to one of the swivel guns, reminded them that those four guns are our only protection against pirates, and that they must be diligent to their duties should we get into a fight. Not that we will. Why, those swivels haven't been fired in years. Burning off a few of the old charges will be good for them. After that there'll be the regular duties of a sailor's mate. Why, I'll have them working as part of the crew long before this voyage is over. They'll be so happy to be on dry land again..." Master Cole chuckled at his own inventiveness, quite pleased with himself.

"Then they'll expect to collect their wages when we reach Williamsburg, Master Cole, have you given that any thought?" added Robert.

That stifled the chuckle. "Well, no, can't say I have. Now see here, they're signed on as passengers, they are, and I don't have any wages to pay them."

"Calm down, Master Cole, calm down. When the time comes I suspect their wages will come to two shillings each, which I will give you to pay them. They needn't know where the shillings originated. So, have we a bargain?"

"Oh, you are cunning, Mister Robert. Are you sure there isn't some pirate in you?"

"Not at all, and it isn't cunning, it's experience. Don't forget I raised three sons practically on my own, plus I have a good memory back to when I was their age. I remember what motivates and captivates them. Aunt Bess, was that you I just heard coughing?"

"It's nothing, Robert, just too much sea air. I think I'll go below and rest some, maybe do some mending. Those boys go through clothes very quickly you know, and there really isn't much for me to do otherwise. Now, stop worrying, I'm fine."

The boys took great delight in spotting every ship that came within sight of the little packet, not that it was all that many. That evening they were a bit disappointed at not having spotted a pirate ship, so Master Cole announced gunnery practice for the next afternoon, assuming they had not been sunk by pirates before then. This fired up their imagination again and they went to bed that night tired and content.

The mothers appreciated Master Cole keeping their boys occupied. In the weeks before departing, they worried about how they would survive two weeks at sea without the boys fighting amongst themselves or causing problems for the ship's crew. Now they were feeling quite safe, learning that most of the crew had sailed with Master Cole for years and none were the hard bitten lot found on Royal Navy ships. Most of them even had wives in Boston, some with children of their own. The two months they were to be employed in this charter for the Jewett family would be the longest any of them had been away from home since the late war.

Mary and Marie spent most of their time with Aunt Bess, sewing and talking. Mary was sharing her dreams of all the things their circumstances had denied them that she would finally be able to get. Marie and Aunt Bess tried to temper her a bit, not to much avail. If truth be told, Marie was feeling almost giddy at the sudden turn in her fortunes as well. Aunt Bess was the one to whom their increased circumstances meant nothing. All she knew was she would again be surrounded by "her boys" and that was all that it took to make her content. Not even the cough that would not go away could get her spirits down, now that she was headed toward that time when they would all be together again.

Marie noticed the change first. The cough seemed to settle deeper into the elderly woman's chest and she seemed weaker, sewing slower and, when she walked, shuffling more than walking. Oh, Aunt Bess laughed it off, saying she shuffled because she could not get used to a pitching deck. But Marie began to take greater note and finally became worried. Then, at dawn on their sixth day at sea:

"Robert, come quick, its Aunt Bess. I'm afraid she's quite ill." It was Marie's troubled voice that caused Robert to rise with a start. Marie was not one to make too much of a thing, so when she became worried, Robert took notice.

He found Aunt Bess in her bed in the main cabin, Mary and Sarah at her side. She was sweating, obviously feverish, and coughing from deep in her chest.

Taking a light hearted tone he did not feel, Robert addressed his aunt. "What's this? Taking to your bed to gain our sympathies? I'd expect that from the boys, but have never known you to remain abed this long. If I didn't know you better I'd think you were looking to have these women take to waiting on you hand and foot. Hey, that isn't such a bad idea. Move over, Aunt Bess, and I'll join you." The smile on his lips did not reach his eyes, nor did he feel it.

"Oh, Robert, how you do go on. I've just had a poor night, that's all, and have a touch of a cough. I'll be fine if you'd all just stop fussing about. Now get out, the lot of you."

They all moved into the passageway and conversed in low tones, all but Sarah, that is. She remained behind, sitting with Aunt Bess and occasionally wiping her forehead with cool water. Aunt Bess tried to shoo her out, but she was not leaving, so the elderly woman gave in and accepted the aid and comfort. By late in the day it was obvious she was taking a turn for the worse and Sarah summoned help.

Each of the women now took turns administering to Aunt Bess, keeping cold compresses on her forehead and wrists, making sure she was propped up and could not slump over. Still the elderly woman failed to show any signs of improvement, though she also didn't seem to be getting worse. The end of the second day Robert brought Master Cole to look in on her for his opinion.

"Well, Mister Robert, it's not consumption, nor is it one of the tropical fevers. I think the fever is a result of her lungs, which are mighty full. It'll be five or six days before we'll reach Williamsburg if these winds hold. While we've passed by New York, we can turn around and put in there so she can be seen by a doctor."

"You'll do no such thing, Master Cole," coughed Aunt Bess. "You are being paid to take this family to Williamsburg and that is where we'll stop. If you turn back for New York, I'll see you aren't paid a shilling..." A fit of coughing ended her tirade.

"Now Aunt Bess, be reasonable. You need a doctor and there are plenty of fine ones in New York. We can take you there, get you well, and then continue on to Williamsburg. Be reasonable."

"No, Robert, what I need are my boys. I've come this far and I won't wait one day longer than absolutely necessary to have them all around me again. So not another word about putting in anywhere but Williamsburg. Promise me, Robert," her firmness giving way, "Promise me, I beg you."

Robert dropped his head, and then gave a slight nod. Aunt Bess smiled, then faded off to a fitful sleep.

So they continued. Robert took to sitting with Aunt Bess most of the time and Master Cole brought out his grog, the only thing he had in the way of medicine. Sitting up, eating broth, and taking an occasional sip of the grog seemed to do Aunt Bess some good, though the fever continued along with the cough and she was quite weak.

Robert, Philip, Charles, and Sarah were on deck with Master Cole as the little packet tacked into The Roads, the entrance to the great bay. The excitement had been building, especially in the boys, ever since breakfast when Master Cole announced they would enter the bay shortly after dinner and could be at the docks serving Williamsburg by morning. At the call of "Land Ho" from the mainmast, the boys scurried into the rigging for a view while Robert and Sarah were content to wait until land was visible from the deck.

Before being rewarded with a view of land, Marie appeared at Robert's elbow and in a hushed, anxious voice said "Father, come quick! It's Aunt Bess."

Chapter 7

"Henry, what are you planning on doing with this?"

"You're the military expert, what do you think? It's a musket."

"I know it's a musket, but I haven't seen one of these in over 25 years when the Tower condemned them and began disposal. Where did you get this man-killer?"

"They issued it to me when we mustered for Louisburg. You really think it is a man-killer?"

"I certainly do. Any man foolish enough to try to fire it is sure to be killed! One things for sure, you can't head west with this antique! And you, Lewis, think we're only going to face birds on the frontier? That fowler is too light to take a round ball."

Both brothers sat looking dejected. Aside from having something to drill with at militia muster, neither brother was proficient at shooting. Now their lives and those of their families would depend on them and it was becoming clear their older brother was not impressed with their arsenal.

"Here, pull those two long crates out. I brought

along these four rifled game guns. They fire a heavy ball, only 32 balls to the pound of lead. And, in this other crate, I have my two officer model muskets. They're better made than the Bess, and have a smaller bore, about 20 balls to the pound, and take ball or shot. With the four of us, we have enough of the rifled guns and, though I'd like a little heavier barrel in Lewis' fowler that also gives us three guns for birds or backup. I do want to replace your very old Bess, Henry. Then we'd each be well armed."

Feeling better now, Lewis added "We also have three strapping boys. Arming them up could provide a lot of extra firepower if we get into a tough scrape. They've never shot, but that puts them about on par with Henry and me."

"Well, we can see if we can find three trade guns, small bored at about 24 balls to the pound. They're light and handy, probably could be handled by the boys you've described. In a real fight, I'd rather have them loading than shooting, but in a running fight it just might make the difference.

"I'm not looking for any firefights, mind you. It's my hope that these just be used for putting meat on the table. That said, we all have to face the fact that we will be far out on the frontier and will have only ourselves to rely on in case of Indian trouble."

Edward looked intently at each of his brothers to make sure they understood what this meant. He had seen war close up and far too personal. They had not and he was satisfied to see them take in his comments very seriously. None of the false bravado he had seen in some new soldiers that usually resulted in early deaths. No, this seriousness coupled with the fact they would literally be defending their families left him confident they would be steady, if not skilled, when the time came. Besides, he still had several weeks to try to teach them shooting basics.

All four siblings were kept very busy preparing everything they would need for the trip. Edward was able to find the extra guns he wanted along with bar lead and kegs of powder and flints. Lewis and Henry looked high and low for horses, finally settling on eight draft and eight riding horses. Together they decided they could find cattle when they stopped at Shadwell. That would put them halfway there before the cattle slowed the progress of the overland portion of the expedition.

Expedition was a good way to label it. Edward was preparing as though he was going on a military campaign. All three men shot each morning and evening with Esther forced to learn loading to where she swore she could do it in her sleep. Lewis and Henry became respectable, if not good shots and were becoming more comfortable handling their arms under varying conditions that included rain, wind, and bright sunshine.

Edward and Colonel Byrd took a sloop up to Richmond Town to arrange for floating their heavier goods up the Fluvanna. It only cost Edward two bowls of punch that day, Colonel Byrd having a powerful thirst on such a warm day. Of course he could only guess about how many boats they would need, none of his siblings having any idea how much would be packed aboard the Boston packet. Based on what they knew of her tonnage, Edward arranged to float that much, lightly loaded as Colonel Byrd suggested, up river. Henry had been right in his observation and all of the boats and crews came from Colonel Byrd.

Lewis had set three saddle makers to work making the saddles and pack saddles they would need. It was the only way they would be done in time. Esther set about gathering trail food for the company. They would be a large group with large appetites and they would be arriving too late in the season to put a crop in. Whatever they needed to carry them through a winter, except for fresh meat if Lewis and Henry ever became hunters, which Esther doubted, they would have to carry with them.

Twice they had dinner with Governor Dinwiddie at the Palace. Edward was convinced the Governor had taken a special liking to Esther, though she always protested loudly when he would bring it up. He was on this very subject one morning after their latest dinner and as they returned from shooting in the fields behind their rented house. As they approached the gate, Lewis saw their father come out the back door and run down the steps toward them. They all broke into a dash to meet him just as though they were young children again.

Robert hugged each of his children in turn, hugging Edward last and longest. After which, with tears streaming down his face, he turned away to compose himself before he continued.

"Esther, boys, your Aunt Bess is gravely ill. We've just carried her up from the Queen's Creek landing, I wouldn't let them put her in a wagon for fear the jolting would finish her. She's sleeping, just waking up long enough as we carried her off the packet to ask if we were in Virginia."

Setting his jaw and looking past his father, Edward spied a boy on the back stoop of the house. "Boy, come here. What's your name? Joseph? Now, Joseph, listen close, run as fast as you can, through the house, cross the street and go past the magazine to the next street. Turn left – show me your left hand, Joseph, good – and go down the street until you come to the Palace Green on your right, run toward the Palace. Just before you get to the gates, there is a large house on your left. That's where you'll find Doctor McKenzie. Tell him I need him and to come quickly.

Now, do you have it? Good, now off with you."

The adults followed Joseph into the house, Robert filling his children in on Aunt Bess' condition as they went. As they entered the room they saw Aunt Bess, still in the ship's bed now set on chairs. Mary, Marie, and Sarah were wiping their tears while Philip and Charles were crying openly. Robert sat down next to his aunt and held her hand as they waited for the doctor to arrive.

He came quickly and examined the elderly woman. He looked at Edward and shook his head, then to Robert.

"I can send for the Parish Minister, if you like."

Robert looked up, shook his head slightly and paused, thinking before he continued. Doctor McKenzie looked to Edward and asked "Dissenters?" Edward nodded. Believing the Church of England had retained too much of the popish trappings, Dissenters like the Jewett family practiced the much simpler form of Protestantism of the Presbyterian, or Scottish, Church.

"Mister Jewett, I am a Dissenter myself and the Scottish Church has been accepted here since the reign of James the First. We have a small congregation and a minister. I could send for him if you like."

"Thank you, Doctor, Aunt Bess would appreciate it very much."

After the Doctor left, Aunt Bess seemed to rally a bit, so Robert, his children and grandchildren gathered around her bed. Her eyes fluttered, and then opened, looking very tired. She first recognized Robert, and smiled, then focused around the bed at each of her family gathered there.

"My boys, all my boys are here. Robert, tell me this isn't a dream, a dream I've had over and over for so many years. It is you, and you're all here. Edward, give your aunt a hug, it is so good to see you."

"Aunt Bess," said Robert sadly, "I am so sorry, I never should have brought you here…"

"Robert you stop that talk right now." Though her voice was weak, it was the aunt they all knew. "If you hadn't brought me I wouldn't be here, now, surrounded by my boys. This is what I wanted, this is all I wanted, and I'm happy it has happened and I've lived to see it." Her coughing cut her off. When she partially recovered, she called to Esther, who had been her constant companion for many years. Taking her hand she pulled Esther close and kissed her hand and held it to her cheek. Rousing again, she again looked each of them in the face.

"Promise me, you're a family and you'll stick together from now on. I mean it. No more running around the world for King and Country, Edward, and no more moving out of town, Henry. You stick together and stay together. Robert, make them promise!"

"You rest easy, Aunt Bess, they all promise."

"Good, good," she said in a failing voice as she again faded off.

Edward looked down at his father, sitting there holding Aunt Bess' hand, and thought how old he looked, how frail. Aunt Bess meant a lot to him, to them all. She had moved into her brother's household, Robert's father, before Robert was born and they had lived in the same house his entire life. This was very hard on him.

Lewis turned toward the window. He was no longer able to choke back his tears. Of the three brothers, he was the one closest to Aunt Bess. She had been there every day of his life and now her life was ebbing away. Henry, tears running down his own cheeks, placed a hand on Lewis' shoulder as Marie moved to comfort her husband.

"How did this happen? She seemed so strong when we left. Why?" asked Lewis softly, to no one in particular.

"I'm afraid Aunt Bess has been frail for quite some time, only she has hid it so as not to miss this moment, when all 'her boys' were gathered around her again. No, it was only her spirit that remained strong," consoled Marie.

They all kept vigil that night. Edward gave Joseph another errand, to bring back the carpenter, and he excused himself just long enough to pass instructions to him. Each time Aunt Bess opened her eyes, she saw she was still surrounded by her family, though she was not able to speak again. Her breathing became very labored by morning when Doctor McKenzie stopped back by and pronounced the end very close. The Presbyterian minister also came by and sat with the family as they kept vigil. To Robert, he offered a place in the Presbyterian burying ground for Aunt Bess, which was gratefully accepted.

Aunt Bess then opened her eyes, looked at no one in particular, and said "Cyrenus?" Closing her eyes, she then breathed her last.

Standing at Edward's elbow, Joseph asked, in a hushed voice, "Who is Cyrenus?"

"He was my grandfather, Aunt Bess' brother."

On only two other occasions had Edward seen his father cry, the death of his father and the death of his wife. Both times it was Aunt Bess who had put her arms around him and whispered in his ear, comforting him. As he listened to Robert's soft sobs, he wished he knew what Aunt Bess had said to comfort him on those occasions. But before he could act, Esther moved to her father and, as Aunt Bess had done before, put her arms around Robert and whispered in his ear. His sobs quieted, he patted her hand, and wiped his eyes.

After each had taken and kissed one of Aunt Bess' hands, the men and children removed themselves while the women began to prepare the body for burial. As they walked through the passage, Robert picked up an old square wooden box from a table and carried it with him as the entered the parlor. A few moments of awkward silence followed, each lost in his own remembrance of everyone's favorite aunt. It was Edward who broke the silence.

"Father, I spoke with the cabinetmaker last night and he said he could have the coffin ready by this evening."

"Thank you, Edward." Then, taking a key from his pocket, he unlocked the box. "I brought this with me from the packet, dreading this eventuality but wanting to be prepared for it." Opening the box, he held it up so all could see the family coat of arms painted on the diagonal on a square piece of heavy English oak plank. "Charles, as the youngest family member able, will carry this right behind the coffin in the processional."

"But, father," whispered Philip to Lewis, a little too loud so everyone heard, "I want to carry it."

Robert responded before Lewis could, "No, tradition has it carried by the youngest member and that's Charles. Your father carried it for my father because he was the youngest able, your Uncle Henry being a newborn then. Aunt Bess always kept this polished. I think it would mean a lot to her to have it carried in her honor."

"Mister Jewett," inserted the minister, "have you considered pall bearers? I could provide them from my congregation if you like."

Looking at his sons, Robert thought a moment then responded, "Thank you, Reverend, but my sons and I will carry it. Aunt Bess isn't, or wasn't, a large woman and I think we four can manage it. She would like that, don't you think, boys?" All three nodded. "We could use some help in getting the coffin onto and off of our shoulders, I should think, if that would not be too much trouble."

"Not at all. I'll be back to check on you this afternoon and to finalize the arrangements. I assume you'll want the service tomorrow afternoon?"

"Yes, that would be fine. Thank you."

Esther had remained sitting beside Aunt Bess after the women had finished and all had retired. She had been her constant companion and while her passing came unexpectedly, it was not completely a surprise. Aunt Bess had confided to Esther before Esther left Rowley with her brothers that she did not expect to live long enough to see Edward's land, only praying she lasted long enough to see them all together again. So, while grieving, she had spent the past weeks steeling herself in case Aunt Bess did not survive the voyage.

As she moved through the passage toward the stairs to the room she was sharing with Sarah, she paused at Edward's door thinking she had heard something. Listening carefully, she heard Edward quietly sobbing and raised her hand to knock on the door, but hesitated. No, it was Edward's way to bear his grief in private and to interrupt him at this time would only serve to make him as cross as an old bear.

With a sigh and shake of her head, Esther thought, "Why can I only think of these plays on words when I'm alone and not while engaged in a battle of wits with my brothers?"

The coffin arrived as promised, a fine oak coffin covered in black leather held in place by brass tacks. There was a silver plate in the center of the lid simply engraved "Elizabeth Jewett." Master Cole had seen to this detail.

The service was held in the Lightfoot House parlor. Master Cole and most of his crew also attended. Afterward the sailors helped hoist the coffin onto the shoulders of Aunt Bess' nephew and grand-nephews, who locked arms and began a slow walk to the burying ground, followed closely by Charles carrying the coat of arms. Behind Charles followed the rest of the family, Master Cole and his sailors, with the minister leading the whole processional. By time they arrived at the burying ground, the well appointed coffin followed by a coat of arms had encouraged many of the townspeople to follow and join in the farewell.

Robert sobbed openly as the minister preached the burial service, as did Esther and Marie. Lewis, Henry, Sarah and the boys cried silently, while Edward stood stoically, although his face showed more of his pain than he realized. After the graveside service, the family began walking back to their lodging. Edward broke the silence.

"I'm sorry, father. If I hadn't proposed the removal of the family to Virginia, this wouldn't have happened."

"Nonsense, you heard Aunt Bess. It was the one thing that brought us all together again and that was the one thing she had hoped for more than anything else. No, she saw this as a gift to her, our being together and her getting to see it. Now that we are all together we still have a long way yet to go. I suggest we begin to discuss the next steps over supper." Though his eyes remained sad, he set his jaw and walked on with his head up and shoulders back, as Aunt Bess would have wanted it.

∽ *Chapter 8* ∽

*T*he day following the funeral found Edward up early, as was his custom, and already walking down Capitol Landing Road when the sun came up. He made his way to the Boston packet and found Master Cole just stirring.

"Master Cole, good morning. I hope I'm not intruding."

"Why, good morning, Colonel, no intrusion at all. Though I must say I have a bit of a head this morning. It was very kind of you to treat the crew to a night at the Raleigh on your tab. I'm afraid we may have lightened your purse more than you anticipated."

"Thirty years a soldier, Master Cole, qualifies me to gauge the quantity of drink a thirsty man can consume in an evening. They'll be no raised eyebrows when I settle the bill, as long as my father is otherwise occupied, if you understand my meaning."

"Aye, never was one to hold with spirits is my guess. But what has you out so early this morning and how can I be of further service?"

Edward then reviewed the plan to use the packet to carry the family's goods to Richmond Town for freighting above the falls. He also advised Master Cole of the goods in need of loading now stored in the lumber house behind the Lightfoot Tenement, things he, his brothers and sister had been accumulating for their trip. Master Cole would handle that transfer for them. Then there was the need to delay their departure for a week while the final preparations were made. Edward knew Master Cole and his crew were anxious to return to Boston and this delay, along with the transfer of goods from Williamsburg to Richmond Town, was not part of the original payment agreed with his father.

"Now don't you worry about the payment. Your father paid us well and in advance and then you treated us to a night ashore. There isn't any balance due on your sheet. Besides, I met a gentleman named Colonel Byrd last night. When I told him what tobacco was going for in Boston, we entered an agreement where I will ship his tobacco there and we'll both make a tidy sum. No, sir, I'll not even be returning home with an empty ship. I've made out quite well on this venture and I've you to thank for it."

Their business concluded Edward started back for the house. Before he had walked as far as the Capitol, he saw his three nephews running toward him, all shouting "Uncle Edward" in unison. He stopped and waited for them to reach him, thinking how good it felt to be called "Uncle Edward" by these three adoring boys.

"Uncle Edward, grandfather sent us to find you. Are you going to teach us to shoot today? You've taught father, Uncle Henry, and even Aunt Esther how to shoot and I want to learn next," panted Philip, the other two immediately piping in with their "Me, too." "I saw you have a lot of guns, more than just for you three and grandfather. Are there guns for us? Are there?"

"Yes, there are guns for you and, yes, if you are to

go to the frontier with us, you will all have to at least be able to load. I am quite sure, however, that your grandfather didn't send you searching the town for me just to find out if I would teach you to shoot today. Unless, that is, you were pestering him so badly that he simply wanted you out of the house."

It was Charles that pushed forward now. "No, it wasn't that. Grandfather had a visit this morning from a man who father said was the Secretary to the Governor. First he wanted to invite us to dine today at the Palace, all of us, and then he wanted to see the coat of arms I carried yesterday. Grandfather showed him and he was very impressed. He made some notes on a slip of paper, thanked grandfather and then left. That's when grandfather sent us for you."

"But," inserted Philip, "it will be hours before we have to go to the Palace. Can't you teach us to shoot before then?"

"First I will find out what your grandfather wants, then I will have my breakfast, and then, only then, will I see if there is time to teach you how to shoot. Though don't expect to learn it all in one session."

With that they started back toward the house, Edward walking with his hands clasped behind his back, an old Army habit, while the boys, now even more excited, ran. Arriving at the house he found Robert in the parlor, looking a bit worried.

"What is the problem, father?"

"Oh, Edward, I'm glad you're here. This man Preston, Henry said he's the Governor's Secretary, came by and invited us to dine at the Palace with the Governor. Then he was quite curious about our coat of arms. You know I don't normally bring it out, except on rare occasions like yesterday, but he was quite persistent about wanting, nay, needing, to see it. I showed him, not knowing what else to do, and he started making notes about it. I hope I did the right thing."

"Father, you did fine. And why shouldn't the Governor ask you to dine with him? After all, your children have dined with him half a dozen times as we waited on your arrival. No, we'll all go, save the boys who can dine here. Sally can see to them."

"Oh, no, Edward, Mister Preston was very clear that the boys were invited also. Master Cole has sent our baggage up, so I will have my black broadcloth to wear, and the ladies are busy gathering appropriately subdued clothing as well."

Surprised, but not protesting, Edward nodded thoughtfully. Then he and Robert joined the rest of the family in the dining room for breakfast. The boys were a bit more boisterous than normal, overly excited in anticipation of the shooting lesson. Edward then announced that Sarah and their mothers would also be participating in the shooting lesson, as befitted frontier women. That sent the boys to rolling their eyes as they chattered among themselves about how well they would do in comparison to their mothers.

After breakfast, they gathered up the shooting gear and guns and headed to the meadow behind the house. As the lessons began, Edward started, much to the boys dismay, with Robert who showed remarkable prowess with the rifle after just a few shots. Lewis reminded the boys that their grandfather was the only one other than Edward who had fired before. In the many Indian skirmishes that had filled his early years, Robert had mustered and marched out in response to uprisings by the Iroquois. He had shown himself quite handy with a musket in those days and today he showed he had not lost all of those skills through the years.

Then it was the boys turn and that is when Edward missed his Captains, Lieutenants, and Sergeants the most. Lewis, Henry, and Robert all helped with the boys, though the calls of "Uncle Edward" were fairly continuous and brought smiles to the faces of the ladies watching. Philip showed the most promise, having stronger powers of concentration, though all three made progress. The big surprise was when the ladies began their lesson.

Marie was first up to the line and Philip was having a bit too much fun predicting where her shot would land. Lewis just smiled and told them to watch and learn. Shooting the short, light trade guns the boys had used, her first shot matched the best the boys had managed and her next was close on the first. Philip was aghast.

"You see, Philip, your mother learned how to shoot and hunt from her father when she was a girl. There remains some things that you don't know, and I would think you'd have learned that by now," Lewis said, barely able to control his delight.

As the lesson continued, Sarah showed some ability, as had Esther earlier, but Esther and Mary were both more comfortable loading than shooting. Edward had anticipated as much and knew that in a standing fight having them load would be better than having them shoot as it would speed the rate of fire of the better shooters.

Then it was time to ready themselves for dinner at the Palace. Much to the boys chagrin, Edward dressed in plain, black broadcloth like his father and brothers and not in his regimentals, as they wanted. This time it took two coaches to carry them the short distance to the Palace and when they arrived there was no hesitancy on Mister Preston's part about seeing them into the parlor.

"Sir Robert, welcome. It truly is a pleasure to make

your acquaintance," the Governor said as he entered the parlor and bowed deeply.

Robert looked confusedly toward Edward who simply nodded that it was alright.

"Why, thank you, Your Excellency. You do me and my family a great honor," was Robert's reply as he, also, bowed very graciously.

Edward smiled, impressed at how quickly his father had picked up the proper, gentlemanly airs in this situation. Of course he knew his father was well known in Rowley for his good manners and way with people that was in part what helped make him successful as a merchant.

"So, Sir Robert," the Governor continued, taking Robert by the arm and escorting him to the dining room, "I understand your family is of Norman origins and you have a crusader in your line. Your family must go back, then to William the First..." The conversation continued throughout the dinner, with the Governor showing considerable deference to Robert, whose grandsons were in awe, never imagining their grandfather being on such easy terms with a Royal Governor.

Back in the Lightfoot Tenement after dinner, the boys pressed their grandfather for an explanation. "What made the Governor think our family was Norman and fought in a crusade, grandfather, and why did he keep calling you 'Sir Robert' all through the dinner?" asked Philip, never one for being shy.

It was Edward who provided the explanation, opening the old box again to reveal the family coat of arms. "You see the main symbol on the crest is a cross? While not every knight who fought in a crusade has a cross on his coat of arms, only knights who did fight in a crusade can use the cross on theirs. Then there is the five fleurs-de-lis arranged on the cross, the symbol of France and indicating Norman ancestry. William the First, or the Conqueror, was Norman and his followers were Norman."

"That makes sense," injected Charles, "but it still doesn't say why he called grandfather 'Sir Robert.'"

"See this helmet, above the crest? That is the sign of a knight, so the Governor assumed that your grandfather had inherited a title with the crest."

"Well, did he?" asked Joseph, not wanting to be left out.

"No, boys, I'm afraid not, though I see no harm in leaving the Governor that impression. Our family does descend from a knight who fought in the First Crusade, it is true, and these arms were presented when Major Jewett was made Forester of Windsor Forest and Parker of Sunnyvale Park over 300 years ago, but these titles aren't ones that are inherited. Your grandfather will be pleased to know that the Heralds had the original of our coat of arms displayed when I was presented at Court." At which Robert gave a satisfied grin.

The boys looked disappointed at this news, though still more than a little bit awed by their grandfather. They were learning a lot of things they had not heard while tucked away in Rowley. It was clear their anticipated adventures had already begun.

The next several days were typical, filled with preparations for their departure. Shooting lessons continued, with Edward stressing discipline and control. All steadily improved and no one was exempt from the practice, Edward included. Joseph and Charles chaffed a bit under the military style training. Requiring the most attention from Edward, they were the ones who were most frequently upbraided for their lapses. The end of each session, however, was always calculated to be on a positive note and even they started coming around.

Marie had a chance to review the horses. All were deemed acceptable and one of the riding horses was claimed as her own. She was doubly impressed upon learning Lewis and Henry had made all the selections. She started spending all of her free time riding again, though there were some in the family who claimed it went beyond her free time and encroached on time she should have been doing other things. One thing she dared not miss was shooting practice as Edward accepted no excuses. The entire family realized quick enough that beneath the gentlemanly veneer was a will as hard as stone formed by his many years of military service.

One day there came a knock at the door and Sally announced Colonel Byrd had come to call. The Colonel was polite but in a bit of a hurry, so he got right to the point.

"Colonel, Sir Robert," for now most of the gentry were referring to Robert as "Sir," "Have you thought of how you will solve your labor problems on the frontier? I have several slaves available for immediate sale that would serve you and your family well for clearing and establishing fields."

Edward and Robert exchanged looks, then Edward responded. "I thank you, Colonel, for your offer. Right now we must decline. We will have our hands full just getting our goods and ourselves to the frontier that to have the added problems of overseeing slaves is more than we're able to take on at this point. Besides, I believe you'll find my father more inclined to pay wages than to own slaves."

"Quite right, Edward. Don't get me wrong, Colonel Byrd, slaves were available in Massachusetts Colony. From my observation, it was far more trouble keeping them than to pay a fair wage for hired labor. I prefer to stay with what

I am familiar with."

"Ah, there you have it then. I think you will change your minds, but there will be time later for you to correct this course of action. If you are more inclined to hire, I might suggest there are in Richmond Town several indentured persons whose time you may be able to purchase at a reasonable rate. I plan on leaving in the morning and will meet you there. Should I hear of any indentures available I'll be sure to appraise you. I'll see you in a few days then."

They doubted Colonel Byrd had taken any offense, though he obviously thought them quite naive to decline his offer of slaves. Edward pointed out that the ones he was likely referring to would be difficult ones he was trying to move off of his properties, though that was just speculation.

Robert remained uncomfortable with everyone referring to him as "Sir." Edward consoled him by pointing out none in the family had started using that appellation, they had just resisted correcting those who used it. Besides, Edward thought the subtle respect had aided them as they made their final preparations.

And it was their final preparations. By the end of the week's time, all was ready. Lewis, Philip, and Joseph would join Edward in bringing the stock while Henry and Charles would join their father on the packet to take care of the floating portion of the expedition. Philip and Joseph had no delusions, their Uncle Edward had made it too clear, should they not work out on the trail, when all reached Richmond Town adjustments could, and would, be made.

After conveying the rest of the family to the packet, they began. Philip and Joseph each led two of the riding horses while Edward and Lewis each led four draft horses, all well packed with the lighter of their goods. The great adventure had begun and they soon realized it was more work than adventure.

Chapter 9

The first couple of hours on the road to Charles City were the hardest. The horses finally adapted to moving along as a string and things did get a little easier. Edward and Lewis traded off the lead after each rest, one always leading and the other trailing with the two boys in the middle. Edward's hopes to get further the first day were thwarted crossing at the Chickahominy River ferry. Instead of crossing all at once, they had to cross in two groups, Lewis and Philip crossing first and then waiting for Edward and Joseph. It was a good break, especially for the boys, and they took advantage of it by eating their meal and thus avoiding a stop later.

The roads in this part of Virginia are generally sandy. If it had been wet the going would have been hard, less for them than for wagons though still not easy. They arrived in Charles City without incident and Edward allowed them to stay in an Ordinary that night. Although ready for a good rest, the boys learned that life on the trail meant seeing to the horses first. They removed the panniers and pack saddles, rubbed the horses down, fed and hobbled them before they were allowed to sit and enjoy the Ordinary's public fare, if enjoy is the right word. Both may have been inclined to complain had it not been for Edward's stern warning at the outset of replacing any complainer with Henry or Charles.

The boys slept in the stable loft, very comfortable on the loose hay, while Lewis and Edward took space in the small Ordinary's garret. The boys got the better night's sleep. By time they arrived all of the bed space had been taken, so they were shown space for two on the floor in a room already housing six men on the two beds and two others on the floor. The noise was loud and the smells beyond description. They were tired so both managed to sleep tolerably well. At first light, Edward had them all up and seeing to the horses, hoping to be on their way by sunrise.

"The boys are moving stiffly and have you noticed how their hands do not seem to want to grip anything," observed Lewis quietly to Edward.

"I've noticed that and something else. Neither has said a word of protest. Their whispers to each other, I suspect, are of their sore physical state. I suspect they do not want to exchange the trail with us for the boat with their grandfather and, worse, the women," was Edward's hushed reply. Both men just smiled at the boys' awkward movements as the packing progressed.

Once the work was done a cold breakfast followed and they were on their way shortly after sunrise. Two hours into their ride, after Edward had passed Herring Creek and while the boys were still in the ford, Edward was startled by the rapid approach of two riders coming up a side road he had not noticed.

"Why, Colonel Byrd, what brings you out this early?" was Edward's greeting to their benefactor.

"I knew you'd be passing and thought I'd ride to

Richmond Town with you to make sure my people do right by your family and maybe talk a little business. My plantation is just here, up this road. When we get to town I might even consent to your buying me a bowl of punch for having roused me this early."

"Yes, I could be so persuaded. And don't you also need to see to the loading of your tobacco on the Boston packet?"

"Not much passes your notice, does it, Colonel? I hope you are not bothered that I have engaged in business with Master Cole, though I probably should have consulted with you first."

"Once Master Cole delivers my family and our possessions, my business with him is done and yours free to begin. He is a good man, so I hope you'll treat him fairly."

Colonel Byrd's absentminded "Of course" ended the conversation as Edward put them in motion again. The two Colonels road together in silence for some time while Colonel Byrd's companion dropped back evidently seeing to the boys while their uncle was distracted. It was Colonel Byrd who finally broke the protracted silence.

"You see, Colonel, I faired poorly at the gaming tables in Williamsburg the other day and find myself embarrassingly in need of some ready money. I remembered our previous conversation about your need for labor and thought we might reach some mutually beneficial arrangement."

"You may recall, Colonel, that I have already declined your offer of slaves as their burdening us too much on the journey."

"Yes, yes, though I do think you right about the journey, you'll regret not having them once you've arrived. But no matter, you can always send for them and I'll sell you the best I can spare. No, I was thinking of Aaron, here, and another, Miles, who is already in Richmond Town. They are both indentured to me and, if you would see fit to purchase the remaining time on their indentures, you would have two good hands not prone to problems."

"Forgive me for being blunt, Colonel, but I can't help wonder why you are willing to part with good hands, aside from your need for ready money."

"If you must know, I have had quite enough with the both of them. Both saw fit to take wives, against my wishes and the terms of their indentures. The women are both at my properties above Richmond Town and Aaron is constantly trying to find excuses to visit her. Miles, on the other hand, at least married a woman near where he works, though now both are bothering me about their separate quarters and couldn't I see fit to build them a cabin. Now, I'm tired of the both of them, though they are good workers, Aaron here being especially good with horses."

Edward remained silent in thought for a long while as they continued down the road. "How much do you want for their papers?" he finally asked.

"I should think £10 per year of their remaining indenture would be a fair price. Aaron has three years and Miles three and a half left, so, say £65 for the two."

"Yes, but there is the matter of their head right. You will be avoiding granting them their 50 acres each when the indenture matures while I will be incurring it. I should think some compensation should be made for that. Perhaps you would throw in the horse Aaron is riding, along with its furnishings as just compensation to me. And a like arrangement for this Miles."

Now it was Colonel Byrd's turn to think, though it did not take him long to see he still would come out ahead. "Done."

"And their wives, what of the price for them? These

two will hardly be content across the Blue Ridge if their wives remain in Richmond Town."

"I hadn't considered that. Yes, I do see your point. Hmmm, Betty has over four years left on her and Mattie just at four. What do you say to another £65 and we call it square. You make out well that way and I have £130 to settle my current embarrassment. You do have £130 in coin, don't you?"

"Yes, not to worry. I'll pay you when we reach Richmond Town and you have delivered papers on all four and their persons, with the second horse and furnishings."

"You drive a hard bargain, Colonel, but a fair one. Done."

Colonel Byrd slipped back and informed Aaron of his change in employment along with that of his wife, before rejoining Edward. At the next stop to allow the horses a break, Aaron was able to quietly slip over to Edward.

"Bless you, sir, you shan't regret it. I'll work hard for you and Betty is as fine a cook as you'll find."

"You're most welcome. Now, here is some salve, would you ask the boys to rub down the front legs of my horse, its knees are swelling a bit."

"Sir, if you don't mind my speaking out of turn, there is nothing wrong with the knees on your horse. He's fit as can be."

"Yes, but a little salve won't hurt him and will do the boys hands a lot of good. This way they get the benefit and keep their pride." Both men broke into large grins before Edward wandered over to fill Lewis in on the change in their party. As he approached he found Colonel Byrd had beaten him to it.

"That brother of yours drove a hard bargain, I'll warrant. I'd hate to face him off in a game of chance, can't read what he's thinking."

"Well, my brother isn't much of one for games of chance, but you couldn't find much better to back you in the game of life. Here he is now. So, Edward, I understand we've added to our motley family since we left the Ordinary this morning."

"Yes, Colonel Byrd was trying to shed himself of his problems and pass them along to us," was the retort, a large grin on Edward's face.

They moved on to Richmond Town without further incident, arriving late in the day. They found the Boston packet tied up to the dock and the work of unloading into the wagons already begun under the watchful eyes of both Robert and Master Cole. The boys started to what they thought would be a grand reunion with their grandfather and mothers when Edward stopped them short and turned them around. Horses had to be seen to first and then they could visit, if they were able. All would spend the night on board the packet.

In the packet's cramped cabin, Robert, Edward, Lewis, and Henry sat with Colonel Byrd and his rude map of the country above Richmond Town. Colonel Byrd thought the best chance of meeting up with Peter Jefferson was to head for his home, Shadwell, even though he now spent most of his time managing Tuckahoe Plantation. He had gone to see to his own interests some weeks before and was not expected back for two or three weeks. They also agreed on meeting the boats where the Rockfish River joined the Fluvanna. Colonel Byrd knew of a passable wagon road that went from a point two days float above there through Indian Gap and onto Edward's land grant. While the road was passable, he recommended they hire two wheeled carts rather than wagons as they were more suited to the narrow, difficult road and steep terrain. Colonel Byrd also knew a freighter at the landing and would send ahead word of their need for carts and oxen.

Their business concluded and supper finished, Robert, his sons, and Colonel Byrd retired to the nearby tavern so Edward could provide Colonel Byrd that promised bowl of punch. As they parted for the evening, Colonel Byrd promised to send Betty, Mattie, and Miles to the docks at sunrise, ready to travel.

Good to his word, the next morning found Colonel Byrd at the docks, a little worse for having drunk the bowl of punch the night before, with the servants and their papers in hand. Edward counted out the money he owed for them after he had inspected the papers, horse and gear provided for Miles, having previously satisfied himself on those given to Aaron. To say these four misfortunates were happy to be included in this family entourage would be an understatement.

The women and Miles would join the family on the boats while Aaron would continue with Edward and Lewis on land, now leading the draft horses Edward previously led. The boys exchanged nervous glances at this point, anticipating their services would no longer be needed and they were to be relegated to the unexciting task of remaining with the boats. When Edward came to announcing a "change in the line-up" for the land expedition, they expected the worst. Instead, another loud Indian war whoop was let out by all three boys when they learned their elders had decided to not only take Philip and Joseph, but to add Charles to their company, now that Robert and Henry had the assistance of Miles with the other company of wayfarers. So the land company departed before the sun was two hours old, leaving the floating company to finish packing the boats for their departure the next day.

❦ *Chapter 10* ❧

They left the dock area of Richmond Town and moved through the town to the northwest road toward Gum Spring. By having Aaron along, Edward was freed up to lead the company and he always kept one of the boys at his side as a sort of aide-de-camp, capable of running messages back along the line. This job was to rotate among the boys, giving each a break from leading horses. The little cavalcade attracted attention of the locals, as it had the previous two days. Once they exited the confines of the town, the land opened up to a mixture of tobacco fields and woodlots with a few scattered farm complexes here and there.

Lewis was up front as they exited the town. Just before passing the last townhouse, he thought he noticed a change in Edward's mood. He shifted from carefree to being watchful and a bit distracted. Not that this change was readily apparent, but Lewis knew his brother and could pick up on his watchfulness. Nothing was said, but throughout the morning Edward would drop back to ride trail now and again, falling a good piece behind several times before catching back up.

The roads had changed as well. From being mostly sandy, they were now heavily rutted red clay. Lewis could only imagine how bad these roads would be in wet conditions. He was in no hurry to find out just how bad, hoping the dry weather held. With a slight breeze from the east, signs were good for several days of good weather. Still, the rutted conditions made for poor footing for the horses and not a very comfortable ride as a result.

The boys were having a great time, now that they could look forward to some break in the monotony of leading the horses. Lewis had to admit Edward's idea had been a good one. It had also resolved a future issue, Charles feeling very left out by having been left behind on the boat. This could have led to further isolating him from the other two, who were already closer to each other than Charles was to either of them because of his previous sojourn in Boston, the other two occupying the same house in Rowley.

During the noon halt, longer than normal so all could rest and a meal prepared, Edward announced it was time to break out the guns.

"From now on we need to carry our arms across the saddle, in readiness. So, Lewis, let's break them out of the packs along with our horns and pouches. Boys, I want you to load a heavy load of buckshot, you too, Aaron. You will use my musket."

Lewis came over to Edward as the boys were unpacking the weapons and, in a hushed voice, asked, "Are you sure this is absolutely necessary, Edward? These roads are difficult and I'd hate to see an accident happen."

"I haven't said anything until now, and would prefer the boys not be told, but I fear there may be trouble in the not too distant future. We attracted too much attention as we left Richmond Town, from two I noted in particular."

Lewis said nothing, just nodded and went to help the boys and Aaron. All made a good show of loading, as Edward wanted. After, they mounted, secured their guns across their saddles, and set out again. Edward continued wary throughout the afternoon but in such a manner neither the boys nor Aaron appeared to notice. The boys were feeling quite grown up to have their guns out and across their saddles. Edward's training, however, ensured they all handled the guns in the proper manner and not like children. They continued at a good pace, not too fast to overly tax the horses, not leisurely either.

When they stopped for the evening meal and, presumably, to camp, Edward again surprised Lewis by announcing they would not unpack the horses. Aaron made the fire and all the boys helped keep it fueled during meal preparation and cleanup. Edward then had a surprise for them all. He ordered the fire put out and ashes scattered, then they remounted and moved on in the growing dusk. It was fully dark when they made a cold camp for the night. The horses were unpacked, unsaddled, and hobbled, the blankets came out and a weary company bedded down in the chill of the evening.

Hours later, while he was soundly sleeping, someone kicked Lewis and ordered him up. Rousing, the full moon gave enough illumination he could just make out two men holding guns trained on him and his fellow travelers. The boys quickly moved to him and huddled around. Edward, however, had not emerged from his blankets.

"Get him up. He's the one with the fat purse I saw in the tavern last night," one ruffian said to the other who was closer to Edward's blankets. Before he could move, he felt cold steel thrust against the base of his skull. "Well, get on with it," the original speaker encouraged. Then, turning his head away from Lewis and the boys to see why his partner had not moved, he, too, felt cold steel rammed into his ear.

"Lewis, relieve them of their weapons, knives as well as firelocks," came Edward's voice with an edge to it none of them had heard before, "and then one of you boys can strike a light."

Philip moved quickly to be the first to get his fire starter, before his father had a chance to disarm the intruders. As he moved, the ruffian in front of Edward's muzzle moved to bring his gun to bear on the boy. Simultaneously Lewis shouted at Philip and the ruffian felt a hard jab from Edward at the base of his skull that caused him to pause in his design, the muzzle of his gun instantly dropping toward the ground between him and Philip, the same direction his head had just been forcibly thrust.

"Move, please move, and it will resolve what I am to do with you," came a harsh near whisper from Edward that frightened his own party as much as it did the ruffians. The gun was immediately lowered the rest of the way, then handed to Lewis as he came near in such a way nothing put peaceful intentions would be construed by the owner of the hard voice behind his head.

Lewis did a thorough job of searching the ruffians for weapons and was rewarded with a good number of knives of various sizes and two hatchets in addition to the guns. Then Edward had them sit and remove their shoes and stockings before he proceeded. Using the light Charles provided, Philip being much affected by recent events, he checked the right hand of both intruders and found a "T" branded below the thumb of the right hand of the man Aaron had been covering. Checking his ears, then, he found the telltale notches caused when one has been nailed to the stocks.

"So, stranger, you have already been labeled a

thief but escaped the gallows by pleading Right to Clergy. You've had your one reprieve. It's the gallows for you. And I dare say your friend as well. For keeping company with a known felon leaves him little room to plead he did not know what would happen."

"What do you plan to do with us?"

"Well, tonight we will string you both up to that tree there, with the strong branch about ten feet up." Edward then had them bound both hand and foot before taking two longer ropes and tying a slipknot in the end of both. Placing the noose around the thief's neck and over the branch, he tied it off in such a way he had to stand on the balls of his feet to avoid choking. He tied his partner in the same manner before proposing his company return to their beds and get what sleep they could.

The boys huddled close between Lewis and Edward, eventually dozing off. That's when Lewis felt he could speak freely to his older brother.

"How did you know?"

"To be honest, I didn't so much know as felt. I saw those two faces in the pub last night, then at the docks this morning. As we left Richmond Town, I saw them again, this time with their guns and wearing traveling clothes. Twice can be a coincidence, but not three times. They were able to stay with us most of the day, losing some ground as we did keep up a pretty good pace. I knew they would overtake us after we had stopped for the night, and we couldn't have continued on with the boys. I tried an old Army trick of moving further after the evening meal, thinking it might throw them off a little. Our disadvantage was, when they found our meal site abandoned, they only needed to continue down the same road and they knew they would eventually find us."

"So you pretended to go to sleep and then slipped

out before moon rise. You could have told me."

"No sense us both losing sleep. Aaron must have seen me make my move and followed. I knew there was someone else out there, I just didn't know who. I was hoping it wasn't one of the boys. When he kept pace with me as I moved in, that's when I saw it was Aaron and you know the rest."

"They certainly aren't enjoying their new neck stocks. You worried me for a moment when I thought you were going to summarily hang them in front of the boys. What are we going to do with them?"

"Tomorrow we'll pack up as usual. As you take Aaron and two of the boys and continue on toward Shadwell, I'll take the third boy and these two in to Goochland. It's a county seat so it should have a Sheriff and gaol for their kind."

"I'll go with you, Uncle Edward," came Philip's voice from under the blankets between them, desperately feeling the need to redeem himself.

"Alright, Philip, but you have to go to sleep so I'll be able to count on you tomorrow. After we drop these two with the Sheriff, we'll have some hard riding ahead of us to catch back up with your father. It's man's work you'll need to do and you can't do it if you're falling asleep." Then back to Lewis, "Just stay on this road. We need to turn back to the turn off to the south for Goochland. We'll catch back up before nightfall, perhaps a little later."

The next morning dawned bright and clear. Edward had allowed them to sleep late, not getting them up until sunrise. By then, Aaron had breakfast prepared and the two ruffians were down, gulping in air but with the nooses still around their necks. The boys were quiet and very quick to follow direction this morning. It seemed all of the competition between them had been overcome during the night's activities.

"Charles, Joseph, when you've finished with your breakfast, take water to our visitors. Allow them all they want to drink, but take them no food. I'll not waste food on dead men." Then, inspecting the weapons from the ruffians, Edward turned toward Aaron, "It seems you and Miles have acquired serviceable guns from last night's intrusion. Neither is new nor fancy, but they are both rifled guns, soundly made and with years of good service left in them."

"And what's to become of their owners?"

"They will have no further use for arms in this world," came the reply in such a cold voice it raised a chill in Aaron.

When they were ready to depart, Edward had Philip bring his horse over near the ruffians. Tying together the opposite ends of the two ropes still fastened around their necks, he centered the knot under the pommel of Philip's saddle. Then he took Philip's blanket and, folding it, draped it across the saddle, over the ropes.

"This may ride a bit awkward for you, but it is better than having the ropes pinch your legs when these two fall. Or worse, having the rope pop over the pommel and pull you from the saddle. This way your weight helps keep the rope securely around the pommel. Now, if they fall you'll feel it but you are not to stop unless I tell you to. Understand? Good. Now, you'll lead and I'll be behind them. Stay at a gentle walk and listen for my instructions. If you should hear a loud noise from behind, it will likely be one of your charges being hurried to his reward. Questions?"

"No, sir, I'm to lead at a gentle walk and not stop for anything unless you tell me."

Edward patted Philip's shoulder then turned to cut the ropes securing the ruffians' feet. He helped them up then turned away, not offering them shoes or stockings. The look in his eye as he helped each to his feet kept them from making any requests or uttering any sound at all.

As this was going on, Lewis had made his way to Philip and, laying his hand on the boy's thigh as he sat his horse, he said in a comforting voice, "You know what's expected of you this day, Philip. Your Uncle Edward will do what has to be done and you need do as he tells you. It's a man's errand you're on. I wish I could have spared you from it..."

"Father, I'll be fine with Uncle Edward. I'm sorry for last night, I just..."

"I know, son, and so does your uncle. That's why he trusts you today. It's his was of showing you it's all right. God speed and we'll see each other again before nightfall."

With that Edward signaled Philip to start back down the road they had ridden last night to the Maiden's Road toward Goochland. At first, the ruffians fell frequently and Edward would allow Philip to drag them several yards before telling him to halt so they could regain their feet. By the time they made the Maiden's Road, about a quarter of a mile, the ruffians had learned that to fall gained them nothing from the tall stranger behind and if they hoped to survive the day, they needed to keep to their feet.

Philip was doing well. They would stop at the stream crossings to allow the ruffians to drink as best as they could from the running water. Other than that, the slow pace allowed them to continue to move without tiring the horses. Still it was after noon when they reached Goochland. Edward found the gaol and the Sheriff, wrote out his complaint, and the two ruffians were locked up, looking much relieved to be away from Edward's grasp. While he was doing this, Philip saw to their horses and made ready to catch up with his father and the others. When Edward came out of the Gaoler's office, Philip was standing by the horses with a bundle under his arm and dark bottle in his hand.

"What's this, taken to drink have you?"

"It's just sweet cider, Uncle Edward, and some ham and biscuits from the Ordinary. I didn't think you'd want to waste any time so I got them for our dinner, to eat as we ride."

Edward turned toward to Sheriff, whose face showed he was mightily impressed with the lad, and beamed, showing the Sheriff his pride in his nephew. Then, adjusting to his serious face before turning back, he patted Philip on the shoulder before helping him mount and handing up their dinner.

"Do I need to stop by and pay for this bounty? We wouldn't want the Sheriff needing to come after us."

"No, Uncle Edward, father has taught me to always have a few shillings in my pocket and I used that."

One pat on the boy's thigh and Edward mounted, then the two rode off down the Gum Spring's Road, suggested by the Sheriff as best for their purposes, at an easy pace while they passed food and drink back and forth between them, both quite cheery on the inside but maintaining a serious demeanor outside.

Chapter 11

*R*obert was glad for the help of having Miles along. Not that he believed Charles would not have been of assistance, only Miles was a well built man obviously used to hard labors while Charles was but a strapping youth. Henry got along well with Miles, who aside from being better built than the perpetually thin Henry, were of similar bents. Of the two women, there could not have been more difference between them. Betty had evidently enjoyed some education, spoke well and was a hard worker. Mattie was coarser, though also a hard worker, and less well spoken. They paired off well with his daughters-in-law. Marie favored Betty and Mary favored Mattie. As he watched, these four paired off and started getting to know each other and by the end of the day there was clearly a teaming up Robert did not care for.

They had gotten a later start than he had hoped for, it taking more time than anticipated to secure their cargo on board the six flat bottomed boats they had chartered for the trip. Once they got underway, things went very smoothly and quickly. There was little for him to do, any of them for that matter, as the watermen took care of the boats. Only when they came to shallows, when all the men were needed to haul the boats above to the next section of calm water. Actually, he found the occasional exercise a fine break in the tedium. Yes, this would have been very hard on the boys and, as a result, they would have made the trip very hard on the adults.

They tied up the first night well short of their goal of making Maidens, near the county seat of Goochland, due mostly to their late start. In fact, they had barely cleared Tuckahoe Island. The boats were tied off to stout trees on the bank and the women set about making supper for the whole company, watermen included. They seemed to appreciate this and Robert saw it as a fine way to build some loyalty beyond the purse between them and his family. He also doubted these hard working men would see much of the charter money they had paid their employer, Colonel Byrd.

Now as he sat against a tree, well fed and contented, looking out across the river, he overheard a commotion off to his left, further from their camp. Going to investigate, he found Mary and Sarah in heated debate, apparently on the various merits of the two women servants. Listening, Robert discovered Mary was upbraiding Sarah for expressing her opinion that Betty was of more use to them than Mattie.

"Why can't I talk to Betty? She seems nice."

"She puts on airs, that's why. You need to spend more of your time with people who won't encourage you to think better of yourself than you are, like Mattie. And you should get used to having her around because I intend to ask her to live with us when we get settled on our land."

As much as Robert would have liked to ignore it, he knew if left alone it would only fester and lead to larger problems further along, so he interrupted. "Mary, I'm sure Sarah is entitled to her opinion. It seems only reasonable she should take a liking to Betty as she is closer to her age. In any case, no good can come from this. Sarah, go and bring the rest of the family here so we may have a family discussion."

Mary clearly wanted to retort, but dared not. Robert, for all of his good nature, was the family patriarch and she could not raise her voice against him without consequences. So she remained quiet, seething, as she thought how frequently Sarah had taken to disagreeing with her of late.

When the others had gathered, out of hearing of the watermen and servants, Robert began. "I feel the need to remind everyone as to the status of our new servants. It seems everyone has already formed opinions and likings toward the three, and that is in part a good thing. What is not good is making favorites. I should not need to remind you all that these servants are not ours, they are Edward's. He purchased their indentures and they are, for the remaining time on them, his property to use as he sees fit. Our opinions as to their qualities or lack of qualities or who should live where is of no import whatsoever and I won't allow their presence to disrupt our family. In Edward's absence, I feel it my responsibility to look after his interests and his servants. Understood?"

He then made sharp eye contact with each of them, first Marie, then Sarah, Henry, Esther, saving Mary for the last and longest gaze. Of his daughters-in-law he had found it more difficult to warm up to Mary. She was more coarse than Marie, more opinionated and vocal about it. He tried to treat both the same for Henry loved Mary and that should be all he needed to know. Yet if there was to be further difficulties between family members, he felt sure

Mary would be found nearby if not at the heart of things.

As the family members moved back toward their beds for the night, Robert noticed Mary had lingered back and was talking rather heatedly to Henry. He chose to ignore it. She was Henry's wife and he would have to deal with it. Right now he was tired and intended to go to bed.

Up early the next day, the women again treated everyone to breakfast, Betty beating even Robert out of his blankets. The family members seemed in generally good spirits, none the worse for the family discussion the night before, even on Mary's part. On the river by full sunlight, Robert hoped to make up some time lost yesterday. They were making good time, not stopping for dinner but eating as they floated, when the few clustered houses known as Maiden came into view.

After they passed the village, Henry noticed a skiff putting off in their wake and brought this to Robert's attention. When it came close enough for a hail, a man in the skiff inquired if this was the Jewett family as he had a message for them. Robert invited the man aboard though he did not dare stop as the current would cause them to lose ground.

The Goochland County Sheriff introduced himself and told Robert and Henry that he had met with Edward just after noon, that the family had just missed him. Edward's message was that all were fine and they were making acceptable, though not fast, time on the roads. He then expanded the message by adding his version of the trouble the trail company had experienced the evening before.

"Were the boys alright?" asked Mary and Marie nearly in unison.

"Well, I only met one, a fine lad the Colonel referred to as Philip. Nothing was said specifically of the others, but as his complaint indicated no injuries, I can only assume them to be faring well."

"Do you have much trouble from highwaymen along these roads?" Henry asked, trying to further dampen the anxiety now apparent in the two women.

"Oh, it happens from time to time, but from what I saw of the party, they are well armed and take no efforts to hide that fact. That alone will dissuade most of the low types we see. They are generally looking for an easier target. And if you could have seen the shape they brought these two in, word of which I have already started to pass, only the bravest sole would take on the Colonel and his party."

"What do you mean?" inquired Robert, now curious.

"They had walked by my estimate seven or eight miles without benefit of shoes and with a rope around each of their necks. If they stumbled, they were dragged by the neck. From the state of their clothing, they had been drug more than once." He continued with the prisoners' version of how they spent the night, which was only slightly enhanced, before adding, "The Gaoler's wife, she's a terrible gossip, so I know this is making the rounds of the county."

Robert saw the effect this had on the watermen and servants, an effect he had hoped for. He did not anticipate any trouble from them but these people were all unknown to him and one never knew. A little preventative medicine could have a good effect, and those not within hearing would hear as soon as they took their next break, if he was any judge of these men.

After the Sheriff had taken his leave, everyone put their backs into making better progress. Here was proof the land expedition was making better time than they were, an unexpected turn of events. Marie lamented not being just an hour or two earlier so she could have seen her son and Mary worried about Charles being out on the roads with other highwaymen about, even if the party was well armed and not likely to become prey again, as the Sheriff had said.

As Robert stood in the bow and tried to gage their progress against the shoreline, Sarah came up and put her arm around him.

"Grandfather, I haven't thanked you yet for coming to my assistance last night. I don't understand why father and I can still get along well, but mother and I are constantly fighting."

"It's nature, plain and simple. You see, you're no longer a girl and not yet a woman. Your mother still sees her little girl and you're looking for her to accept you as a woman. Yet you don't always feel like a woman, so those times you're feeling like a girl again and your mother then says something that shows she still thinks you are a girl, you resent it. It's all part of growing up."

"So why does father accept me for whom I am?"

"That's easy, Sarah. There is a bond between fathers and daughters that causes both to overlook the petty and forgive the slights, not always but generally. If you'd like another opinion, just ask Esther how it was for her at your age. And I dare say if Marie had a daughter your age, I'd be having this same conversation with her. It's best to accept what is and not bother yourself so much with the why of things."

Sarah stretched up and kissed her grandfather, then laid her cheek against his chest. She had missed him so much while they lived in Boston.

They put in that night at the head of Elk Island. Once the camp was made and supper started, Henry came to where his father was sitting, thinking, and sat with him a few minutes.

"Father, Mary meant no harm last night, I hope you realize. It was good for everyone to hear what you said, it cleared things up that needed to be cleared up and I don't think there will be any further issues."

"Mary and I are fine, Henry. I hold no animosity against her or anyone else, as you know. She does have a sharp tongue on her, though, and I do worry what its effect will be on our small company. We are here amongst strangers we must rely on to get us where we're going. Any fracture on our part could cost us everything, even our lives. That is why I had to take quick action last night."

"Do you think us in danger?"

"Of course we're in danger; danger from the river, from river pirates, danger from our own human failings."

"River pirates? Are you saying we should arm ourselves as Edward has evidently done with the others?

"I'm thinking what the Sheriff said about making a good show. Now, I am a peaceful man and don't want to overplay it, Edward knows better about these things, but I think if one of us were always under arms, it would send the desired message. It is just you and I, Henry. That is all that these women have to count on. Miles remains an unknown in these matters. I think we should take prudent precautions."

"I'll get the rifled guns and we can make a small demonstration of loading them before supper."

"A small show, yes, though let's not overplay our hand. Then we must be ever watchful. If needed, I'm sure any adversary would be taken completely by surprise when the women take up arms and demonstrate their proficiency. No, I must thank Edward for ensuring our preparedness. Now, go get the rifled guns before they call us to supper."

❧ *Chapter 12* ❧

*E*dward set a hard pace as the two weary travelers moved north on the Gum Springs Road. When they had again returned to their original route, he estimated they had covered more than 14 miles and were no further along than five miles from whence they started. Evening was approaching, they and their horses were tired, and Lewis would likely be 15 miles further down the road from where they now stood. No, he was no longer confident of catching up by nightfall.

Lewis and Aaron, with Charles and Joseph, had spent an uneventful day on the trail. The road remained dry, the farms more scattered, and they could have made excellent time. Instead, Lewis held them to a slow pace. None of them, Aaron included, knew exactly how far Goochland was and thus how far Edward and Philip would have to travel. At Gum Springs they learned the most direct route to Goochland was eight miles. Assuming Edward learned of this road, and did not retrace his steps up the Maiden's Road, it would help, though still a very long ride.

They decided to have a hot meal in the Ordinary

at Gum Springs while the local Ferrier checked the horses for loose shoes. It was not only a treat for the tired travelers it bought extra time for Edward and Philip. After their experience of last night, Lewis was careful to follow Edward's advice to make a good show of being well armed, especially in the village where they were under careful scrutiny.

For Charles and Joseph it made them feel grown up. It also helped them deal with the fright they had suffered. Having spent their lives in town, they were used to accidents and tumbles, not having guns pointed at them in a threatening manner. Now neither boy was ever more than a short arm's length away from his gun. As much as they made light of it between themselves while eating, Lewis knew this bravado was to cover up just how much it had affected them. Yet he had to smile at the slight swagger they had adapted, even to the point of remaining aloof from the local boys who came to see the strangers moving a pack train in the wrong direction.

Gum Springs was used to its share of traffic as the farmers all along the road moved their crops and herds to Richmond Town and the markets. The wagons carrying the tobacco crop went east heavily loaded with hogsheads and returned lightly loaded with necessaries and delights. These strangers were somehow different. They had loaded pack horses moving west with a decided military air about them. If it were not for the two boys, the townspeople speculated, they would have thought it was a military expedition of some type. Instead of coming right out and asking, the townspeople gave the travelers their space, remaining cordial but not engaged. They knew they could ask the Ferrier and owner of the Ordinary later for more details.

After the longer than usual delay in Gum Springs,

Lewis moved them on toward Shadwell. He kept the rather leisurely pace he had set that morning for what was left of the afternoon. Before dusk he announced they would go into camp along the road where a strong spring gushed forth its fresh water. All the normal evening activities were seen to, a light supper prepared and eaten, and all settled down for an evening's repose under the stars. Lewis remained watchful, concerned about his son and Edward being able to overtake them. At length, when full darkness had fallen about their campsite, he decided they would linger a bit in the morning, prepare a hot breakfast, then proceed at their leisurely pace again tomorrow. If the two had not caught up by time they stopped for dinner, he would ride back along their route to find the reason.

Edward and Philip learned in Gum Springs of the passing of their little company, so continued on without undue delay, only long enough to purchase another cold meal to take with them as they continued on their way. Edward was watching Philip closely as they went, the lines of fatigue readily apparent in his young face. As they started to lose the light, he noted Philip's head drop and come up quickly. He was falling asleep in the saddle.

"Philip, I am far too tired to take another step. What say you to stopping here for some sleep? We can start again after the moon rises and we have light enough to see. Would you grant an old man his rest?"

"Well, Uncle Edward, if you're tired then we should stop. But we must be up very early as father will be worried our not catching them tonight," he replied, not suspecting his uncle had caught on to just how exhausted he was.

They moved off the road to the banks of a small brook with sweet water, cared for the horses and then fell asleep nearly as soon as they had lain in their blanket.

Edward was awake shortly after moonrise, but hesitated waking his nephew, deciding to allow a few hours more sleep. Finally it was time, though still well before first light. It took a little effort to wake Philip but once up they were quickly ready and on their way again. Shortly after sunrise Edward called a halt.

"Do you smell that, Philip my boy?"

"I smell wood smoke, if that's what you mean."

"Wood smoke isn't all you smell, is it? Can't you smell bacon as well?" When Philip nodded after taking another sniff, he continued, "What say you to a hot breakfast with your father?"

Puzzled at first, Philip's face brightened when he realized what his uncle meant. A short, quick canter put them in the middle of his father's camp and the little company was reunited again amid hugs and handshakes all around. As they ate Edward filled Lewis and Aaron in on what had transpired in Goochland and that his inquiries on the river company had met blank stares, meaning they were behind schedule. Philip told his tale of hard travel to Charles and Joseph who in turn told Philip of their travels and the adventures in Gum Springs, suitably embellished for their listener's enjoyment.

Packing the horses quickly, they started on toward Shadwell at a brisk but not overly taxing pace. Edward thought they could make it by nightfall if the weather held and they did not lose their way. Before they took their break for dinner, however, the weather was starting to change, with clouds covering the sun and occasional light showers. The little bit of water left on the roads was not enough to soften them, only enough to make them quite slippery, forcing a slower pace. At length they had to clear the road for a herder taking his cattle toward the market in Richmond Town.

This final delay convinced Edward they would not make Shadwell that night and they should start thinking of a campsite where they could stay reasonably dry. Passing his thoughts on to Joseph, it being his turn at Edward's side, he asked him to pass the word back along the line to Lewis. As boys will do when entrusted with what they see as a mission of some import, Joseph turned his horse too sharply for the slippery conditions, causing the horse to stumble, slip, and go down, pitching Joseph from the saddle.

"Here now, Joseph, are you are right, boy?" shouted Edward as he dismounted and moved quickly to the boy who laid face down in the road. Aaron, who followed Edward in line, also dismounted and went to the horse struggling to regain its feet after being relieved of its burden. The rest moved forward to where they could see what was happening.

Joseph pushed himself up and said, "I'm alright, sort of."

"What's wrong, you're not hurt?"

As Joseph turned to face Edward and the others, they all saw what can happen should one be thrown onto a road where cattle have recently passed. The men all showed large grins at the revelation, but the two other boys broke into peals of laughter. Joseph just stood there, now red faced, not really knowing what to do next.

"Aaron, lead the others up that rise. If it is as it appears, it should be dry ground for our camp. I, in the meantime, will take young Joseph here to that creek, just there." As Edward moved away with the boy he asked, "Can you swim, Joseph?"

"Swim? Yes I can, father taught me."

"Good," and with that Edward picked the boy up and tossed him into the creek. "Now, scrub yourself and those clothes good, so there's no smell left. I'm just going to sit here and make sure you don't come out until I can no longer smell you." Now laughing himself, Edward picked a rock on the bank and sat down to watch the boy scoop up handfuls of sand to rub on his manure covered clothes and face. When he had finished and rinsed well, they both walked up the hill toward where the others had set up the camp. By now even Joseph could laugh about his tumble.

On reaching camp, Aaron informed Edward that Joseph's horse was fine, no harm done. Lewis, however, held up Joseph's muddy gun and announced it was sound, but they would have to pull the charge as it was ruined. Edward made quick work of pulling the charge and then handed it back to Joseph with instructions to clean it thoroughly and to allow Edward to inspect it before he reloaded. This done and the rain now becoming steady, they wrapped themselves in oilskins and settled in to get what rest they could.

The sun rose the next morning to what promised to be a clear dry day. After their damp sleep, all of the travelers started the day moving rather stiffly. They soon loosened up and everything was made ready to continue their journey. Before starting, Edward had all of the weapons discharged, cleaned, and fresh charges loaded as a precaution following the damp weather.

The road was now sticky from the night rains, although those portions where the sun reached it were drying quickly. Their progress improved as the morning became warmer and the roads dryer. By noon they approached a cluster of farm buildings, a story and a half house typical of the area fronted by two service buildings. In the yard was a large, red headed man and a boy of about nine, also with red hair and both well freckled.

"Excuse the intrusion, sir, I am Colonel Jewett and

we are in search of Shadwell and Mr. Jefferson. If you could but direct us we'll be on our way."

"Don't be so quick to move on, for if it is Shadwell you seek, it is Shadwell you've found. I am Jefferson. What business can you have with me?"

Alighting, Edward made proper introductions and handed Peter Jefferson the letter from the Governor. After quickly reading it, he signaled for all to dismount and called for a slave to see to the horses.

"You are lucky to find me here. I spend most of the year at Tuckahoe Plantation overseeing affairs there for the orphaned children of William Randolph, my good friend now departed. This is my son, Thomas. We had planned on leaving this morning to return to Tuckahoe, delaying only because of the rain last night. Come, I have some sketches and notes in my office that might help you locate your grant."

They entered one of the small buildings making up the forecourt and Peter pulled papers and notes out of a trunk to review with Edward and Lewis. The boys were entertained in a fashion by Thomas who was younger than the three and a bit shy.

After being satisfied he had provided his guests all the information he had, he suggested, "The man you really should talk to is Doctor Thomas Walker, up at Castle Hill. He has traveled extensively through the Valley and much further to the south and west. Castle Hill is just five miles to the northeast and should prove well worth the detour. You can leave the boys and horses here with your manservant and it will hasten your trip."

Lewis and Edward thanked Peter for his hospitality, then departed for a quick trip to Castle Hill, their departure marred only by the protests of the boys not pleased with being left behind to see to the horses. Unencumbered by the pack horses, they made the five miles to Castle Hill before dusk and found Doctor Walker at home.

"You'll find your grant to be made up of good land, rolling hills and bold streams," he told them. He also had sketches of the area and allowed Lewis to copy them as they talked. "In fact I have just returned from my spring hunts in that region. It is not uninhabited and I am afraid you'll have to deal with some squatters. The Scots-Irish have been moving up the Valley from Pennsylvania, most continuing on to the Yadkin Valley, but some remaining along the route. There is now even an academy some 20 odd miles north of where you'll be. Augusta Academy they're calling it, a small thing, but a classical school nonetheless."

Returning to Shadwell the next morning armed with all the information available on the site of his Royal Land Grant, they were now eager to rejoin the rest of the family at the rendezvous point where the Rockfish River joined the James. Saying their goodbyes to the Jeffersons, they set off across the Rivanna River and followed the valley running southwest, as Peter Jefferson had advised them. They were aimed, he told them, toward Rockfish River. When they made it, they need only turn south by southeast to reach its junction with the James and the rest of the family.

Chapter 13

*R*obert was feeling better. Since passing Maidens their pace had picked up and the rains the next day had raised the water level. Though this made the current, and hence working the sweeps, harder, the raised water level helped them over the shoals with much less work.

With them were 18 watermen working the boats. Billy Watson was the foreman and made sure things continued to run smoothly. Being included in the meals had gone a long way in winning Billy, and thus the others, over and it no longer seemed to Robert like they were two groups traveling together as it was one company. Miles and Henry took turns at the sweeps, Robert at the steering oar, and the women passed water and refreshments around to all hands.

"Mister Jewett, can we talk for a moment?" Billy asked one afternoon.

"Mister Watson, you look concerned about something. Of course we can talk," replied Robert, more than a little concerned.

"We're now past what's called Big Island and should be at your rendezvous point tomorrow. Problem is, from here on the waters can be dangerous and unpredictable and the men are a bit nervous."

"What, are there rapids ahead?"

"Oh no, sir, we can handle the river obstacles fine as any watermen you'll find on the Fluvanna. It's the pirates. You see, this is the area where those who've run away from their indentures feel safe and they've taken to piracy to make their living. They are a bad lot, from Newgate Prison mostly, and we're likely to run into them before we run into your sons and grandsons. Especially if we spend any time camped along the mouth of the Rockfish."

"Do you propose to abandon us, here, when we are so close to our destination?"

"Oh, that's not it at all, sir. It's just that we've taken stock and between us we all have knives and some have a pistol, but we've no long arms beyond the two we've seen you and Mister Henry with. Now, I think your showing yourselves with them has been a good thing, but if that's all we have, we may be in a bad way should we happen upon them pirates."

"I understand now. We are better supplied than you have seen. In addition to the two rifles, both my son and I have a fowler apiece and all four women have fowlers. Don't be fooled by the women, they know how to use them."

"Ah, that makes things some better. Between the eight long arms and our pistols and knives, we should make a good fight of it. We are an above average sized party to begin with. If you don't mind, sir, I'll pass that word around the men. It'll make them feel better."

"Please do, and if there is anything else, Mister Watson, do not hesitate to bring it to my attention. We're in this together, all of us."

After supper that evening, Robert gathered the family along with Miles, Mattie, and Betty, and relayed the conversation he had with Billy earlier. All sat silently while the import of the conversation sank in. Then Henry spoke.

"Might it not be wise to pass our fowlers to two of the watermen? Surely there are two who are handy with long arms?"

"And," added Mary, "perhaps they should have Sarah's and mine as well. Marie is a good shot but Sarah and I are more comfortable loading than shooting. And if I'm aiming at a man, well I just don't think I could do it." Sarah nodded in agreement and Esther did also, simply saying "Make that three."

Robert thought for a moment. "Yes, that makes sense. It would give us seven long arms on the line and we'd be a formidable force to deal with."

"Eight," interjected Marie, "there'd be eight long arms on the line."

"Actually, Marie, I was considering putting you back with those watermen who have pistols in defense of the boats and women. If it gets close on the line, you've not the strength or size to wrestle with a man." Marie indicated she understood and agreed.

"Now, Miles, how handy are you with a long arm?" asked Robert. "Before I start offering them to the watermen, the first would go to you if you can handle it."

"No, sir, I'm no good with a long arm. I am good with a boatman's pike, though, and would propose being up on the line with the seven. If things got close, I would weigh with the pike where needed and be an extra set of strong arms."

"That's fine. So, I assume we're all in agreement?" Robert saw nods from all. "Then I will discuss this with

Mister Watson in the morning. Just remember, we have no idea when Edward and Lewis will make the river, but we are more than well supplied with powder and ball and Edward trained us well. Anyone trying to cause us mischief will find a warm welcome waiting for them."

The next day dawned bright and clear. As they were close to their rendezvous point, they didn't push off from the bank until the sun was up. Robert had discussed their defense plans with Billy and found the waterman very comfortable with them. As Robert had hoped, the women preparing and offering meals for all, rather than letting the watermen fend for themselves, had gone a long way in forging a closeness between the family and the watermen. There now was genuine affection between the two groups that made up this, the largest, of the two expeditions bound beyond the Blue Ridge.

No further problems occurred as they made steady progress up the river. At one point, Robert realized they had nearly doubled back and Billy confirmed they had just traversed a large loop in the river, covering six river miles to end up just one mile from where they started the loop. Robert just smiled and shook his head. Just in floating up this river he had gained more travel experience than in all of his previous travels about Massachusetts.

They reached the Rockfish River late in the afternoon. Robert, Henry, and Billy all went ashore to scout for the best place for a camp, one they could defend. They all finally agreed on a spot about 100 yards down river from the mouth of the Rockfish. There they found a beach of 20 yards or so, a cut bank, shoulder high and curved away from the river, and a treed ledge above the bank, clear of underbrush, nice and dry for camp. By tying the boats in the center of the arch formed by the cut bank, they could be protected from approach by the main line at the cut bank.

Plans were laid that, should an alarm be sounded, all would make their way back to the river. Robert, Henry, Miles, and those watermen now armed with the fowlers would take position at the bank, Robert and Henry, because they had rifles, on the right and left of the line respectively. Everyone else would move to the boats where Marie and those with pistols would back up their line and provide the last line of defense.

With all in readiness, they settled into camp life while waiting for Edward and Lewis to arrive with the boys. As was their habit, the watermen slept on board the boats while the family and their servants slept ashore. The boats were rigged with awnings in the stern and the family put up awnings among the trees so all were protected from the dews and damps of that region. River traffic was light this time of year. They did note some small craft plying the waters and that made them all the more watchful.

The second morning in camp, Betty and Mattie were up before first light and went to the spring they had found with clear, sweet water. On the way in the darkness, they heard voices where none should have been. At first they thought it must be Edward and Lewis and their part of expedition. Only a few moments of listening told them otherwise. Moving as quietly as they could, they quickly returned to camp. Moving through the camp they quietly passed the alarm. Everyone started moving back toward the bank and the boats, exercising as much stealth in their movements as possible.

By the time the pre-dawn light allowed them to see about them, all was in readiness. The line was formed with the seven men armed with long arms plus Miles and his pike. The rest were on the boats, crouched behind the cargo. All were listening and waiting, hoping Betty and Mattie were wrong but fearing they were right.

The instant the sun rose above the western mountains, 12 or more armed men burst into the camp howling and discharging their guns into what they thought were the sleeping forms of the family. There was, in fact, nothing but empty blankets under the abandoned awnings.

Robert, using Miles to spread the word, urged all to hold their fire until he fired the first shot. The intruders soon realized their error and, in the moment they stood with empty guns absorbing the turn of events, Robert fired and downed the first intruder. With that six other guns barked in unison and sent their deadly missiles into their former camp, several more of the intruders falling.

Now that the element of surprise had shifted and then dissipated in a cloud of white smoke, the intruders took cover behind the large and scattered trees to reload. The intrepid few behind the bank needed no encouragement to do likewise. Now the fight, which had begun with a volley, became one of sniping as each side looked to pick off any unfortunate who exposed himself. Here the two rifled guns in the hands of Robert and Henry had the advantage with their accuracy and both made themselves felt by downing another intruder apiece. The numbers now were looking pretty even to Robert and, not at all liking the work he found himself forced to do, he hoped for a speedy conclusion.

Rather than being discouraged by the sudden change of events and the loss of their companions, the intruders became enraged that their intended prey had turned the tables on them. Now they called on their leader for blood, clearly heard by those behind the bank. A few shouted commands and the intruders began moving forward, carefully moving from tree to tree. Shots from the bank claimed two more of their number and caused the leader to call a pause where they were.

That was when Miles appeared at Robert's elbow offering water from a canteen. He then moved down the line, stopping at each in turn to allow them to quench their thirst. It had barely been half an hour since Robert took the first shot, and the first life, yet it somehow seemed much longer, like they had been in this situation for hours. Robert's eyes now moved across their former camp trying to discern why the intruders were holding their ground. What were they waiting for?

He suddenly heard a sound, maybe movement, but from where, their left? Before he could tell for sure, the intruders began another general push all across their front. Firing again became general as the distance between the two opposing forces closed to 25 yards, in some places less.

From the boats, the watermen and women were becoming nervous. The intruders, while bloodied, were steadily advancing on their line and would soon be at the very edge of the bank. Pistol priming was checked and those without handled either a boatman's pike or knife, ready for the final phase of the battle.

Marie had been taking aim at first one intruder than another, holding fire as the distance was further than she felt comfortable with. Now they were less than 60 yards away, coming within her range, and she was wondering when she should add her fire to the fight.

Mary, at her side but without a gun, was focused on Henry, worried for his safety. She silently cheered each time she saw his shot find its mark. It was while watching Henry that she saw something further down the bank that drew her attention, where it bent away blocking their view further upriver. What was it, a reflection off the water? A bird perhaps? As she watched a man's form stepped out from where it had been hidden by the bank. Her heart leaped into her throat as she saw him take careful aim and fire. As quick as her eyes returned to Henry, she saw him spin to his right and fall, face down to the ground.

She was up in an instant, leaping the short gap from boat to shore and running toward her husband with no thought for her personal safety. Sarah and Esther both shouted for her to come back. Mary did not really hear them, hearing the words but not able to understand their meaning. Her only thought was Henry was injured and she must go to him.

She had covered half the distance to Henry when a movement to her left caused her to freeze in her tracks. The intruder had finished his reloading and now was taking aim directly at her. She stood for what seemed like forever, looking down the barrel of that gun, no other sound or sight making any impression on her. Nothing existed except the muzzle of that gun. She knew she must move, only she could not, not a muscle, she was not even breathing.

Then came the loud crack of a shot.

⨴ *Chapter 14* ⨵

*A*aron had things ready when Edward and Lewis returned from Castle Hill so they could get started. All said their goodbyes to Peter and young Tom Jefferson, the Jeffersons starting out for Tuckahoe Plantation as the Jewetts started toward the southwest and the Rockfish River's junction with the Fluvanna.

Now they were off the roads all together, following woodland trails instead. Rather than impeding their travel, they found the pack train moved easier on the hard packed trail than the rutted roads they had been using. It was also clear that to attempt these narrow trails with wagons or even two-wheeled carts would have been the height of folly. The pace picked up as they followed this natural valley toward their destination. Both Peter Jefferson and Dr. Walker had told them to keep Green Mountain to their left until it ended at Green Creek, which flowed into the Rockfish River. Here they would find easy passage around the mountain into the Fluvanna River basin.

The boys were more animated than Edward had seen them. It seems young Tom had made quite an impression on them. It did not matter which of the three was riding next to him, the chatter was constant and the same. "Tom reads really well; Tom attends school at the plantation; Tom is learning Latin, should we learn Latin; Reverend Benson wouldn't teach us Latin because he says it's a Papist language; Tom took us up a little mountain where you can see for miles…"

Edward road back along the line and joined Lewis at the end. "Who's leading us if you're back here?" asked Lewis.

"I gave Joseph my compass and told him to plot our course to the southwest. I just had to get away from those boys! All they do is talk about Tom this and Tom that. Who would have thought a boy three years younger than the youngest of them would have such an affect on them?"

"He may be younger, and skinny, but he's nearly as tall as they are and a sight better educated, once you get past that shyness."

"His father sure isn't shy or skinny either. That is a large man with a very outgoing disposition. And he has quite a head for the lay of the land. If he hadn't told me otherwise, I'd have sworn he was a King's military engineer."

"Yes, but listen to you, you're sounding as bad as the boys!"

They both grinned and Edward slapped Lewis on the back. "Yes, I guess we were all impressed with the Jefferson family. Now I'd better get back up front before we end up in New France, considering who's leading us." With that, he headed back to the front, picking his way around the trees lining the narrow trail they were following.

Able to make very good time on the trail, they came to what they supposed was Green Creek. At least it matched the description and, on following it, found easy passage around Green Mountain. By time they made the river and turned south, it was dusk so they made camp at the next creek to flow into the Rockfish, preferring the cleaner creek water to the muddy river water.

Up before first light and on their way before sunrise, they took an easy trail just across the creek they had camped along that headed south when the river looped to the northeast. As they cleared the rise and started their descent, Edward stopped short and listened before hurrying back along the line.

"What is it, Edward?" Lewis asked, concerned by the look on his brother's face.

"Do you hear that popping sound? That's gunfire, coming to us from the south, from the same direction father is to be waiting for us. I'll take Aaron and ride ahead..."

"No, Edward, we'll leave Aaron here with the boys and I'll go with you. He's my father too."

"I've no time to argue with you. Aaron, help me break out the muskets. Now, Lewis, we'll sling the muskets across our backs. When we get close, if it's needed, we'll take the first shots with our rifles, then un-sling the muskets as we move in close. Muskets are quicker to load and I've a cartridge box for each of us with twenty rounds in them already made up."

Aaron handed up the muskets as Edward belted on his cartridge box and handed the other to Lewis. The boys watched this in concerned silence, making no protest about being left behind.

"Now, Aaron, if we are not back for you by mid-day it'll be because we're not coming back. If that should happen, take the boys back to Dr. Walker's. It's no good stopping at Shadwell as the Jeffersons are gone from there. Philip, here, take my satchel. In it are all the papers you'll need to establish your claim to the Royal Land Grant, plus Aaron's papers. Oh, may as well take my purse as you may have need for ready money. Lewis, we ride!" Spurring their horses they were down the trail and out of sight in a flash.

This was not the first time Edward had ridden to the sound of the guns and, as the sounds became more distinct, his demeanor changed to pure soldier. This was Lewis' first time and he found it both drew him toward it and repulsed him away. By the tight set of his lips, though, one thing was certain – he was just as determined as Edward to rescue their family.

Edward signaled a halt in a depression formed by a spring and, in hushed tones, explained their next step to Lewis.

"We leave the horses here, out of the line of fire, and work our way to the right. We don't want to come up right behind them as that would put us in danger of fire from father and Henry. The other reason is most men will come around the right side of a tree to fire, exposing as little of themselves as they can. If we are to their right, they will be more exposed to us. Once we've made our presence known with the rifles, drop it where we can claim it later and use the musket. Fire as quickly as you can while making every shot count. Advance from tree to tree as I advance, pull back if I pull back, and if I fall make it back to the horses and get the boys to safety. Understood?"

Lewis nodded then followed Edward, trying to emulate his crouched run as they advanced to the right from tree to tree. It did not take long before they heard the sound of ball impact the trees to their left and Lewis understood the wisdom in Edward's approach. Then he could see them, to his front left, and they were doing just as Edward said they would, exposing themselves as they took aim at the riverbank. Only then did Lewis see heads popping up and down along the bank, each time accompanied with a flash of flame and smoke as the defenders returned fire.

Edward signaled a halt when half a dozen attackers were plainly visible and signed that it was time to take the fight to the enemy.

Mary saw the flame come toward her from the muzzle of the gun, saw the gun rise, felt its heat on her cheek and something pull her hair. Then she realized the gun continued to rise and the man behind it was falling over backwards. Stunned, she looked back and saw Marie as she began to reload, then six watermen jump from the boat and head in her direction.

"Henry, I must get to Henry," she thought as she again found the strength to move. When she got there he was still face down, the back of his shirt bloody and his face ashen. No sooner had she reached him than the watermen were there as well, four lifting Henry for the run to the boats while two with pistols covered them.

Just as they started their run for the boats, a second intruder appeared around the bank and fell just as fast to a waterman's pistol shot. They never saw the third, for from her vantage point further out, Marie saw and dispatched him before he came into their line of sight.

That was when they heard Miles calling from the right. Several more watermen left the boats and moved to Robert, who was now seated against the bank clutching his right arm, his sleeve red with blood. Sending one waterman back to the boat with Robert, Miles put Robert's rifle, pouch, and horn into the hands of another before hurrying to the left with three others. Henry's rifle was then put back into action and Miles moved with the remaining two to claim the guns of their fallen adversaries.

As Miles rounded the bank to collect from the last intruder downed by Marie, he came face to face with a fourth. Both completely taken by surprise, it was Miles who reacted first and drove his boatman's pike through the intruder before he could bring his gun to bear. Quickly recovering, he claimed all the guns and ran to the boats. Giving these two guns to Esther and Sarah, he instructed them to keep a close watch on their left for any more surprises from that quarter.

Just as he was about to turn, heavy firing was heard to their left, only up beyond the bank in the trees. "If this means more of them, we could be in a tough spot. Watch close on the left."

Following Edward's lead, Lewis fired as quickly as he could. Still, Edward was able to get off more shots, three to his two, and yet this rapid rate of fire had the desired effect of making their adversaries believe there were more than just two of them. Instead of giving up, once again the intruders fought more desperately, neither asking for nor receiving quarter. Well they knew, as the defenders did not, that it was either die here or at the end of a rope in Williamsburg. At least on this field, as long as there was fight left in them, there was a chance.

On Edward's signal they shifted, not an advance exactly but a move more to their right. What Lewis did not know was Edward hoped to make their presence known to the defenders. This would help minimize the danger they were in from their own party as well as encourage them if they needed it. After two such maneuvers, firing all the while, Edward was seen by Marie and Esther and they shouted the news to Miles. Then and only then was Edward ready to push the intruders across the front of the makeshift breastwork.

Moving through downed intruders, Lewis heard Edward's warning shout but did not understand it until he felt the knife slice down his left calf as Edward dispatched the wounded man, too late to save his brother from being wounded. Lewis was now down, unable to move further, but he could still fire so he kept up his shooting from behind the tree. Only now there were fewer targets to shoot at and for the first time he realized how sporadic the firing had become.

A whoop from the watermen along the bank signaled the end of the intruders. That was when Edward made his way cautiously to Lewis. "Here, let's wrap that leg to stop the bleeding. We'll tend to it better at the boats."

"Me, and what of your wounds?" asked Lewis.

Edward was totally unaware he was bleeding from just above his right temple, his right upper arm, and his right thigh. Looking himself over and feeling the wound above his temple, he pronounced, "I'm just grazed, no solid hits, all where I was exposed in firing at the vermin. They're not my first and I know from experience they'll heal nicely. Now, try to stand and I'll help you to the boats."

Upon reaching the boats, Edward found the Jewett family had sustained the most serious of the wounds. Mary and Esther were with an unconscious Henry while Sarah sat with her grandfather and Marie rushed to Lewis' side.

Edward bent to examine Henry first. He found the ball had entered and been stopped by Henry's shoulder blade. Betty was at his elbow, suggesting they should remove the bullet before she stitched the wound closed. Edward agreed and, using his patch knife, the bullet was quickly out and Betty set about cleaning around the wound so she could sew it. Esther was not looking well so Edward suggested she get some air on shore until she felt more up to tending the wounded. "It's fine," he said as he gave her a reassuring pat on the shoulder and sent he on her way.

He then moved back to Lewis. "You're lucky, little brother, it looks worse than it is. His knife slid neatly between your shin bone and calf muscle. I think when Betty's done with Henry, sewing you back up should be enough to make you whole again." This brought a small smile to Marie's face.

Marie then asked of her boys. "Surely you didn't allow them to expose themselves to hostile fire. Where are they?"

"They're safe about a mile north, with Aaron. I'll bring them in once I've seen to father." Then, to Robert, "And what happened to you?"

"I can't say I know," responded Robert, "although I know I am mighty glad to see you. Did you need to wait for such a dramatic entrance?"

"Naturally, I wouldn't have it any other way. Now, let's see how badly you're hurt. What's this? You have a medium size ball stuck in your elbow! How in the world did you get wounded in such a way?"

"What I remember is taking aim, then being hit in the elbow. As I spun, I saw Henry down, Mary standing in the open, Marie lowering her gun, and one of these pirates falling just beyond where Mary was standing. Does any of that make sense?"

By then Edward had popped the ball out of his father's elbow and was examining it closely before nodding to Sarah who applied a bandage. "Well, father, it would seem you were struck by a spent ball, probably a ricochet. And good thing, too, or it would have shattered your arm."

"So, grandfather will be normal again?" asked a very concerned Sarah.

"I don't know if I ever was what one would call 'normal,' Sarah darling, but I think your Uncle Edward was saying I'll heal," came the response, with a good natured grin from her grandfather.

"I must go reclaim your grandchildren before they head back to Rowley, so if you'll excuse me, father, Sarah," said Edward as he stood to leave.

"Not before I've seen to your wounds, Colonel," interjected Betty. "Now sit back down and let me see them. My lands, you're all cut up and down your right side like someone went at you with a knife. Sit still and this will go a lot faster," she commanded.

After Betty released him and returned to Lewis to finish sewing him up, Edward went ashore and found Miles directing the watermen in collecting arms, powder, ball, and anything else the intruders had that might prove useful, then dragging the bodies to a point down river and away from their camp.

"Tell me, Miles, you seem to be a man with military training, the way I saw you directing the fight and now the recovery. Were you a soldier?"

"Oh, no, sir, and don't you worry, I'm no deserter. I did a tour on board a Royal ship-of-the-line before being discharged and making my way to these shores. That's why I'm no good with a long gun. Give me a cannon, though, and I'll show you marksmanship!"

"I knew it had to be something like that. Now, come with me. You can bring Lewis' horse and rifle back to camp while I go in search of the boys and Aaron."

⊙ *Chapter 15* ⊙

Edward and Miles recovered the rifles and started moving toward where they had left their horses when movement ahead caught Edward's eye and he signaled Miles to take cover. Both were behind trees instantly. As Edward carefully scanned the woods ahead, he picked up the movement again, closer this time, and moving toward them with some attempt at stealth. Edward checked his priming.

"Philip, Joseph!" Edward had allowed them to walk past him before hailing them, a hail that caused the boys to nearly jump out of their skins. "What are you two doing here?"

Recovering their fright, Philip responded, "We couldn't stay on the ridge waiting when you might need our help, so we followed. Why is Miles with you and not father?"

Edward's face darkened as he replied, "Your father, grandfather, and Uncle Henry are all lying wounded. Now, explain yourselves, why aren't you with the pack horses and where is Charles?"

"Father's wounded?" replied Philip, "Where, I need

to go to him?!"

"I asked you a question." The look on Edward's face now frightened the boys more than the news their father had been wounded.

"We slipped away from Aaron when he stepped behind the bushes for some privacy. We came on foot as quickly as we could to help, all three of us. We lost Charles somewhere back before we came upon the horses. Now, please, can I go to father?"

"Why, so you can tell him how you deserted your post? How you left the pack horses we worked so hard to bring this far to the wolves? How you lost your cousin Charles in the woods and left him to fend for himself? No! You're coming with me, first to find Charles and then back to bring in the pack horses."

The look on Edward's face silenced any objection the boys may have been thinking of making. Without taking his fearsome gaze from them, Edward spoke to Miles. "The horses are just ahead. When you return to camp, I want you to move it about a mile upriver from the mouth of the Rockfish. Though you've done a fine job of clearing the carnage, it will draw wolves and I'd rather not bring the horses there. We'll find Charles and then gather up Aaron and the horses. We'll cross up river where it is shallower and make your camp, probably mid-day tomorrow."

Philip was crestfallen. He desperately wanted, needed, to go to his father and yet he knew his uncle was just containing his rage and he dared not push him. As much as this felt like punishment for leaving his post, he also knew this would not be the end of it.

When they reached the horses, the two men mounted, the movement causing Edward's wounds, which had dried, to crack open. Miles departed back the way they had come. Now Philip and Joseph knew they were at the mercy of their uncle with no one around to appeal to for leniency.

"Now," Edward's voice caused the boys to jump again, "did you follow our trail down?"

"Yes, sir," came the response in unison.

"Good, it's an easy trail to follow. Now, Joseph, I want you out to the left, Philip to the right. Stay only so far out as you can both still see me. We need to sweep up this trail and find Charles, no matter how long it takes. Let's move."

It was an hour later when they found Charles. From his vantage point on the back of the horse, it was actually Edward who saw him first. He had evidently dropped down off the narrow spur and lost the trail. He had done well, though. Edward saw he had gone to ground at a spring where he did not want for water. When Philip finally saw him, he stopped and gave the signal. Edward passed the signal on to Joseph and moved to Philip.

"I think he's crying, Uncle Edward."

"And you're to say nothing more about it," came the harsh, whispered reply. Then, in a lighter tone than Philip had heard from his uncle all day, "Ah, Charles, there you are, lad. How about giving me a hand with the horses? Are you up to it?"

Charles was thrilled to see his uncle. "Uncle Edward, I'm sorry, I know you said to stay with Aaron and the horses, but we were so worried. I'm sorry I got lost. Uncle Edward, you're bleeding!"

Edward told Charles the wounds were nothing to worry about, then dismounted and took a long drink from the spring, inviting Charles to join him. Charles understood and took the opportunity to wipe his face with the cool water without calling undue attention to it by his cousins.

"Now, your father, Uncle Lewis, and grandfather have been wounded. We, with Aaron's help, are all that's left to move the pack horses to the river and the new camp. Can I count on your help, Charles?"

"Yes, and I won't disobey you again, Uncle Edward. I truly am sorry."

As Edward turned back to the other boys, they saw his face harden again. "Well, boys, we found Charles. Off with you to find Aaron and the pack horses."

They found Aaron where they had left him, greatly relieved when he saw his charges coming up the hill. Then he saw Edward.

"Colonel, I started after them as soon as I saw they'd gone, but I couldn't leave the pack horse to the wolves. I wasn't sure what you'd want me to do. I hope I did right."

"Yes, Aaron, you did all you could, given the unruly nature of the boys." He then added, more for the boys' benefit, "I fear not one of them will survive this journey as they do not follow instructions."

After checking and tightening the packs, they started out, Edward in the lead, then the boys, with Aaron bringing up the rear. Rather than continue the way they had just come, from the Fluvanna River, Edward led them due west, or as due west as the ground permitted, toward the Rockfish River. They found a suitable ford before dusk, crossed over and made camp on the west bank.

Philip spent a very restless night. While all were worried about their fathers and grandfather, Philip was feeling especially sensitive to having disobeyed Uncle Edward and the consequences that might hold. This was not like before, when he had moved and nearly drawn the fire of the ruffian. This was far more serious. He had not only disobeyed, he had lost Charles and left Aaron unable to fulfill the instructions from his master, endangering him and the horses. Uncle Edward had warned them all that lives would depend on their following instructions. He had not and had nearly cost Charles his life. He knew he somehow had to regain Uncle Edward's trust and that was not going to be an easy task. No, whatever punishment Uncle Edward had in mind, Philip knew he deserved it as much as he was so not looking forward to it when it came. The waiting was the worst part.

They found the new camp of the river company at mid-day. Before being allowed to see the wounded, Edward had the boys see to the horses, unpacking them, rubbing them down, all the normal chores when they went into camp. Their mothers watched with not a little pride showing and while knowing not to interfere with Edward. He had his methods and was too much "old army" for them to get involved.

Edward left Aaron to supervise the boys as they hobbled the horses and went to see his father and brothers. Betty caught him before he got there.

"All are doing fine. Lewis' leg is the worst of the three. I had to drain the poison out of it this morning but it is doing much better. He is in a lot of pain. Henry and your father are both doing well. Henry can't move his left arm all the way, but I don't want him to so the wound will heal. Your father can't fully straighten his right arm, and may never be able to again. His wound is also healing nicely."

"Thank you, Betty, you've been a big help with our wounded." Then, entering under the boat awning he said, "Lewis, I hear you're in some pain."

"Quite a bit, actually," came the reply.

"Well, I have a solution for that. You just need to convince our sister to share her medicinal rum with you is all," throwing a grin in Esther's direction that became a chuckle with her indignation.

"Listen, Edward," continued Lewis, very seriously, "Miles told us what the boys did and I'm very sorry. Have you punished them?"

"That might depend on who you ask. I'm sure they think that my not letting them come to you yesterday was punishment, or even making them tend the horses now before being released to see you is punishment. I see those things as lessons in discipline. Other than that, I have not punished them. I am not their fathers."

"I see you found Charles so he must have been alright. Mary was worried sick when Miles told us he was lost in the woods," added Henry.

"He went to ground as soon as he knew he was lost, at a spring where he had water and stayed put until we found him. No, he did fine and I think being abandoned has helped him learn his lesson. The other two probably have as well. I'm just not convinced it's been as lasting a lesson as Charles had. Here come the boys and I don't want my presence to spoil your reunion with them as I doubt I'm their favorite person right about now." With that, Edward left the boat as the boys came bounding in to see their fathers and grandfather.

They spent the next four days in camp allowing the wounded to heal before starting again. First Edward inspected all of the arms taken in the recent fight. Some were found to be, like Henry's musket, condemned arms that he discarded, but he also found many serviceable rifles and muskets. He first offered pick to Billy Watson and his watermen, who mostly preferred pistols to having to haul a long arm around in their line of work. The remainder he had packed away to be taken with them.

Edward and Aaron rode ahead to check out the trail for the pack horses to the river landing site. They found a freighter had a permanent establishment there for hauling mostly crops to the river and, to a lesser extent, moving supplies inland. They arranged with him for eight two-wheeled carts each pulled by a brace of oxen, all the man had, to move them from the river through Indian Trail Gap. They then returned to move their party along.

They found the party ready. Henry was much recovered, though still stiff in his left shoulder, and Robert was going around showing everyone the dimple the spent ball had put in his elbow, a mark he likely would never lose. Lewis was improving, but he still was unable to walk and healing slowly. He asked to speak privately with Edward after supper.

"I've spoken with Philip and he is terribly sorry for leaving the pack horses when you told him to stay. He desperately wants to make it up to you, to win your confidence back. Joseph as well, but it is Philip feeling the worst about what happened."

"I'm glad to hear it. I sensed Philip was the leader of the three, with Charles a reluctant follower and Joseph probably giving Philip added encouragement."

"Then you'll make up to the boys?"

"Of course, but it will not be tomorrow. I want them to remember the lesson and reduce the chance of it happening again. What they did could have cost them their lives. Tomorrow, when the pack horses start, I intend to take Charles and Marie along. Marie is anxious to get back in the saddle and asked if she could ride when I returned this afternoon. I could use the help. Philip and Joseph will ride the boats up as a way to reinforce the lesson we hope they've learned."

"They will both hate that!"

"I don't doubt it. I'll make it up when we start up toward Indian Trail Gap. We'll be able to tie the pack horses off to the carts so I can take the boys and scout ahead."

"Thank you. That should set things right between you. By the way, you should also know what they have been saying about you. Philip let it slip that he agreed with his Aunt Esther. With Aunt Bess you got a bear hug, with Uncle Edward you get the whole bear." Both men laughed before Lewis continued, "Charles added that he was just glad you are on our side, and of course that you weren't mad at him!"

Laughing, Edward observed, "Charles is a smart boy, but we're going to have to keep a closer eye on our sister!"

The next morning they set off. The pack horses had the more direct and thereby shorter route while the boats had to follow the river and all of its curves and loops. Philip in particular was beside himself with grief when told he would be part of the river company for this leg and his mother would take his place with the pack horses. He tried appealing to his father and then his grandfather, both of whom gave him the same answer, "The Colonel makes the assignments."

The result of the pack horses, the slower of the two companies, having a shorter distance to cover was both groups arrived at the landing just before supper time and they all made camp in a wooded glen. The next day was spent unloading the boats, a task accomplished before dinner. At Robert's suggestion, Mary, Marie, Esther, and Sarah, with Betty and Mattie helping, prepared a big farewell dinner for all the watermen. As it concluded, Billy Watson approached Robert and Edward.

"Gentlemen, it has been a real pleasure for us to make your acquaintance. Just so you know, the men all agreed that if you was to need anything you can call on any one of us and we'd give you the shirt off our back and glad to do it."

Robert, speaking for the family, replied, "And that goes for us as well, Mr. Watson. Tell the men that if they ever find themselves in need to look us up. They've helped us through trying times and we now consider them a part of our family." With that there were handshakes all around and not a few of the watermen asked for and received a hug from the women. As the boats pulled into the current, Edward came up next to Esther.

"Are you sure you don't want to go back with them? I saw the hug that big one gave you."

"Would you just stop that!"

∽ Chapter 16 ∽

After watching the boats drift around a bend, Esther and Edward turned and walked back to the camp arm in arm. In spite of the light teasing, they had always been close, or was the light teasing an indication of how close they were? Naturally, she was closer to Lewis, having lived close these past 30 years. She felt much closer to Edward than Henry, even though she had seen more of Henry over the years than of Edward. She could not explain why, so she did not try and just enjoyed the stroll with her brother. Once at camp, Edward excused himself to go find their freighter.

"Mister MacDonald, I wonder if you could be of further assistance."

"Colonel, I'd be more than happy to try. Your family has brought me substantial business at what is normally my slow time."

"With my father and brothers wounded in our recent misfortune, we will be needing labor when we reach our lands and I wondered if I could hire it through you."

"But of course, Colonel. I could easily lease out eight good hands for up to two months at, shall we say

£160?"

"I asked to lease, not to buy! We both know £20 per year is a good wage, and we are talking just two months of labor. I was thinking more £80 for the lot."

"Why, Colonel, I must have some profit for my making the arrangements. Can we agree on £130? I'll even provide for their needs, all but fresh meat which I'll ask you to provide."

"I'll go £100 with the stipulations you just added and no more. As with the carts and drovers, we'll pay in coin. How often do you even see that much coin this far west?"

"That is a hard bargain. What if I don't agree, how will you get your labor then?"

"Then I will start our little band on the road while I visit the surrounding farms offering to lease labor at half what I just offered you. What's more, you know these coin starved farmers will agree to it. So, do we have a bargain or will you lose the business?"

MacDonald looked closely into Edward's eyes to see if there might be some more negotiating room. When he found only a cold, determined look in return, "We have a bargain, hard as it is. I'll have them ready tomorrow. Shall we say nine of the clock?"

"Good, only have them ready to move by dawn. I'll pay you when you deliver them to me. And I'm expecting first rate laborers, no sick or infirm."

Not looking entirely pleased, Mister MacDonald nodded his assent. After Edward left the shack MacDonald used as an office, MacDonald's mood actually lightened as he considered the tidy profit he was still about to make on the labor. He had thought he could gain a little better deal than he got, but all in all he still felt he came out ahead on the deal. He then went out to make arrangements for the laborers.

After supper, the family and drovers gathered around Edward as he reviewed the order of march for the morning. Edward, with Philip, Joseph, and Charles, would ride ahead and scout the trail, an announcement that brought large grins to the boys' faces. Robert, sufficiently recovered from his wound, would mount and lead the carts. Each cart would have one pack horse tied behind. After the first four carts would be the laborers, on foot, with a mounted Henry overseeing them. Betty with Lewis would be in the first cart where Betty could signal a halt if Lewis' condition warranted it. Aaron and Miles were to ride trail. Esther demurred when offered a chance to mount, choosing to ride a cart instead, so Sarah would mount and ride with Henry. Mary and Mattie would also ride carts. All of those riding the carts, except the invalided Lewis, would walk when the going became difficult.

Marie would be mounted and Edward gave her rein to ride from point to trail as she wished, cautioning her not to disrupt the carts in passing but to give them right of way on the trail. Having missed her daily rides for most of their journey, this arrangement pleased Marie and she shot Edward a broad smile to thank him.

Then Edward continued, "All are to be under arms from here on. The women in the carts should have their arms loaded and in the cart they intend to ride. I do not expect them to carry them while they are walking. All who are mounted are to have their arms across the saddle ready for action at all times. We have recently dealt with the river pirates and though we leave this scourge behind us, we are moving into a region frequented by the Indians. Some will no doubt be friendly enough, others will not. I am not experienced enough to know the difference until they show their hand, so we must all be ready for any eventuality."

The next morning everything was ready for a dawn start except the promised laborers. Mister MacDonald finally arrived, half an hour late, with the laborers, slaves all. Edward looked them over, checked their provisions and paid Mister MacDonald for their services. That taken care of, they started.

The oxen made the main party move quite slowly. Horses would have been faster but there was no matching the oxen's pulling ability. Marie seemed to enjoy riding the several miles separating Edward in the advance and Robert with the main party, so much so there was little for the boys to do, Marie taking all the messages back and forth for them. She really was a good horsewoman and negotiated the rough trail with ease.

They made a halt for dinner and then moved on trying to get as much trail behind them as possible. Edward found a good meadow for the evening camp with ample grass for the beasts and water for everyone, just before the ground began to rise to the foothills of the Blue Ridge. This was one time Marie was not with the advance, so he sent Joseph back to inform Robert a campsite had been selected.

"Charles, we're about an hour or an hour and a half ahead of the main party. Would you be alright waiting here for them while Philip and I scout on ahead? We don't want them to miss the campsite for we know little of what is ahead and this could be the last promising spot. It's an important task I'm entrusting you with if you're up to it."

"I'll wait for them here, Uncle Edward," replied Charles, beaming with not a little pride. The last time he found himself alone he had been scared and crying so this he saw as an opportunity to show Uncle Edward he was stronger than that. This is, of course, what Uncle Edward hoped to do.

Moving further down the trail, Edward called a halt after a mile or so as the trail started to climb. Tying off the horses, he took Philip off the trail a piece, to the edge of a small brook where he sat at the base of a tree. Philip did the same. As he tried to ask what they were doing, Edward signed him to silence and signaled the need to be watchful. Not knowing what the matter was, Philip did as bid with tense anticipation.

After little more than half an hour, a large buck stepped into view and halted at a distance, wary of its surroundings. Edward motioned for Philip to shoot. He hesitated, whispering, "But deer are out of season, we can't preserve the meet this time of year."

"We've a party of thirty, there will be no need to preserve anything and we need the fresh meat."

The deer sniffed the air and listened carefully. The wind was in their favor so it did not detect Edward and Philip. Moving a bit closer, drawn by water, the deer finally stepped into the open at a comfortable range for Philip. He took careful aim and, after what to Edward seemed like an incredibly long time to aim, he fired.

When the smoke cleared from in front of his face, Philip saw the place where the deer had been, empty. Dropping his head, he apologized, "I'm sorry I missed, Uncle Edward."

"Missed? Are you sure? How can you tell from here?"

With Edward's encouragement Philip went forward to the spot and found blood, quite a bit of it. Turning with excitement, he froze when he found his uncle was aiming directly at him! "Uncle Edward, what did I do?"

Edward slowly lowered his rifle. "Philip, I'm now an Indian. Are you prepared?"

"I don't understand."

"You left cover to check on your game without re-loading. Any Indian hearing the shot would move in your direction to investigate if it be a friend or foe. We are in a hostile land, or are about to be, and such carelessness could cost you your life. Worse, it could cost me mine!"

"I'm sorry, Uncle Edward. It seems I just can't get things right. I don't mean to be such a problem." His eyes filled but he held back the tears. Edward re-primed his rifle and closed the steel, having rendered his rifle safe before pointing it at his nephew, and gave his nephew opportunity to regain his composure.

"Philip, I was taking an opportunity to teach you another very valuable lesson. An empty rifle on the frontier is worthless, even dangerous. Now, reload so we can go and recover your kill. Our party will be hungry and tonight you're feeding them."

Edward showed Philip how to track the deer, finding it less than 20 yards from where it was hit. He then kept watch while talking Philip through the field dressing.

"No, I didn't kill it so I'm not field dressing it. It's as simple as that. Starting now, this is how we'll be getting our fresh meat so you may as well learn now how to properly prepare it." Philip made a face and started rather tentatively. It was not long before he realized it was done and not as bad as he thought it would be.

They returned to Charles before the main party had arrived and found he had taken a defensive position. "I heard a shot and not knowing what it was, I thought it'd be wise to be prepared."

"You did right, Charles. You have good instincts for the frontier. The other day you stayed put where you'd have water and today you heard a shot and took cover. I'm quite pleased. Now, let's get a fire started, a big one, so we can roast this deer Philip shot."

"Philip shot it? You mean it and aren't just saying that?"

"Yes and the next one is yours, Joseph the one after that. While we're on the trail you boys will be responsible for providing us all with fresh meat."

It was a road weary group that arrived with the carts half an hour later, just about sunset. Finding a deer already roasting gave them the energy to go about caring for the stock and preparing the camp. When all was in readiness and the deer properly roasted, the company gathered around.

"Father, would you honor us with a prayer and then taking the first serving from your grandson's first kill?" began Edward.

"Philip shot this deer? My, my, well, my grandsons are growing up right before my eyes." With that, Robert led them in prayer, they ate, and the company retired for the evening.

As they ate, Edward made his way over and sat down next to Henry and Mary. "I left Charles alone today, here, telling him it was so you wouldn't miss the meadow. In reality it was for him to build his confidence about being alone."

"And how did he do?" Henry asked, with a little apprehension. He knew how much being lost had affected his son.

"He did great, even taking cover when he heard Philip's shot. He's got good instincts. Enjoy the venison, I told Charles the next one is on him." Edward left two beaming parents as he went over to finish his meal seated with Robert and Esther.

The next day started at first light and they were on the trail by sunrise. The trail was now getting steeper and the pace for the carts was slowed as a result. In a couple of places, Edward and the boys had to do makeshift repairs to the trail to permit the carts to pass. They managed to find a small meadow just barely large enough for their dinner break. After the carts arrived, Edward moved ahead with all three boys while dinner was being prepared.

They had not gone far when they met someone coming toward them on the trail, the first they had met in a day and a half. It was a young man, well mounted and leading two pack horses. As the stranger approached he hailed them, "Hallo, would you happen to be Colonel Jewett, late of His Majesty's Army?"

"I am Colonel Jewett, sir, and to whom do I have the pleasure of addressing?"

"Sir, I am Major Washington," was the reply accompanied with a most graceful bow. "Governor Dinwiddie asked that I survey your grant in advance of your arrival. I thought you might come by way of Indian Gap Trail and, having finished my survey, came to meet you and guide you in."

∞ *Chapter 17* ∞

*M*ajor Washington and Edward rode back the trail toward where the rest of the party was preparing dinner. Joseph was entrusted with the Major's pack horses and Charles was sent ahead to inform the others of their guest.

"Surely, Major, you didn't survey my grant this fast by yourself?"

"No, sir, I have five assistants who aid me. When we finished, I sent them back down the Valley to Chester while I came in search of you. It wasn't that hard to survey your grant as I have laid it out, with the North River forming two of your boundaries. It makes for a long, rather narrow track but I was able to avoid land already occupied in the process."

"That sounds fine. You can fill me in this evening, but, here now is the rest of the family. Let me introduce you around and get some food into you."

With that, Edward introduced their visitor to his family. He noted that, while Sarah seemed especially taken with the youth, he blushed and stammered when introduced to her. The dinner break was short, as was their custom, and the whole company was set into motion again. The Major traveled now with Edward and the boys, talking as they worked up the ever steeper trail.

"I think you'll find yourselves over the summit mid-day tomorrow at the rate the oxen travel. Once over, the descent is shorter than the climb and you'll soon find yourselves at the North River. The far side is quite steep and not conducive to crossing with the carts. There is a place I found to the southwest where all can cross safely. Once over, you're on your grant as I've surveyed it. Once you've had a chance to look over my work, and approve, I can take a copy of it with me and file it for you."

"You're being most helpful, Major. What do I owe you for all this special treatment?"

"I did the survey at the request of Governor Dinwiddie to be paid by the Crown, it being a Royal Grant. As for the rest, I simply hoped to meet you and, perhaps, learn how you were able to succeed in the Royal Army. I have some aspirations that way myself, you see, and I thought I could benefit from your advice."

Now Edward understood the motivation. They chatted about all things military as they moved up the trail. As daylight began to wane on this eastern slope they looked for a suitable campsite for the party. The ground was quite steep and a large, flat meadow was out of the question so they settled on a narrow table where at least there was some grass and room for a long, narrow campsite. While the Major remained with Philip and Joseph, Edward proceeded on with Charles.

"We're going to have a bit harder time of it than Philip did last night I'm afraid. There is less deer sign so we'll need to work smarter. I've always preferred working smarter than working harder. How about yourself?"

With a shy grin, Charles answered, "I've always

preferred not working to working, if truth be told."

Edward was still chuckling when he found a likely spot and signaled a halt. They dismounted and tied the horses before he continued in a soft voice. "Unless the horse has been accustomed to gunfire, only in an emergency should you ever fire while seated on its back. You have no idea how the horse will react to a shot that close and you could be hurt. Now, lets move along this game trail as quietly as you can, slowly, pausing often to listen and look."

Moving with the light breeze generally in their faces, they found an area of large oaks rimmed by pine. Edward signaled a halt behind a deadfall pine. Although they did not have long to wait, it seemed forever to Charles. Instead of a deer stepping into the clearing, it was a rather large bruin. Charles looked at Edward who nodded assent then whispered very softly and close to his ear instructions on where to aim. Sighting carefully, he squeezed the trigger and the bear disappeared behind the cloud of white smoke. Then he heard the bear let out an awful, angry howl and there was another shot.

Both quickly reloading, Edward slapped Charles on the back and congratulated him before they moved forward to the mound of fur where the bear had previously stood.

"But I didn't really get him, you did, Uncle Edward."

"Nonsense, Charles, you bagged him fairly. I simply added a coup-de-grace because I'm saddle weary and didn't want to have to drag this fellow any further than necessary." Like the night before, Edward kept watch and gave instructions as Charles went about the task of field dressing the bear. Then he brought up the horses and they hoisted the bear onto Charles' horse, which was not all that happy with its new cargo.

Back in camp, Charles lead his horse with its cargo right to where Henry and Mary were standing with Robert. Beaming, he announced that tonight's supper would be roasted bear meat. Robert, Henry, and Mary were quite impressed but a quick glance would have told anyone looking that Philip and Joseph were more than a little envious.

While the bear was roasting, Major Washington pulled out his maps and started reviewing his surveying results with Robert, Edward, Henry, and Lewis. "It follows the North River in a northeast/southwest direction and is generally a rolling valley. The western boundary is a ridgeline that runs, with a few interruptions, two miles to the northwest and parallel to the river, also in a northeast/ southwest direction. The North River takes a turn, here, as I've shown, to the south and two mountains are on the west side of it, the only mountains on the west bank of the river. Your grant ends at the southwestern base of the southernmost, largest of the two mountains."

After some questions as they looked over the map, it was time for supper. During supper, Sarah sat quite near Major Washington, who pretended not to notice except his red face gave him away. Presently, she asked him how long he had been a surveyor. He responded, more to the group than to Sarah directly for it seemed to pain him to look in her direction, that he had been doing it for four years, since he was 16, mostly for Lord Fairfax between the York and Potomac Rivers and along the lower Shenandoah River. Even at that he seemed to have difficulty getting the words out.

At length, Sarah was able to approach Robert somewhat off from the others and ask, "Am I so terrible to look at that the Major can't stand the sight of me, grandfather?"

Although forced to laugh, Robert comforted her. "Not at all, Sarah, and don't be thinking that way. The Major is just very shy. I can't say I've seen a case of shyness quite this bad, unless it was your Uncle Lewis at his age. Just be nice to him and don't hold his shyness against him. But not too nice, young lady, you're not of age yet, only to look at you he'd never know it." That got Robert a hug and a kiss on the cheek before Sarah returned to the group gathered around the Major, seating herself right next to him and now almost enjoying the discomfort this caused.

The next morning Edward announced a slight change to their normal march. He, with the boys, Major Washington, and Marie, would move on ahead at a good pace. Once Major Washington had shown them the ford onto their grant, he would send Marie and Philip back to guide the rest to and over the ford. That raised a protest from Philip that was quickly silenced by a single look. Edward would send Charles back to wait at the ford with directions to that night's camp site within the boundaries of their property. He and Joseph would arrange for their evening fare.

With that they started. They continued to do any repairs to the trail where it would halt the carts, still making good time up to the crest where they spied the Valley of Virginia for the first time. Major Washington had been correct. The descent was easy and much shorter than the ascent. Once on the valley floor, the Major pointed out where the trail continued toward the north and west to cross the shallower South River. The more populated areas were in that direction. The party continued to the southwest, coming to the ford the Major had selected in just a few miles. Here Marie and Philip were sent back to guide the main party to the ford.

Just across the ford was a good meadow with excellent grass near the banks of the river. Edward pointed it out to Charles as their first campsite and left him at the ford to direct the main party to it. Now down to three, they continued at a brisk pace up the rolling hills and deeper into the grant Major Washington had laid out.

First moving to the north, this being the closest of the borders, they located the Major's blazes and followed them back to the southwest. When nearly opposite the ford, they cut across their grant to join the main party, stopping to locate meat on the way. They found a bold stream and a likely spot for deer, Edward repeating the hunting lessons of the past two nights given to his other nephews. Once again rewarded in short order, Joseph managed to put a well aimed shot on a large buck and receive the same lessons in field dressing as his brother and cousin.

Moving up from the stream toward the east and the campsite, the three came to a spring at the edge of a large meadow of perhaps 50 acres. Looking around, Edward and Major Washington conferred before pronouncing this a good spot to move the main camp tomorrow. The tired trio returned to find the camp established and hot fire in anticipation of fresh meat. While the venison was roasting, the family men again went into consultation over Major Washington's map of the grant. While Robert moved the main camp to the selected site, with Joseph as their guide, Edward would continue the boundary scout with Major Washington. This time they would move along the river to the southwest, working their way around to the point they had left the boundary this evening and back to camp.

As this would likely take all day, Edward explained the form of the camp to Robert. There was a large marquee to act as a warehouse for all their goods. If he set this up first, they could unload the carts and allow the drovers to depart the following day. He had also included ten wedge tents; one each for the four married couples, one for Esther and Sarah to share, one for the three boys to share, one each for Robert and Edward, leaving two for the hired laborers.

"I can not help but observe how you provide for your servants as if they were family," said Major Washington. "Even the slaves you have hired eat from the same game as the family and now you'll house them as you house the family. I can attest this is not the custom of the country and find it curious."

"Well, Major," was Edward's reply, "I have found the men grumble less and work harder if their officers share the same conditions with them. I have also seen many a unit ruined when the officers saw to their comforts first, caring little for the conditions their troops faced. On the field of battle, these latter units invariably are the first to break while I have seen those officered in the former manner stand beyond when there was any hope rather than abandon their officers. Remember that when you command in the field, Major." Robert was nodding through this explanation, looking pleased as these were lessons he tried to teach all his sons, even before Edward had seen them employed in battle.

With that, the women announced the venison ready and all lined up to receive their portions. The Major then realized Edward had, as he had last night, taken his place at the very end of the line, not being served until everyone else had received their portions. Perhaps he could learn more by watching and understanding how this experienced officer conducted himself for it was true, the entire expedition had a very military feel about it, yet all were content in spite of the hardships of the trail.

After the meal was consumed, Sarah approached the Major and, with a big smile, "Come, Major, you've been riding all day and should stretch your legs before retiring for the night or they'll be stiff in the morning. Let's take a walk along the river." Then, not giving him a chance to answer, she took his arm and led him, as red-faced as he ever had been, toward the river.

Robert made eye contact with Esther and made a quick tilt of the head in the young couple's direction. Esther knew immediately and fell in behind them, far enough back not to inhibit their conversation, should the Major ever regain his ability to speak, but close enough for her presence to be felt, as a good chaperone should.

The others then settled into their evening routine. Betty changed Lewis' bandage, checking the wound, while Marie sat close. Henry and Mary, after watching the young couple and Esther walk off, fell into a hushed conversation before turning into their blankets. And the boys, yes, they excitedly discussed their day's events while the rest of the camp settled in for some earned rest in the hopes for an easy day on the morrow.

Chapter 18

dward was up before first light, as was his custom, only this morning he had company. Henry joined him as he stood near the river away from the camp. "What do you make of the character of Major Washington?"

"He seems a fine young man, terribly shy but hard working and quick learning. Why do you ask?" responded Edward.

"Well, we, that is Mary really, was wondering about his prospects. What do you know of his family?"

"The Major comes from one of the principal families in Virginia, one that has been on these shores nearly as long as our own. He had the misfortune of having an older brother who inherited the vast bulk of their father's estates so he turned to surveying for his living and has aspirations for the military, as is traditional for men in this circumstance. His brother just died without increase, they were very close, and he stands to inherit a sizable estate. Both Governor Dinwiddie and Lord Fairfax think quite highly of him and from what I've seen, their opinion is well founded. I still do not understand why you're asking."

"This is a bit awkward for me. I think you've seen

how Sarah and Mary are together and it is not a good situation. Mary thought, perhaps, if the Major would be a good match, and as Sarah has shown an interest in him, their marriage would be a good thing..." Henry then fell silent, obviously uncomfortable with the subject yet compelled to bring it up.

After suitable reflection, Edward spoke softly, "I would not presume to speak for father and you would need to take this matter up with him. For me, I would advise against it, strongly, not because of any faults in young George but because Sarah has just turned fifteen on this trip and is too young to marry. No, Henry, this is no way to resolve the turmoil in your household." Both men fell silent, lost in their own thoughts. Several minutes passed before their contemplations were interrupted.

"Ah, Henry, here you are. Good morning Edward," came Robert's soft voice. "Henry, I want to talk to you about something, something rather sensitive."

"Of course, father, anything."

"No, you can stay, Edward. Henry, it's about Sarah. She and Esther have grown very close on this trip, I think you'll agree, and now that we are here and will be preparing our separate lodging over the next weeks, I was wondering if you and Mary could see your way clear to letting Sarah come stay with Esther and me. I know Mary will miss Sarah's helping hands around the house, but it would mean a lot to your sister who is feeling the loss of Aunt Bess and, frankly, I'd love to see more of my only granddaughter. There's no need to make a decision this instant, think it over, talk to Mary and Sarah, and let me know your decision."

"Thank you, father, I'll take it up with Mary and Sarah today," came Henry's response. After a few more minutes in silence, he excused himself and walked back toward camp comforted to have an alternative to present to Mary.

Several more minutes passed before Edward spoke. "You heard our conversation, then?"

"Every word and I thank you, Edward, for what you said." The two stood in silence, listening to the sounds of the river and enjoying the other's presence until it was light enough to see to waking the camp. They walked, still in silence, back to the camp where they separated to see to their own morning tasks.

Joseph was all grins to be leading the main party to their new campsite. Edward gave him a few encouraging words before Joseph took his place with Robert at the head of the column. Robert nodded to him and the boy signaled the start. The other two boys had chosen to join their uncle and the Major on their ride around the grant boundaries. Philip was a little out of sorts when his mother announced her intention to join them on their ride, looking forward to the excuse to be mounted for most of the day.

The small group made good time down to where the North River fed the Fluvanna River. Turning west, the Major showed them his blazes at the southwest flank of the larger of the two mountains where the grant left the river in a northwesterly direction. After about a mile, the Major called a halt.

"Colonel, I would like to show you a natural formation just west of here, perhaps half a mile. It is a rock bridge, quite high, and well worth the detour. I found it quite sublime."

"I'd love to see it," came Marie's voice before even the boys could speak in favor of it. "We can spare the time, can't we, Edward?"

Looking into the three excited faces of his family companions, Edward knew there really was no option open to him. "Well, I suppose there'll be no denying you three or peace if I try. So, Major, lead on."

They lost little time locating the formation and were all struck by its grandeur. As Marie and Edward admired the sight, the Major took the two boys to show them where he had carved his initials in the rock. As they returned they were in an animated discussion.

"I say I can," the Major was saying.

Philip turned to Edward, "Uncle Edward, the Major says he can throw a rock clean over the rock bridge and we say he can't. Who's right?"

"Well, if the Major says he can, who are we to say naught? Of course, if the Major is up to a little sport, I suppose he could demonstrate and give you each a chance to match him. Then we need to be moving on. We still have some ground to travel."

They watched as the Major carefully picked out his stone, weighed it in his hand, positioned himself to his liking, then with a powerful throw, tossed the stone up and over the rock bridge. Marie and Edward smiled as the boys both stood with their mouths open in absolute amazement.

"How tall would you say the bridge is above where we now stand, Major?" asked Marie.

"I went to the top and dropped a weighted line, all I had with me, 250 feet worth, and it was 20 feet or more shy of the bottom." Then, looking at the boys to make sure they were listening, he turned back to Marie, "That's why I threw the rock to clear 272 feet. Seems to have been just about right," he concluded with a smile.

Edward allowed both boys one throw each to try to match the Major before ordering a resumption of their journey. It is of little wonder neither throw had the slightest chanced of succeeding, both falling pitifully short of the bottom arch, let alone being able to clear it. This left the boys in even bigger awe of their companion, if that was possible.

Major Washington quickly got them back to the boundary line and they began moving to the northeast generally along the crest of a broken ridgeline about two and half miles from the North River. From a few high points along this route they did see an isolated cabin in the valley to the northwest, but none to the southeast where it would have placed them on the grant as the Major had surveyed it. This pleased Edward for he hated the thought of driving someone off land they had improved for their own use, even if it was his right to do so.

Coming to the point they had concluded their ride yesterday, the small group paused to let the horses rest and discuss the maps of the grant. Edward was satisfied the boundary had been well planned and well marked and he was very satisfied with the quality of the land within these boundaries. This came as somewhat of a relief to the young man who, even though he found he was warmly welcomed into the family circle, had been unable to ignore the Colonel's position and his own desire for the Colonel's approbation.

Now late in the afternoon, as they went to resume their mounts, Philip asked the question he and Joseph had obviously been debating while the three adults had consulted the maps. "Who will bring down the deer for tonight's supper, Uncle Edward? I say it's my turn as Joseph provided the meat last night."

With a smile toward Marie and the Major, Edward said, "Why, Philip, you've forgotten your mother. Tonight it is her turn, though I dare say she will allow you and Joseph to practice your field dressing once she has it fairly downed."

The look of total shock and surprise on both boys' faces sent the three adults into fits of laughter. Good to his word, as they came to a likely spot, Edward took Marie off in search of game. It was not long before the boys heard a single shot. Following a short pause, they heard Edward call them to him where he put them to work field dressing another fine, large buck. Marie, Edward, and the Major conversed during this process, with Edward keeping watch on their progress and adding an occasional correction to their procedure as needed.

Returning to the spring they had found yesterday, they found the main camp already erected. Robert had chosen a relatively flat piece of ground to the south of the spring, quite near a smaller spring and closer to the strong stream. The horses were picketed beyond camp, down stream, then came the large marquee, and a double row of wedge tents, pitched in perfect alignment to form a wide alley leading to the marquee. To the streamside and beneath a large sycamore, they had erected a large awning for taking meals and other group activities.

"Colonel, your family never ceases to amaze me."

"How so, Major?"

"Why, to look at this camp one would expect to see a squad of Regulars about, so perfect in its alignment and layout."

"I would say that is not such a bad impression to leave someone observing the camp from a distance, perhaps a native of these woods and hills. Wouldn't you agree, Major?"

George had to agree, when viewed from a distance an Indian would think twice about approaching, expecting to find regular army troops in residence. This Colonel was proving a sly one indeed, thinking of, it would appear, everything, and his father was no less impressive, having led the main party from the beginning.

The men again went into consultation while the meat was roasting. With George's help, they prepared all of the necessary papers to be filed with the county court to finalize the boundaries and conditions of the grant. As they were concluding their business, Mary approached.

"So, where are Henry and my lands located in this grant?" This caused Henry no small discomfort as Robert and Edward both first looked to him and then each other before Edward responded, George quickly and quietly removing himself.

"I have written the papers so that you are guaranteed your acreage but to be worked in common until such time as it becomes prudent to divide the land. We will spend this first winter, and probably the next, in the structures we will erect over the next few weeks, here, where we are mutually supportive in case of trouble."

"Well, that is not what I agreed to! Edward, you promised us our own land. That's what brought us all this way. And now you go back on your word."

Robert saw the anger building in Edward so he took over the conversation. "Mary, Edward has been true to his word and the grant that will be filed with the county court provides Henry every acre as agreed. It is impracticable at this point, having seen naught but the boundaries and a few acres in between, to make any equitable division of the land. Now, Henry has been provided for, as has Charles as his heir, we will go into the winter quarters here, all together and there will be no more said on the subject." Robert's voice had been gentle, as always, but firm, becoming firmer by the end and the look in his eye closed any chance for compromise.

After a moment for her defeat to sink in, Mary

turned and returned to where final meal preparations were underway. It was apparent she was not pleased with her defeat and yet realized to bring it up again would not be prudent. Henry broke the silence.

"Edward, father, I'm sorry about that. Mary has been quite on edge lately. She means nothing by it, I assure you. She'll be better after a few days rest."

"Yes, son, I'm sure you're right. All she needs is some rest," Robert responded, casting a skeptical look to Edward and Lewis. "Now that we're here, what's to be done tomorrow?"

Edward explained his plan to first build a blockhouse over the spring, then to build five cabins to see them through this winter and likely the next. Robert, Henry, Lewis, and Edward would each have a cabin with the servants sharing the last.

"Edward, I've been of very little help with this leg and I'm tired of being waited on. What can I do to be useful?" asked Lewis with some pleading in his voice.

"Well, brother, if I don't miss my guess you've split a rail or two and riven a shingle or two in your day, and that should come in handy," said Edward with a wicked smile toward Robert and Henry.

∽ *Chapter 19* ∽

*A*fter their supper, Major Washington requested leave of Edward to depart in the morning, which was granted. This made the evening rather bittersweet for all had come to like the young man who had helped them so much. Sarah sat next to him as Philip and Charles goaded him into retelling and retelling the story of throwing the rock over the rock bridge for the benefit of Joseph and Sarah and anyone else they did not think had heard it enough. Her nearness made it difficult for George to concentrate on the story and the boys had to keep pressing him to continue.

The next morning at first light, the camp stirred and breakfast was made. George said his goodbyes and prepared to leave, saving Robert and Edward for last. "Sir Robert, it has been my pleasure to meet and assist you. Should you ever require my services in the future, I am at your disposal."

"Why, thank you, Major, but please, Robert will do. You've always a home here, should you ever need it."

"Thank you, sir. And Colonel, I can't thank you enough for all you've shared with me over these days riding together. I have learned far more than I ever dared hope. I would be honored if I could serve under your command one day."

"Nonsense, Major, it is I who has been honored. I do hope we see each other again. Best of luck to you."

Turning to his horse he found young Sarah standing, holding his bridle. He immediately turned red and cast his eyes about as if not sure how to proceed. After a moment's hesitation, he moved to his horse and bowed deeply to Sarah.

"You will come visit us again, won't you, Major? I should be just devastated if you left never to return. You will promise, won't you?"

"Of course, Miss," stammered George, "I would be honored to visit again." With that, he mounted quickly and, with pack horses in tow, he was off.

Edward then gave out the day's assignments. The laborers would be divided into two groups, one group of four headed by Miles would cut and haul oaks to a spot near the spring. The other group, headed by Aaron who professed some knowledge of the task, would set to work squaring the logs for a blockhouse. Edward wanted two lengths, 16 feet and 24 feet. The blockhouse would have a 16 foot square ground floor and a 24 foot square upper floor. The cabins, to be built after the blockhouse was finished, would be 24 feet wide by 16 feet deep. The women's assignment would be to make mud for chinking the logs.

Turning to Lewis, Edward said, "So, you want an assignment. I've saved the most difficult for you. Henry, father, and I will busy ourselves cutting cedars while you oversee the boys splitting them into rails for a corral for the horses and then shingles for the roofs. I am very glad it is you that now has charge of the boys, as I have had them for day after day and am ready to hand off the responsibility," grinning widely at Lewis.

"Hey," yelled Philip. Then "Just how many shingles do we have to make until we're done?" chimed in Charles.

"Oh," said Edward, thoughtfully, "I suppose a million should do for now. We will need more later, though." That elicited the expected response from all three boys as the groups split up to their appointed tasks. Edward did approach Marie and ask her to take a few moments to mark out an appropriate corral for the horses, something Lewis could use to gage how many rails would be needed in fencing it.

The work progressed quickly with so many hands working on it. Robert twice reproached Miles for his treatment of the laborers before Miles understood the way this family worked with hired labor. Though all were slaves, they belonged to someone else and to the Jewett family they were hired laborers. Robert insisted they be treated as such. Once ahead of the boys in providing cedars for them to work, Robert, Henry, and Edward were able to clean out and line the spring with stones so it created a pool that would be inside the blockhouse. This ensured, in case of an attack, they would have water inside.

The laborers squaring the logs were very good and made very precise dovetail joints so little chinking between logs was needed. The blockhouse took shape and was finished in ten days. Then work began on the cabins. Robert and Edward laid out a street with three houses on one side facing three on the other. While the original plan called for Miles and Mattie to share a cabin with Aaron and Betty, work on the cabins progressed so quickly they had decided to build two smaller, 16 by 16 foot cabins, one on each side of Edward's cabin on one side of the street facing a cabin for Robert flanked by cabins for Henry, and

Lewis, thus bringing the total from five to six cabins.

Robert and Edward noted the improvement in Mary's disposition since work began on their familial community. Having even just the privacy afforded by their separate tent apparently satisfied her for now. And it was not like she was doing any more, or less, than anyone else. Seeing how all were sharing equally in the work also helped. The hard work they were all doing also meant little time for much of anything else and little energy when there was time.

Edward and Henry moved between cutting cedars for the boys to work on to building stone fireplaces and chimneys. Then, as the boys caught back up, the men would move back to cutting cedars. Lewis, who was still having problems with his leg, spent his days with a knife finishing the shingles the boys had riven. There did come a day when, as Edward brought up another large cedar for them to work, the boys complained.

"Uncle Edward, I think we've cut all the shingles you asked us to cut," said Philip, obviously the spokesman and with more than a little complaining apparent in his tone.

"Well, I thought we said a million would be the number needed and you've only cut five thousand three hundred and," making some show of counting the ones they had stacked near Lewis, "twelve. That still leaves nine hundred ninety four thousand six hundred and eighty eight yet to do. At the rate you boys rive shingles you'll be old men before you're done!" The boys looked at each other in amazement before moving off to continue their work where they could converse without their uncle overhearing them.

"Edward, I had no idea you were keeping such a close count on how many shingles the boys had turned out!" said a very surprised Lewis.

"Actually, I have no idea how many they've made and neither do they. But you can see my very specific answer has had the desired affect. Now, how is that leg of yours doing? Not that you're likely to tell father or me when it's healed, fearing we'll assign you much more difficult tasks than the one you 'carved' out for yourself."

"Very funny, very funny! I'm hobbling around pretty good, though I can't walk too far. At night, though, it aches, interfering with my sleep. That's why I always seem so tired."

"Try riding some and let me know how that goes. I'm thinking, with your limited ability to do heavy work, we should send you and one of the boys to take our laborers back to Mister MacDonald when the time comes. Think about it and let me know."

"It might be a good time for Philip and me to work together on the trail, relying only on each other. I like the idea."

"Good, then assuming you're able to ride without hurting that leg, that's what we'll do."

The cabins, being one story, went up fairly quickly, all six being up in six weeks. This now put them at the end of the two months they had hired the laborers for and it would still take another week to walk them back to the river landing. Lewis' leg was well enough now that he was able to lead them back and, no surprise to anyone, he chose Philip to assist him, though he did put on quite a show in the selection. The night before their departure, after the communal dinner under the awning, the laborers approached Robert and Edward with one called Sam acting as spokesman.

"Master Robert, Master Colonel, we've been talking and you're going to need a lot of help turning this land into farms. We're all strong workers and were wondering, well, if we might be able to stay on with you here. Not go back tomorrow."

Robert looked at Edward before he spoke, "You've helped us a great deal and we're very pleased with how you've fit into our family. However, we hired you from your master for a set amount of time and that time has come and gone. We can't just keep you, much as we'd like to, for that would be the same as stealing."

"Now, having said that," inserted Edward, "I understand you all belong to the same man, correct?" They all nodded. "Good. I wrote a letter last night that Lewis will give to your master telling him how pleased we were with your work and how we want to hire all of you, no one other than you eight, next summer, directly from him and not through Mister MacDonald."

This brought a large grin from each of them. Robert then continued, "And, if any of you gain your freedom, come here and you'll find a job waiting for you where you'll work for wages." This had a very dramatic, positive effect on these eight simple men who, after thanking Robert and Edward profusely, moved off by themselves and were soon heard softly singing.

Robert turned to Edward and asked, "So, do you still intend to do what we discussed last night?"

"More determined than ever that it is the right thing to do."

"Good, I agree."

The next morning, after breakfast, Lewis, Philip, and the eight laborers prepared to depart. Standing outside the awning, each of the laborers thanked the women one at a time, doffing their straw hats and then shaking hands with the boys and men. Edward stood last and, as each laborer shook his hand, they found a shilling pressed into their palm, more hard money than any of them had ever held before. This had an even more dramatic effect than the night before. Robert, who had been leading the group in regular prayer from the outset, then offered up a prayer for their safe journey before the group set out.

There was still a lot of work to be done on the cabins so the family and their servants set to the task of finishing fireplaces and chimneys for each and moving their supplies from the marquee into the blockhouse which would serve as their main warehouse. Edward had stipulated that each cabin would keep one gun, pouch, and powder horn, the rest kept inside the blockhouse. Behind the door, which faced down their street, would be the boys' guns, pouches, and horns while the rest, including those taken from the river pirates, were safely stored on the second floor along with their supply of powder and lead. In this way, Edward explained, there were enough weapons to provide cover as everyone moves to the blockhouse and none at risk of falling into the hands of "unfriendlies."

Once the cabins were ready, requiring less than a week to finish, the process of moving from the tents began. The first cabin ready was Henry and Mary's, by agreement between Robert and Edward. Edward's was the last one completed so, by time it was done, his was the only tent left in their old campsite. They then moved the awning up from the old campsite to sit at the opposite end of the street from the blockhouse. The weather still being warm with only occasional rain, the family continued to gather under it for their meals.

Shortly after Lewis departed those that stayed behind started receiving visits from neighbors from the valley on the other side of the ridge forming the grant's northwestern boundary. At first it was just the men who came by, mostly on foot, a couple mounted, to introduce themselves and inquire about the purpose of the block-house. It seems this was the only blockhouse in the area. On learning this, Robert invited them to bring their families here in case of trouble. The cabins were built stout and all of their openings, doors and windows, faced into the street with only shooting loops high up on the back walls making them useful for defense as well. In total, there were some ten families in reasonably close proximity to them. Once the offer of mutual defense had been made and the men saw the six women in the Jewett extended household, they started bringing their families for short visits to get acquainted. All were hearty Scots and Scots-Irish stock who had moved down from Pennsylvania.

Soon it was learned the Jewett's were also dissenters and that Robert had been ordained an Elder. With that, these women pressed him to conduct Sunday Sabbath services. Travel and work being what they were, Robert finally agreed to conduct one service a month under the awning for which he would accept no payment and collect no offering. Robert afterwards suspected it was Esther who had told of his stature back in the Rowley church but never brought it up in her presence.

❧ *Chapter 20* ❧

*L*ewis was walking much better now and he tried to walk as much as he could, mounting only when his leg would bother him especially bad. He also had Philip walking except when crossing the fords or when Lewis would send him ahead to scout the trail. He felt a little self-conscious riding while the laborers were walking. In addition to the two riding horses, they had taken two draft horses to serve as pack horses with their rations, as Edward always called them.

Without the carts they found they made very good time, reaching the summit and beyond their last campsite on the east side of the Blue Ridge the first day. After a good supper they settled into their blankets for the night. After moonrise, there came a horrible cry that bothered the horses terribly and caused the laborers to huddle together in fright.

"What was that, father?"

"I have no idea, Philip. It woke me from a deep sleep and I didn't get a fix on the direction it came from. Could you tell?"

"I was sleeping, too."

"Well, we need to see to the horses and somehow calm them down…" Lewis was interrupted by another, louder cry that seemed closer than before. This really alarmed the horses. Lewis and Philip did their best to calm them but they remained very nervous and on the alert.

"Catamount," said several of the laborers. When questioned they told of a large, fearless cat that haunted these mountains. It feared not man nor beast and it terrified these otherwise strong men.

"Father, I wish Uncle Edward was here. He'd know just what to do."

"You're not alone in that wish, Philip. I wish Uncle Edward was here, also." And then, more to himself than Philip, "I really do."

Building a large fire to illuminate the little glen they had camped in, Lewis and Philip checked their priming and decided they would move the horses well within the light of the fire and take turns keeping watch. It was going to be a long night.

Philip tried very hard to stay awake. It was not long, however, before his head started to droop and then he fell asleep. Lewis, too, was having trouble staying awake. He tried to busy himself stoking the fire, but the long walk and warm night, plus the even warmer fire, was taking its toll on him and he found himself nodding off. The horses rearing and neighing brought both of them fully awake.

"There it is, father, the other side of the horses. Do we shoot it?"

"Not until we have a clean shot without hitting one of us or one of our horses…"

That is when the cat leaped onto the back of Lewis' riding horse. The frightened horse reared, bucked, and spun, coming closer to the men. One of the laborers quickly grabbed a burning brand from the overlarge fire and shoved it close to the cat's face, singeing both the cat's whiskers and the horse's mane. This caused the horse to let out its own terrible cry while the cat snarled and turned its attention from horse to man.

Time for Lewis seemed to slow. He saw the cat shift as it prepared to leap from the horse to the man still brandishing the burning brand. He knew he would have the briefest of moments where he could take a close range shot. Lewis took his shot just as the cat leaped clear of the horse and before it reached the man. The cat dropped to the ground between Philip and the laborer, stunned and bleeding but clearly not dead.

"Quick, Philip, shoot!" shouted Lewis, who was already in the process of reloading. Philip hurried his shot and missed the cat completely, which, with a swipe of its paw, knocked Philip off his feet. The laborer kept the cat from pursuing his attack on Philip by again shoving the brand into the cat's face until Lewis finished loading and finally shot the cat a second and final time. Everyone was quite shook up over the affair, not realizing how much until it was over. Lewis, Philip, and the laborer were all out of breath and sweating profusely.

Recovering somewhat, Lewis thanked the laborer, who went by Sam, for all his quick action that likely saved the horse and at least one life, Philip's. While Lewis and Philip were reloading, remembering Edward's lesson on never leaving your gun empty, Sam and two of the others checked the horses. They were all fine except Lewis' horse which was bleeding from where the cat clawed it. Assuring themselves the wounds were not serious, Lewis suggested they all get some sleep. Turning to Philip who seemed troubled by something, "You, too, Philip."

"I don't understand how I missed. I was so close. How did I miss him when I was so close?"

"That's a question best answered by your Uncle Edward, not me. Tell you what, though, I won't tell Uncle Edward you missed your shot if you don't tell him it took me two shots to stop a cat. Agreed?" Philip just nodded as the two settled into their blankets, staying very close to each other. With a nudge and a grin, Lewis continued, "I'm starting to think you're accident prone."

"Ah, father!" Philip muttered as he drifted off to sleep.

It was well after sunrise when the camp roused itself the next morning. After the excitement, they all needed the extra rest and Lewis was not worried about the lost time. They ate, packed up, and started down the trail. Philip had given up his horse to his father because Lewis' leg was bothering him and they did not want to saddle the injured horse. All the horses remained a little nervous, improving as they settled back into the trail routine.

The next night, after going into camp and eating their supper, Sam came up to Lewis and presented him with the dressed skin of the catamount.

"I didn't see you skin out the cat. When did you do it?"

"Right after you fell asleep last night. I was still wide awake when everyone else fell asleep and needed to do something. It didn't take me long and I got to sleep not that long after you did."

"Well, I may have shot it, but if it wasn't for your quick thinking, I never would have had the opportunity. You were the hero of the evening and I think you should keep the hide as testimony to your courage and faithfulness." This brought a large grin to Sam's face and Lewis knew he had settled the question the right way. Sam stepped back among the other laborers who were all grinning and slapping him on the back, indicating they also concurred with Lewis' decision.

The rest of their walk was tame by comparison. They started getting some afternoon rain but continued to make good time. In just four days, they had covered the distance to the landing. Their first stop was the plantation where their hired laborers lived. Lewis and Philip parted with them here after Lewis delivered Edward's letter to their owner. He also took the opportunity to add his own thoughts on the merits of these men who had helped him and his family so much. While Philip waited outside with the laborers, Lewis pressed their master on these men's behalf.

"Do you think we'll see them again, father?"

"I certainly hope so. They were good workers and we could sure use their help next year as we work on creating farms. That's what your Uncle Edward wrote their owner about in that letter and that is what I was discussing with him. I think we have a deal arranged where we will lease them again next year. I sense their owner may have some debts and I helped him see the profit in leasing out his men, directly and not through another. We'll know in the spring if your uncle's letter and my talk had the desired effect."

Proceeding on to the landing they found Mister MacDonald, concluded their contract for the laborers and the carts, oxen, and drovers. Lewis was vague when Mister MacDonald questioned him on whether his family would want to hire more labor again next year. From his discussions with Edward, he knew Mister MacDonald had made more than a reasonable profit from them on this contract and while they had paid this time, it was not something they wanted to make a habit of doing. Mister MacDonald also held a letter for Robert from Mister Prentiss that had come up river. They collected it, wrapping it tightly

in a leather wallet, before starting back toward the Blue
Ridge.

   With both now riding they thought they should
be able to make good time in spite of the occasional rain.
The rain continued to increase, turning to bands of storms
passing through with some regularity. This made the trail
rather difficult, more difficult the higher up they traveled,
and freshened all the streams they had to cross. Their second day out, as they worked their way up the east slope
of the Blue Ridge, they found the trail especially difficult
in a storm with lightening and high winds, to the point
they needed to call an early halt and seek shelter in a rock
house they saw a short distance off the trail.

   The overhanging rock provided a small shelter,
large enough for the two travelers, their gear and packs,
and a small fire. It was damp, but by no means wet like
everything beyond its gaping mouth. They picketed the
horses as close to the entrance as possible, still remembering their experience not that far from here on their way
to the landing, and settled in for dinner and an early night.
The wisdom of this move, and the fortuitous placement
of this rock house, was brought home shortly when the
storm's fury intensified. Lightening flashed in rapid succession, the wind whipped the rain across the opening,
and the thunder was deafening.

   Lewis enjoyed the opportunity to sit and talk with
Philip. They reviewed all that had happened to their family in the past several months and he was able to gain a
perspective on how the boys viewed the events. Once he
started talking, Philip continued on for hours with little
encouragement. Only when they spoke of Aunt Bess did
they mutually lapse into a moment of silent reflection,
each shedding a tear they kept hidden from the other.

   As Philip talked on, Lewis could not help but be

struck by how much his son had grown up in just five months' time. All of the boys had. And yet it would not surprise anyone that Lewis was especially proud of Philip and the changes he saw in him. In spite of the hard work and toils of the trail and frontier life, the boys still saw this as much of a grand adventure as when he and their grandfather first announced Edward's offer and their decision to accept it. Only now listening to his son, he realized the boys had gained a healthy respect for nature and a more mature attitude. He reflected on how he, too, had changed.

The next morning dawned clear. To say it was dry would be a misnomer for while the rains had moved on the ground was saturated and there was running water at every turn. The trail was very difficult to negotiate being deep with slippery mud and cut quite deeply by the runoff. Lewis decided to lead and keep both of the pack horses, allowing Philip to concentrate on keeping up and the footing of his horse alone. Both were eventually forced to dismount and walk their horses, it just not being safe to do otherwise in this steep country.

Here is where, harkening back to their conversation of last night, Lewis reflected on how his life to this point had so ill prepared him for frontier living. His skills were improving but, like his leg, there were limits. Trudging through the slippery mud brought home just how weakened his legs had become with all the sitting his injury had forced on him these past weeks. Breaks were frequent as he found himself out of breath and his leg aching. Because of the switchbacks in the trail, they found themselves crossing the same streams twice or more.

After crossing one such bold stream the second time, a bit more difficult here where they were higher and the ground a bit steeper, Lewis stopped for a breather and turned to watch as Philip negotiated the fast moving water. He was picking his way gently through when his horse shied, causing a tug on the lead rope Philip was holding. Nothing out of the ordinary here, it happened frequently on this trail and both were used to it. This time, however, it came at an especially inopportune time, when Philip only had one foot firmly planted as he sought firm footing with the other.

To Lewis' horror, he watched as Philip lost his footing and went with the water off the edge of the trail and down out of sight in the underbrush below.

❦ *Chapter 21* ❦

After supper, Robert approached Marie and asked if he and Edward might have a word with her, in private. She could hardly refuse so they retired to Edward's cabin. Marie was more than a little concerned about the nature of this conversation and it showed as they made the short walk from the awning to the cabin.

Once inside, Robert started the conversation, "Marie, you're doing a marvelous job caring for the horses and seeing to their needs."

"I sense you did not bring me here just to tell me that, Robert," she replied. "Why don't you just say what is really on your mind?"

Robert looked a little nervous and he glanced at Edward before continuing, "If Lewis were here this is something that we would have taken up with him, but as he is not due back soon and the issue is not going away, I felt it necessary to bring it up directly to you. It's about your daily rides, Marie. I fear with everyone else engaged in cutting fodder, your riding is causing some discontent. I wanted to talk to you about it before this discontent grew to something more difficult to deal with."

"This is about Mary, isn't it? She doesn't think I'm pulling my weight because I take rides. That's it, isn't it?"

"Now, Marie, you know how things are. And I'm afraid the discontent has already started to spread beyond just Mary. All I'm asking is that you reduce the time you spend riding and spend that extra time in the meadow with the rest of us as we cut and gather the winter fodder. After all, if we don't, we'll end up eating the horses once they starve to death."

"It takes two grown men to ask this of me? Well, Edward, are you also discontented with my riding?"

"Actually, Marie, I have a different subject to address with you concerning your riding. You've been riding alone, which was fine in the country around Rowley, but here it is dangerous, quite dangerous."

"So, one wants me to reduce my riding and the other not to ride at all?"

Both men responded "No" before Edward continued, "If you are riding out of sight of the blockhouse I must insist you take someone along, someone armed, even if it is only Joseph. I was speaking with Tom McCrary who arrived in the Valley mid last year. We are entering the season when both the Cherokee from the south and the Iroquois from the west venture into the Valley for their fall hunt. A woman riding alone may be too tempting for them. And despite what you might now be thinking," smiling at her, "we really don't want to lose you."

"Ah, I see," pausing thoughtfully, "this actually makes some sense to me. Alright gentlemen, I will reduce my riding, help with gathering the fodder, and will not ride alone beyond sight of the blockhouse. Is there anything else of my behavior you wish to address at this time?"

"Please, Marie," said Robert. "Don't be upset. We really do love you and only bring this up for your benefit."

"I know, father," as she laid her hand gently on Robert's arm, "and it is not you who I am mildly displeased with, or you, Edward. I will get over it and do as you ask."

The next day all got an early start with Marie seeing to the horses first, as was her custom, while the others moved into the meadow to continue cutting fodder. Miles, Aaron, Henry, and Edward wielded the scythes while the women gathered the cut grass into bundles and put them on sleds they had fashioned. Charles and Joseph guided the horse drawn sleds from meadow to the makeshift barn they had constructed to keep the fodder from the weather. Here Robert and Sarah were charged with unloading the sleds.

After just over an hour, Marie joined them in the meadow and offered a break to Mary while she took over for her. The shock was apparent and Edward had to smile at the way Marie had chosen to very dramatically, yet subtly, make her appearance. He knew it had so disarmed her critics that the issue would not likely come up again.

After working in the meadow for several hours, Marie went with Betty to help prepare dinner. Only after dinner did she take her ride, and then not without asking Robert if it would be alright. With a nod to Edward, she took her gun, horn, and pouch with her while announcing her intention to just ride in the general area of their village.

This became the routine over the next few days until they had finished cutting the meadow. Marie looked at the supply of fodder drying in their barn and announced, if the winter were not too harsh, she thought they had enough to last them. She would, however, like to gather acorns when they dropped this fall to supplement the fodder and what oats remained of what they brought with them.

With the last of the major communal jobs finished, the village sank into their individual routines. Each of the men worked for an hour or so each day splitting firewood for the winter. Edward took the boys out for some bird hunting in advance of the regular deer season, and all started wondering about Lewis and Philip.

One day, Marie came to Edward and asked to take Sarah to see the rock bridge and young George's initials. Edward agreed but with conditions attached. She was to take both Joseph and Charles with her and all would carry their arms. He also wanted them to keep a close watch about them for any signs of Indian hunting parties. Agreeing to the conditions, she prepared to set off when Mary raised an objection.

"I don't think it wise for Charles to be riding around the countryside when there is the possibility of Indians. Edward, I don't understand how you could suggest such a thing. Two boys would by of little help should they meet up with the savages." Charles, who had been enthusiastic about going, tried to interject something but was quickly hushed into silence.

"You know, Mary, you make a good point. Why, just having the boys along isn't the best course. I could use a little ride myself, so I'll take the boys, Sarah, and Marie with me. Joseph, saddle my horse and, Charles, here, take my musket back to the blockhouse and bring my rifle, horn, and pouch. Father, you and Henry keep a sharp eye out here for any trouble and get everyone into the blockhouse if you even suspect it."

The family crisis was thus averted. Betty supplied the little band with a packed dinner to eat and they set off in good spirits. The day was one of those perfect early fall days, sunny, dry, and not too warm. They covered the eight miles easily enough, though Edward had the boys ever vigilant, and enjoyed their dinner in the shadow of the rock bridge. Sarah was awed by this natural rock formation and took to sketching it while the boys pulled their shoes and stockings to enjoy the cool water of the creek.

Riding back down the valley on their way home, Edward called a sudden halt and dismounted, checking the trail closely as the boys crowded in. "We've trouble now. See these prints coming in from the west, hitting our trail. Well, they first mill about, then head off down the trail toward home. I'm not good enough to tell you how many, but it looks like five or so."

"Why did they move up our back trail and not follow us?" asked Marie.

"My only guess would be, with five horses and not knowing there were two women, they may have assumed we were five men out hunting them. In any case, we must be wary of an ambush. Joseph, I want you to ride off the trail to the left, about 20 yards, as far as you can and still keep me in sight, just like when we were looking for Charles. Charles, you do the same to the left. Look sharp to your front and sides. I'll stay in the center of the trail. Stay even with me and don't fall behind. Marie, Sarah, you follow me by about 20 yards. If something should happen, cut to the left, over the ridge, and make for the McCrary cabin as fast as you can ride."

The next four miles were very tense as the little group felt their way along, each expecting to hear an Indian whoop at any moment. As they approached the last hill between them and the blockhouse, Edward signaled a halt and dismounted. They approached the top of the hill cautiously and when they had gotten to where they could see the blockhouse, they saw a lot of activity around it. The horses were being led by Henry and Miles toward the cabins and others were moving about the door to the blockhouse.

Edward drew their attention away from the scene below and pointed out how the footprints they had been following stopped where they had, then moved off to the northeast, toward the North River, keeping just below the backside of the hill. Here Edward changed the order of march, putting Marie and Sarah in front with the boys on their flanks while he would bring up the rear. When all were ready, they started riding as fast as the country would allow toward the blockhouse and shelter.

Reaching their little village without incident, they found Tom and Jenny McCrary and the four McCrary children already there.

"Edward, we're really glad to see you," said a much relieved Robert. "Tom and Jenny saw Indians this morning and headed our way. We were just thinking about going out to find you when we saw you coming over the hill."

"Leaving the blockhouse would not have been a wise plan, father, for it would have weakened your defenses too much, what with me and the boys already out. We picked up the trail of several Indians about five miles back. They followed our back trail to the top of the hill, there, and then moved off," indicating their direction with a sweep of his arm.

Robert, Edward, Henry, and Tom McCrary then set about the task of deciding their course of action. Their conclusion was all would stay in the village tonight with a strong watch kept, moving to the blockhouse before first light. They believed it likely that, should an attack be made, it would come at first light, before sunrise. The horses, theirs and the McCrary's, would be penned in the street, between the cabins. The women then went about putting supper together while the men and boys checked and loaded all of the guns and distributed them around the blockhouse at the shooting loops. All told they had 26 guns, a number that both surprised and comforted the McCrarys.

Each of the men stood their watch, with Edward taking the last watch for himself. When he judged it to be near a half an hour before first light, he quietly made a circuit of the cabins, telling everyone to move into the blockhouse. He was pleasantly surprised with the speed this was done and how little noise they all made in the process. First light then sunrise came and passed with nothing happening. The women prepared breakfast, which the men and boys ate while watching through the loops.

With the sun fully an hour up, Edward called a counsel. He would make a circuit of their meadow, looking for any signs they had been visited. The others were to keep close watch for any movement in the woods, using Edward's telescope to help them. They were to fire a warning shot if they saw Edward moving into an ambush. In spite of some objections to his plan, the main being his going alone, they agreed with the stipulation Tom would go along.

Tom and Edward moved quietly and cautiously on foot just inside the fringe of woods looking for any signs they had been visited in the night. When they returned, it was with bad news.

"They were out there, alright, quite a number of them," Tom told his anxious listeners. "It looked to be three groups. One was just opposite the creek to the west, another over the rise to the north, and the third was to the northeast, between here and the North River ford. They all appeared to move in from the west as one group before splitting up."

"Then why didn't they attack?" asked a very concerned Mary.

"It may be they didn't anticipate the strength of the blockhouse and withdrew rather than risk attack. None of the groups were very large, maybe five or six in each," responded Edward.

"So, they've gone then?" asked Sarah.

"Not necessarily so, young Miss," answered Tom. "They may have just gone for help to hit us with more tomorrow."

"Edward," interrupted Robert, "what of Lewis and Philip? We expected them yesterday. Could they have been intercepted by these Indians and..." his voice trailing off.

"No, father, these Indians came in from the west and Lewis is coming in from the east. It is unlikely they met unless Lewis was foolish enough to try to ford the river during the night, something he would never do, after they had moved to that side to hem us in. That said we don't want him riding into a trap. I'll saddle up and ride out to meet them. Three of us, well armed and expecting it, should be able to get through."

To the general cry against his plan, Edward held firm. Lewis and Philip had to be intercepted and warned. He would use speed and surprise to ride to the North River ford and afterwards he should be beyond the Indian's immediate reach. He would meet Lewis and Philip on the trail and, based on what signs they saw, would devise their course accordingly. This won him reluctant acceptance of his plan from all except Joseph.

"Uncle Edward, you can't do this alone. That is my father and brother out there. I have already lost one father. I won't sit idly by and risk losing another. I'm going with you. Don't say it, I'm going. Sorry, mother."

Edward hushed the dissent with a wave of his hand. "Well, Joseph, it's a man's job you're taking on. You'll have to ride hard and possibly fight hard to see this thing through. If you're determined, we must arm ourselves and be off within the half hour. Betty, please put together some field rations for us."

Taking just what would be needed for an extended fight and the food Betty prepared, the duo was soon ready. Miles had their horses saddled, shielded from view by the cabins. Before slipping from the blockhouse to their horses, Robert put a hand on Edward's shoulder, "Be careful, son. I can't spare any of my sons."

Marie had just given Joseph much the same message when she turned to Edward, "Thank you, for what you are doing and what you are risking to save my husband and son." With that, she reached up and gently kissed his cheek. With that they were off, last seen riding fast across the meadow toward the North River ford, a chilling Indian whoop from the hill to the southwest hurrying them on their way.

⊘ *Chapter 22* ⊘

*L*ewis could not believe his eyes. One second his son was making his way across the stream and the next he disappeared down the mountain. He quickly plunged into the underbrush, following the stream down the side of the mountain. It was hard going but nothing was going to stop him. He kept as close to the stream as he could, looking in vain for Philip. He came to the lower portion of the trail and paused, looking around in the hope Philip had regained his footing before cascading with the water further down the mountain.

Just as he was about to follow the stream further on down, something just above the trail caught his eye and stopped him. Looking carefully, he saw it was the muddy butt of a gun sticking out of the greenbriers next to the stream. Leaping the stream and slipping in the mud, he reached for the gun which seemed to have stuck in a mound of mud the tangle of greenbriers were growing out of. As he took hold of the gun, the mound of mud suddenly had two eyes looking right at him and very close to his face, causing him to recoil.

"Uncle Edward told us never to lose our gun," came

a weary, pained, familiar voice. "I hung on to it, all the way down."

"Philip? Are you alright? Don't move and I'll cut you out of the briers."

"I hurt, father, in places I didn't even know I had."

Lewis gently cut Philip out of the briers and sat him on the trail with his back against the uphill bank. He was one large mud ball, almost unrecognizable. First wiping mud from his face as best he could, Lewis then check his limbs for breaks while Philip just sat there, eyes closed, wincing occasionally.

"I can't find anything broken, but you're all cut up by the briers. We need to get the mud cleaned off before I can tell the extent of your injuries. Do you think you could stand if I helped you?"

"I'll try," was the pained response. Lewis was very gentle and slow as he helped Philip rise. Once on his feet and apparently whole, the sight of him coupled with his relief caused Lewis to laugh. Philip chuckled and then, "Stop, it hurts when I try to laugh!"

"I can't help it. You are such a sight! If you're able, there is the bold spring where we filled our canteens at not ten yards up the trail at the switchback. We'll go there and get you cleaned up."

Painfully Philip, with Lewis' help, covered the distance. Lewis helped him remove all his mud soaked clothing and washed him down with the clear spring water. Bruised and cut, he appeared to otherwise be whole and sound.

"Here, take my coat and wrap yourself in it. I'll go and bring the horses back here. We'll stay until you feel well enough to go on."

Returning with the horses, Lewis went about wrapping Philip in a blanket before making camp and starting a fire. Philip watched as his father washed the mud out of his clothing and laid them on bushes to dry. He then went about cleaning Philip's gun, not an easy task as the bore was filled with mud and water. Keeping busy with camp chores helped calm his mind after the fright he had suffered.

Checking yet again on Philip, his son began to laugh at him, "You should see your face, father. I'm not the only one cut up by briers."

Until then Lewis had not realized he, too, had been cut on hands and face as he plunged down the slope in search of his son. And by pointing it out, Lewis knew Philip was obviously feeling better. They remained in camp that night and all the next day so Lewis could assure himself Philip had suffered no serious injuries he could not detect. Though stiff and sore, Philip was able to move about the camp well enough and no fever had developed, so the following morning they started again.

By now the streams had subsided and the road was much drier. Even so, Lewis set a slow pace and called a halt for the day after dinner. They had by now cleared the summit and started their descent. Both still looked like they had been beat about the face with briers, which they essentially had been, though most of the ill effects were passing. Lewis decided a regular start the next morning would have them home around dinner time.

Reaching the cutoff where they would head to the south and the ford to their land the next morning, they were hailed by what turned out to be a large group of their neighbors.

"You two are headed into trouble and you best watch yourselves."

On questioning, they learned the man was named McNulty and they had left their cabins yesterday afternoon trying for the blockhouse. Finding the way blocked, they had retraced their steps, crossed the South River on the trail, and planned to leave their families at the cut-off. If they could reach the blockhouse from the east, they would gather their families and move that way. If not, they were intent of quitting the valley through Indian Gap.

They were six extended families, the McNulty's, Stuart's, Gordon's, Bennett's, Thompson's, and Fisher's, from farms just beyond the Jewett Grant and, with the addition of the McCrary's, represented the sum total of the Jewett's neighbors. All told there were eight men, eight older boys under arms, six women, and 16 girls and younger boys. "We tried to get to Tom McCrary's cabin, but the savages blocked our way. We have no idea what has happened to them or your family, though with the blockhouse we assume your family has fared the best."

They decided Lewis, Philip, and three of the men would scout ahead to the ford. If the way was open, they would send Philip back for the rest. If not, all would proceed through the gap to safety. Even though he had agreed, Lewis had no intention of returning to the east. He was determined that he and Philip would find a way to reach their family, somehow.

Moving watchfully down the trail, the little party was nearing the ford when they reined up sharp at the sound of pounding hooves coming from the ford. Dismounting, all guns were at the ready when, from around the bend into view came Edward and Joseph, riding hard until they saw their welcoming committee and stopped suddenly.

"Edward, Joseph, has some disaster befallen our family?" called out Lewis, the first to speak.

"They were fine when we rode out. You and Philip are the cause for our ride. We didn't want you falling in with the savages on your return. I recognize Mister Mc-Nulty with you so I assume you've fallen in with our neighbors."

After being quickly appraised of the situation, Edward was ready to act. "We can send the boys back to bring up the rest of the party. We need to return now to the ford to push the Indians following us back to the far side and give us some room to plan and act without observation."

Edward was now all quick action. Dismounting and spreading out after the boys left back up the trace, they had covered about half the distance to the ford when they saw five braves running toward them, still thinking they were in pursuit of just the two horsemen. Five shots proved them wrong and dropped three of their number, the final two retracing their steps even quicker than they had been moving forward.

"Well, that's not good," said Edward. "Those two will bring a force to watch the ford and block our path."

"Do you think we can reach the blockhouse from the ford?" asked McNulty.

"No, I don't. But I do think we can move further south to where the land flattens out and can make the blockhouse more from the southwest. That, however, will depend on how well we trick our savage friends."

"But our families, they're on their way here. Shouldn't we stop them, send them on through the gap?" asked Stuart.

"I can't tell you what's best for you and yours, but for me, I propose to set up a camp the Indians can see on the other side of the river. Then we'll move out in the dark and cross further south. If things work like I think they will, my brother, his sons, and I will be with our family before noon tomorrow, although it will mean a hostile river crossing at night."

"Colonel, have you ever done that, made a hostile river crossing at night?" asked McNulty.

"I have, more than once, each one successful."

"Then," seeing nods from Stuart and Gordon, "we're with you."

In short order, the boys arrived with the rest of the neighbors and Edward outlined his plan. It required four men to stay behind, two to keep the cook fires going until moonrise and the other two keeping watch. The rest would move south at full dark, staying back from the river for about three miles. There the ground on the west bank was low and flat. They would throw over a group of men to secure the crossing. The rest would wait to cross after moonrise. Once across, all would rest and wait for the ones tending the camp. If all went well, the Indians would be convinced the group was staying by the ford and they would be unopposed further south. Once across, they would wait for first light and then ride hard for the blockhouse.

All agreed to the plan and all that remained was selecting the four to tend to the fires. Philip and Joseph were quick to volunteer for that task.

"It's hazardous duty, young men, and I'm not sure your father will approve," responded Edward. They were firm and not to be dissuaded.

Lewis approached Edward thoughtfully, "Well, Colonel, if the boys are staying, then I am staying also. All you need now is your fourth man."

"You know I'd rather stay with you and the boys, but I'm needed to force the river crossing. Are you sure about this, Lewis?" With Lewis' nod, Stuart came up and volunteered to stay with them.

"You got a taste for how badly Gordon and McNulty shoot today" he said with a grin. "At least with me, you've someone who can shoot straight."

The group then set about making a show of going into camp. They did take advantage of building the cook fires and all enjoyed a hot meal and some tense rest before the night's activities. As arranged, once it was fully dark, all but the four volunteers slipped deep into the east woods and prepared to move south. Edward had arranged for all to ride, doubling up the children with the older boys and women while leaving the men free to move and, if necessary, fight. Before leaving, Edward loaned Joseph his belt axe to use in keeping the fires fed.

All went well. They marked their path with patches of white cloth so the volunteers could easily follow in just the moonlight. Once they reached the place Edward planned for the crossing, he and four men hurried over and checked out the far bank. Finding their way unopposed, the rest of the group crossed without incident after moonrise.

Back in the camp, the two boys followed Edward's instructions. By moving constantly and from fire to fire, they purposefully threw their shadows against the trees and gave the impression of more people moving about than just the two. The men stayed well out of the firelight, not wanting it to affect their night vision, and watched for any hostile trying to get a better look. They did see two come close to the far bank, just shadows, really, and return, evidently convinced nothing was amiss. Before moonrise, the boys stopped feeding the fires, letting them start to die down, but kept moving about. On a signal from Lewis, all four made for their horses and followed the others. The trail had been well marked and they had no trouble finding and joining the larger group now on the other side of the river.

Edward gathered all around him before first light

and gave them their marching orders. Lewis, Philip and Joseph would lead as the advance. Stuart, Gordon, McNulty, and Bennett would be flankers, two on each side. Thompson and Fisher would join him as the rear guard, with the elder Stuart and McNulty protecting the women. The unarmed women would ride at the center with the armed boys on both of their flanks, close in, and all of these last riding at least double, even on Lewis' pack horses, so all would be mounted. All agreed except Joseph.

"Uncle Edward," he started, "I began this mission with you and plan on staying with you. I'll therefore be in the rear guard with you."

"Joseph, think about that. It's the rear guard who'll be the most likely to have to fight their way in. I'd feel better, as I'm sure your father would, if you were in the advance with him." Lewis nodded but Joseph was unmoved, so Edward acquiesced, sending Fisher forward with Lewis in the advance.

Lewis set the pace as they moved forward at first light. Slow at first, then picking up the pace after sunrise and full light. That was when the first popping sounds reached them, indicating the blockhouse was, indeed, under attack. He called a halt before they broke from the woods into the now cut meadow. The sounds of gunfire were clear and they could see puffs of white smoke around the roof of the blockhouse, the only part now visible.

Looking to both flanking parties and the main body and receiving head nods to indicate their readiness, he pulled his hat tight on his head and gave the signal. Breaking from the wood line at a gallop, they were quickly among the attacking Indians, causing the Indians more than a little consternation to have this large group of armed men appear, as it were, out of nowhere. Shooting from horseback, Lewis, Philip, and Fisher cut a gap in the Indian's loose line and the flankers held this gap open for the main party to make their way through.

As predicted, the Indians recovered and began pressing in quickly on the rear guard. Joseph was a little ahead of Edward and, as he looked back, saw Edward jump from his horse, roll, and come up on one knee in a shooting position, letting his horse continue on after the others. Thompson, also, was dismounting, a little less quickly, and the two were providing covering fire for the families to make their way around the blockhouse and into the cover provided by their little street.

Joseph now dismounted and fired his gun at an on-rushing Indian. Then he saw an Indian come in from their right holding a small axe over his head to strike Edward and from too far behind Edward, who was reloading, for Edward to see him. His gun empty, Joseph did the only thing he could think to do, he pulled Edward's axe from his belt and with a mighty heave, threw it at the Indian, striking the Indian on the head, only not with the blade. Edward had turned at this point and Joseph saw he was holding his gun in his left hand and knife in his right as the Indian fell forward into him. Edward pushed free, slid his now red knife back under his belt, scooped something up from the ground, and signaled it was time for all three to make for the blockhouse now near at hand.

Running now, and with renewed and heavy fire coming from the blockhouse, the rear guard made the door and was ushered in, the door being slammed and barred behind them.

Chapter 23

Robert, Esther, and Marie watched Edward and Joseph's dash across the field and out of sight from the second story of the blockhouse. All were tense, not so much about their own situation as much as the four family members now outside the protection of the blockhouse.

"Why did Edward have to go, father?" Esther sadly asked Robert as they looked at the now empty field.

"Because he's a soldier, daughter, and he knows he can best affect our safety out there, fighting, than in here with us, immobile," was Robert's thoughtful reply. "Besides, you know he and Lewis have always been close. He can't sit here with us while Lewis is in danger."

Esther understood. She just did not like the answer. She was frightened for her brothers more than for herself. It was not having them here, knowing they were on their own and in danger that bothered her most.

Now they had work to do. The horses were crowded into the street and needed to be cared for and better secured from wandering off. Miles and Marie would take care of seeing to these tasks while Tom McCrary, Henry, and Aaron went along as guards. Robert would remain in charge in the blockhouse. He placed everyone else at the shooting loops on the second floor, each armed, to watch for movement in all four directions. The four McCrary children huddled together in the middle of the floor, crying softly.

As Marie fed the horses, checked their hobbles, and put water out for them, Miles fashioned temporary fences between the houses to keep the horses from leaving the street. Coming to the end opposite the blockhouse, he asked Henry to help him take down the awning. Marie took Henry's gun and stood his watch while the two men worked. They then used the poles and ropes to fashion a fence across this wider opening. Their work done, the five then returned to the blockhouse to wait.

While the work was in progress, Robert was kept busy inside. They were seeing Indians moving around beyond their meadow and every time an Indian showed himself, Robert moved to whoever spotted them and used Edward's telescope to try and ascertain the Indian's intentions. What he determined by all of their observations was they were being closely watched and it was being done on all sides of them. They were not seeing many Indians, just one or two at a time. Robert thought this might mean they were not as numerous as feared. Perhaps they had not intended on taking the strong blockhouse, may not have known it existed, but rather were here to hunt and annoy any whites they came across.

Robert was not an Indian fighter and had not grown up on the frontier. That did not mean he lacked all experience. He found his thoughts going back to when Edward and Lewis were very young boys and before Henry was born, the winter of 1704, when he was called out with the rest of the Massachusetts militia first to protect the frontier and then to respond to the attack on Deerfield. There were 200 Indians with nearly 50 French involved in what was a true war party. He had seen plenty of Indians that winter, fought them on more than one occasion, but it was not something he bragged about. Rather, he had rarely mentioned it these past 46, near 47, years and had never told the boys about those experiences. Those who knew him now would never have guessed he had once fought Indians on what was then the frontier.

Once Henry, Marie, Aaron, Miles, and Tom returned to the blockhouse, their task completed, they sat to discussing their situation. Miles was sure he had heard a short burst of gunfire from the direction of the ford. It was too far away to know more other than it was more than two guns firing. Then he asked whether some should move to the houses to provide better protection for the horses. The houses were as stoutly built as the blockhouse, though they lacked the benefit of a spring, and had shooting loops high on their outer walls.

"What you say makes some sense," Robert said to Miles, "and it is something we should do if there were more of us. With just five men and a boy, plus the women who can shoot or load, we have barely what we need to defend the blockhouse. For that reason I say we abandon the cabins, and the horses if need be, to their fates. We must all stay here and, through long range shots, try to keep the Indians from reaching the cabins."

His reasoning was sound and no one moved to argue with him. It is probably best for he could point back to Deerfield where the inhabitants had mostly been murdered in their cabins, thinking themselves safe. The harsh winter weather and the militia guard they had posted lulled them into this fatal lethargy. No, he would keep them all here where he could ensure their watchfulness and readiness.

Robert arranged them into three watches, four

always being on watch, each facing a different direction, from the second floor. The others could eat and rest as best they could. He kept himself out of any of the watches, always remaining on the second floor where he was readily available if something needed his attention. Food would be prepared and eaten on the first floor and only those not on duty were to eat. Robert did not want his lookouts distracted by trying to eat, the risk of them thus missing something was too great.

Late in the afternoon, after they had all eaten their dinner, Henry spotted more movement than they had grown accustomed to along the wooded creek to the west of the blockhouse. Robert agreed that their besiegers were up to something and called everyone to arms. No sooner had they all taken their places than a group of half a dozen Indians burst from the creek and ran forward as if to make the end of the street opposite the blockhouse.

"Cut them down or it'll be close fighting this night," called Robert as he carefully aimed and fired the first shot, tumbling the lead warrior. Turning, he found Sarah at his side, reaching for his now empty rifle while handing him a loaded one.

More shots rang out, dropping three more Indians and forcing the last two into retreat. "There," said Tom McCrary, "that'll keep them away for a little while."

"Yes, but they'll try again in the dark when we aren't as effective detecting or hitting them," added Robert. "Come morning we can expect them to be among us on that side while we should be able to hold them off some distance on the other three."

"Well, we could still put some of us in the cabins," said Miles, still trying to sway them toward his idea.

"I'm afraid anyone we place in the cabins won't live to see morning. If there were more of us, it would be different. I've said it once, we must stay in the blockhouse. It is all we can effectively defend. If we spread ourselves too thin, they'll pick us off as effectively as we picked them off just now." Robert was not about to give in and they all realized it though none knew the real reasons why.

Tom then added his thoughts. "What if we built a bonfire at the other end of the street, where the awning stood? We could then at least see them approach and, with the light, might even get a shot or two off at them. We'd only need the fire up to moonrise, so we should be able to build it once and leave it."

There were several who nodded in agreement with this suggestion. Robert stayed thoughtful for a few moments before adding his thoughts. "Is it wise to give the Indians such easy access to fire when we are dependent on wood dwellings for our defense?"

All saw the wisdom in what Robert said and they agreed that if the Indians made the cabins they would just have to deal with it after moonrise or in the morning, whenever the Indians decided to try to exploit this advantage. So they settled back into their watch routine. After sunset they became especially watchful, looking for any signs of movement in their direction but spying none. Once the moon rose, they felt better at their ability to detect movement.

During Marie's watch, she kept a close eye on the horses. She knew they would signal anyone trying to move up the street by becoming agitated, if not neighing and kicking. All remained quiet, though.

When Robert determined it was about an hour before sunrise, he woke everyone and, after all had a chance for a quick meal, in shifts, he had them all at the loops at first light. This was good for they had barely gotten ready when a whoop sent three groups running toward the blockhouse from three directions, only the cabin side remaining clear.

Shooting began immediately. Robert resisted the urge to move those facing the cabins to the other three sides, suspecting the rush was a diversion. As the rush started to waiver, then recede, he was sure he was right. Henry's shout as he shot down the street proved it. Several Indians had evidently secreted themselves against the far wall of Henry's cabin, the furthest on the left side of the street, and now were trying to sneak through the horses to the blockhouse door. Henry had dropped the last one to come into view.

With the horses now milling about the street, neighing and kicking, the Indians found they could not make progress even though the defenders were holding their fire for fear of hitting the horses instead of the Indians. As the horses worked themselves into a frenzy, the Indians began to pull back down the street, seeking shelter from these kicking beasts. Two were being dragged after receiving especially hard kicks that evidently incapacitated them. Marie smiled to herself. Her faith in the horses had been rewarded.

There was now a lull in the action and Robert made the rounds, checking on everyone. Esther moved with him, carrying water so all could quench their thirst. The Indians seemed to be armed mostly with bow and arrow and a few trade guns, making the wounds of the defenders very slight indeed. Satisfied they had bested their attackers, for now, Robert reinstated the watch system used throughout the night. In this way, he hoped they would be better rested when the struggle continued. The real question was when the next attack would come.

It was nearing noon when it finally came. It started with the rush, as they had experience earlier, only this one seemed different, more determined. This time the rush was not meant to be a diversion, it was the main event. The Indians were running and dodging, making themselves very hard targets to hit as they came closer and closer to the blockhouse.

As the distance closed to under 50 yards, Robert shifted some of the men from the second floor to the shooting loops on the first floor. This gave them a more direct aim at their attackers and, as a result, the Indians began to take more casualties. He took a chance and reduced those watching the street to just Marie, leaving clear instructions to sing out loud if she saw any signs of an attack from that side.

Charles' alert brought Robert back upstairs to the boy's side. As soon as he got there, he saw what had excited the boy. There, coming over the rise in the meadow, was Lewis and Philip in the company of a fairly large number of other settlers. Robert shouted to all to pick up their rate of fire to provide cover to their friends trying to make the blockhouse. He then turned to Miles and sent him out to make an opening in his fence so their friends could make it into the street and blockhouse. Henry went to provide him covering fire.

Fire from the blockhouse now came fast and unrelenting with everyone shooting as fast as a loaded gun could be placed in their hands and the women loading as fast as possible. Robert alone was pausing between shots, searching the faces of those riding fast toward them for those of Edward and Joseph. Then he saw them. And just as fast, he noted the Indians recovering from the initial shock, turning their fury on the three figures following the others, Edward, Joseph, and Tommy Thompson.

Shouting now, Robert focused his shooters on providing cover for these last three. Then he saw Edward dismount, roll, and come up on one knee, shooting down an Indian in the act of shooting at Tommy Thompson. Thompson rode on only a few more steps before he, too dismounted and, to Robert's horror, then Joseph, instead of finishing the last few steps to safety, dismounted and shot as well. Now there were three empty guns outside and they were still more than 15 yards from the blockhouse.

Robert yelled for a fresh gun and Sarah was there putting it into his hand as he watched an Indian rise and move toward Edward, weapon raised. Before he could thrust the gun through the loop he saw Joseph throw something and the Indian stagger and fall into Edward. Then the three were moving again and Robert shot another Indian hot on his son's heels. Moments later, the slamming of the blockhouse door told him all of his sons were with him again. He had not time to feel relieved.

ᐁ Chapter 24 ᐁ

"Quickly, everyone who can shoot to the loops." Robert's voice was clear above the din of the now very overcrowded blockhouse, "They're making a rush and they're too close."

The addition of 20 gun-wielding men and boys caused every loop to be manned and a withering fire delivered at close range on their attackers. The result came quickly as the Indians melted away from all three sides of the blockhouse at once. They had stood the fire when there were but five men and six women providing for the defense, most of the women loading and not shooting. This, however, was completely different. There were 20 loops, not counting the five facing the street, and every one was belching flame and smoke with hardly a pause between shots. No, it was time to call a halt to what was turning into a slaughter.

As they disappeared, for it seemed they were under 20 yards from the blockhouse one second and gone the next, Robert's voice was again raised above the din calling a cease fire. Once the shooting had stopped and it was easier for all to hear, Robert again called out, "Who's wounded? Sing out."

"Thompson's got an arrow in the shoulder;" "Bennett's got a ball in his leg;" and "McNulty's been hit in the side, but it passed clear through." All the wounded were those who made the dash for the blockhouse, for once inside the stout walls proved too tough for the Indian's weapons. Only some splinters to the face when they came close to getting a shot through the loops befell the defenders. Betty and Esther took over seeing the wounded were cared for while Mattie, Marie, and Mary tried to make room for their neighbors.

Robert moved through the blockhouse gathering his sons about him. When they were all together, he gave each a heartfelt hug. This seemed to surprise Henry a little, after all, he had not been out of his father's reach like Edward and Lewis had been. He then brought Edward and Lewis up to date on what had happened and they, in turn, recounted their experiences. Then the discussion turned to their current situation.

"Father, we have way too many people jammed into this little blockhouse," said Edward, stating the obvious. "I propose to take six each men and boys under arms and six women and place them in the cabins. This will spread out not only our fire, but also the crowding in here."

"We had discussed this before and I said no. That was when we were but six men and boys under arms with seven women and four children. Now things have changed and we've the people to do it," was Robert's reply.

"Good. Lewis, Henry, I'll want you each in your cabins. Lewis will take Philip and Marie. Henry, you take Charles and Mary. Each take two guns apiece, even the women. Betty's too valuable here nursing the wounded but we can send Miles and Mattie to their cabin, maybe Joseph can go with them..."

"I stay with you, Uncle Edward, remember? This isn't over yet," came Joseph's voice. That was when the men realized the three boys were huddled close, not wanting to miss out on anything that passed between the men.

"I'll go. I'm not a boy but an old man should meet your purpose just as well," said the elder Stuart. "And I'll volunteer my son, grandson, and daughter-in-law to fill another of the cabins. That's four done."

"I'm not as old as Stuart," inserted the elder Mc-Nulty, "so if you could spare one of your women so my daughter-in-law can stay by my son, my grandson and I will take the fifth cabin." Esther said she would go, so Edward assigned them to Robert, Esther, and Sarah's cabin.

The Gordons, father, son, and wife, filled the sixth requirement. After all had gathered their guns, powder, shot, food, and water, they prepared to move to their assigned cabins. Edward led the way, taking first the cabins on the one side, then those on the other, Joseph constantly at his heels. Henry's was the last of the cabins.

Edward opened the door, perhaps a little less alert than he had been, having found all well in the other five cabins, when he felt a knife graze his ribs and strong hands pull at him. Then there were two gunshots very close by, close enough for him to feel the sparks on his face as he was drawn roughly into the room and the door forced closed behind him.

A quick glance around the dark cabin showed there were five Indians inside. Two had crumpled into a common pile just to the side of the door, another still had a firm grip on Edward, and the final two, after barring the door, were turning to help their now overmatched compatriot with Edward. As they struggled over Edward's gun, Edward managed to align the muzzle with one of the Indians by the door and trip the trigger, evening the odds considerably. Now both Indians were on him and it was all he could do to keep hold of their knife hands, one in each of his, precluding any chance for him to gain his own knife. Pushing and shoving, all three tried to gain an advantage. Knocked to the floor at one point, Edward just managed to avoid a knife thrust to his body by rolling over the other attacker.

Just as the struggle looked to be going against Edward, there was a loud crash of splintering wood and light filled the cabin from the now open doorway. Miles and Henry burst through the broken door and each grabbed for one of the Indians, pulling them off Edward. Now free, Edward quickly dispatched the first Indian with his knife. Turning to the second, he saw him slump from Miles' grip.

"I'm afraid he accidentally broke his neck, Edward," said Miles with a grin. "I heard the shots and thought you could use a bit of help. Besides, you hold my indenture and I really would hate to have it passed to one of the boys. I couldn't abide having a minor as my master."

"I thank you for your help. And for Henry and Joseph, whose fast shooting helped even the odds up so I could hold on while you worked on the door." Looking at Joseph, he saw an odd look on the boy's face, more in his eyes, really, a look of mingled anger, resignation, and determination untainted by fear. Edward had seen it before in men's eyes when, in battle, they went from being a green troop to being a veteran troop. This boy had just grown up very fast.

Henry, Miles and Edward went about the task of relieving the Indians of their weapons and hauling the bodies out of the cabin. They tossed them over the fence Miles had crafted at the end of the street to await burial after the crisis had passed. Improvised repair of the door complete, Henry, with a shaken Charles and Mary, then took up their positions in their cabin, Miles crossed the street to his, and Edward and Joseph turned toward the blockhouse.

"We need to get you patched up, Uncle Edward. You're bleeding pretty badly from your side and arm."

"So I am," responded Edward, noticing for the first time where the sharp knives had cut his clothes and flesh. He reflected on how odd it was that a sharp knife cuts the flesh and only later does one truly feel the cut. "And Joseph, I'm really lucky to have had you with me today. Twice you've saved my life." Joseph thought a second, nodded and then continued on. No, thought Edward, he is not a boy any longer.

Then, with a grin, Edward added, "Of course, if I knew you were going to throw my belt axe, I'd have taught you how to do it without breaking the handle," pulling the blade with its now much shorter handle from his belt. All Joseph could do was look in amazement. So that is what he saw Edward stop and scoop up from the ground.

Robert had everything in readiness in the blockhouse, expecting another try before dark, and he was not disappointed. Edward was still being sewn up by Betty when the attack came, if you could call it an attack. The withering fire from the blockhouse, which the Indians expected, coupled with the unexpected fire belching from the cabins, squashed the attack almost before it got started. The Indians quickly faded back into the woods or over the rise in the meadow from whence they had come.

When it was full dark, Robert implemented his watch system once again and things settled down into a routine. He took this opportunity to seek out Edward and ask his opinion of what would come next.

"I'm not an Indian fighter, father, but if this were the French, I'd say the fight had gone out of them after their aborted attempt this evening."

"Well, I have had some Indian fighting experience… don't look so surprised, you don't know everything about your father. They lose their ardor for the fight once casualties mount with nothing to show for it. Not having any scalps to show their martial prowess, nor an easy way now to obtain them, my guess is they're done."

"We'll still need to stay forted up for a day or two, until we can do a reconnaissance to ensure they have, in fact, quit the Valley."

"A day or two and we'll be up to our eyeballs in horse manure. What's to be done with all of them? They fill the street to the point they can barely move. It was all we could do to get those you brought in unsaddled and unpacked."

"In daylight tomorrow, when we can keep a sharp eye, we should be able to picket them around the cabins. We really do need to rethink our setup here. It doesn't work badly for us, but when you add in the neighbors, it is quite difficult."

"What if we add pickets to the roofline between all the cabins, along their outside walls," suggested Robert. "That way we gain the space between the cabins to picket the horses. We'll need to add a gate as well, best done on this end under the loops of the blockhouse."

"We'll also need quarters for our laborers. When they return next year, we can close the end of the street with a cabin for them."

The two sat thinking over their plans to turn their village into a frontier fort. Edward broke the silence, "You were very good today, father, very good." Then both fell back into silence.

Sarah came over, took her grandfather's hand, and sat down close to Edward, causing him to wince from his wound as she put pressure against it. She moved when she saw his pain but he pulled her back and she sat for some time with her head against his shoulder while still holding Robert's hand. Yes, it had been a hard day on everyone.

Robert had everyone up and to their positions before first light the next morning, just in case the Indians decided to renew the struggle. As they had surmised the night before, no attack came. By mid morning, Robert and Edward decided they needed to send out a patrol to check on things. Henry volunteered to go, as did both Stuart men and Tom McCrary.

Not venturing far, their circuit of the area immediately around the blockhouse yielded no fresh sign of the Indians. Even the bodies dumped next to Henry's cabin had been stealthily removed during the night. With this intelligence they decided to move the horses out of the street and a little distance from the blockhouse where they were guarded by two mounted men, Henry and Tom taking the first watch.

They returned everyone and all the horses to their little fort well before sunset and were prepared in case the Indians wanted to try them again. It turned out to be an unnecessary precaution but their recent experience had reinforced that caution often meant the difference between life and death.

Edward mounted a patrol the following day with four of the neighbors, Tom, Jim Stuart, Ben Gordon, and Able Fisher. They took a wide loop beyond the Jewett Grant and to the farmsteads of their neighbors, all without seeing a single Indian. That did not mean there was not sign of where the Indians had been.

When the patrol returned around dinner time, all

gathered to hear the results. The McNulty farm had been burned while the others were only ransacked. There were a few swine found roaming in the woods but the rest of their stock had been butchered. All the gardens had been vandalized though they thought enough remained to see them through a meager winter, provided they could harvest enough meat to last them. All in all they painted a bleak but not desperate situation.

Robert immediately offered the blockhouse to the McNulty family until they could get a new cabin erected on their land. All of the neighbors volunteered to help erect it. When the appointed day came, they all arrived early and started on the task immediately. The logs had been cut in the days before, so all was in readiness. The women busied themselves roasting two deer the McNultys provided for their communal dinner. The evening ended with music as the elder McNulty and the elder Stuart brought out their violins and played a few tunes before all headed back to their homes.

On the way back to their village, Esther rode next to Edward. After a while she looked over with a smile and said, "You know all the women were lamenting the fact that such a fine man as yourself, not to mention rich, is still a widower."

"Esther, would you just quit!" came the response, accompanied by a wide grin as brother and sister enjoyed their moment together.

∾ *Chapter 25* ∾

fter Esther cleared the supper dishes, Robert sent Sarah to find her Uncle Edward. He then took out the letter from Mister Prentiss and looked it over again. This is how Edward found him. "Ah, Edward, come, sit, we have some things to discuss in private."

"Yes, father, I thought you'd want to discuss the news from Williamsburg and possibly London, but shouldn't Lewis and Henry be here as well?"

"Yes, yes, but not before we've had a chance to discuss things. Frankly, after my debts to Mister Hewitt were satisfied, I've fared quite well. Lewis is very comfortable as well and your resources are, well, just let me say you have done far better for yourself than I had realized. Well done, son. And Mister Prentiss says the Colony's Treasurer is holding your retirement pay in coin for you whenever you want it, so you are wealthier than even Mister Prentiss indicates. The issue we need to discuss is your brother, Henry. I took their provisions for the trip out of my warehouse at my own expense as he had no real estate to sell, nothing, really. And his account reflects just that."

"I knew he wasn't faring well. I just didn't know it

was as bad as all that."

"Well, it isn't, really. Because of the gift of land you've made him a not unsubstantial landowner. As such, Mister Prentiss is willing to carry him on credit against his future earnings. As an alternative, I thought I could split my account with him. In that way he is not dependent on credit. I feel the need for your approval. As the eldest son, you stand to inherit all my property, so it is really coming out of your inheritance."

"Father, you know I care not for your money and estates. Any funds I would inherit I intend to give to Esther for her maintenance anyway and she will have life tenancy to your estate. So give Henry what he needs. I would only ask two things: that you keep enough for you to live very comfortably as the gentleman you deserve to be and that you oversee any expenditures against the portion you intend for Henry. Please preserve as much of his estate as possible for Charles."

"Thank you. That takes a heavy load off my mind. I wasn't even sure how to bring it up to you. And then I asked myself what Aunt Bess would have advised me, I often sought her help in such matters. She would have told me to just put it to you plainly, so that is what I've done. I always found Aunt Bess to be uncommonly wise about how to deal with people."

Both men fell silent as they remembered this very special person. Their business done, they shared some of the news Mister Prentiss included in his letter. It seems young Major Washington had used his payment for surveying the Jewett Grant to purchase over 1400 acres in the lower Valley and he had taken full possession of his late brother's estates. Before saying their goodnights, they decided that they would discuss tonight's events with Lewis and Henry in the morning.

Edward stepped from his father's warm cabin into the pleasantly cool night air. He had taken but a step or two when Esther was at his elbow. "Thank you, Edward, for what you said in there."

"Why, sister, I'm sure I haven't a clue what you are talking about."

"Oh, no, of course not," and then in a serious, low voice, "Really, Edward, thank you. This is for Charles, also, even though he'll never know what you've done for him tonight. Thank you." No more words were spoken as they shared a few minutes in silence. She leaned up and kissed his cheek and he gave her an affectionate hug before they parted.

Work began on the pickets between the cabins in earnest. At Edward's suggestion, they concentrated on the four, two on each side of the street, and reserved the gates between Lewis' and Aaron's cabins and the blockhouse and the end of the street for when the laborers arrived. In the meantime, they built portable sections like Edward had seen used on the battlefields of Europe to fill these areas which, when tied together, both kept the horses in and made it difficult for hostiles to pass through.

They also shared the job of scouting the area for further hostiles with their neighbors. Two men made the circuit each day looking for fresh Indian sign. Weeks passed with nothing to report. Then Tom McCrary and Able Fisher rode up to let them know fresh sign had been spotted coming in from the south, the Cherokee lands. The patrols were increased to two per day and everyone stayed on the alert, ready to head for the blockhouse at a moment's notice.

The next day Marie came racing back from her ride shouting an alarm. She had spotted Indians heading in their direction. The family quickly assembled in the block-house and made ready to repulse an attack. What they saw coming over the rise was somehow different than before, four Indians walking toward them. They stopped about 50 yards from the blockhouse and sat down on the grass. After a quick consultation with Robert, Edward decided to go out to find out their intentions. As he went to leave the blockhouse, he found Joseph right on his heels.

"Not this time, Joseph. If this is a trap you'll be needed here." Joseph at first looked as if he would protest, but the firmness in Edward's voice caused him to rethink things and reluctantly return to his assigned loop.

From the blockhouse, they watched closely in all directions for any indication this was a trap. Edward approached the Indian group and, at a gesture, sat opposite what appeared to be their leader. A pipe came out and was offered to Edward after the Indian leader had ceremoniously smoked it. Robert was in agony for his son's safety as the conversation in the field seemed to go on and on. Then he saw them all stand, so he shouted a warning to everyone to be ready. Instead of hostilities, Edward and the Indian shook hands before they turned, each heading on their own way.

On returning to the blockhouse, Edward was besieged by questions. He waved them all off and then gave an account of his conversation with the Indian.

"These are Cherokee, not the Iroquois we fought before. One of them spoke better than passable English and translated. They heard about our fight with the Iroquois and saw the graves of their dead, 'more than the days between full moons, more than three men can count on their fingers.' They wanted us to know they mean us no harm and will not molest us. They only want to hunt. I told them they are welcome to hunt, but if any ill was done we would smite them as we had the Iroquois. They seemed to take this strong talk as gospel and I don't think we have anything to fear from them. All the same, Lewis, you and Philip ride over to the McCrary's and get the word out. Everyone is to be on their guard but no one to molest the Indians unless they molest us. They should be prepared to make for the blockhouse quickly if they suffer any insult."

Patrols were stepped up even further, now three men twice a day. All of the families began to find game left on their stoops every few days, a deer one day, a brace of rabbits another. The Cherokee were only spied at a distance, never approaching close to the settlers in daylight, never giving them cause for undue alarm. This went on for a few weeks, everyone relaxed somewhat, though not completely, and the visits from the neighbors to the Jewett's picked back up again, returning to the pattern established immediately after the fight.

Women would come to visit with Esther, mostly, and along came their older sons and their marriage age daughters. The boys were interested in Sarah, who was not interested in them in the least. The daughters they hoped would catch Edward's eye. The most common way for a family to increase their prospects continued to be marrying one of their daughters just reaching marrying age to an older widower with an estate. Younger men would then court the young widows who were near their age as a way to increase their circumstances, frequently acquiring an instant family in the bargain. It was quite common in the more settled parts of the country and back in England though the opportunities were rarer here on the frontier where widowers of means were few and far between. This accounted for Edward's instant popularity.

Robert would just chuckle at Edward's discomfort. He well recalled his years as an eligible widower and how the mothers of Rowley would come for tea with Aunt Bess, solely to parade their daughters in hopes he would take a shine to one of them. It was an odd custom, but it had worked for generations and many a family of limited means had advanced as a result. It appeared to him the effort was as wasted on Edward as it had been on him all those years ago. Edward for his part escaped as often as possible, taking his nephews, one at a time, hunting. Naturally, no one visited when he was scheduled for the patrol.

Edward enjoyed his hunts with his nephews, particularly with Philip. Charles was a little younger and it showed, though he listened well and did as Edward told him. Joseph had become quite serious since the attack, not sullen, but he now took everything very seriously. Hunts with him turned into work as Edward tried to lighten the boy's mood. No, he and Philip seemed to mesh uncommonly well.

As the weather cooled, the family took more of their meals in their own cabins rather than communally as had been done during warmer weather. Still, each evening Robert and his sons would gather in Robert's cabin and discuss the business of the family, work to be done, or, frequently, just joke and chat, enjoying each others company.

Finally, as November waned, the patrols showed the Indians had moved on and the settlers had the Valley back to themselves. This freed a lot of time for other tasks that had previously been scheduled around the patrol schedule. One pressing matter was getting a list of supplies back to Mister Prentiss so they could be brought up river early in the spring. Henry felt it was his turn to make the ride to Mister MacDonald's landing with Charles. They set off the first week of December with Robert's letter to Mister Prentiss and another from Edward for Mister Gladstone who owned the laborers. They hoped to arrange for them to be rented from spring to fall next year so they could get the farms started in earnest.

Robert was finding the early winter weather a very pleasant change from the winters he was used to in Massachusetts Bay Colony. Cold weather had come and gone several times and did not seem to last as long nor the cold turn as bitter as in the more northern climate. He especially remembered back to that winter of 1704, the winter of the Deerfield massacre, and how bitter and cold that was. Since the fight with the Iroquois, he found himself reminiscing of those days more and more, though he still refrained from sharing these memories with his sons.

He also found his household quite pleasant. Esther and Sarah got along well, making his life much more pleasant than should it have been otherwise. In fact, it was not unlike earlier when it was Aunt Bess and Esther looking after him. Meat was plentiful and the woods yielded a nice crop of blackberries and wild cherries, though they had to rely on the flour and dried goods they brought with them for their normal fare. If they got the laborers early enough, they would be able to get in a crop of beans, oats, wheat, and corn, some of it naturally going to animal fodder. Orchards would have to come later, so for their fruits they would remain reliant on what the wilderness offered.

Robert did miss his riding chair, though. He never missed a chance to make this point to Lewis and even enlisted Esther, who had also never seen the rock bridge, to put pressure on her brother. He seriously thought that Lewis and Henry could start making carts for the locals and do quite a good business with it. He was considering opening a small store himself to help satisfy some of the needs of the locals a lot closer than going up to Beverly's Mill Place or all the way down to Mister MacDonald's landing on the Fluvanna River. Long term these enterprises were likely unnecessary for their support once the farms were up and running. In the near term, however, he thought it would provide them a ready income that would help preserve the credit they had with Mister Prentiss. After all, Williamsburg was a long way to have to go for everything they needed, but if they had some local income, even if in the form of promissory notes, it would simplify things.

It was not long before Edward announced his intention of riding out to see what was keeping Henry and Charles. The hunting was done and he could use the ride, or so he claimed. In reality, he was worried about his little brother alone on the trail with only Charles to aid him. So, he set off early one morning with Joseph, heading toward the ford and the Indian Gap Trail.

❧ *Chapter 26* ❧

*H*enry and Charles got off to a fair start. They found ice starting to form among the rocks at the North River ford, though the river itself was flowing free and cold. They rode on talking about the major changes this year had yielded them. Henry had to stop frequently to stretch his sore legs, a problem that plagued him more in the colder weather.

Talking idly, they found the trail crossing another river, smaller than the North but one neither of them remembered from before. They stopped, looked around, thought, and finally determined they had mistakenly followed the Indian Gap Trail west instead of turning east. Sheepishly remounting, they turned around and headed back east. Passing where their cut-off joined the main trail, they felt more confident they were heading in the right direction.

Expecting to clear the gap before dark, they found their little detour and slow pace had them well shy of the summit when dark overtook them. In fact, dark came upon them so unexpectedly they had a difficult time establishing their camp and getting a fire going. Finally succeeding, they sat there quietly while their pot of chocolate heated over the fire.

Henry was experiencing some loss of confidence as he sat there. He knew he was not an experienced frontiersman, had never claimed to be. When he volunteered for this trip, however, he had not expected his skills to so immediately come into question. He must do better, for Charles. When they left, Mary was still very upset that they were going, Charles in particular. Lewis' tale of Philip's slide down the mountain only added to her apprehension. For Henry, he was determined to pull his weight. The last thing he wanted was to have Charles see his father as a failure who depended on his grandfather and uncles. No, he had to do better tomorrow.

"Father," Charles broke the silence, "can I ask you something?"

"Of course."

"What are you and Uncle Lewis doing down in the barn? The two of you have spent much of the past week down there alone and neither of you have said a word about what you're up to."

"And we have good reason for keeping quiet. So if I tell you, how can I be sure you won't talk, telling our secret to everyone else? Or worse, tell your mother who would be sure to tell everyone who would listen."

"I can keep a secret. Is it something bad?"

"What, your Uncle Lewis doing something bad? Think about what you're saying! No, it's nothing bad, just the opposite, in fact."

"Then tell, tell!"

"Alright, but if word of this gets out you'll have to take your meals standing up as your bottom will be too sore to sit on! Understand?" Charles nodded. "We're building your grandfather the riding chair he's been asking for."

"You're helping build a riding chair?"

"Hey, I'll have you know I worked with your Uncle Lewis when he first started his carriage building business, before you were born! Actually, I've built the platform and chair while your uncle has built the axle, wheels, and tongue. We haven't iron or a forge, so we're at a loss as to how to rim the wheels, but other than that, it's coming along quite well. Right now I'm working on some chairs for the McNulty family to replace what they lost in the fire. Uncle Lewis, once he finishes putting all the parts of the riding chair together, is going to make them a couple of chests and a table."

"Where will you get the iron and the forge? The wheels won't last long without rims."

"Well, we saw some iron and a forge in the McNulty farmstead ruins. When we're ready we thought we could ask Mister McNulty for his help. Hard money is scarce, we're about the only ones around who have it, you know. We thought we could help them by providing them a little hard money while they'd be helping us with the iron and a forge we'll need to finish the chair."

"How have you been able to keep this secret?"

"Oh, it's really been pretty easy. We work on the back side of the shelter barn and hide our work in the hay when we finish for the day. We enlisted Esther as our look-out."

"That's why she's taken to reading in the field near the barn! And she said she just enjoyed the early winter sunlight!"

"Yes, and you didn't even notice she said it in a loud voice so we would hear her. You and your cousins are so easy! Your Uncle Lewis and I have often talked about how much harder it would be to keep secret if we had smart children!"

They dozed off chuckling, enjoying the father-son moment. The next day Henry had especially stiff legs, causing a later than normal start to the day. They crossed through the gap and had their cold dinner on the eastern slope. Remembering their experience of the night before, Henry decided to make an early camp. His legs had continued to bother him all day and he was ready for a rest. They had now covered the distance they expected to cover the first day out.

Getting a good start the third day, they ran into snow by late morning and it continued to increase in intensity until their dinner break. The trail was now snow covered and slick so Henry called another early halt, remembering again Philip's recent experience. The fourth day dawned clear with warming temperatures, turning the trail from slick frozen to sticky mud as the day progressed. They talked about how different the weather was here than in Boston, where the temperatures would not have risen so quickly and the snow would likely have been on the ground until late spring.

Henry's legs did not bother him as much today and they managed to make fair time on the trail in spite of the changing conditions. Be that as it may, it still took them a full week to make it to Mister MacDonald's landing. Mister Gladstone, owner of a middling plantation, was very hospitable and invited them to stay the night. In this way, he would be able to write out a letter to Edward to send back with them.

After supper, while Henry sat in the small parlor visiting with the Gladstone women, Charles made his way down the farm lane to visit with the laborers. He found them all very glad to see him and especially pleased when he told them they had asked to hire them for most of the year, from spring until fall. He remained with them as they sat around their fires singing until Henry came to find him and hustle him off to bed. Though only a mattress on the floor, it felt really good to young Charles to be in a warm room after a week spent on a winter's trail.

The next day, they packed up and made their way to Mister MacDonald's. Here Henry left their letter for Mister Prentiss and bought two tanned deer skins.

"What are those for, father?"

"Now, what is the secret you're keeping? How do you expect me to give your grandfather a comfortable seat without something to cover it? Besides, these are tanned far better than we can do so they will hold up better."

Their business done, they got a late morning start up the trail, making better time going west than they had coming east. Henry's legs were not aching like they had been, having grown more accustomed to riding. He had frequently been plagued by sore legs and joints over the years and he accepted it as something that just had to be borne.

Starting up the west slope, they again came into snow. It started as flurries but progressed rapidly to a good snow storm. As they ate their dinner they discussed stopping but, as there was little wind, they decided to keep moving as long as they could see the trail. This became harder as the day progressed and evening came on. Days were much shorter now and, with the snow falling, dusk came early.

Making camp on a flat piece of ground, Henry pulled out the small tent fly they had carried and set it up as a shelter while Charles gathered firewood. Using a pine branch to sweep the snow out of the shelter, Henry then cut more pine branches to make a nice nest under the fly.

Charles was having a difficult time gathering firewood. Snow covered the ground so he had to brush it away just to find likely wood. Then there was the slippery footing. After falling for what seemed like the hundredth time, he staggered back into their camp, dumped his final armful of wood, plopped down and declared himself "finished."

At first all Henry could do was laugh. His son made quite a sight, his now red face poking out of his clothing all covered with snow. He laughed so hard it first made Charles angry. The angrier he got, the harder his father laughed at him until he, too, was laughing, only he did not know why he was laughing. Still laughing, Henry started brushing the snow from Charles' clothing which turned into lighthearted wrestling, both continuing to laugh and now Charles was also squealing. A voice from outside the firelight startled both and brought the fun to a quick and frightened end.

"You two are the sorriest excuse for frontiersmen I've ever seen," Edward said as he leaned against a tree near their camp.

"Edward! You sneaking up on us almost scared me to death! What are you doing here?"

"Looking for you two, and from the looks of things, I found you just in time to save you both from yourselves!" They saw the big grin on Edward's face as he now entered the firelight.

"Who's that with you?"

"Oh, Joseph came along to keep me company on the trail. You were overdue and father was worried about you, so I came out looking. I just didn't realize I'd need to go all the way to the landing to find you!"

"You can't fool me, dear brother! You're running away from all those women trying to link you up with their daughters is what you're doing. Oh, you'll charge through attacking Indians quick enough, but in a room full of skirts you turn coward."

Looking over his shoulder, Edward saw that this exchange had even brought a smile to Joseph's face. Wasting no time setting up their winter lodging, Edward and Joseph joined Henry and Charles' winter camp. The jocular evening continued well into the night as they all enjoyed the warmth of the fire while the snow piled up all around them.

They awoke early to a very cold morning. The snow stopped during the night and the now clear skies had caused the temperatures to drop. They got a good start with Edward and Henry leading, breaking the trail through the snow, while Charles and Joseph followed, each leading their packhorse. When the two men were a little distance ahead of the boys, Henry broke their silence.

"What made you bring 'Ol' Sourpuss' with you? I'd have thought Philip would have been better company for you."

"There's no doubt about that and I would have enjoyed it more. That said I'm worried about Joseph. Not only has he become my shadow since the Indian fight, pouting every time I take Philip or Charles hunting and not him, he has also become so serious. Did you notice how last night, no matter how hard the three of us were laughing, the most we got out of him was a smile?" Henry thought and nodded his agreement. "That's not good. It's more than we've seen from him in weeks, so I'm not completely discouraged. I was just hoping I'd be able to draw the boy in him back out on this trip."

"The way he's latched onto you, if you can't do it I don't think Lewis or father could either. It's good of you to try, at least. Since that fight he's got being a boy and being a man all mixed up inside his head. So, you want is to bring the boy in him back out? Maybe, just maybe, you can't do that. Instead of you hauling him around while you do your business, force him to be with Charles and Philip, to kind of remind him what being a boy is all about. I think it's a better way to go about it."

Edward gave his little brother a long look before saying, "You know, Henry, you surprise me sometimes. Every so often you say something that makes perfect sense."

"Why does that surprise you?"

With a bold chuckle and good natured slap on his brother's shoulder, Edward explained, "Because you do it so infrequently, of course!"

❧ *Chapter 27* ❧

"**G**randfather?"

"What is it, Philip?"

"Is Uncle Edward upset with me?"

Robert laid aside his account books where he had been diligently entering all of the information from Mister Prentiss. "Not at all, Philip. What ever gave you that idea?"

"Well, he took Joseph with him again this time. I understood why he took Joseph when they came looking for me, but I wanted to go with Uncle Edward this time."

"Now, Philip, hasn't Uncle Edward taken you hunting plenty of times since the Indian attack?" Philip nodded. "And haven't you and your uncle had good times on those hunts?" Another nod. "So, just because he takes Joseph with him on this trip you think he's upset with you?" Again a nod.

"No, you need to get that out of your head right now. Your uncle and I have discussed this. Haven't you noticed a difference in Joseph since the attack?" Nodding again. "Well, your uncle, father, and I have noticed it as well. We've also seen how Joseph has latched onto your uncle and wants to go everywhere he goes. No, it wasn't because he was upset with you that he took Joseph, it's because he's looking for a way to help the boy overcome whatever it is that has been troubling him."

No nod this time, just a thoughtful look. Like when they were in Rowley, Philip spent most evenings sitting with his grandfather, sometimes talking together but as often just sitting close and enjoying each others company. Marie and Lewis always knew that if Philip was not with Edward, they could find him near his grandfather. Robert enjoyed having his grandson close, wished he could get closer to Charles as well. He worked hard to resist showing any favoritism, even with Joseph who was adopted into the family, but had to admit that he continued to feel closest to Philip.

"Grandfather?"

"I'm still right here."

"It's good of Uncle Edward to try to help Joseph."

Robert smiled and patted Philip on the leg. He was pleased the boy had thought through the issue and come to the right conclusion. They both looked up as the cabin door opened and Lewis walked in.

"Is it snowing again, Lewis?"

"It's snowing hard. No wind, though. That's lucky for anyone on the trail this night. Philip, your mother sent me to bring you home. It's bedtime. Stop with the faces, you know I can make funnier faces than you can, so just get your coat on and get home to your mother. I'm going to sit with your grandfather a minute or two."

That stopped Philip in his tracks. He never wanted to be left out of anything and now was no exception. "I can wait."

"You say that now, but as soon as you see the look on your mother's face you'll be putting the blame for not coming home right away on me. I'm in enough trouble, so you just get your coat on and move along."

Once the boy was out of the cabin, the two men just shook their heads and grinned, neither needing to say anything about Philip's ways. Sarah, sitting across the room while Esther brushed her hair, could not hold in her laugh.

Looking around rather embarrassed, "I can't help it if it's funny the way he is around you two, and Uncle Edward, too," then looking at Esther who was struggling to hold in her laughter, "and, see, Aunt Esther thinks so as well!"

"Don't get me into this!" By now they were all laughing loudly at poor Philip's expense. They laughed so hard Lewis forgot what he wanted to discuss with Robert and ended up going home, still chuckling.

After Sarah had gone to bed, Esther sat down next to Robert and waited for him to close his account books before saying what was on her mind. "You know, father, that if you don't start these boys, and Sarah for that matter, on some lessons, they'll forget whatever they knew about reading and ciphering."

"You think I should start schooling them? I've never been a school teacher."

"No, and you'd never been a preacher before coming here. You've now held two prayer meetings and I haven't heard any preacher back in Rowley or in Williamsburg who gave a better sermon or offered a more touching prayer. If you don't, who will?"

Robert looked closely at his daughter in the candlelight and was struck by how much she really did resemble Aunt Bess. And this is just the kind of thing Aunt Bess would have brought to his attention as well. For as much as it misted his eyes thinking of her, it warmed his heart twice as much.

"You're likely right, but there's no sense doing it for just three boys and Sarah. Let's get word out to our neighbors and invite them to join in as well. Let's see, it's Tuesday, we could be ready to start on Monday?"

"I know we can. We can hold classes right here, Sarah can help me. We'll use shingles and charcoal for slate boards and chalk and I'll ask Lewis and Henry to nail together a couple of rough tables and stools."

Robert just rolled his eyes, saying, "You children always did manage to make more work for me," as he kissed Esther good night on the cheek and shuffled off to bed.

Esther chuckled as she watched him shuffle, knowing full well it was an act. Oh, he would act old and infirm now, but earlier today he was showing Philip how strong and young he was as they were splitting kindling for the cook fires. No, he could be quite the actor.

The next morning it was clear and cold and the ground was covered in deep snow. Robert was up early and went to see Lewis as soon as he had finished his breakfast. He had been thinking hard all night about what Esther had said and he now needed to talk it over with Lewis. Of course this also meant talking it over with Philip, who was right there as his father and grandfather tried to talk. He liked to read and liked learning but had been enjoying the exciting life of a frontier boy. He was not too sure he wanted to go back to regular schooling when there was still so much adventure to be had. It was at this point that his mother shooed him out to get her more wood.

"I think you should do it, father. They've already called on you to lead prayer meetings and it is a natural extension of that. Don't listen to Philip. If we want to get him into the College, he needs it."

"Can you make it over the ridge and pass the word

to our neighbors? I don't have school books. I did bring my books and Edward has a good library. Between these two sources, I suppose I'll have enough material to teach them something."

"You suppose? You're going to do this community a great service."

It was after dark when Henry, Edward, Charles, and Joseph straggled into the village after a hard day on the snow covered trail. Mary, who had been beside herself with worry, raced out when Sarah brought the word that Aaron had spotted them from his watch in the blockhouse.

"Oh, my boys, I missed you both so much. Come give mother a hug and kiss. I've been so worried about you!"

Henry acted a little embarrassed by his wife's reaction but both submitted to her hugs and kisses tolerably. Marie went to give Joseph a hug. He shied away until she grabbed him and basically forced it on him.

"Yes, we found these two last night hopelessly buried in the snow and hollering just in hopes someone would come along to save them," said Edward with a wide grin that all knew meant he was stretching things more than a little.

Miles and Aaron took the horses and the weary travelers accepted Esther's invitation to come in and warm themselves. In Robert's warm cabin, Esther and Sarah served up hot mugs of chocolate and rabbit stew all pronounced the best they had ever eaten. Philip was unable to get any satisfactory answers out of Joseph so he moved over to Charles who cheerfully filled his cousin in on the events of the trip. Philip had news for them, too. When he told about the school their grandfather was going to start, Joseph let out an audible groan while Charles just shrugged. He liked learning, as did Philip, and preferred it over life on the trail.

The following morning Edward joined Lewis on his ride over to the neighbors to invite them to send their children for Robert to school. Naturally Philip had to come along as well, not wanting to miss out on any conversation between his father and uncle. When they arrived at the McNulty farmstead, Lewis took the opportunity to address use of his forge and the purchase of iron for wheel rims while Philip was distracted by the McNulty boys. The deal struck, they sat their horses waiting for Philip to join them.

"It isn't disrespect for you, Edward that had me keep my project from you. I wanted it to be a surprise."

"I'm sure it will be. I should be honest and tell you I knew before I went in search of Henry what you two were up to. Hiding your handiwork under the hay may keep it from father's prying eyes, but not mine." The surprised look on Lewis' face pleased Edward. He liked it when he could keep his brother and nephew guessing. "I think what you're doing is wonderful."

Riding on, they met a stranger, well dressed on a well groomed horse and accompanied by a like mounted servant. As they approached, he bid them to halt and asked their business in a rather demanding tone.

"I'm Colonel Edward Jewett, late of His Majesty's Army and now Military Advisor to the Governor of this Colony. State your business with me, sir, and be quick about it as I do not take kindly to being stopped on the road in this manner," was Edward's brusque response, his years as a colonel showing in the ease in which he upbraided the questioner.

Taken aback, the stranger quickly regained his composure and his tone became very respectful, "Oh, sir, we have not had the pleasure. I am James Bordon and own this sizable tract, which adjoins your property to your west. I saw your claim posted at the courthouse in Beverly's Mill Place and have been looking forward to making your acquaintance."

"Mister Bordon, my brother, Lewis, and nephew, Philip. I didn't realize you owned this land. I thought it was owned by these small farmers who occupy it."

"Oh, I do a bit of land speculating and have sold them their tracts alright. Until they satisfy the terms of the sale and I sign over their deeds I still technically own the land. I have been meaning to ride over to meet you but my affairs have kept me most occupied. You must come to Beverly's Mill Place some time. I'm sure you'll need to sell some of your land to satisfy the requirements to retain it and Thomas Lewis, Nelson Beverly, and I would enjoy playing your hosts and helping you with your transactions."

"I'm afraid you are misinformed, sir. I have already satisfied the requirement for one freeholder per thousand acres necessary to retain my lands. Governor Dinwiddie has witnessed this fact personally and it has been properly filed with the Colony's Clerk." Edward continued to use his officious tone that kept his questioner on the defensive.

Bordon found this stranger different than the Scots-Irish and Germans he had grown accustomed to dealing with in the Valley and he suddenly felt much overmatched. "I see, I see, you are in a most enviable position then, sir. Naturally, you have a smaller holding than any of us three so I'm sure it was easier for you to satisfy the requirement. I mean no offense. My invitation is still good. We'd like to meet you and perhaps share a bowl of punch as we discuss the situation in the Valley. And, of course, we'll need you to sit on the County Court come April as befits someone of your standing," finishing this statement with a gracious bow.

"I shall take you up on your kind invitation, sir. As for the County Court, either I or my father, Sir Robert, will attend to sit court. Now, we have business elsewhere. Good day to you."

Once they were out of earshot, Lewis broke the silence, "You were a little curt with him, weren't you Edward?"

"Just two old dogs circling each other, sniffing. Remember what Governor Dinwiddie said about the three large landholders in the Valley? They style themselves after English Country Squires and prey on the poor coming up the Valley from Pennsylvania or over the Blue Ridge from the tidewater region. They are powerful men who purchased their large tracts at a penny an acre and who are looking to turn a tidy profit. We need to deal with them, but I won't let them think for one moment I'll bow to them or take up their ways. Mister Bordon will get the word to the others that I'm unimpressed by them or their holdings. I believe that will give me the advantage in our next meeting."

"Uncle Edward?"

"Yes, Philip?"

"You referred to grandfather as 'Sir Robert.' Why did you do that when he isn't really a 'Sir?' I know you let the Governor use it, but you said it was because he came to that conclusion on his own and you just weren't correcting him. Here you started it. Why? Isn't that telling a lie?"

"Well, Philip, that's something you may find difficult to understand. These men are easily impressed by titles. I bear one given me as the result of my military service to His Majesty, something I included in my introduction to distinguish my title from the local militia 'Colonels' who take up these titles with regularity, like Colonel Byrd. Father, that is your grandfather, is the head of our family. For these people to afford him the respect he deserves, it benefits him to imply he has a title in his own right. It is purely to ensure these wealthy men do not try to take advantage of him." And then, turning to Lewis, "It probably is telling a lie. Do you object?"

∽ *Chapter 28* ∽

*T*he Virginia winter continued to baffle the New England transplants. The first week in January found them shedding their coats it was so warm. Edward, Lewis, Henry, Miles, and Aaron went to work on the creek bottom where they hoped to plant a large vegetable garden to provide for their wants.

It was a four or five acre section along the creek to the west of the blockhouse. They cleared the brush, felled the trees, trimmed and cut them to length, and hauled them near where the cabin for the laborers would be built. All that remained was for the squaring and notching. Then it was pulling stumps. Having the draft horses made all this work possible. The cedars that came out of this section were prepared for the boys to rive into shingles when they were not in school. This did not seem to meet with their approval.

Robert's school, as predicted, was widely popular among their neighbors. Well, that is to say among the parents, the children not being too sure about the mental efforts expected of them. Many of the children, including those near the age of the Jewett boys, had never learned how to read so Robert had a large class for beginning reading. The influence of the Jewett boys and their ability to read helped the class progress quickly. Joseph was somewhat behind Philip and Charles, but not significantly, and the association with the other boys seemed to help his disposition, returning a little of the Joseph they knew from before the Indian fight.

One Sunday in early March, after Robert had held one of his monthly prayer meetings, Mrs. Thompson and her eldest, a daughter, sat to visit with Esther. After some small talk while she looked around to see if Edward had noticed her daughter, Mrs. Thompson leaned forward and took on a serious tone.

"I can't tell you how much your father's school means to me," she said, tearing up. "My boys will be the first in the family who are able to read and cipher. I'm happier than I've ever been in my life and I've your family to thank for it."

Although these conversations, of which this was not the first, made Esther a bit uncomfortable, she always graciously thanked the women. She also never failed to point out how great a man she thought her father was, each time the woman agreeing wholeheartedly. All had begun referring to Robert as "Sir Robert."

By mid-March, the riding chair was complete. The family gathered at Edward's cabin for a family dinner and, after dinner, Edward introduced his brothers.

"Father, Lewis and Henry have a surprise for you."

"You have repeatedly remarked how much you miss your riding chair," started Lewis.

"Yes, but I know, out here, I'll need to wait until we are better situated and have access to all the parts and tools you need," interjected Robert.

"Not so fast, father," said Henry. "Lewis is a magician, didn't you know that?"

Now Robert was very confused. Lewis and Henry led him outside where Miles had drawn up the new riding chair, already hitched. Robert was speechless and they saw tears running down his cheeks. After turning to wipe his eyes he turned back toward his sons.

"Oh, my, just look at her! Where did you get the green paint? And look at the leather seats, just beautiful! Iron rimmed wheels, how did you do it?"

"Well, father, Henry did the platform and seat. I did the wheels and running gear. And Mister McNulty did the forge work for us. Do you like it?"

Words would not do so he grabbed both of them and gave them a long hug. Then, at Lewis and Henry's insistence, he climbed aboard before inviting Esther to join him. Once she was seated, they were off at a canter across the meadow.

Now it was Philip's turn, "How did you do all that and why didn't you tell me what you were doing?" he demanded of Lewis.

"Well, I wanted it to be a surprise and we both know you can't keep a secret."

Robert thoroughly enjoyed riding about in his riding chair. Now that spring chores had started, he had adjourned school until after fall harvest, so he had more time to ride. Esther was his constant companion on these rides and Marie took delight in riding next to them and showing them the sights. She even took them to the rock bridge, the first time either had seen this natural wonder, and a few days later Robert took Mary, again escorted by Marie, so she, too, could see the wonder. He also visited their neighbors where his riding chair was quite the novelty and much admired. When he visited the McNulty farmstead, he made sure to thank Mister McNulty for his contribution to the riding chair.

In early April the County Sheriff came by to see Edward. After the Sheriff departed, Edward gathered the family to discuss the latest developments.

"The County Court will meet in two weeks, on the 15th, and I'm asked to sit as a Justice, requiring my presence in Beverly's Mill Place. Aaron will attend me on this trip. I want to arrive a few days early so I'll depart next week."

"Uncle Edward, is it only Aaron who will go with you?" asked Philip.

"Why, Philip, did you have someone else in mind?"

"Well…"

"Lewis, do you think you can spare your son, Philip, to accompany me to the County Court? I've noticed how useless he is with farm chores, so I doubt you'll miss him much as far as work goes." This caused everyone but Philip to laugh.

"Well, it's as you say," responded a still laughing Lewis, "if you take him for a couple of weeks, we're likely to get more done without him than if he stayed."

"Good, that's settled. Now we need someone to go to MacDonald's Landing to bring back the laborers and, hopefully, the supplies we requested of Mister Prentiss. Henry, are you up to that?"

Henry hesitated, a hesitation prompted by a sharp look from Mary, so Lewis stepped in, "I could take Miles with me and bring them back. I assume we should both leave about the same time?"

With the assignments agreed to, the family members returned to their chores. Philip walked around with a huge grin, one you could not slap off his face, though several family members thought seriously about it. Edward calculatingly went bird hunting first with Charles and then

Joseph, not with Philip, before the day came when he needed to depart.

The day came and Philip was ready. In addition to trail clothing, he had carefully packed his best clothes to wear to court. Marie had groomed the four horses they were taking. Miles had repaired all the tack, polished the brass, and rubbed the leather to a satin sheen. After saying their goodbyes, all five mounted and headed toward the ford.

Where their trail joined the Indian Gap Trail, they paused. Marie had given Philip specific guidance on how he was to conduct himself and Lewis chose not to repeat it. He did, however, after giving Philip a hug, point his finger in his face and said one word, "Remember!"

"Lewis, it is likely Mister MacDonald will not be pleased the laborers were not hired through him, as we did last year. Just be prepared for it and try to sooth his ruffled feathers the best you can."

"I expected as much. You be careful in Beverly's Mill Place. I'm not sure who has the more difficult task but my hunch is it is you."

"That may be, but no more sliding down any mountains for you, is that clear?" Both men laughed. Then Edward and Lewis shook hands before Edward, Philip, Aaron and their one pack horse headed west and Lewis, Miles, and their two pack horses headed east.

Arriving at Beverly's Mill Place required only one night on the trail. It was a crude frontier settlement, though the mill did afford more buildings, notably the Court House, to be made from sawn lumber instead of logs. There were several taverns and Edward chose the largest one for them. Paying in coin overcame the proprietor's reluctance to rent them a private room during his busy time. They had a room with fireplace, two beds, and a pallet on the floor for Aaron.

They had barely gotten settled and the horses bedded in the stable when a slave boy brought a note from Nelson Beverly inviting Edward and Philip to join him for dinner at Beverly Manor, a short distance from the village. His information system was very good to know so soon that Edward had brought Philip along.

Dressing in stylish though plain clothes, Edward and Philip, accompanied by Aaron, arrived at the appointed time. Beverly Manor was a comfortable, though not large, country house of post and frame construction with a porch where Nelson Beverly awaited his guests.

"Ah, you must be Colonel Jewett. I've heard much about you. And this, I assume, is one of your nephews?"

"Good afternoon Mister Beverly. Yes, this is my nephew Philip, my brother Lewis' son. He's been good enough to keep me company on the trail and is looking forward to carrying tales of court back to his brother and cousins."

"You're a fine looking lad, welcome. We are joined today by James Bordon, whom I believe you've met, and Thomas Lewis. They are waiting in the dining room. We four will be sitting as justices over the next week or so and I thought this a good way to get acquainted before court begins."

Entering the manor, they made their way to the dining room where introductions and handshakes were exchanged. Aaron remained at Edward's left elbow throughout and performed perfectly as a valet. In fact, he would not allow the Beverly slaves to serve Edward or refill his wine, reserving this for himself. Several bottles of wine were consumed even though Edward took only a few sips with each course.

Attempting to be coy about their questioning of

Edward, the three self-styled gentlemen were nonetheless very curious about their new neighbor and the dinner conversation was more interrogation. Edward took it in stride and divulged only what he wanted to divulge, deftly changing the subject to suit his desires, not theirs.

Thomas Lewis in particular was not shy about trying to influence Edward's decisions in court. It was clear to Edward these three were out to maximize profits from their land speculation and cared not a bit for those who bought their lands. Having found his neighbors to be simple but decent people, Edward did not allow himself to be drawn into their harangues of the Scots-Irish or German families moving into the Valley. He instead sat thoughtfully, making mental notes much as he had done at military war counsels. As was the case then, he chose to keep his opinions to himself until he was ready to reveal them.

Following dinner, the punch bowl was brought out. All drew full cups while Edward drew less than half a cup. After several toasts requiring the refilling of their cups and not Edward's, he remained sober while his host and the other guests were showing signs of their insobriety. The dinner concluded on a very amiable note, should the three landholders be able to remember anything of their leave taking, and Edward, Philip, with Aaron in tow, rode back to the village.

Returning to their rooms in the tavern, Edward turned to Philip and asked, "Did you learn anything at the dinner?"

"I noticed you drank little and retained control while they drank a lot and lost control. Is that what you mean?"

Edward just smiled and patted his nephew on the back.

❧ Chapter 29 ❧

*L*ewis and Miles made good time after parting with Edward, Aaron, and Philip. Truth be told, Lewis would have preferred to make this trip with Philip. Nothing against this burly former Royal Navy Gunner, it is just they were very different people with not a lot in common. It was nice, as they made camp the first night, to have Miles preparing the camp for him rather than his preparing the camp for Philip. They both basically kept to themselves, not because of any rift between them, they just did not socialize much.

Arriving on the third day, they first went to see Mister MacDonald. Their supplies had arrived with another letter from Mister Prentiss and Lewis arranged for the hire of carts, oxen, and drovers. When the conversation lagged, Mister MacDonald turned it to the hire of laborers.

"So, Mister Jewett, does the Colonel wish me to engage laborers for him again this year?

"I'm afraid, Mister MacDonald, my brother has already made arrangements for labor for this year. Mister Gladstone, when we returned his laborers last fall, contacted my brother and offered to lease them again this year. My brother has taken him up on it and we are to gather them up once we are done here."

Mister MacDonald was taken aback. At first he was angry, but then he reconsidered venting his anger on a family who were good, cash paying customers. "I will admit to being disappointed. But, as I reflect back, I'm sure Mister Gladstone made him a deal it would have been impossible for the Colonel to pass up. Alright, then, what else can I possibly do for you?"

Concluding their business and agreeing the carts and drovers would meet Lewis at the Gladstone plantation, Lewis and Miles road out to meet with Mister Gladstone. The owner was very glad to see them, invited them to spend the night, and asked Lewis into his plantation office with his overseer to discuss "some details" while Miles ensured all was in readiness for a morning departure.

"Mister Jewett, I have a proposition for you. I agreed to lease you the eight slaves for six months for a total of £56 in ready money. The problem I have is two of the slaves, Sam, the foreman, and Jubal have 'jumped the broom' and would like to take their women with them. Now, before you answer as I can see your skepticism, these women are good workers and would take the burden of cooking and cleaning from your wives and daughters and place it on the slaves where it belongs."

"Well, Mister Gladstone, my family isn't used to having slaves, as I'm sure my brother Henry informed you in the fall. We do need the labor, but treat them as hired laborers, which to us they are. I further assume the labor of these two women would not come without a cost."

"Of course, but I am not out to cheat you. I'm letting you have the other slaves at £8 each. These are for sturdy men worth between £70 and £80. The women are worth just £25 each. Shall we say £8 for both?"

"The value of a human being is not something I am comfortable discussing and we are not looking toward a purchase, so their worth is of no real concern to me. I'm sure the two laborers would be more content if their women would accompany them and I can see how they could be useful. I am willing to give £4 for the two, you to provide for all their needs save fresh meat."

"Oh, you drive a hard bargain, that you do. Can we agree to split the difference at, say, £6 for the two?"

"We can. I'll pay you tomorrow, in coin, when I see all ready for the trail and Miles informs me they are all properly equipped."

"I can't tell you how much I enjoy doing business with your family, sir. It's a real pleasure. And when you're ready to purchase slaves instead of hiring them, I'm your man and will make you a fair bargain."

"I'm not sure we'll take you up on that offer, Mister Gladstone, but I thank you for the sentiment."

"Now, you will join me for dinner, won't you? And pass along any news you picked up at the Landing?"

Mister Gladstone was a gracious host and the table fairly groaned under the abundant foods his wife laid out for their guest. The household consisted of Mister and Missus Gladstone, their three daughters, from their mid- to late-teens, and one son about Philip and Charles' age. Finally excusing himself after a very long dinner spent in lively conversation, Lewis went to find Miles and ensure their readiness for tomorrow's rendezvous with the carts and drovers.

Miles relayed how Lewis' decision to allow the women to come along had a very positive effect, not only on Sam, Jubal, and their women, but on the others as well. All of the original eight were pleased to be spending six full months hired out and there were several others who, having heard the tales from the last season were willing to go in their stead.

Mister Gladstone had perhaps 20 field slaves to work his plantation and was hiring out eight. This left him short handed, true enough, but profits in tobacco were not what they were in hiring these slaves out for hard money. Those left on the plantation had been on short meat rations, relying on their own gardens for most of their sustenance. In addition, though Mister Gladstone was not a harsh master, the overseer was more demanding and less forgiving. No, all in all, there was not one left behind who would not have preferred to go along with Lewis and Miles.

The entire Gladstone household turned out to see Lewis and Miles off the next morning. They had now met two of the brothers and found them easy people to like. The carts and drovers arrived about an hour after sunrise so, after saying their goodbyes, the little band got a reasonable start on the day. Along with the four carts for the Jewett supplies were four additional carts. A note from Mister MacDonald asked Lewis' indulgence as these were for Misters Bordon and Beverly and he hoped they could travel along with Lewis' company over the Blue Ridge.

Unlike the fall, the April weather had thus far been rather dry, allowing them to make good time over the dry trail. There were similarities between this caravan and the one from last summer, to Lewis' mind. Both had eight carts and eight laborers. What Lewis missed the most this time was the family camaraderie he had enjoyed the first time over these ridges. Granted, then he was confined to a pallet in a cart due to his injury, so he received a lot of special attention without the accompanying hard work of life on the trail. Be that as it may, having family around him had always been important to Lewis. Were it not for his whole family taking part in this adventure, he would have remained comfortable running his small carriage works in Rowley.

This trip was easier for him than the one he made in the fall with Philip. His confidence as a "trail boss" had improved and it showed. No, he was not a frontiersman, not by any stretch of the imagination, but he was adapting well to living on the edge of civilization. His black charges, after he had killed the catamount in their camp last fall, looked upon him with a renewed respect and trusted him. Miles was not hurting Lewis' reputation at all as he told Sam and Jubal about the Indian fight and how Lewis, returning from seeing them home, had lead a charge right through the main Indian attack on the blockhouse. The more Lewis tried to downplay his role, the more the legend of his role seemed to grow, so he eventually just gave up his protests, resorting to "If that's how Miles says it happened, it must be so," instead.

Marie met them at the ford, a little further out than she was supposed to be alone, and rode back next to Lewis, sharing all of the happenings from the past ten days. They had put up the awning and tents for the laborers, except they had not counted on two bringing women with them so Marie suggested they set up two more of their tents to give the two couples a little privacy from the other workers. When they arrived at their little family village and started getting settled, Sam approached Lewis.

"Mister Lewis, who cut all these trees and dragged them up here?"

"Why, Sam, we did, Miles, Edward, Henry, and I."

"Why did you do that? I thought that's what you hired us to do, the hard and heavy work. Now you've gone ahead and done most of it, does this mean you won't need us for the whole summer?"

Lewis then understood Sam's concern, that they might not stay the full six months but be returned early. "Well, Sam, you just didn't give me a chance to explain the work for this year. We cleared out the garden area, so we'll need that plowed and planted. These logs need squared up because we're using them to build a house for all of you."

"We get to build a house for us?"

"Yes, though we hadn't thought of you having women along so we didn't make any provisions for separate lodgings for you and Jubal."

"That's alright, we know how to make do. How big do you want this cabin to be?"

As Lewis showed Sam the stakes he and Edward had set marking the corners of the building, Sam's eyes grew quite large, realizing it was to be, next to the two story blockhouse, the largest cabin in the village. That's when Sam became all action. He gathered the other laborers around him and started making assignments, some to unload the carts into the blockhouse, some to start the plowing, and others to start squaring up the logs, each according to his particular skills.

Miles, who thought little of the slaves but had learned to respect the ways of the family he was hired on with, looked on in amazement. Approaching Lewis, "What has Sam so fired up?"

"I just showed him the stakes marking the dimensions for their cabin and explained the work to be done. Now he's getting everyone organized and working."

"Well if this doesn't beat anything I've ever seen in my life. Most of the time, on Colonel Byrd's plantations, we couldn't get the slaves to work. Here, they're working harder than I've ever seen in my life. Why, it's as if you offered them their freedom."

"Don't tempt me!"

Mattie and Mary oversaw the supplies being put into the blockhouse, Henry and Joseph went to the creek bottom and helped there, while Lewis and Miles stayed with those working on the cabin, explaining to Sam how he wanted the cabin configured. Sam also looked over the piles they had placed between the cabins and told Lewis he would, when he had time, see to properly tying them together by notching them up high and down low so he could install a log across them to hold them firmly in place.

As Sam went back to supervising the work on the logs, Lewis thought how they were lucky to have Sam as their foreman. He may not have been able to read or write, nor was his speech always proper English, but he was a good worker and very smart in the rural trades, exactly what the family needed to start turning their patch of wilderness into farms.

That night Henry took great delight in retelling the story of the fight in his cabin. He was very animated, acting out the main parts and bringing Joseph up to help, all to a very receptive and impressed audience. As Lewis sat watching, with a full belly and his arm around Marie, he could not help but smile to himself. He was content and happy here.

◌ Chapter 30 ◌

*P*hilip had been the first in the courthouse in the morning. After taking breakfast with his uncle and Aaron, he had dressed and come down here while Aaron helped Edward dress. He had staked out his place just behind the bar, right in the center, so he would not miss anything. Rowley was not a court town, that honor having gone to Ipswich, so this was to be his first experience in a courtroom. He was very excited.

He was not alone in the courtroom for long. People began filing in until there was little room left and he was glad he had arrived extra early. He recognized the Sheriff from when he came to notify Edward of the court dates. Today he looked very official with his long staff and polished boots. A few of the other faces he recognized but only from seeing them around the village yesterday or this morning. There were two men who were past the bar only Philip did not know them or what they did. Evidently, they were supposed to be there because they talked to the Sheriff and he kept addressing them as "sir."

Philip jumped when the Sheriff suddenly banged his staff on the floor and shouted in a loud voice, "Make way for the Justice, make way there." The people really were not making way. Rather, to him, they looked a little upset with the man who had just entered the door and there were things said that he did not think his father would like for him to hear. When he could finally see, it was Mister Beverly, who went past the bar, talked to the two men, and then took the center seat at the front of the room facing them.

Again the Sheriff banged his staff and another Justice entered, receiving much the same welcome as Mister Beverly. This turned out to be Mister Bordon, who also went past the bar and spoke to the now three men there before taking a seat next to Mister Beverly. The third time the Sheriff banged his staff it was for Mister Lewis. While the spectators were not overly respectful for the first two Justices, they were outright disrespectful for Mister Lewis.

Now anxious for his uncle to arrive, he quietly worried about the reception Edward would receive. He had been a Colonel in His Majesty's Army and was used to being afforded a degree of respect that this crowd did not seem likely to offer. Philip hoped this would not put his uncle in too bad of a mood. As much as he worked to control it, Philip could always see when the anger was building within him. Though he had never truly seen his temper erupt, watching the look in his eyes as the anger built made Philip wish never to see it.

Bang, bang, "Make way for the Justice, make way."

Philip could not believe it. The room, which had been so noisy just a moment before, went quiet. He knew this had to be Edward, but was not tall enough to see exactly what was happening at first. Suddenly he saw it, the crowd was making way, and the men were bowing. Then he saw his uncle. He could not believe what he was seeing at first. His tall, erect figure with his square shoulders alone was quite impressive. He was dressed all in black in the finest suit of clothes Philip had ever seen, with silver buttons and silver braid. While the other Justices were wearing boots, Edward was wearing shoes with silver buckles. His black hat was trimmed in silver and pure white feathers. Pinned to his breast was a Royal Order Philip had never seen before, all glittering silver and bejeweled. Across his chest and under his coat was a red silk sash with two white stripes.

Looking neither right nor left, Edward passed through the parted crowd to the bar where one of the court officers held open the gate. As he passed the bar the three other Justices all bowed deeply, clearly moved by the vision before them and Edward returned their bow, only his looked more graceful, more natural. Mister Beverly then stepped aside and indicated the central seat for Edward to take. Declining at first, he accepted as soon as the three other Justices all joined in encouraging him to take it. Edward stepped in front of the tall chair, turned, paused to allow the other Justices to take their places, then sat and nodded toward the Sheriff.

Philip had never been to the Royal Court, had never seen the King, but imagined if the King were to make an entrance, it would have been exactly like the one his uncle had just made. He was so thrilled he tingled. His only regret was Grandfather could not be here to see this, he would have been so proud.

Feeling a firm but gentle hand on his shoulder, Philip turned slightly to see his grandfather standing just behind him, tears flowing down his smiling face. And Charles was there, also, at their grandfather's other elbow. He could not believe his eyes at first, but, no, he was really here. Before he could ask, the Sheriff's staff banged again calling for silence in the court and calling the court to order with "God Save the King."

One of the men who had been past the bar then called the first case and read the complaint. Philip listened intently, trying to learn all he could about what Court was all about. What impressed Philip was that, after hearing from one making a complaint and then from the person the complaint was against, the other justices seemed ready to make their decision. But, no, after listening, Edward asked each party several questions, good questions, Philip thought.

"Then it would appear to me the complainant has misstated the facts in his original complaint. Gentlemen, I would suggest this case be dismissed as groundless. Don't you agree?"

From the hushed voices that filled the courtroom before the Sheriff banged them to silence, Philip learned the complainant was acting on behalf of Mister Lewis and the people could not believe this new Justice was deciding on the merits of the case and not on who it would benefit. The other three Justices looked uncomfortable but all nodded their assent to Edward's announced position and the case was dismissed.

And this is how it went the rest of the day. Edward waited to hear everything, even opinions from the other Justices, before asking a few very pointed questions, the answers always resulting in revelations that clearly decided the case one way or the other. Sometimes, from what was said around him, Philip learned that Edward had found to the favor of one of the other Justices, other times against, the common theme being the people supported each of these decisions and with a growing admiration.

Finally the Sheriff announced the day's session was over, banged his staff again, and shouted "Make way for the Justices, make way." Edward led the four Justices through the crowded court room and, like when he arrived, the people made way. Again, the men bowed their heads as Edward passed, but did not repeat the bows for the other three Justices. Philip was tired, tired of standing, tired of listening, and thirsty. He was so tired, in fact, he almost forgot to ask his grandfather what he and Charles were doing in Court after they left them back home.

"I think I can answer that," came Edward's voice from behind Philip as they exited the courthouse. "You see, the only way I have found to keep my father away from events his children are participating in has been not to tell him about it until afterwards. It's like when I was to be presented to His Majesty, I didn't write him about it until afterwards for, even though I knew there wasn't time for a ship to take the letter to him and he to return on the very next ship, it would be just like him to flap his arms hard enough to fly there, just to see one of his children doing well. How are you, father. I knew that riding chair would be nothing but trouble!"

"Son, you were great up there. I'm very proud of you. Charles and I left shortly after you did and found lodging just outside the village last night at Mister Steele's Tavern, coming in just in time for court this morning. I hope I haven't caused you any trouble, Edward."

"Well, Sir Robert, you have been invited to join me and the other Justices at Beverly Manor for dinner. Do you think you are up for a trip into the lion's den? I can't imagine they are as proud of me at this moment as you are."

"That's only because they couldn't hear what the people were saying about this new, and I must say elegant, Justice. The people are very pleased with what they called real justice."

Edward changed into a suit of clothes less formal,

though still finer than his host's, and they enjoyed what proved to be a surprisingly amiable dinner. Robert was his charming self, making it impossible for the conversation to stray into areas that may result in disagreements. The evening ended on a very pleasant note, with the Jewett's being invited back for dinner the next day following court.

As they rode back toward the tavern, Philip observed, "They drank more tonight than they did last night, Uncle Edward. Do you suppose they will be able to sit court tomorrow?"

"Well, Philip, you and Charles would do well to learn from their example. Strong drink does not produce a strong mind."

Court the next day and the dinner that followed was much the same as the first, with Edward making the court's decisions after asking pointed questions and the others agreeing. It was the third and last day of court, the last case brought before the Justices that really caused a stir.

"Mister Michael Miller of Augusta County brings charges against Mister Thomas Lewis of Augusta County," read the clerk.

"Just a moment," interjected Edward, "Am I to understand this suit is against one of the seated Justices?"

"That is correct, sir."

"Mister Lewis, I think in the interest of justice it only appropriate for you, at this time, to excuse yourself and take a position on the other side of the bar for this case, as befitting your status as defendant."

Thomas Lewis was obviously angered by something, only Philip was not sure if it was the suit or Edward's request he give up his position as Justice for this case. To Mister Lewis' credit, he kept his anger under control, stood, bowed toward Edward, and made his way behind the bar.

"Now, then, Mister Miller, state your complaint against Mister Lewis," continued Edward.

"Yes, sir. I purchased of Mister Lewis 160 acres of land along the Cowpasture River three years ago. I have satisfied my obligations to Mister Lewis, only he has yet to provide me with a deed to the property. I'm asking you Justices to compel Mister Lewis to provide me the deed to land I have already paid for."

"Mister Lewis, your response," said the Clerk.

"I am a very busy man and have not had the time to survey the land. Without a survey I can hardly produce a deed, now can I? He'll just have to wait his turn, like the others, and I will survey his property as soon as I can."

This resulted in a murmur running through the crowded court room and Philip realized Mister Miller was not the first, nor the only to have similar problems with Mister Lewis. Before the crowd became unruly, the Sheriff banged his staff and brought the crowd back into order.

"Am I to understand that you do all of the surveying of the lands you sell to others?" asked Edward.

"I do."

"How many parcels of land have you sold since acquiring your lands here in the Valley?"

"I don't have my books here but I believe it is around 60."

"And how many have satisfied their obligations to you for the purchase of that land?"

"Again, without my books I can not be precise but believe the number to be around 12."

"And how many of the 12 surveys have you completed and filed with the County Clerk's office?"

"Why, I can't be sure. That's not the point. I'll get

to Mister Miller's survey when I get the time. That will just have to do."

"How many?" this time addressed to the County Clerk.

"None, sir."

The murmur of the crowd was louder this time, hardly a murmur at all, and the other two Justices were sweating, obviously uncomfortable with the way the questioning was going. In truth, they were also quite glad it was not them who were being subjected to the iron gaze of their new Justice. The Sheriff again had to bang the staff to bring the crowd back to order.

Edward turned first to Nelson Beverly and addressed him in low tones, then did the same to James Bordon. Both men nodded. Then he rested that iron gaze back on Mister Lewis, who was now less angry than he was uncomfortable. After a pause, Edward continued.

"It is apparent to this court that Mister Lewis, with all of his other civic responsibilities and business interests, lacks the time to go traipsing through the woods conducting these surveys. It also seems to us that a more fair survey could be had by the hire of a surveyor rather than to rely on the owner of the property to do the surveying. Therefore, we instruct Mister Lewis to hire a surveyor, at his own expense, and to produce the 12 surveys before this court reconvenes in October. Mister Clerk, please place this case on the agenda for our October session."

The crowd now went wild, shouting huzzahs for Colonel Jewett and slapping each other on the back. The banging of the staff went on for a full five minutes before order was restored. The Court adjourned and Edward found himself surrounded by well wishers upon exiting the courtroom. That afternoon as they dined at Beverly Manor, Thomas Lewis was notably absent. Both Nelson

Beverly and James Bordon assured Edward and Robert that the case had been decided fairly and Thomas would come around. He just needed some time alone to deal with his "disappointment."

As Aaron took the horses and riding chair to the stables upon their return to the tavern, a man approached Edward, "Forgive my interruption, your Lordship, but you are Colonel Jewett, aren't you?"

"I am."

"Well, your Lordship, I am a miller who came west with my late wife after our indentures were up hoping to find a situation where I could ply my trade to the advantage of myself and an employer. What I've found is they already have all the mills they want here at Beverly. I listened to you in court today and take you to be a fair man. If you were in need of a mill, either for grinding or for sawing, I'm your man and I'd be proud to work for you if you're of a mind."

"I currently have no mill nor do I know how to construct such a complex structure."

"Oh, I know how to build them as well as how to operate them. If you've a stream with a good drop and some skilled builders, we can make a mill that will pay for itself in no time at all, based on the rates I see being charged here."

"Let me think about it and call on me at my estate the first of June. What is your name?

"Agner, your Lordship, Mark Agner, and bless you, sir, bless you."

∽ Chapter 31 ∾

obert and Edward had the boys up and ready to depart right after breakfast the next morning. Aaron brought the horses and the riding chair around to the front of the tavern. As they emerged from the tavern's doorway, they were met by a small crowd of well wishers. The two men felt awkward, not knowing how to respond and not wanting to further alienate the three other major landholders who held the other Justice positions. The boys, noticing their elders' discomfort, found the scene all the more amusing for it and considered it great fun.

"Colonel, Sir Robert, we just wanted you to know how much we appreciate your sense of justice. We now have more hope that the way things have been isn't the way things will stay," said Mister Wilson, the spokesperson for the gathered group and the local blacksmith. "We thank you for all you've done for us."

"Well, Mister Wilson, I really did nothing other than my civic duty to sit as a Justice. We thank you for your kind words, in any case, and look forward to having you all as neighbors for a very long time."

They took their leave and started up the road toward the south end of the village and home. After clearing the last cabin, they saw Mister Lewis sitting his horse, waiting. As they approached, he raised his right hand and hailed them.

"Colonel, I see you're leaving. May I ride with you a ways?"

"Mister Lewis, good day to you. You are of course welcome to ride with us, though I'm surprised as we're not exactly heading toward your estate."

"Oh, I just want to ride and talk a bit." Looking over the little group, Philip and Aaron mounted and Charles and Robert in the riding chair, all armed with long arms, he observed, "I notice you all travel well armed. Are you expecting trouble?"

"Not at all, which is when I've found trouble usually finds me. Shall we ride on ahead so we may talk in some privacy?"

"We'll follow along behind," said Robert, "staying just within rifle shot." This latter was added as a warning that was not lost on Mister Lewis, even though Edward waved it off indifferently.

They rode on a ways before Mister Lewis finally spoke. He seemed to be agitated and trying to find the right words to begin. "At the end of Court yesterday, I was very angry, mostly with you, sir."

"I sensed that, sir."

"Your findings in general, and your final ruling, stands to cost the major landowners in this Valley and benefit the lower sorts who are moving in after failing in the more civilized portions of the colony, or in Penn's Colony."

"I did nothing more than apply English Common Law to free born Englishmen who are entitled to it, sir."

"I just wanted you to know that, having reflected

on the events and your part in them, I realized you did me no injustice by finding how you did. Nelson, James, and I had become used to running things in a certain manner, which was how it needed to be in the beginning. Now that we are organized and recognized as a county, I know it's time we ran things in a more formal, proper manner."

"I, of course, have no idea how things were run prior to this week but I am very glad to hear you are comfortable with how I ran the proceedings, at least in hindsight. I can also tell you that the effect on the other residents of the county has been very positive. I would think that having contented neighbors would only help you as you continue to sell off parcels of land."

"You're right, you're so right. I just have an Irishman's temper, inherited from my sainted mother and sometimes need time to cool down to see the way of things. So there I've said it. I'd like to call you my friend and offer you my hand on it, to take or slap away as you see fit."

"I'll shake your hand and proud to do it." With that, the two men shook hands and Mister Lewis took his leave, turning and riding back toward Robert and the boys. He turned again and rode along next to the riding chair a few paces before speaking.

"Tell me, boy," Mister Lewis directed his question to Charles, riding next his grandfather, "how good a shot is your grandfather?"

"Fair. He can only hit a fly at one hundred paces. Uncle Edward can shoot the wings off a fly at that distance, so grandfather is pretty good only not quite as good as my uncle."

Mister Lewis' face showed his initial surprise, then changed to respect before he bowed toward Robert. "Good day, Sir Robert. I hope you'll have a pleasant journey home and am most pleased you weren't called upon to demonstrate your marksmanship." Then he rode off.

After Mister Lewis had ridden off, Edward rejoined his father and nephews. "Your conversation seems to have gone well, Edward," said Robert. "I trust he bears no hard feelings?"

"He says not, though I think he really does. He just doesn't want us as enemies. Mister Beverly and Mister Bordon represent us in the House of Burgesses while Mister Lewis is the Colonel of the county militia. If he were a Burgess I'd be more concerned. As it is, he bears watching, but I'm not overly concerned. What did he want with you?"

"He asked me how good of a shot grandfather is," replied Charles.

"Yes," said Robert in a firm voice, "and I'm afraid my grandsons and I will need a little time alone when we get back home to discuss the merits of honesty."

This sent both boys into peals of laughter that was so infectious Robert and Edward could not help but to join in. Looking back, Edward saw even Aaron had succumbed and was laughing heartily.

They arrived home the next day, late in the morning. Cresting the hill just to the north, their little village came into full view. Pausing, they took in the whole scene. There was the blockhouse with the cabins, awning, and tents to one side, the Blue Ridge in the distance beyond. On all sides there was activity. Logs were being squared near the one end of their little fort, for it was now hardly just a street; the creek bottom was being plowed. Carts were lined up for unloading near the blockhouse and a little knot of women were washing and hanging clothes. Robert, who had started to worry about Lewis, relaxed. He was obviously home and well as they could see him now riding toward them.

Pulling up as he reached them, Lewis dismounted and he and Robert exchanged warm hugs of greeting. "You surprised me, father, when I returned to find you gone. I had no idea you planned to follow Edward up to Beverly's Mill Place."

"You know me. I just can't resist good drama. And you, your trip looks to have been most successful."

"Well, yes. That's why I came out here, to brace you for the surprise I brought back." Lewis looked around and saw the curiosity he hoped for. "It seems Sam and Jubal had both 'jumped the broom,' so I liberally spent Edward's money to hire their women for the summer as well."

"Now do you see what I've been telling you, father?" said Edward with a merry look on his face, "Lewis just can't be trusted with money! Especially mine!"

As they rode toward the village all the activity they had observed ceased and they were greeted by a small sea of smiling faces. Only Marie was absent, being off on one of her daily rides. After receiving greetings and hugs from the family members and Miles, Mattie, and Betty, Robert and Edward greeted the laborers warmly, glad to see all of them back.

As Sam introduced his woman, Rachael, Robert asked, "So, when do you expect the baby?"

Sam was confused, not sure what Robert was talking about. Rachael, however, looked demur and said, "Should be about five months more, now, Master."

"Hush, young lady, we don't use those slave terms here. So, you'll give birth while you're still here. Good. Depending on how you're doing, we may just have to keep you and the baby here until you're both strong enough to go back over the mountains."

Now Sam understood. His Rachael was with child. Everyone else was a little ahead of him reaching that conclusion and he was impressed with Robert's ability to see it right away. There were congratulations for the happy couple all around, though Rachael remained a little embarrassed by the whole situation.

"Lewis, were you able to purchase that keg of sweet cider for me from Mister Gladstone?" His nod confirmed it to his father. "Ah, good, then I think we will all partake of a glass with dinner today to celebrate the news of Sam and Rachael's child."

As the family gathered in Robert's cabin, everyone else returned to their work. Philip was first to tell all about their experiences in Beverly's Mill Place, suitably exaggerated and, when he did not feel Philip had gone far enough, enhanced by Charles. Esther brought Robert and Edward up on the changes made to accommodate the two women and how they were already working hard, doing the laundry for all in the village.

Lewis gave a sketch of his trip, retaining the specific business details until the others had all gone back to their chores, leaving just the four men around Robert's table. Esther, though, was never out of hearing as she went about her household chores where she would not draw the men's attention to her presence. That was when Lewis went over the negotiations that resulted in the two women accompanying their "husbands" for the summer.

"You made what appears to be a good bargain, Lewis," commented Edward. "Sam and Jubal will be much more contented and, as they are the natural leaders of that little band, it should have the same effect on the others. Besides, it is unlikely we would be able to get them to wash their own clothes, so this will benefit the air about our village as well," he concluded with a smile the others immediately picked up on.

At about that time Betty announced dinner and

told them the drovers had chosen to start on their way rather than eat, now that the carts had been unloaded. They were to wait at the Indian Gap Trail for the other drovers before all heading back to the landing together.

Dinner proceeded without Marie as she had failed to return from her ride. Lewis and Robert were concerned but Edward was becoming irritated with his sister-in-law. When Lewis told them she had met them at the ford as they returned, Edward asked pointedly, "Didn't we agree she would remain within sight of the blockhouse unless she was accompanied by armed men? Has she so soon forgotten our experience of last fall? Please send Philip and Joseph out to bring her back. We need to talk to her!"

As soon as the toast to Sam and Rachael ended, the two boys took off, happy to have been trusted with what they saw as a mission of importance. Sarah told them she thought Marie was going exploring over toward the Thompson homestead to the west so the boys began by heading in that direction while everyone else returned to their chores.

Robert and Edward were standing with Sam just over an hour later, discussing details of the new cabin, when the sound of pounding hooves caught their attention. Looking toward the hill to the northwest they had traversed just this morning, they saw the two boys riding hard toward them, shouting. By time they drew up where Robert and Edward were standing, Lewis and Henry were running up from the creek bottom and Esther, Sarah, and Mary came from their little fort.

"Where's your mother, boys?" asked Robert, not bothering to mask the concern in his voice.

"We came across Indian sign and saw smoke coming from the direction of the Thompson farmstead," said Joseph, breathlessly.

"And we found this where we found the most sign," interrupted Philip, handing his grandfather his mother's riding crop and bonnet.

"We rushed back here as soon as we found them," concluded Joseph.

Edward sprang into action. "Betty, get the boys some water. Mary, Esther, get us food for the trail. Lewis, Henry, see to your rifles and horses. Quickly now, we haven't a moment to lose. Boys, you're going to take us back and show us exactly were you found these things. Father, it's time to fort up again. I'll leave that in your capable hands."

⌘ *Chapter 32* ⌘

*E*dward was pushing them all hard as they raced to where Philip and Joseph had found Marie's bonnet and riding crop. As they crested the last hill before the site, they could see the smoke hanging over what looked to be the location of Tommy Thompson's farmstead, just as the boys had said.

A quick search of the ground told the story. The Indians had laid in ambush for Marie to come by, jumped her, and then moved off toward the Thompson place. They had kept Marie's horse with them and, as there was no sign of her footprints beyond the capture site, they assumed she was again mounted. Edward now pushed them hard onto the Indian's trail.

They came across the creek and entered the clearing to see the Thompson place burned to the ground. There was no sign of anyone having been there at the time, meaning they found no bodies in their very quick search of the area before starting off again at a fast pace. The trail was now basically following Buffalo Creek toward the northwest when it suddenly turned southwest and crossed the creek. Here Edward called a halt, studied the ground for a moment, then turned them around and started back the way they had come. Lewis and Henry started to ask what he was doing but he signaled them to silence. After moving the 50 yards or so that took them out of sight of the crossing point, Edward dismounted and signaled them all to do the same.

With everyone gathered close around him, Edward talked in hushed tones, "I can see no reason for them to cross the creek where they did unless it was to draw any followers into an ambush. We've made up a lot of time and I think we're now close on their heels."

"So now what do we do?" asked Lewis, looking at the boys as he whispered it.

"We can't continue with the horses. They're too large and make too much noise, making us easy targets. Philip, Joseph, your horses are about played out. I need you two to take all of the horses back to the blockhouse. Go straight there and once there, you stay there. Understood?"

Both boys hesitated before they nodded. "I mean it, straight back and stay put." This time they nodded instantly. "Good. Now, off with you both. Keep a sharp eye out. I think this is just a raiding party, probably out for vengeance after the thumping we gave them last fall. I may be wrong, so be careful."

After they watched the boys start back up their trail toward home, Lewis and Henry turned to Edward with questioning looks. "Now it gets interesting," stated Edward. "I propose to slip up and over this wooded ridge so we can't be seen from where they crossed the creek. We'll rejoin the creek a couple of hundred yards beyond the crossing point. Unless I miss my guess, those with Marie won't be waiting in ambush but will continue on. I think we can pick up their trail."

"Won't that put us between the two bands of Indians?" asked Henry.

"And Lewis says you're the dumb one!" chuckled Edward sarcastically. Then he led off up the slope to the north, over the summit, then down the other side where they angled back to the northwest and rejoined the creek. Moving as stealthily as they could, they kept a sharp eye out for any sign of a trail coming back across the creek.

Henry saw the trail first, a horse and what looked like two or three Indians and a small shod foot. Neither of the three being true frontiersmen, they were not expert at reading the signs but were fairly confident of what they were looking at. The ground around the tracks was still wet, indicating the Indians were not too far ahead. They moved on, not as quick as before but more quiet and more watchful. After going only another couple of hundred yards, they heard the distinct clopping of a horse's hooves very close ahead.

Now they spread out. Lewis off the trail to the left, Henry off to the right, and Edward keeping to the trail. Just before they split up, Edward cautioned them to use the knife or axe if at all possible. A shot would only bring the other Indians running to help their friends, putting the brothers in a very bad spot.

They were so close now that they moved more apace with the Indians than gaining on them, trying to find some advantage that would allow the brothers to rescue Marie. Then the horse stopped. After taking a couple more steps, all three brothers as one dropped to their knees, having come just in sight of the Indians and the horse which was carrying not only Marie but the Thompson girl as well, a girl of about 15 years. Missus Thompson was leading the horse and there were three Indians guarding them.

It looked to Edward like they were halting to wait for their compatriots to complete their business of thwarting any pursuit and then catching up to them. The Indians' focus was on their prisoners as Marie and the Thompson girl dismounted. Now was the chance they had been waiting for.

On his signal, all three brothers rushed into the small glade. The Indian with his back to Edward saw Henry just as he sunk his axe into another Indian's skull. Before he could react, Edward used the butt of his rifle to deliver a fatal blow to the back of the Indian's skull. Lewis managed to sink his knife into the third Indian almost simultaneously with the other two Indians dying. He then quickly hushed the women to silence before their screams could give them away. Time was now of the essence.

Not taking any time to bask in their success, the group moved quickly on foot to the north, up a small, narrow valley. Edward had not allowed the women to remount. Now he removed the bit from the horse's mouth and gave the horse a hard slap on the rump, watching it disappear into the woods at a hard gallop. To Marie's whispered protest he said, "Just as we used the horse to find you, the Indians can use it to find us and retake you women. If the wolves don't get him he'll find his own way back to us. For now, we have to move and move fast."

They headed due east, heedless of the terrain they had to cross. This had them moving further away from the creek with every step they took, trying not to meet up with those Indians who had laid in ambush. Edward took the lead with Lewis and Henry bringing up the left and right rear, the women in the middle. The women knew not to complain or ask for a break as any halt could be their last.

They crossed into the narrow Spring Valley, the

mouth of which was nearly opposite where the Indians had crossed Buffalo Creek to set up the ambush. Edward allowed them to pause only long enough for each to take in a couple of mouthfuls of water before pushing them on. This time, however, he had Henry take the lead while he moved further off to their south to keep an eye out for any Indian movement from the creek crossing.

About the time the group made the summit of Spring Valley's eastern ridge, they heard it, the sound of horses galloping off to their right, from the direction of the creek. They all stopped and listened, trying to determine where the horses were coming from and if it were Indians, not known to do much riding of horses, or someone else. As soon as it was clear the horses were coming from the southeast and there were several of them, the little group quickly huddled.

"This is very bad," said Edward, once all were close enough for low voices. " It is likely our neighbors are heading right into the ambush set for us. Henry, you and Lewis take the women back to the blockhouse. I have to go try to warn our neighbors of their danger."

"Edward, I don't see how you'll reach them before they cross the creek. You'll be too late," responded Lewis.

"I have to try. Even if I'm a little late, my entering the fight may cause just enough confusion to give our neighbors a chance to get out of the ambush."

Henry put his hand on Edward's shoulder, "You're too important to us to risk like this. You go with the women and I'll warn our neighbors."

"No, I must do this. Neither you nor Lewis have much experience in a close fight. It's what I used to do for a living. Now, off with you both." Edward turned and started moving quickly down the ridge toward the creek and the sound of the horses.

"Henry, it's up to you. Get them home. I'll watch Edward's back. Don't argue, just move!" Lewis ignored Marie as she reached for him, instead moving quickly in Edward's wake without even a glance over his shoulder.

"Come on, there's no time to lose," Henry said more to Marie than to the others. These four started moving fast over the crest of the ridge and down the other side, keeping to their original route of travel to the east. This was not the direct course to the blockhouse, but as Edward had pointed out, it was the safest as with every step it put more distance between them and the last known location of the Indians.

They were making good time when a faint Indian whoop followed by the popping of gunshots caused them to pause, but only for a moment before taking up their line of march again. They all knew what these sounds meant, that the ambush had been sprung. There was no way for them to know whether Edward and Lewis had reached them in time or if their friends and neighbors had blundered into the ambush unawares. They could not think of that now. All they could do was to make their way as fast as they could toward the blockhouse. And now there was precious little daylight left. It was unlikely they could make it before full dark.

Henry's mind was racing. There was a good moon but it would not rise for two hours after they lost the light. What to do for those two hours? He could push them on, but it was dangerous to travel in the full dark. An injury could halt them and ultimately prove fatal to all. They could stop, but if the Indians were on their trail now, they could be caught before they started to move again. He then saw it and his decision was made. In the distance was the McNulty cabin, dark and evidently abandoned. They would halt there until moonrise. They all needed the rest and if the Indians were on their trail, the stout log walls would buy them a little time at least, perhaps dissuade the Indians from attacking at all.

Edward and Lewis headed not directly for the crossing, the sounds of the horses told them they could not reach it before their neighbors, so instead they angled to cross the creek to the northwest in the hopes of coming in behind the Indians lying in ambush, maybe making it before the trap was sprung. Both men were already very tired but they could not slack their pace, lives depended on them. When they hit the creek, Edward scooped water into his mouth as they crossed and signed for Lewis to do the same. He knew from experience that fighting was dry work and you never passed the opportunity to quench your thirst when it presented itself.

Now they were very close, the horses were clopping toward them from their left, slower since crossing the creek. They were straining their eyes in the gathering dusk to see where the Indians were lying in wait as they moved now very cautiously forward.

Lewis could not remember ever having been as scared as he was at this moment. He looked toward Edward and wondered if he, too, was scared. No, probably not. While he could see tension on Edward's face, there was also an unyielding determination in his eye. As close as they were as brothers, Edward had obviously seen things that had hardened him to battle. Lewis shook off these thoughts and went back to concentrating on the task at hand.

The Indian whoop was so close it caused Lewis' heart to skip a beat. He now saw the Indians rise, they were right in front of him, and that was when he realized he could see the horsemen as well. The Indians fired before he had his rifle to his shoulder and he noticed out of the corner of his eye that there were now empty saddles. That was when he heard a blood chilling shout from Edward and turned his head to see what had caused his brother to make such an unnatural sound.

☙ *Chapter 33* ☙

*T*he Indian whoop was immediately followed by a couple of gunshots and a barrage of arrows that cleared four saddles. No sooner had the barrage occurred than the Indians came out of hiding and swarmed into the very small glade. One Indian leaped onto the chest of the victim closest to Edward, pulling his knife in preparation to take the scalp. That was when Edward let out his horrible cry.

The Indian's head snapped up and, just as fast, Edward sent a heavy lead ball into his head just where the nose and eyebrow ridge come together, hurtling the Indian off his intended victim. Even before the lifeless body of the Indian had hit the ground, Edward was moving forward through his own gun smoke. Lewis saw him drop to one knee next to the victim, scoop up the victim's gun and shoot another Indian. Pulling his knife and belt axe, he charged forward again, into a knot of Indians who had paused, shocked at the sudden attack from an unexpected quarter. He slashed one with the knife in his left hand and hacked another with the axe in his right hand, moving swiftly to dodge blows intended for him.

Lewis shot, tumbling an Indian with a gun who was

taking aim at Edward, and immediately began to reload, glad that Edward had drilled them in fast reloading. Edward again dropped to one knee, taking up the gun just dropped by the Indian Lewis shot to kill another Indian at very close range. Now he was again among them. Lewis shot another on the edge of the group, not daring a shot into the knot of Indians for fear of hitting his brother. Just as he started to reload, he saw an Indian running toward Edward from behind him and to his right. Loading as fast as he could, he just knew he would not be loaded in time.

As Lewis quickly primed, he saw the Indian raise his tomahawk to strike. Just as he did this, Edward bent double at his waist and shifted backwards to his right, hitting the Indian with his body just below the Indian's belt. The Indian's momentum carried him across Edward's back and as he thumped onto his back in the dirt Edward's knife pierced his heart.

With Edward bent low, Lewis risked a shot over his back and into an oncoming Indian beyond Edward. With that shot, more shots were heard from Lewis' left as the surviving farmers recovered from the initial shock and joined the fight that had thus far been carried on by the two brothers. This was all it took to end the Indians' ardor for the fight and, just as suddenly as it began, they disappeared into the darkening woods.

Now reloaded again, Lewis came cautiously forward and into the glade, meeting Edward by the body of the first victim. His brother was covered in blood and gore so that Lewis could hardly recognize him.

"Lewis, I am so sorry," came Edward's melancholy voice, looking down at the body between them. Only then did Lewis look down.

Looking now upon the lifeless body of his son, two Indian arrows stuck in his chest, Lewis was overcome with grief. He sunk to his knees, his mind not fully comprehending the scene before him. "But how, you sent them home with the horses? What is he doing here?" Tears flowed freely down his cheeks as he put a hand on the boy's shoulder, as if perhaps it was not real, this horrible vision that was before him and by touching him the reality might change.

"I can answer that," said the elder McNulty, joining the brothers. "We met up with the boys and they told us what you had found. Tommy there," indicating the lifeless body of Tommy Thompson, "begged the boys to guide us to where the Indians crossed the creek. The one boy, Philip, would have no part of it, stating plainly that his uncle had told them in no uncertain terms to go straight to the blockhouse. The other boy, young Joseph here," gesturing to the boy's lifeless body, "barely hesitated. He just handed the horse he was leading over to Philip and joined us."

Looking around, Edward saw the elder McNulty cradling his wounded arm, and standing near Mister McNulty and his two oldest sons. Lying on the ground in addition to Joseph and Tommy were Tommy's two sons. Tommy Thompson's rash behavior had cost him his life and those of three innocent boys.

Turning back to the elder McNulty, Edward said, "I'm going to wash in the creek. Wrap the bodies in their blankets. Gather up all the guns, powder, and ball, steel knives and tomahawks. Leave them their bows and arrows. Do not molest the Indian dead, but lay them out on their backs, respectfully." Looking down at the grieving Lewis and lifeless Joseph, he sighed heavily and then moved to the creek to wash.

They had lit pine knots to light the clearing as they went about their work. When Edward came back, he saw they were in the final stages of readiness, just loading the blanket wrapped Thompson bodies over the backs of their horses. Lewis had pulled the arrows from Joseph's chest and wrapped his body in a blanket.

"I'll put him on his horse and we'll be ready to go," he said sadly as Edward came next to him.

"No, I've got him." With that Edward handed Lewis his rifle, bent, and scooped the boy up in his arms. Turning back toward the creek, Edward began the walk home, carrying the boy and not saying another word.

They walked slowly by the moonlight, Edward in the lead, carrying Joseph, then Lewis, leading Joseph's horse, followed by the McNulty's leading the Thompson horses and their burdens. Edward never stopped, never put Joseph's body down. He staggered twice, but before Lewis could move forward to reach him he had stopped, squared himself, and moved on again. This was the sad procession that came across the meadow toward the blockhouse just after sunrise.

All of the little fort's occupants gathered around to meet them as they came up the rise from the creek. A weary, heartbroken Edward walked right up to Robert, the others gathering around them. Tears had started to flow down Robert's cheek as soon as he had seen Edward carrying his burden, expecting the worst.

"It's not Joseph, is it?" he asked.

"I'm sorry to have to say it is," came the melancholy reply.

Marie let out a sob and shouted, "What have you done to my Joseph?" Lewis grabbed her by the upper arm and jerked her to his side, cutting off any further exclamations.

Sobbing, Philip looked from the blanket to Edward and said, "I'm sorry, Uncle Edward, I..."

"No," came the loud, harsh reply. Continuing in a hard, firm voice for all to hear, "this is my fault!"

At that, Robert took Joseph's blanket wrapped body from Edward's arms. He wanted to say something, wanted to disagree with Edward's acceptance of blame, but now just did not seem the time. As soon as he was relieved of his burden, Edward again squared himself, paused, and walked directly to his cabin, banging the door behind him.

Robert carried Joseph to his cabin where Esther, Betty, and Mattie prepared it for burial. The McNulty and McCrary women did the same for the Thompsons using Henry's cabin. McNulty, McCrary, Miles, Sam, and Jubal worked to fashion crude coffins for the four bodies.

Philip's natural inclination was to go to his father for comfort, but his father had taken his mother and headed for their cabin. He knew now was not the time, so he stayed with his grandfather. This too was a natural thing for he and Robert were very close. They sat on a bench outside the blockhouse door, Robert's arm around Philip's shoulder. Words were not necessary as the two just sat and grieved together, comforted by the other's closeness.

Marie still wanted to blame Edward. Actually, anyone would do but Edward had just become the natural person for her to blame. Lewis would have none of it and was much harsher with her than he had ever been, his grief coming out in the form of anger he really did not feel. He placed the blame for Joseph fully on Marie. Had she not been out riding for her own enjoyment, had she not gone far beyond where they had agreed she could ride unescorted, she would not have been captured and they would not have been out looking for her. The Thompsons were not her fault. They were going to do what they were going to do regardless. But Joseph and Philip were only out because she was not where she was supposed to be and had to be rescued.

There was no doubt Lewis was right, only she desperately needed him to be wrong. If he were right, then she caused Joseph's death and she did not think she could deal with that. Finally the harsh words subsided and both gave in to their grief, holding each other and crying for what seemed a very long time.

It was a melancholy group that gathered under the awing in response to Betty's call to dinner. Everyone was there except Edward, who had not emerged from his cabin since that morning. No one spoke much and while none were very hungry, all ate. It seemed they really had not thought about food until they took a couple of bites and realized they actually were hungry. Betty prepared a plate and took it to Edward, but he declined it through the door and sent her away.

Supper was passed much the same, without Edward. Later, after Philip, who had stayed close to his grandfather all day, went home to be with his father, Robert made his way to Edward's door. He knocked lightly and Edward asked to be left alone. When he found it was Robert, the door opened and Robert was invited in.

"Son, Joseph's death is not your fault. Forget what Marie said, she was hurt and angry with herself more than anything."

"It is my fault, father. These boys are town raised. They don't have any business being out here in the first place. Look at how the first Indian fight affected Joseph. I knew it then, only I did nothing about it."

"What could you have done that you didn't do?"

"Just what I'm going to do now. As soon as we bury our dead, I want you to all pack up. I'm taking you back."

"Back, back where? We belong here now."

"No you don't, none of you. I've taken a group of New England townsfolk and brought them to the frontier.

First it was Aunt Bess and I didn't learn my lesson. Now it's Joseph. I'll be damned if I'm going to let you all stay only to be killed off one by one. I'll see you all back to Rowley, or Williamsburg if you'd prefer that, but you can't stay here, it's too dangerous."

"Nonsense, that's just your grief talking. You didn't take anybody, we came of our own. And because of that, you can't send us away. We're here and here's where we're staying. Joseph died of exactly what you told him he would die of, not following your instructions. You did what you could to protect them, both of them. One listened and lived, one didn't and died. It was out of your control. You're an officer, what's the first thing an officer has to learn?"

"In war, young men die."

"That's right. There's nothing you can do to stop it. And there was nothing you could have done to stop this."

The two men sat together in silence long into the night. The next morning they buried their dead.

↷ Chapter 34 ↶

*T*he day after they buried Joseph, Marie's horse wandered in much the worse for wear. It had sores from having the saddle on all this time and the saddle itself was in need of repair where the horse had tried to rub it off against a tree or two. Marie went to work treating the horse's sores while Henry offered to repair the saddle for her.

The daily patrols were still turning up significant Indian sign, so they basically stayed at their little fort. Plowing and planting continued under armed guards as did work on the cabin for the laborers. At night, they were all locked in the little fort before sunset, not to come out again until after full sunlight.

Edward remained distant, taking his patrol only with Lewis and eating alone in his cabin. Robert was the only one who he welcomed in, so they sat together each night when they were not on the watch. Sometimes they talked but most often they just sat shoulder to shoulder and remembered.

The only time Philip was beyond arm's reach of his father was when Lewis was on patrol with Edward. Those times Philip stayed close to his grandfather. Joseph had been his best friend as well as his adopted brother and he felt his loss keenly. He was also mourning for his Uncle Edward who continued to take Joseph's death very hard. Even Charles was subdued, having grown quite close to Joseph. Truth be told, Joseph and Charles were more alike than either was with Philip.

One morning, the fourth day after they buried Joseph, Marie and Henry came running up from the barn, frightened. Hanging from one of the fence posts by the door, they had found a bear claw on a leather thong. Running into their little fort, Henry noticed four more hanging from the post next to the unfinished gate and Mattie found two more by the back corner when she and Betty carried the laundry over to where they had the large laundry kettle set up.

Edward mounted and led a patrol of four out to check their immediate vicinity. There was a lot of sign showing how the Indians had approached, probably under cover of full darkness before moonrise, but no Indians were seen. Everyone was now even more on edge. The patrol not turning up any immediate threat, the horses were let out to graze near the fort.

As they sat down to dinner, the watch called that there seemed to be something wrong with the horses, they seemed agitated. Everyone turned out and Edward again led four men out to bring the horses in. What they found was every horse had a bear claw on a leather thong around its neck. A quick conference was held and no one could come up with any explanation for this. The Indians were obviously close, watching, and had something in mind. The watch was doubled and everyone stayed inside the little fort that afternoon.

An hour or so before sunset, the fort was hailed

by a small group of Indians approaching from the south, where the creek flowed closest to the blockhouse. Robert had everyone at their assigned posts while Edward prepared to go out to meet them. Lewis waited for him and was about to leave the fort with him when Edward stopped him.

"Not this time, Lewis. If this is treachery, father can only afford to lose one son today, not two."

"Wrong, father can't afford to lose any of his sons. You're not going out there alone and that's all there is to it."

Putting a hand on Lewis' shoulder and giving him a familial shake, the two brothers walked out together. Both were well-armed but knew there was no cover in the field should Indian treachery occur.

The head of the Indian delegation spoke broken English and identified himself as Black Fish, the war chief of the Shawnee. They sat and went through the pipe smoking ceremony like the one last fall with the Cherokee. Then he asked how Great Bear was.

"Great Bear? Who do you mean by Great Bear?" asked Edward.

Black Fish indicated Edward was Great Bear. He went on to explain they had named him Great Bear because he does not seek to fight, but fights with terrific violence when he or his kin are endangered. By not taking scalps of their dead but treating them respectfully, even leaving them bows and arrows to hunt with in the next life, he showed he was not afraid to meet them when he passed into the next life. This had earned their respect and gratitude.

He then explained how each of Great Bear's horses had been marked as being his by the bear claw and another had been left for each of Great Bear's women, so any

Shawnee coming upon them will know they are of Great Bear's clan and are not to be molested.

Black Fish then said Edward should come back to their village with him. He would be Black Fish's adopted brother and take the wives of those warriors he had slain. They were young, strong women and would give Great Bear many sons. And Great Bear's sons would make the Shawnee strong and he would live forever through them and their tales of his great victories.

Edward looked at Lewis who was as surprised as he was. "Thank you, Black Fish, I would be honored to be your brother, but my place is here, with my people. I am sorry there are so many Shawnee wives without husbands. As you have said, I did not seek out the Shawnee. The Shawnee entered my lands and assaulted my family. That is why so many wives weep."

Black Fish was disappointed but not surprised at Great Bear's decision. In any case, he would be Black Fish's brother. And all the Shawnee will know to sing their death songs before doing any mischief to Great Bear's clan. He closed with a warning. Should Edward venture over the mountains except alone and then only to visit his brother Black Fish, his protection ended with the mountain forming the Valley's western boundary.

Black Fish rose and drew his knife. Lewis tensed and cocked his rifle which was in the crook of his arm. Making a small cut on his left palm, Black Fish then offered the knife to Edward, who understood he was to do the same. This done, Black Fish grasped Edward's hand, the blood flowing together to the ground. After a minute or so, he released Edward's hand, acknowledged Lewis, and turned, leaving the way they had come.

Walking back to the fort, the tension now eased, "So, Great Bear, how many wives do you have, anyway?"

Lewis asked with a laugh.

"How many wives do you suppose you could handle, dear brother?" was Edward's grinning comeback.

"Oh, I don't suppose I'm able to handle the one I've got very well, but you are the war chief Great Bear. Surely a little woman would be no match for you!" Lewis could hardly get this out he was now laughing so hard. He was most enjoying the fact that Edward was grinning, something he had not seen since before the fight.

"Just what I need, an Indian lodge full of women arguing among themselves and demanding I do this or that to show how I favor one over another. If that's heaven, I think maybe it's not someplace I want to go!" Both were laughing hard as they crossed into the little fort.

Keeping a strong watch posted, Edward gathered what Lewis was now calling the Bear Clan and reviewed the nature of his discussion with Black Fish, omitting the part about the Indian wives waiting for him in the Shawnee town. The Jewett women plus Betty and Mattie were instructed to wear the bear claw necklace at all times but not to rely on its protections too much. All it would really mean to a Shawnee warrior is that he was bringing pain and suffering onto his tribe if he were to molest them, not that he could not molest them. The horses, also, would always have the bear claw around their necks. Edward thought this might lessen the chance of them being stolen.

Tom McCrary wondered what this meant for the rest of them. "I don't think they've extended this to all the whites who occupy the valley, Tom," Edward responded. "I do think they will refrain from attacking us here, so if you and yours can make the protection of the fort, I think you'll be safe. None of us can count on this being more than a warning to an Indian warrior. The best protection will continue to be our watchfulness and our ability to shoot straight."

Edward's mood had lightened considerably following his meeting with Black Fish. After their meeting broke up, he grabbed Philip and Charles and took them over to the pile of logs and gave them a lesson in throwing a belt axe or tomahawk. They now had a good supply of tomahawks to choose from and he presented each of the boys with one to carry with them. They were very proud of their new weapon and, as they all gathered for dinner, could not resist showing them off to their fathers and the other boys in the fort.

Edward joined everyone for dinner this time. When he sat in his normal place, Jenny Thompson and her daughter sat next to him. He acknowledged their presence but really did not talk much to them until Jenny thanked him for bringing her husband and sons home and seeing they got a good Christian burial.

"Well, Missus Thompson, it's just a shame it happened. It didn't have to end that way," said Edward, feeling the conversation a little awkward.

Dinner over, Edward suggested to Lewis they should do a quick patrol around the fort, leaving in half an hour. He then walked toward his cabin with Jenny and her daughter walking alongside him. This made Edward very uncomfortable though he said nothing.

"Did you notice how Jenny Thompson is playing up to Edward?" Marie asked Lewis as they walked toward their own cabin.

"I'm glad to hear you put it that way, because Edward didn't seem to be encouraging the attention at all," observed Lewis.

"The poor woman has lost her husband and sons and everything she owns in the world except the clothes on her and her daughter's backs. I think she's looking to the only eligible widower as a way out of her current impoverished state."

"Marie, she just buried her husband!"

"This is the frontier, Lewis. If she doesn't find a suitable match, either for her or her daughter, right away they'll likely starve. She knows that as do all the others. It's different for men on the frontier. Life's hard on women who lose their husband unless they have older sons to continue to provide for them."

"So you think Jenny Thompson and Edward..."

"I'm only saying that's what she has on her mind. And Edward could do a lot worse. She's still pretty and only 34, even if those have been hard years."

"Marie, you stay out of this! I mean it, don't you encourage her!"

∞ *Chapter 35* ∞

*E*veryone stayed at the Jewett's fort for the next several days even though the signs were clear the Indian raiding party had left the area. It could have been a ploy to get everyone out from the protection of the stout walls. The mood was lighter, though, since the immediate danger seemed to have passed.

After their communal supper, stories of their Indian fights were told and retold. The laborers sat taking it all in with wide eyed amazement. The elder McNulty told the story of the ambush, how they knew Edward suspected it from what Joseph and Philip had told them. They thought they were proceeding cautiously enough, though Tommy Thompson was anxious for his wife and daughter and was pushing them on. His account of the Jewett brothers coming as if from nowhere to their assistance was told in graphic detail. Edward was fierce and merciless and Lewis covered his back to buy time for the farmers to recover from the initial shock.

Edward usually excused himself when the storytelling began, using the excuse of needing to check on the watch. Robert would usually join him. He had taught the Thompson boys how to read over the winter and felt their loss a waste. He also continued to mourn for Joseph, knowing Edward and Lewis had sent them to safety and that he was beyond the reach of the Indians, when he foolishly joined into Thompson's rash dash after the Indians.

Philip kept looking for his chance to catch his uncle alone but that had proven difficult. Either he was absorbed in the duties of keeping them safe or Missus Thompson was hanging about. Edward seemed to pay her little attention beyond politeness when she would approach him. Philip was not sure what was going on here other than it was interfering with his desire to talk to Edward alone. Then one night he saw Edward return to his cabin alone and there was no one else around.

"Uncle Edward? It's Philip. Can we talk, I know it's late but I really want to talk to you," he said through the door. The door opened and Philip was let into the darkened cabin.

"I'm afraid I haven't been much company lately, Philip, and I'm sorry for that. I really haven't known what to say to you since costing young Joseph his life."

"That's just it, Uncle Edward, you didn't, I know you didn't. I know what you said when you brought him home, that it wasn't my fault, but it was. I should have stopped him. You were very clear that we were to come back here and I didn't stop him." Tears now ran down Philip's face and Edward pulled him close.

"It wasn't up to you to stop him, Philip. Ever since that first Indian fight there had been something going on in Joseph's mind. I knew it, I could see it. He always wanted to be with me at the point of the most danger, like he no longer cared if he lived or died. For that reason I should have left him here once you two had found where your mother had been taken. I knew it was dangerous to take someone who has lost his fear out after an Indian raiding party and I did it anyway. No, it wasn't up to you to stop him."

"Does the sadness ever go away, Uncle Edward?"

"I hope not, Philip, because when it does it means we've forgotten him. Aren't you still sad about Aunt Bess?" Philip nodded. "I am also, because we both remember her. No, I hope we never get over being sad about poor young Joseph. But," he took Philip by the shoulders and held him away, stooping so their faces were close together, "that doesn't mean we let the sadness keep us from enjoying the fact that we are still here. Does that make sense to you?" Philip nodded again and Edward drew him back to him and they stood there quite a while, remembering.

Edward noticed over the next couple of days that the laborers were talking among themselves and looking in his direction whenever he was near them. Finally having enough of this, he called Sam over, out of earshot of the others, and asked straight out what was going on.

"Well, Colonel, it's like this. You are the most powerful man any of us have ever been around. Not in the way Master Gladstone has power over us because he owns us and can do with us as he pleases. You're more powerful than he is. When someone does you wrong, they have a way of not staying alive very long. And yet those you care about and are under your protection seem to live. We just want to make sure none of us do you a wrong."

"Sam, are you saying I scare you?"

"Yes, sir, Colonel sir, you scare us a lot. Not in a bad way, no, in a good way. And all of us hope you'll continue to hire us out from Master Gladstone. Even this far out on the frontier and with Indians all around us, we feel safer here than in the quarters at Master Gladstone's."

"Thank you, Sam. You are all good workers and I

hope we can continue to labor together." He then extended his hand to Sam, who hesitated. He had never been offered a hand by any other white man except here with the Jewett's. Then, with a big grin, he took Edward's hand in his big paw of a hand and shook it heartily.

The patrols continued, both ensuring the Indians had not doubled back and taking stock of the damage done to the farmsteads so the owners knew what they would be returning to. Only the Thompson place had been burned, the others just ransacked. A lot of the stock had been driven off but most were simply in the woods surrounding the farmsteads. This had been a vengeance raid and very little in the way of looting had been done.

As they sat around under the awning after supper one night, as a light rain pattered against the canvas, Tom McCrary casually mentioned, "It sure would be nice to have some help making furniture to replace what the Shawnee broke up. You've got some nice furniture in your cabin, Jim," referring to Jim McNulty. "Tell me again where you got that?"

With a big grin, Jim McNulty said, "I'll have to think. Now, let me see. Mother, do you remember where we got that furniture after our cabin burned last fall?"

"All right, you two, knock it off. Everyone knows what you're hinting at. I'm sure Lewis will agree to help me make some furniture for you," said Henry, starting to feel he had started something when they helped the McNulty's out, something that was going to mean a lot of extra work.

Later, Edward finally made peace with Marie, at Lewis' urging. One day while she was in the barn, Edward sought her out and sat down on the hay. She looked very nervous, almost like she wanted to run away from him, but she did not.

"Marie, there were things said when I brought Joseph home for the last time, things we need to get out in the open. I will start by admitting I was very angry with you for having disregarded your own safety and thereby putting the safety of Lewis, Henry, Philip, Joseph, and me at great risk. It was poor, young Joseph who paid for your disregard and I was powerless to stop it. For that I am angry with myself."

Marie sat down on the hay next to Edward and started to cry. "Those things I said, I didn't mean them. I know it was my fault Joseph died, only it was too hard for me to admit it, even to myself, that I lashed out at the one person who did more than any to save me, to save us. It tears me up inside to think that Joseph died because of me!"

"Marie, Joseph died because of Joseph. You made a bad decision that put us at risk, yes. He made a bad decision that cost him his life. He was beyond all of our control when he made that decision. By then there was nothing any of us could do."

He gave her a hug and patted her shoulder before getting up to leave. As he came out of the barn he signaled to Lewis, who entered and comforted his wife. Things between them improved to where they were back to normal, only Marie did not ride these days.

When it was decided safe for the neighbors to return to their farmsteads, Missus Thompson came to see Edward at his cabin.

"As you know, I am destitute, I have nowhere to go and nothing to go to, yet I have my daughter to provide for, my eldest child is all that's left me." She choked back a sob and composed herself before continuing. "So I'll speak plain. I'm told I'm not without some appeal and thought, if you'd have me, I could stay with you, provide for your needs, make you a good wife. It is unnatural for you to be alone and I need a husband, so it could work well for us both. There, I've said it."

Edward had been expecting as much. He had noticed she was paying him uncommon attention and hoped it was something that his indifference would cause to pass without having this type of confrontation. He did not want to hurt her feelings any more, after she had already lost so much.

"Now Missus Thompson, Jenny, have I done anything to make you think I was pushing my affections on you? No? Good, because while you are a handsome woman and I'm sure would make any man a good wife, I am not ready to take another wife at this time."

He could see her deflate, a great disappointment come over her. It was not that there were true feelings for him. It would have been a marriage of convenience, something very common on the frontier and not all that uncommon even in the more settled portions of the colony. Now she had no idea what was to become of her and her daughter and the world suddenly looked very cruel indeed. She turned to leave.

"Don't go just yet, Jenny. Sit and let's talk a bit." They took chairs opposite each other and Edward went on, choosing his words carefully. "You own three horses, the three I brought back to you. We've seen your cow and a few hogs around your farm on our patrols, those are yours as well. And then there is the land itself."

"Oh, but Colonel, we haven't satisfied Mister Bordon on the land yet, so we don't have a deed. We needed to make the last payment this fall, only now I won't be able to do so."

"Think, you may not own the land outright, but you have made payment on it and Mister Bordon is not an unreasonable man. I'm sure we can persuade him to purchase back the land for what it is worth today. You also have three guns, two of them rifle guns, and all the accouterments that go with them. So there are options for you."

"Yes, I suppose I can sell the farm back. I have no idea how to do that or what would be a fair price. And what am I to do when it's sold? Where am I to go then?"

"First things first. Now that you know you're not destitute, there's no reason to make hasty decisions. As with the McNulty's last fall, you are welcome to remain with us for the time being. We'll bring in your livestock so that they are here and under your control rather than risk them being claimed by others in your absence. I'll ask my father to take you over to see Mister Bordon, not to sell your land, not just yet, but to see what kind of offer he would make. It might be better to sell to another and pay Mister Bordon out of the proceeds. Father can advise you best on these matters."

Dabbing her eyes with her kerchief, Missus Thompson felt a lot better. Yes, it would have been good to marry someone as rich and prominent as the Colonel to secure their future, but this may be just as well. While he seemed a good man, she knew how terrible he was fighting the Indians so he could be prone to beat her just as Tommy had regularly done. Maybe, just maybe, remaining a widow a little while would be better. And if they had the protection of the Jewett's, she knew they would be safe.

She looked up at Edward's kind face and nodded, then stood and walked to the door. He rose and followed. Opening the door, she paused and looked back at him, giving him her best, most fetching smile and said, "I would have made you a good wife, you know." And with that she was gone.

Sarah and Rebecca Thompson had become friends, so the Thompson's moved into Robert's cabin. With now four women under his roof, he spent more of his time either in the blockhouse, where he had set up a small office to do his books, or at Edward's cabin. This was fine with Philip. Now when he was spending time with his grandfather in the evenings he was also spending time with his uncle. One evening, as the three of them sat quietly reading in Edward's cabin, Robert closed his book and looked up at Edward.

"I'm taking Missus Thompson over to see Mister Bordon tomorrow to discuss options on her land."

"Good, let me know how it turns out," said Edward, rather distractedly.

"You dodged a bullet this time, son. And it came close!" Robert said, chuckling. Philip started laughing harder than he had laughed since the Indian fight.

Chapter 36

"What do you think you're doing, sending Charles off like this?" Mary screeched at Edward. "Joseph is dead and now you're putting my Charles out there for the same thing to happen to him. You can't do this to me!"

"Mary, Charles is going along with his grandfather and Philip as they drive Missus Thompson to see Mister Bordon. That's all. The patrols have returned no Indian sign in well over a week and father is hardly Tommy Thompson. He won't be rushing into any Indian ambush."

"Charles shouldn't be out of the fort! He needs to stay here where he's safe. He's all I've got and you can't have him!"

Edward looked over at Henry, who was looking very uncomfortable at Mary's outburst. "Mary, have you forgotten your daughter?"

"What? What do you mean by that? We're talking about Charles, not Sarah. I won't allow Charles to leave the walls of this fort, where I know he'll be safe."

"Mary, Charles wants to go with his grandfather. Edward didn't tell him to go. I really think you're making too much of this," inserted Henry, not wishing to further aggravate his wife but unable to remain quiet any longer.

Mary now turned her attention to him, "You want him to go off and get killed like Joseph? Are you that heartless and uncaring?"

"That's not what I said!" retorted Henry, in an unusually curt response to his wife. "We can't lock him in the cabin to keep him safe. He's just as safe with his grandfather as he is with me, maybe safer."

"Oh, I'll say he'd be safer! Don't think I've forgotten you nearly getting him frozen to death last winter when you got stuck in the snowstorm on the mountain."

"Enough!" Edward had finally had all he intended to take. "Charles is riding out with his cousin and grandfather this morning and will be back, safe and sound, tomorrow morning. That's all there is to it. If you were still back in Boston, he'd be starting an apprenticeship and under his master's control. Here, his apprenticeship requires him to learn how to survive on the frontier. I won't allow the boy to be endangered because you coddle him out of your own fears. Now, get out of my cabin, both of you!"

Edward hated being so rough with Henry. He really did not deserve that harsh treatment. Ever since the latest Indian problem, Mary had not allowed Charles to leave the fort, barely even allowing him out of their cabin except for their communal meals under the awning. So when Charles learned Philip was accompanying their grandfather to Mister Bordon's "to protect him," Charles begged Edward to be allowed to go. He hated being locked in the fort and even felt he had been left out when Joseph and Philip went with Edward, Lewis, and Henry to recapture Marie from the Indians.

"Is it safe to come in?" asked Robert as he stuck his head in the door, grinning.

"Oh, father, come on in. Safe? Probably depends on who you ask."

"I understand things did not go well and Mary is very angry about Charles going with me today. Of course, you're who she's angry with, not me."

"She has become obsessed with protecting Charles, doesn't want him to go anywhere or do anything," observed Edward. "The poor boy can't live that way and I can't allow it. I do hope you agree. I told her that Charles was going and then invited her to leave."

"Threw her out is a better description. What, I can't help overhearing when you shout like that! I'm glad you did. Charles needs to get out and I want to spend more time with him. It's pretty hard when she has him locked in their cabin most of every day."

"You know the boys think I'm sending them along to protect you, don't you?" Robert nodded. "I see no harm in them feeling important in this way. And besides, after barring Marie from riding alone, I can hardly allow you out without suitable escort."

Robert first patted Edward on the back, then pulled him in for a hug. "I'll take care of them, Edward, not to worry. Remember, they're my grandsons. You're only their uncle, a very special uncle, it's true, but I love them both, also."

"You know I'm right, father. If we didn't come out here, both of them, and Joseph, would have been signed out for an apprenticeship by now. I can't help but believe this will be better for them, even if there are more risks."

"If we doubted it, we never would have left Rowley. Now, I'm off. Good luck with 'her majesty' while I'm gone. Oh, and look in on your sister and the girls now and again. There are too many women in that cabin and they need a steadying hand from time to time." The two men enjoyed a laugh, and then they walked out of the cabin into the morning light.

Philip and Charles were armed and mounted, ready to go, and Missus Thompson was sitting on Robert's riding chair, holding Robert's gun. Everyone was there to see them off, except for Mary who was nowhere to be seen. Henry's last words to Charles were "Behave yourself and listen to your grandfather."

The whole family turned out to see them off. The mothers waved goodbyes to their sons who were too proud of having a grown-up assignment to wave back. After they had driven off and everyone started moving back to their chores, Edward approached his brothers. "Well, Lewis, with Henry building furniture for the entire Valley and the laborers' cabin finished, what are we going to do to keep you busy? How big is the biggest wheel you've ever made?"

"Biggest wheel? What do you mean?"

"Well, a Mister Agner is a miller I met in Beverly's Mill Place. He couldn't find work at Mister Beverly's mills and asked if we could use him. I told him to come by the first of June, so we're likely to see him any time now. Do you suppose you could build us a mill down the creek a little piece?"

"Oh, I can build a water wheel, with the help of our laborers, and I can put up the building, but I have no idea about the inner gears of a mill. I can make them. I just don't know the size or orientation of them."

"Well, Mister Agner claims to be an expert on mills and capable of putting one together if I could supply people to build the building and wheels."

"Okay, then, I'll start looking for a site. May I suggest we use the creek here below the fort? I think keeping it close will serve our interests better."

"I agree and leave the actual site selection to you. Talk to Sam, I think we can spare the four laborers who just finished work on the cabin to start the mill. Then there will be a miller's cabin, don't forget."

Robert's visit with Mister Bordon was not exactly successful, though they all returned without incident, as expected. Mister Bordon purchased his large land holdings for a penny an acre and sold it for a shilling an acre. The Thompsons still owed £4, due in October. If he did not receive it, the land reverted back to him and he saw no need to purchase it back for even a portion of the £4 the Thompson's had already paid. Jenny Thompson had been devastated. Robert told her not to panic, they would work out something.

"Missus Thompson, what if I was to buy the farm from you for the full £8. That would give you the money to make the final payment and, once you have the deed, you sign it over to me," Edward proposed. Robert smiled having been confident Edward would do exactly this. "I have two indentured families whom I owe 50 acres each at the end of their indenture, so you see, I can use your farm to satisfy this requirement."

Knowing Edward could have deeded the 100 acres out of his estate at no cost made this offer all the more unexpected to Jenny. She did not know what to say at this obvious generosity from a man who had previously declined when she offered herself to him. She was confused. "Are you sure? You needn't buy any land to give them their lands and yet here you offer to purchase my farm. I don't understand why."

"I have my reasons and the £8 will work no hardship on me and will allow me to meet my obligations without reducing my estates. So, Missus Thompson, have we a deal?"

Jenny looked to Robert, saw his approving smile and then nodded her agreement. Both men rose as she did. She first moved to Robert and, placing a hand on his shoulder, leaned up and kissed his cheek. Then, as she passed Edward, she paused, put her hand behind his head and kissed him full on the mouth before passing quickly out the door.

"She may land you yet, Edward. You need to be more careful!" laughed Robert.

Returning to Robert's cabin and finding Esther alone at the table sewing, Jenny finally got up the courage she needed. "Esther, forgive me for asking such an indelicate question, but why is the Colonel so opposed to marriage? Is it me or is there more to it?"

Esther slowly put her sewing aside, weighing the words she would use carefully before beginning. "Edward married young to a woman he had known most of his life. He loved her deeply, still does if truth be told." Here she paused to find the right way to proceed. "After a while it became apparent that she was slowly going mad. Edward did his best to help her, but nothing worked. In the end, she died by her own hand. He blames himself for it. We all hoped he would get over it, would see that he had done all he could, but it's been nearly seven years and he still can't bring himself to talk about her."

"Oh, Esther, I had no idea about any of this! I feel so foolish"

In the loft, Sarah, who had been listening and learning of her uncle's sad story for the first time, muffled her sobs into her pillow lest Aunt Esther discover she had been listening.

Lewis picked a site for the mill downstream from the fort, where the stream curved and there was a low place suitable for a mill pond. Mister Agner showed up, as scheduled, ready to go to work to build a mill. He came complete with all the tools he needed to cut millstones and maintain a mill. Edward put half of their laborers to work building a mill and cabin for Mister Agner near the mill site, the other half continuing their field work. They would be able to get two cuttings off the meadow this year.

Henry worked on building furniture to order for the neighboring farmers. Charles and Philip would help by splitting down the larger pieces of wood Henry would then shape or plane. Philip also helped his father on the mill, though Charles was not permitted to venture that far from the fort. It was surprising Mary allowed him as far as the barn, where Henry was doing his work. Charles really chaffed under these restrictions, all the while knowing neither he nor his father could successfully argue against his mother.

Mary had started taking her meals in their cabin instead of joining everyone else under the awning. Henry and Charles would eat with them, and then Henry would take a plate of food to Mary. Robert was not going to insist she take her meals with them, but he did insist she come out and do her share of the work, both in preparing the meals and in helping gather the hay the laborers cut. The whole time Mary was in the field, she was noticeably nervous and as soon as the work was done, she practically ran back into the fort and her cabin.

Robert and Henry discussed the problem and found no solutions. She was gripped by fear, fear for her safety and especially fear for Charles'. Robert tried to talk to her only she would not talk to him. She simply brushed him off saying, "I'm doing my share of the work and that's all you need concern yourself with."

Mary and Sarah no longer spoke. Sarah could not

understand what the problem was, at first thinking it was something about her, but Esther assured her the problem was with her mother, not her. Over the past year, Esther had become more Sarah's mother than Mary, both Esther and Sarah seeming very content with the arrangement. Henry still stayed close to Sarah, or as close as he was able without angering Mary for she watched him closely when he was in the fort. That was why most people talked to Henry while he was working in the barn these days, it was easier.

"Edward, I'm really worried about Mary. We thought she'd come around after a while, but she hasn't shown any signs of it, none at all. In fact, it seems worse rather than better," Robert told Edward one evening while Philip was spending time with his father instead of them.

"I'm worried as well. Her fears are totally unwarranted and unreasonable and nothing any of us have said or done has had any effect at all. Joseph wasn't even her son, she had barely gotten to know him, and yet Marie has recovered from the loss while Mary has not."

"What this is doing to Charles and Henry, well, I'm worried and don't know what to do. This helpless feeling bothers me more than anything."

"Forgive me for saying this, but you know I've been through something like this before. I fear she may be going mad."

They sat in the gathering darkness, both trying to think of how to help their kinswoman, hoping for the best but fearing the worst.

☙ *Chapter 37* ❧

The boys were captivated by Mister Agner's work to create the grinding stones. First he had them searching for a stone of a certain size and shape. They found several that they thought met his criteria, only to have them rejected upon his inspection. Why remained a mystery to them. Finally they found one that met his approval and he set to work, first rounding the stone and flattening the top side with his heavy hammers. Once rounded, he called in the laborers and, using trees as fulcrums, they rolled the stone onto the now flattened side and he went to work on the bottom, making it as flat as the top.

With this done, he again needed help to set the stone on its side where he had it braced securely before using his chisels to split the stone almost perfectly in half, making two round stones each with one flat side. He went to work now on making the grinding sides of the stones and cutting a square hole in the center of each. He was at this work for many weeks, working slowly and accurately.

Charles had found he could go with his father to the barn as if he were helping in making furniture. Once there and using the barn to shield him from view from the fort, he would slip down to the creek and follow it to the new mill site where he met up with Philip. As long as his father did not let it slip and he stayed out of sight of the fort, he felt safe from his mother finding out.

Lewis made good progress on the water wheel, having it ready when the mill building was ready to receive it. Mister Agner sketched out the interior gears and shafts and Lewis set to work making those. It would not be a large mill, but it would be a well-built one.

The neighbors got into the habit of stopping by to see how the mill was progressing. Having one close by would save them a lot of time hauling their corn and wheat to Beverly's Mill Place for grinding. The very fact the mill would be done by harvest had caused all of the local families to plant more corn this year than they had in the past, previously planting little more than what they needed for their own use. Now their ground corn would become a cash crop for them. With their debts for the land coming due, they all needed as much credit or cash as they could get. Having the Jewett family for neighbors was working out to their advantage in more and more ways.

Tom McCrary brought his new neighbor by one day to meet the Colonel and see the fort. The Rice's had just purchased 160 acres bounding the McCrary's and the McNulty's farmsteads and were just starting to build their cabin. Jim Rice was stout and strong and carried a rifle gun he claimed to be fairly good with. His wife was Melinda and they had one teenage daughter, Caitlyn, the same age as Sarah and Rebecca Thompson. The three girls hit it off well and Melinda and Caitlyn came by as often as their chores would allow. Henry was, naturally, enlisted to build them needed furniture items.

After supper one evening, Esther found Edward sitting alone outside the fort walls and joined him.

"Have you noticed how the number of visits by the local women with marriage age daughters has decreased significantly since Jenny Thompson moved in?"

"I've been busy supervising planting of orchards and cornfields, so I can't say I've really noticed who has, or hasn't, been visiting. I assume you have a point to make."

"Well, it seems the local ladies have the mistaken idea that you and Jenny will now marry, her being a destitute widow and all. I know, I know, you're not interested and you've told her so. That hasn't stopped the others from assuming it and she isn't doing anything to dissuade them of their beliefs. I just thought you should know."

Edward sat thinking for a moment before answering. "Now let me see. Jenny knows I'm not interested and is leaving me alone now that I've made my intentions clear. The other women of the county have stopped parading their marriage age daughters by me hoping I'll select one of them. I get left alone by all. I must say, I fail to see a problem here."

Both enjoyed a laugh before Esther got serious again. "You know, Edward, it has been a long time and it wouldn't hurt you to start thinking about marrying again. I'm not suggesting Jenny or any of the local women, what with all you've done and your education they are hardly who I would see you with, though Jenny still has eyes for you. You shouldn't be alone."

"You're a fine one to talk, Esther Jewett! Here you are, well-off and single yourself, you'd be a fine catch for a widower of means," Edward retorted, laughing again before turning serious. "No, dear sister, we won't be alone, not as long as we have each other." He took her hand and patted it. She laid her head against his shoulder, and they sat watching the stars which always seemed so brilliant in the time between full dark and moonrise.

Robert had started up lessons again for his grand-children and Rebecca, an hour in the evenings after daily chores were done and before supper. He enlisted Edward from time to time when one of his experiences fit with the lesson they were studying. Like when he gave them lessons in geography, he had Edward tell about the different places he had been, including his mission to the Dey of Algiers in North Africa. Philip and Charles were especially spellbound by their uncle's experiences.

The end of July brought a stranger to the fort looking for Edward. It turned out he was a post rider for the Governor and delivered to Edward a summons to come to Williamsburg for a special session of the Governor's Council to discuss Indian problems on the frontier. The Governor considered Edward's presence vital to the success of the meeting and his letter urged Edward most emphatically to attend if at all possible. The meeting was set for mid-August, giving Edward just over two weeks to make the long journey to the capital.

Edward sent Sarah to gather Lewis from the mill site and Henry from the barn as he went to the blockhouse to find Robert. They all gathered in Edward's cabin and Robert read them the Governor's letter.

"You really have no choice, you must go," Henry said, the first to speak.

"Everything is under control here. Miles is a good overseer for the farming, I'm working with Mister Agner on the mill site, and Henry is busy building furniture. None of these require your immediate presence," added Lewis.

"You're both right, of course. I'll take Aaron, naturally, but who else is to go?"

Henry was again the first to speak, "I've been covering for Charles for weeks now to give the boy a little freedom. That's one thing. Asking Mary to allow him to accompany you to Williamsburg? Well, that's not something I want to bring up."

"Philip could go, though it might seem like you're choosing favorites by always taking him along with you, like when you went to Court in April. Charles got to go, but only because father followed along," Lewis pointed out.

"I guess that settles it, then. Father, you and I shall go to Williamsburg. You can sit with Mister Prentiss and go over your books with his while I'm occupied with the Governor and his Council."

Robert was taken by surprise at this turn in the conversation, but recovered quickly and smiled, "Who knows, while you're off with the Council, I might just find some merry widow to keep me company." They all laughed, knowing this was a kidding reference to Jenny Thompson kissing Edward with thoughts of improving her circumstances.

When the announcement was made at supper, Philip was beside himself. He could go, wanted to go, and did not want to be left out. Lewis calmed him telling him he needed Philip's help to get the mill running on time and, besides, they could not spare another in case the Indians made another vengeance raid on the fort. He would be sorely needed here should that happen. This placated Philip, a little, though not enough for him not to raise the question again as he, his uncle and grandfather were sitting in Edward's cabin reading that evening. The answer, however, did not change.

The next evening, as these same three sat around Edward's cabin again reading his books, of which there were many, there came a knock at the door. Answering the knock, Edward welcomed Sam and Jubal into his cabin. Both men had very serious looks on their faces portending the importance they gave the subject.

"Colonel, you'll be going right by Master Glad-stone's plantation on your way to Williamsburg." Edward nodded and Sam continued, "Well, we were hoping you would see your way clear to stop in on Master Gladstone and ask if you could purchase me, Jubal, Rachael, and Sally. We really want to stay with you and, now with the baby close, I don't want Rachael and my child to have to go back to that plantation." Jubal nodded his agreement in emphasis at all the key points.

Edward first looked to Robert, who was taken aback by the request and really offered no assistance or opinion at this point. Edward then dropped his chin in thought for a few minutes. The two men stood, feeling awkward but knowing better than to interrupt Edward's thought. After what felt to them to be hours though really only a minute or two, Edward spoke.

"Sam, you and Jubal are much prized by Mister Gladstone and I'm not sure he'd be willing to sell you, even if I could afford the price he'd ask for you. I'm more confident I could arrange to purchase the two women and, by extension, your child. You know, however, that I, like my father, am against owning other human beings and to purchase you goes against my convictions. And what of the other six, how can I arrange to purchase only you two and not them without their feeling betrayed?"

Jubal now spoke for the first time, "Colonel, we talked, all of us and not just Sam and me. The others want to stay with you as well, that's true. They also know it would be very expensive for you to purchase us all and would reduce the chance of Master Gladstone agreeing to the sale. As long as you bring them back again next year, they're willing to wait, hoping you could purchase more of them next year until all would be able to stay." This time it was Sam's turn to nod in agreement at the important points.

"Edward, I can talk to the others and satisfy myself on the depth of their agreement with this plan. In any case, it doesn't solve our immediate question of how we are to resolve the conflict between our beliefs and purchasing slaves." Now turning to Sam and Jubal, Robert continued, "While we are willing to consider your proposal, it would be very difficult for us to actually purchase another human being and remain who we are. So while it seems a simple request to you, involving only money, to us it involves our conscience and we'll have to think and pray hard to come to our decision. I see you're disappointed. Don't be. We will consider your request and try to find a solution that will be best for all concerned." He then told them they could go assured they would work to find a solution.

"Philip?"

"Yes, grandfather?"

"Please run home and ask your father to join us here. Oh, and there's no reason for you to come back. You can stay with your mother this evening."

Showing his disappointment, Philip paused in the doorway. "Do you want me to send Uncle Henry also?

"No, we don't need you to go for him. Just ask your father to join us and your task is done." Reluctantly, Philip left the cabin and headed across the little street toward his home.

Waiting for Lewis to arrive, Robert and Edward sat looking at each other in silence, weighing the importance of what was being asked of them. When Lewis arrived, Robert gave a quick summary of Sam and Jubal's request before they fell into intense discussion. It continued late into the night and, the next morning, Robert found opportunities to talk with each of the other six laborers and confirmed what Sam and Jubal had told them the night before.

Meeting again after supper, they weighed this new information and refined their plan on how to proceed. Then they called Sam and Jubal to Edward's cabin.

"Sam, Jubal, I will meet with Mister Gladstone and discuss the purchase you proposed last night. It goes against our beliefs, but we are willing to enter into a discussion. I can not tell you I will affect your purchase. It is dependent on Mister Gladstone. All I can tell you now is that we will discuss it with him and see if some accommodation can be reached," Edward explained

Sam and Jubal were happy beyond description. Robert tried to dampen their hopes, again pointing out that ultimately it would be up to Mister Gladstone, to no avail. The next morning, as Robert, Edward, and Aaron left the little fort, all of the laborers were there in high spirits as they saw them off. After goodbyes to the family, the three travelers began their long journey to the Colony's capital.

❧ *Chapter 38* ❧

*L*ewis was, as usual these days, working at the mill when Tom McCrary rode up with a large boy in tow. "Lewis, this boy here needs your assistance with a broken down wagon."

Lewis noticed the boy was mounted on a draft horse still wearing harness. "What's your name, boy, and what seems to be the problem?"

"My name is Boone, Daniel Boone, and I'm moving some of my family down the Virginia road to join my father and the rest of the family in the Yadkin River valley. I skirted a boulder in the road but my cousin, driving the following wagon, hit it hard and broke a wheel. McCrary here says you're accomplished at repairing wheels and thought you could help us."

Lewis looked the boy over. He was large, about 17 or maybe 18, his size made guessing his age uncertain, dressed like a hunter and carried rather carelessly a well-used rifle. He had an air of a braggart about him and Lewis took an immediate dislike to him. Be that as it may, the boy's family was in trouble and he might be able to help them.

Turning to Philip and Charles, "Go saddle my horse and two packhorses to carry my tools. Bring them here so we can load up the tools."

The two boys, who had been eyeing the stranger closely, broke into a run toward the meadow by the stockade where the horses were grazing. Lewis saw Charles' mistake but there was nothing he could do about it. The boys had barely cleared the rise when Mary's voice could be heard calling at Charles. Lewis could not see what was happening as he packed up his tools, but Mary continued to call and each was more frantic than the one before.

It was not long before Philip and Charles were back, mounted on their own horses and leading Lewis' and the packhorses.

"And just where do you two think you're going?" asked Lewis.

"With you," they both answered together as a breathless Henry came running into their midst.

"Charles, you've really done it now! Your mother saw you come, not from the barn, but from the mill and she is hopping mad."

"Father, I've been practically a prisoner and I want to get out, to go with Uncle Lewis, and not be trapped within sight of mother and the blockhouse."

"I know, I know. Go ahead then. We'll both be in for it when you return, but go ahead." Looking to Lewis, "I may need a place to sleep tonight, if you've room in your loft."

Young Boone looked on humorously at this exchange, as did Tom McCrary. Tom had the advantage over Daniel, however, in that he knew Mary and also knew what had been going on around the little fort with Mary desperately trying to hold Charles to her while he looked for ways to escape.

Henry headed back to his furniture making when Lewis, the boys, Boone, and McCrary left for the Virginia Road. He was in no hurry to face his wife and if he could put it off until Charles was safely back, so much the better. At least then he would not have to listen to her voice her fears of all the things that might happen to the boy the whole time they were gone.

Lewis rode next to Daniel and their conversation soon turned to hunting. Daniel confirmed what Lewis had already surmised, that he had taken up hunting as his profession. True to his suspicions, Daniel also added that he was an amazingly good shot, at least according to the boy.

"I hope the repairs won't take long as I'm anxious to get back to hunting. The deer hides taken while they're still red, before they take on the winter's grey color, command higher prices in Philadelphia," Daniel told Lewis, who was unfamiliar with the fur trade particulars.

"You've been to Philadelphia?" asked Philip, never far from any conversation his father was having.

"I'm just returning from there. Sold my winter pelts at a good price before helping my uncle and his family remove to the Yadkin."

Daniel let it out that while he had made a good profit from the sale, he was returning home with nothing left, having gone on a spree after buying powder, lead, and a new shirt that left him with nothing to show for his efforts. Lewis looked over his shoulder, now regretting having the boys along. He now knew Daniel would not be a good influence on them.

They arrived at the two wagons soon enough, were introduced around, and then looked to the wheel. As he had been told, the left front wheel of the following wagon was well broken. Looking it over, he announced his findings, "Well, I'll need to fashion a couple of spokes and re-place the wood rim. You're lucky in that the iron rim is only bent. We'll still need to take it to the McNulty farm. He has a forge and can straighten it out for us. Tom, if you wouldn't mind doing that for us, it would speed up the repairs considerably. By time you get back, I should have the rest of the wheel about put together."

George Boone, Jr., the uncle to young Daniel, stayed by Lewis, helping him as he went about his task of rebuild-ing the wheel. Lewis noted the strong contrast between uncle and nephew. While Daniel was already a tough back-woodsman, even at his relatively young age, George was more refined and a member of the Society of Friends, as were his wife and children. Lewis did not ask but it was clear Daniel was better categorized as a "former" member of the Society.

The boys stayed with Daniel, eventually setting up a shooting contest between the three of them and Daniel's two cousins. After soundly beating all four competitors, Daniel then went on to demonstrate some trick shooting, like holding his rifle in only one hand and still hitting his mark. Lewis continued to work but managed to keep an eye on the boys at the same time.

"Friend, your nephew seems a bit vain and vulgar, quite unlike what I would expect from a distinguished fam-ily such as yours. I do hope he won't have too negative an influence on my son and nephew."

"Daniel is a handful for his father, that is true. Of course, his father was a handful for our father in his day as well. The acorn doesn't fall far from the oak. He is all you say, but he does have his good qualities. No, he prefers the woods to the field and reading animal sign to reading books, and is perfectly at home with the long hunters. He has taken his first long hunt and did quite well, not that he has anything left to show for it. I think your children will be fine in his company, so long as you correct any of Daniel's ways that may rub off."

Lewis worked quickly and soon had the disassembled wheel reassembled waiting for the iron rim to tie all the parts together into one. Tom McCrary returned with the rim late in the afternoon and Lewis, with the help of George and Tom, fitted it to the wheel. Once all was reassembled, it took all three men to heave the wagon while Daniel set the repaired wheel into place. Philip and Charles had the job of greasing the hub, which they seemed to relish, and before sunset the job was done.

Waving aside the offer of payment, Lewis simply asked that they remember the kindness and return it should the opportunity ever present itself. Then the three headed back for their cabins and to face the wrath of Charles' mother.

Arriving back home just before full dark, they did not have long to wait for Mary was pacing at the entrance to the stockade and started shouting for Charles before they had even alighted from their horses. Once assuring herself Charles was fine, she started in on Lewis.

"How could you take my son out of the protection of this fort? How you endanger you own son is your business but you have no right to endanger mine."

"Now, Mary, Charles has been in no danger today and, as you can see, I return him to you unharmed," replied Lewis, trying to avoid prolonging the scene. He looked to Henry, who was standing nearby with Marie, but Henry kept his head down and would not return his look.

"In no danger!" Mary shrieked. "How can you say such a thing when you yourself have already lost one son to Indians and nearly lost another to a wild beast?"

Turning her attention now to Charles, "And you,

young man, I now know you have been sneaking around, going beyond the barn with your father. From now on you will stay within the walls of this fort!"

Charles was about to protest but Lewis, who felt his own anger rising, cut him off. "No, Mary, he won't! He has chores to do just like Philip and those chores take him outside the walls of this fort. The same goes for you. Ever since father and Edward left, you have stayed inside the fort and neglected your chores. From now on you will do your share just as Charles is going to do his! Enough of this. Marie, we're hungry, is supper ready?" With that he turned and walked away from Mary and toward the awning where everyone else was gathered, pretending not to be noticing the scene over near the blockhouse.

Charles and Henry joined them for supper but Mary was noticeably absent. Later, after everyone had turned toward their own cabins and Charles and Henry could put it off no longer, they returned to theirs. Mary's loud voice could be heard for hours after they entered their cabin, berating her husband and son.

The next day Lewis was good as his word, sending Charles with Philip to bring in the horses and Mary to the creek to fetch water. That finished, he then sent Mary off with Jenny, Esther, and Sarah to help gather the cut hay from the far meadow.

When they all gathered for dinner, Mary was again absent, choosing instead to take her meal in her cabin. Before Henry could take a plate of food to her, Lewis intervened again.

"Henry, she had the chance to eat with us, she chose not to. Taking her food will only encourage her behavior. If she wants to eat, she is welcome to join us."

"She is not going to like that," came Henry's nervous reply.

"I know, and I also know I am setting you up for another berating like you received last night. For that I'm sorry. However, you know father and Edward would say the same thing. She has to learn that this behavior is not going to gain her anything. Then she will stop. Just like she went and did her chores today. Now, please tell her the horse trough needs filled for the night."

Henry rolled his eyes before slowly walking to his cabin to deliver the message. After a short pause, the door was flung open and out stormed Mary. She grabbed up the water buckets and brushed past Lewis on her way to the gate, nearly knocking him down in the process.

"You know," Marie said as she came to Lewis' side, "likely as not all the water will have boiled out of those buckets before she gets them back up from the creek." She then smiled up at Lewis who could not help but smile back.

Chapter 39

Edward rode part of the way over the mountain on the riding chair with Robert so they could talk easier about their upcoming meeting with Mister Gladstone. At these times, Aaron always followed a respectable distance behind so as not to intrude on the conversation. Aaron had grown to like and respect both of these men and as much as he would relish his release from the indenture, he was not looking forward to having to leave their service. They had been kind to him and never had asked of him anything they were unwilling to do themselves. Quite the contrary, usually they worked together, something he found both unusual and refreshing.

Though the weather was warm, they had a pleasant trip over the Blue Ridge and down the other side. After several days, they came to Mister Gladstone's plantation where they were warmly greeted by the entire household. After a fine dinner, Robert and Edward followed Mister Gladstone to his office to discuss business. The immediate outcome was Mister Gladstone's slaves would remain with the Jewett family until Edward and Robert returned from Williamsburg. At that time, after Mister Gladstone had sufficient time to reflect on the proposal, they would decide what was to be done. Mister Gladstone wrote out the note authorizing the extension and promised to pass it to the next rider heading toward the Valley for delivery to Lewis.

Invited to remain the night and refresh themselves, Robert spent a pleasant evening regaling the Gladstone sons with the stories of their Indian fights. Edward, on the other hand, was cornered by the women of his household to tell of London and His Majesty's Court. And when he mentioned spending a year and a half in Algiers among the Mohammedans they just could not believe all the things he had seen and done. The questioning continued all through supper and up until Mister Gladstone drove them from the room so their guests could relax before turning in.

From the Gladstone's plantation, they made their way to Mister MacDonald's landing and found two boats about to return to Richmond Town empty. Hiring them to carry the riding chair, horses, and themselves, they found half the crews of these boats had participated in the fight against the river pirates and were very glad to have fallen in with them again. This made the days on the river pass very pleasantly and, traveling with the current, they made excellent time.

Arriving in Williamsburg at mid-day, they made their way directly to Mister Prentiss' store where they found him engaged in business in his office. With a large grin he invited them in and introduced them to Mister John Dandridge.

"We can't stay long, Mister Prentiss, as we still need to arrange lodging for our stay," Robert said, trying to gracefully exit so Misters Prentiss and Dandridge could continue their business.

"I might be able to help you there," said Mister Dandridge. "I inherited a house just up the street from my father-in-law and where I stay whenever business brings me to town. There is his office just adjacent that I do not use. It has a large room on the ground floor and another in the garret. Please, accept my invitation to use it for as long as you need it."

"If you are sure it would be no inconvenience," replied Robert after getting a nod from Edward.

"It's settled then. I'll send my manservant over to have it readied for you and in the meantime perhaps you'll join me for dinner at the Raleigh. Mister Prentiss, you're invited as well."

Before leaving the store, Edward wrote out a note for Aaron to deliver to the Governor's secretary announcing their arrival and informing him of where they would be lodging. After delivering the note, Aaron was to get his dinner and then help prepare their lodgings and see to stabling the horses.

Over dinner, Mister Dandridge told how he and his wife, Fanny, had nearly sold off her father's Williamsburg house because they came to town so infrequently. Now, however, since their daughter Patsy had married Daniel Parke Custis, they were coming to town more frequently to see the young couple and, now, their grandson. Although the couple had inherited White House Plantation in New Kent County on the death of John Custis, they spent more of their time at their house in Williamsburg. Mister Dandridge promised an introduction as Daniel Parke Custis was now one of the richest men in the Colony and sat on the Governor's Council as a result.

The following morning Edward called upon the Clerk of the Colony to inquire about his pay. He found waiting for him £5,000 in coin, quite a bit more than he was anticipating, and a letter from Lord Halifax. In the letter, Lord Halifax stated that, as he had agreed to serve as a military advisor to Governor Dinwiddie, Lord Halifax had petitioned to have him reinstated at full pay for as long as he continued to serve in this capacity.

The letter continued informing Edward of Lord Halifax's fear the French were intent on cutting the English Colonies off from the Ohio Country. This had to be countered and he hoped, as this region primarily fell within the charter of the Virginia Colony, Edward would help Governor Dinwiddie find a way to counter this threat to English interests.

"Edward, you look perplexed. Is it bad news?" asked Robert.

"No, not really, and yet it could be very bad news for a certain family living on the frontier. It seems London believes the French will try to cut us off at the mountains just west of us, retaining the Ohio Country for their Indian allies. The only way they could hope to do this is by using those Indian allies against us, principally the Shawnee down where we are."

"That would mean more raids like the one we just endured. I'm not sure how much more our neighbors will take before they start leaving the frontier. And that would leave us very much exposed, don't you think?"

"It would indeed. Our little fort has served us well against a hunting party and intimidated a small raiding party. Against a concerted attack by a large war party, I don't think we'd fare as well. Though I think we'd give a good account of ourselves. No, if we're out there alone, the best thing for us would be to join our neighbors retiring east of the Blue Ridge. That would leave the entire Valley open to the Indians and, ultimately the French."

"Then I suppose that will be the focus of your discussions with the Governor and his Council."

Meeting in the Council Room of the newly rebuilt Capitol, that was exactly the thrust of the discussion. Edward found himself called upon frequently, not only because of his military experience in general, but because of his recent experience fighting these same Indians. The state of affairs as Edward relayed them did nothing to ease the anxiety over the difficulty of the situation.

Edward and Robert were invited to dinner with the Custis' and found them to be quite the odd couple. Daniel was in his forties, had never been married previously, and was a bit dour. Patsy, a pet name for her given name of Martha, was nearly half his age and full of life and spirit. She liked bright colors and decorated their home with bright, colorful fabrics. She was taken by Robert's riding chair and had to take him out to the carriage house to show him her London-built carriage she used only in Williamsburg and never over the rough roads outside of the village, even though their plantation was not far.

Remaining his charming self, Patsy became very fond of Robert and father and son found themselves invited to the Custis house on a regular and frequent basis. After dinner or supper, Daniel and Edward usually excused themselves to continue their discussions from the Council meetings while Patsy and Robert would sit and chat or, occasionally, take a ride either in the London coach or sometimes on Robert's riding chair. Frequently these rides ended at the Dandridge house where they would visit with Patsy's parents.

Governor Dinwiddie had Edward pen a bill that would create a Virginia Regiment to protect the settlers in the Ohio Country. He then had Edward, resplendent in his regimentals, meeting with key members of the House of Burgesses to convince them of the need to authorize and fund the regiment. He also wrote out an organization for the regiment and included recommendations on arms and equipment. All this drug their stay in Williamsburg out until the beginning of November when they finally were allowed to quit the Capitol and start their way home.

By now Robert and Edward were both anxious over the safety of their family. The hunting season was in full swing and they had no news of whether the Indians had returned to molest either the Jewetts or their neighbors. Indian deprivations further north and west were being reported, especially for those settlers who had moved west of the Alleghenies into the Ohio country. They determined the quickest way was overland in this season and planned to get started as soon as possible.

Before they could leave, the Governor insisted on hosting them at a ball in the Palace. Edward and Robert had everything packed and ready to go before attending the ball. It was a grand affair with the entire Council and their ladies attending. Despite their interest in departing, they were unable to leave the ball until well into the early hours of the next morning. Neither would let their lack of sleep keep them from departing Williamsburg at first light the next day, while some of their fellow revelers were still on the streets heading home from the ball.

They kept up a fast pace, as fast as they could without killing the horses. When they finally made it to Mister Gladstone's plantation, they were all bone weary and the horses were nearly played out. Looking up at the Blue Ridge not far distant, they could see snow had already blanketed the upper reaches. Therefore, they accepted Mister Gladstone's invitation to remain a few days while their horses recovered.

This also allowed Mister Gladstone and Edward to discuss the status of the slaves. It was no longer a secret that Mister Gladstone was in need of ready money to cover his debts brought about by the falling tobacco prices. That is what inspired him to lease out his slaves in the first place and the tobacco market had not improved very much. The large planters, who had access to fresh acres, had weathered the low prices by planting more tobacco. This had done nothing to stabilize or raise the price and was especially hard on the middling planters who lacked access to more land.

Mister Gladstone wanted £660 for all ten slaves while Edward thought the value of the lot was closer to £450, not all of the men being worth the same amount as Sam and Jubal. It was Robert who finally broke the impasse.

"Now Mister Gladstone, I ask you, are you better off with, say, £450 in coin or with £650 in tobacco credits? I believe if you reflect on it in this manner, you'll find Edward's offer to be to your own advantage."

After pondering what Robert had said, he knew him to be right. The deal was struck and all ten slaves became Edward's property. Mister Gladstone went to draw up the bills of sale and Edward counted out £450 in coin.

"I think we're doing the right thing, son," said Robert after they were alone.

"While I agree with you, father, why does the right thing always end up costing me more money?"

The next morning, the horses having fairly recovered, as had Edward, Robert, and Aaron, they determined to be on their way. The clouds were low and the top of the Blue Ridge was lost to view, which could only mean more snow and a hard trip through Indian Trail Gap, but they were determined to waste no more time waiting on the weather. Taking along extra provisions and blankets, they set off for home.

✑ *Chapter 40* ✑

*T*he Gladstone's eldest boy, a lad of about 17, had delivered a note from his father telling Lewis the laborers were to stay until Robert and Edward returned. Needless to say, all of the laborers took this to mean some agreement as to their future had been reached and they were all well pleased. This also saved Lewis from having to further reduce the fort to take the laborers back over the Blue Ridge now, when the hunting season was full upon them.

The mill was in full operation now and their neighbors were daily bringing in their crop of corn to be ground into flour. Mister Agner turned out to be a first rate miller, knowing his trade well. The arrangement was that Mister Agner would receive half and Edward the other half of all proceeds from the mill. As there was no ready money in the Valley outside of the Jewett family, most of the payment was by a share of the corn brought to be ground. Lewis put the laborers to work building a storage building capable of holding their corn as it would have soon overwhelmed the already full blockhouse. Some of the corn remained in kernel form for the animals and some was ground for the family's use.

Mister Agner was in the most exposed position, his house and mill being some distance from the fort. Lewis thought it prudent to bring him into the fort at night, so that if there was trouble, he was with them and they did not have to risk going to his aid. A widower, he grumbled a bit at the "fussy" women in the Jewett household but put up with the arrangement tolerably well. Esther confided to Lewis that she thought Mister Agner actually liked having the evening meal prepared for him. She also asked if Lewis could talk to him about his cleanliness, something he lacked entirely.

Tom McCrary and Jim Rice rode in one day and announced there was Indian sign in the Valley again, although no one had seen them and no one had been molested. Regular patrols were again implemented and fresh sign was seen every day and on every patrol. None of the neighbors moved into the fort yet, just prepared to do so at a moments notice.

One morning as the family sat down to breakfast, Charles, who had the watch in the blockhouse, sounded the alarm. As Lewis strode toward the blockhouse, a group of Indians entered the fort by the gate next to the blockhouse and strode down the little street toward him. Taken completely by surprise and now with Indians between the family and the blockhouse, Lewis chose to continue on toward them while signaling Henry and Miles to get everyone else under cover. "At least," thought Lewis, "we're all armed, even at this hour."

As Lewis met the group of Indians in the middle of the street, between Robert's and Edward's cabin, they all stopped and at first just looked each other over. The Indian directly facing Lewis, who he took to be their leader, then said something to the Indian beside him. This Indian spoke English and began to translate for his Chief.

"The Cherokee came last fall and made peace with Great Bear. Now we return to find the Great Bear has become blood brother to our enemies, the Shawnee. Is this how Great Bear repays the Cherokee for not attacking him last year?"

Lewis knew he had to think fast and answer well or it was not going to be a good day. "My brother, Great Bear, did not mean to offend his uncle, great chief of the Cherokee nation. The Shawnee returned in the spring, took my wife captive, and we again made them pay in blood for their transgression. It was only after they agreed to bury the hatchet with us that my brother agreed to become blood brother with the Shawnee Black Fish. We did not need to shed blood with our uncle's people to make peace and we therefore value and honor our ties to the Cherokee. With the Shawnee, we made a peace with them, but we trust them not."

The deference Lewis showed in both his manner and his words worked well with the Cherokee Chief and he seemed much placated by the response. They all then sat in the middle of the little street and the discussions continued on a more amicable note for nearly an hour. Lewis told the story of the capture and rescue of Marie, the ambush, and the death of Joseph. He also relayed how many Shawnee had fallen, a number the Cherokee found impressive.

The Chief then explained to Lewis how he came to learn the name the Shawnee had given Edward. Evidently they had posted "signs" around the Jewett property announcing the presence of Great Bear. Lewis had seen these "signs" without knowing what they meant. He also learned from the Cherokee that the Shawnee were a much smaller tribe, in overall numbers and in the number of braves, than the Cherokee and thus they could ill afford the heavy losses the Jewett's had inflicted on them in the two fights. The Chief then warned Lewis to be on his guard for the Shawnee would wait only a few seasons before trying to again extract revenge for the dishonor they had suffered at the hands of these few white men. He also told them the Shawnee were much taken by the gifts they received from the French and the French were encouraging them to attack any white English settler they found.

Their conversation ended, they all stood and Lewis and the Chief shook hands, or, rather, in Indian fashion they each grabbed the other's right forearm near the elbow. Referring to Lewis as "Wise Owl," they were gone as quickly as they arrived. Charles called down when they were completely out of sight and all breathed a little easier, all that is except for Mary.

Mary came out of her cabin nearly hysterical with fear, calling for Charles to make sure the boy was alright. Then she turned to Henry and told him to get their horses, that they were leaving this instant, going back to Boston where they were safe from the savages. Henry looked to Lewis, not knowing what to do, and found his brother had no answers for him.

"Are you deaf? I told you to get horses for you, me, and Charles. We're leaving, now!" With that she ran back into their cabin, dragging a protesting Charles with her.

"I don't know what to tell you, Henry. She seems completely deranged by this," offered Lewis.

"Maybe I'd better get those horses and take her out of here. This has been building up all summer and I just don't see her making it through the winter with her fears. At least she isn't including Sarah in this. You'll look after her, won't you?"

"You know we will. But you also know there's been

snow in the mountains. Do you honestly think you can make it through the gap with her in this state?"

They all stood listening to the ravings coming from Henry's cabin as Mary set about gathering what she intended to take with them. When she looked out and found Henry still just standing there, she screamed at him to get the horses again, only more frantic.

"Maybe it's best if you take her at least over the mountain to the landing. Then, if she calms down, perhaps you can talk reason with her," observed Lewis. "I just don't see how you're going to make it through the gap in the snow. Remember the last time you were up there in the winter."

In the meantime, Marie and Esther had gone to try to calm Mary down a little and talk reason to her. Neither thought they should attempt the gap until the weather in the mountains broke and the snow melted some. All of them now knew the snow would only stay a week or so. Their attempts at calming had no effect. Mary was beyond all reason and was intent on running as quickly as she could. When they reported this to Henry and Lewis, the men just shook their heads and Henry went to saddle three horses. Miles went along to help.

Mary emerged from the cabin about the time Henry returned with the horses. She ran to them, tossed her quickly packed bags over the horses back, and mounted, urging her son and husband to do the same. Once all were mounted, she tried to hurry them along, only not being very good on horseback, had some difficulty pushing Charles in front of her. Once out of the little fort, she urged them into a gallop toward the river and they were lost from sight.

Sam broke the silence, "That woman's lost her mind. She'll never be right again."

Lewis only nodded. He feared Sam was right.

Henry tried reasoning with Mary the whole mad dash for the river, to no avail. She crossed recklessly, nearly falling into the cold water before reaching the opposite shore. There she paused only long enough to get Charles again in front of her and she urged them into another gallop in her desperate attempt to escape her fears. Only the fatigue of the horses caused her to slow the pace, but once the horses had recovered, she was off at a brisk walk, the most the horses could now manage.

They hit snow not long after starting the ascent and it became more and more difficult to see the trail. Henry and Charles were now holding back while Mary continued to urge them to hurry. By time it was dark, they had reached the gap where the snow was belly deep to the horses and still coming down. Henry and Charles stopped here but Mary continued on, refusing to halt for any reason. They lost sight of her in the snow.

Knowing of the rock houses off to their left, Henry directed Charles to the first one, where they set about making a fire to warm themselves before looking to the horses. Periodically, Henry would step out of the rock house and call for Mary, even telling her they had made a warm camp for her. No answer.

Having been forced to pack quickly, father and son were little prepared to face a winter storm in the mountains. They took stock of what they had, a little food, one blanket, one leather bottle of water, and the horse blankets. Henry spread the horse blankets out over the horses backs in hopes to keep them somewhat warmer and then wrapped their one blanket around both him and Charles as they huddled close to the small fire trying to stay warm.

By full light the snow had stopped. They ate what little food they had left before breaking camp to go in search of Mary. The snow had filled in their tracks and no sign remained of where she had gone. They started down the trail, staying as close to it as they could now that it was completely covered in snow. The horses having gone without fodder were moving slowly, their energy about spent even though the snow depth was decreasing as they moved further down the mountain.

Rounding the side of the mountain, they met Edward riding toward them.

"You don't know how glad I am to see you, Edward."

"And I you. After we found Mary, I feared the worst and came on ahead to see if I could find you."

"Then you've found her? Is she alright? Where is she?"

"I'm sorry to have to tell you this Henry, Charles. We found her this morning as we came up the mountain, just about a hundred yards back, frozen to death."

☙ *Chapter 41* ☙

"**I** should have stopped them," Lewis told Marie as they looked out of the little fort to where Henry, Mary, and Charles had disappeared moments before. "They took nothing that they'll need to get through the gap with the snow we know has been falling there for more than a day."

"There was nothing anyone could have done to stop Mary. I've never seen anyone in such a state as she was. I wish she hadn't insisted on taking Henry and Charles with her. Why endanger all three for the fears of one?" Marie responded.

"They didn't even care what became of me," came Sarah's voice, startling the two as they thought the others had already dispersed to the cabins.

"Not true, Sarah, not true at all. Your father asked me to take care of you, not wanting to take you out with them, not really wanting to go himself. You're far better off here with us than out on a winter's trail with little in the way of provisions." Lewis then put his arm around Sarah's shoulders to comfort the girl.

After a few moments in silent reflection, Lewis continued, "Well, we need to make some changes in light of this morning's events. Our strength is markedly reduced and I'm not sure how long we can rely on the benevolence of the Cherokees. Let's gather everyone together so we can make our preparation."

Once all had gathered, Lewis outlined his plans. The fort gates were to be kept closed at all times. As the grain had all been ground, Mister Agner was to move into the fort full time. A sharp watch needed to be kept from the advantage of the blockhouse, so he increased it from one to two at all times. Then came the question that caused Miles to recoil instinctively.

"Sam, can you or any of the others shoot?"

"Well, sir, Jubal and I have hunted rabbits, birds, and such, and have also kept wolves and foxes out of the barns. None of the others have so much as held a firelock before."

"Well, that's something, anyway. Miles, provide Sam and Jubal with a musket each from our stores and see they have powder and ball."

"I think that ill advised, Mister Lewis," was Miles' reply, not without some emphasis but in a low tone meant for Lewis' ears alone.

Lewis responded for all to hear, "There are some who would advise me against arming men held in bondage, and they may well be right. I also know that we are far out on the frontier, surrounded by the Cherokee who would not think twice about lifting the hair of any intruder, be he black or white. Our only security lies in the goodwill we have with each other and in our mutual defense of this little outpost."

Looking from face to face, Lewis saw this had made a great impression on the laborers. Miles still did not understand these Jewett's, only he had to admit their methods seemed to work more often than not. Lewis told Miles he wanted him to be in the laborers' cabin should there be a fight, directing the action there, with Mister Agner as well. They would only man the blockhouse and the laborers' cabin in case of attack.

"Might I suggest," injected Miles, "That we hang short strips of cloth on the inside, above each cabin door? When we clear the cabins, we should close the door so the cloth is on the inside. Anyone opening the door would then close it back on the cloth, leaving the cloth on the outside to show us there has been unwanted entry."

"Good idea. Then we avoid the problem we had last fall with the Shawnee in Henry's cabin," concluded Lewis. "Mattie, would you see to this and make sure everyone knows how to use it?" Mattie nodded her agreement.

Philip came up to Lewis after the meeting ended. "When will grandfather and Uncle Edward return? They've been gone now over three months."

"I wish I knew. We sure could use them here."

The rest of the day passed quietly. The snow was only flurries in the valley, but all knew it was heavy in the mountains as they could not see the peaks to the east at all. The work now that it was winter centered mainly on caring for the animals and keeping warm. Several of the laborers knew how to tan leather and occupied their time tanning the deer hides Lewis, Philip, and Miles had brought in during their fall hunts.

After dinner, Philip approached his father, "Do you think I should ride out and try to find Uncle Henry and Charles? I know you said Aunt Mary wouldn't come back, but I'm worried about Charles. Did you know they didn't take any blankets with them?"

"I know, and I'm worried, also. Only adding you to the list of those outside the fort won't help me much. Besides, with all the Indians around I might need you here more than Uncle Henry and Charles need you. I'm sure, if they can, Uncle Henry and Charles will be back."

Near dusk, Tom McCrary and Jim Rice rode up, having completed their patrol.

"I don't like it, Lewis, not at all," said Tom. "The Cherokee are staying longer than normal and there seems to be more of them than in years past. I'm not sure what's up, but I'm thinking we may want to bring our families into your fort, if that's alright with you."

"I have no objections, and with Edward and my father gone, and now Henry leaving…"

"Henry's gone?"

"Yes, we had a visit this morning from the Cherokee and Mary insisted they leave right after that. They took Charles with them, of course, so we're rather short-handed here. I'd welcome the help, to be honest."

Tom looked at Jim and gave a low whistle of surprise. He then looked back to Lewis, "We'll come in tomorrow morning, then."

Thoughtfully, Lewis added, "Aren't you concerned what might happen to your farmsteads if you abandon them?"

"I am, but I'm more concerned about the safety of my wife and the kids."

"You all have stock to tend. What if we went out in a group each day and made a circuit of the farmsteads to tend the stock and check up on things. We could take along a couple of our laborers to do the work while the rest stand guard. We'll need a strong guard here, but it might forestall any problems at your places."

Both men liked the idea, so Tom and Jim left in the gathering darkness to spread the word to the Fishers, Stuarts and McNultys. Lewis set Mattie, Jenny, Esther, Sarah, and Rebecca to work preparing to receive the other families into their little fort. In addition to the spring in the blockhouse, all of the water barrels were filled and hay was brought up from the barn for the livestock. It was going to be tight again, like in the spring, but the fort was well made and could accommodate them all, if not in complete comfort.

That night as Lewis and Philip watched from the blockhouse, waiting for the moon to rise so they could see the fields around their fort, Esther joined them, bringing them each a mug of hot tea from their now dwindling stocks.

"Sarah is still feeling abandoned, even after what you said to her this morning. I can't say I blame her, watching her father, mother, and brother head off for Boston without so much as a goodbye to her. I've tried to talk to her, but think she needs more. I wish father were here to comfort her."

"I can't say I blame her. I just wish she believed me when I told her that the last thing her father said to me was to take care of her. I'm not sure what else I can say."

"Father has a way of getting through to her. I think it's harder raising a girl child than a boy child. Father has experience raising me that I think he uses when comforting Sarah."

"Have you thought to ask Jenny's advice? She's raised Rebecca, who's close now to Sarah. Maybe she could advise you."

"You just don't want Marie to see you talking to the young, attractive widow, that's why you're sending me to do it," laughed Esther, and then more seriously, "But it is a good idea. I'll talk to her tonight."

The two sat quietly while Lewis finished his tea, enjoying each others company. When he was done, Esther collected the two mugs and left to seek out Jenny Thompson.

It was mid-morning when the neighbors began arriving at the Jewett's fort. First came the McCrarys, the closest, followed closely by the Rices. The Fishers, McNultys and Stuarts followed about an hour later. Although it made the little fort crowded, Lewis felt better now that there were enough guns to put up a good defense should anything go amiss with the Indians.

Previously, it was Robert and Edward all of them had turned to for organization and direction. Now Lewis found they were turning to him. It was a different role for him and while he did not necessarily feel his abilities compared well to Edward's, he was growing more confident. He organized patrols and the watch, assigned living quarters, and made sure everyone knew where he wanted them should danger occur. By dinner time they were as ready as they had ever been to face an attack and Lewis took some time to relax.

"Uncle Lewis, can I talk to you?" asked Sarah as she slipped into Lewis' cabin that evening.

"Of course, Sarah, anytime, you know that."

"I've been talking to Aunt Esther and just wanted you to know how much I appreciate what you're doing for me."

"We all love you, Sarah, and only want what's best for you. I'm just sorry your grandfather isn't here to help you through what must be a difficult time."

"I do miss him terribly, but what you said my father asked you to do, is that true?"

"Why, yes, Sarah, it is. If he could have, I'm sure he would have left Charles here as well. As long as your mother wasn't insisting you go along, nothing could get your father to place you in danger by suggesting you go as well. He loves you very much."

"I guess I know that, it just doesn't always seem like he does. Sometimes I feel more like you or Uncle Edward are more father to me than he is. Is it awful to feel that way?"

"It's not awful, but I do hope you understand your father has had to deal with a lot of different issues and he has tried his best to do what is right by you, by Charles, and by your mother. He might not always get it right, but he is always trying to do the very best he can. Promise me you believe that?"

After thinking for several minutes, Sarah moved and gave Lewis a big hug. "I promise," she said, starting to cry softly. "And Uncle Lewis, I love you very much for all you've done for me."

Lewis patted her shoulder and leaned down to kiss her hair as she buried her face in his chest. Then they heard the alarm being sounded from the blockhouse.

Moving into the street, everyone was rushing to their assigned posts. Lewis moved swiftly to the second floor of the blockhouse to assess what had caused the alarm to be sounded. What he saw caused him to pause. From both the east and west, they could see bands of Indians moving quickly along the woods on paths that would have them converge to the north, where their little trail to the ford came up from the river. Whatever they were doing, it did not look good for the little band in the fort.

ᴄᴏ *Chapter 42* ᴄᴏ

"**D**id you notice the horse, Uncle Edward?" Charles asked.

"The horse, I don't know what you mean, Charles."

"Mother was riding the same horse Joseph was riding when he was killed. Now she has died," Charles pointed out sadly, looking at the blanket wrapped form his grandfather and Aaron had secured over the horse's saddle. "I don't think I would want to ride that horse, ever."

Edward looked sadly at Robert, who had heard everything his grandson said. "Charles, now it's time for you to eat and drink. You need to rest and warm yourself before we start for home."

Moving to one side, Robert and Edward talked in soft tones. "It's a good thing we brought along extra blankets and provisions. What possessed them to leave home so poorly provisioned for winter travel?" Robert asked.

"Henry told me the fort was visited by the Cherokee yesterday morning. Mary became extremely frightened and insisted they leave without allowing him to make any preparations at all."

Looking back toward the lifeless form in the blanket, Robert continued, "I hope she has at last found a peace she never seemed able to find in this world."

Once Henry, Charles, and the horses that came out with them had been fed and warmed, Edward announced it was time to move on. He and Charles rode side by side in the lead, followed by Aaron and Henry, each leading a horse, the six horses breaking a trail through the snow for Robert and his riding chair. Although cold, the weather was clear and the little party made good time to the summit of Indian Trail Gap.

Charles was understandably quiet as they rode, saddened by the loss of his mother and numbed by the events of the past day. First it was Joseph, who rode out one evening and never came back. Now it was his mother who had ridden on ahead and would never be seen in this life again. He reflected on how quick life could take unexpected turns. His mother had been excited about the prospect of having their own land. When they were alone in their cabin she would speak of being respectable, and then the fear took hold. It, and not the frontier, had been what caused her death.

"Uncle Edward, mother died because of her fear and Joseph died because he had no fear. How can both be true?"

"Well, Charles, Joseph died because he was running toward something he had stopped fearing and therefore stopped respecting the consequences. Your mother was running away from something in such haste she failed to stop and respect the consequences. It may on the surface look like they were doing the opposite, but really they were doing the same thing. Both failed to respect the consequences of their actions, failed to stop and think of what could happen. I hope you'll remember this."

Charles went back to his own thoughts as they continued on over the summit and started down the other side.

They stopped early for dinner to give the horses a break. They were now past the deep snow and the sun was already starting to melt the snow on this western face of the mountains. Charles and Henry again ate hungrily and both appeared to be in improved spirits, now that they were relatively warm, well fed, and among family. Edward was able to get Henry to give a more complete account of Lewis' meeting with the Cherokees the morning before.

"Father, I don't like it. This is very late in the season for the Cherokee to be hunting this far from their homeland. Something must be going on that we don't know about."

"I agree, though it doesn't at this point sound hostile. You've been talking to Charles, how is he holding up with his mother's death?"

"He's quiet, thoughtful, but not overly melancholy. He seems to have a grasp of how this happens. I am concerned about his comment on the horse. I hope he isn't becoming superstitious."

"We'll need to watch him over the next few weeks. Henry, on the other hand, seems almost relieved. I think Mary's constant fear wore on him more than Charles. He covered for Charles and bore the brunt of her fury."

"I can only imagine how her fear increased all this time we've been gone to drive her to this. Poor woman, when she was safe, warm, and loved with bright prospects ahead of her," Edward lamented.

Their break over, they started again toward their ford. The snow was all but gone now that they were at a lower elevation and the afternoon sun had done its work. All well-mounted and Henry and Charles' horses fairly recovered, they made good time. Before crossing the river, Edward gathered the little party together to give instructions.

"We know the Cherokee are in the vicinity of home. They have not molested us before and probably won't today. That said, it would be prudent to take due precautions. See to your priming and make sure you have a sharp flint just in case. If we're confronted, we'll form a line abreast and keep moving toward the blockhouse. Father, you'll be in the middle of the line with Charles and then Henry to your left, Aaron and I on your right. Ride upright, showing no fear, and look straight ahead, moving only your eyes to keep them in view.

"When we arrive at the gate, father enters first with the riding chair and then Charles, Aaron, Henry, and I'll enter last. We'll be under the guns of the blockhouse, but there are very few guns left. If the Cherokee mean to take us, they've picked a perfect time for it. In any case, I'll be the first to fire if it comes to that. I want to avoid an altercation if at all possible."

"Edward, I'll ride in Charles' place and he can drive my riding chair," Robert offered. "That will put the boy through the gates first. I'm not young any more, but can still hold my own. Charles' size would put him at a distinct disadvantage should it come to a fight."

"Alright then, but you follow the riding chair into the fort in Charles' place. Anyone have any questions?"

They had none. All could tell when Edward ceased being son, brother, and uncle and resumed his role as Colonel. From this point on, they knew he would be pure soldier.

Crossing the ford quickly, the water being quite cold, they formed their line on the other bank and moved at a fast walk toward home. They saw the Cherokee just as the top of the blockhouse roof came into view, coming toward them from both the southeast and north-northwest, converging on them.

It was a strange sight. The Cherokee were running, but not whooping, nor were they painted as if for war. As they came abreast, they began moving with them, jogging to keep pace with the horses, not closing closer than about 50 yards or so, as the terrain permitted.

Clearing the rise that brought the blockhouse and fort fully into view, they found their way blocked by another group of Cherokee, a smaller group, and Edward recognized the Chief he had spoken with the year before and the English speaking Cherokee at his side. Passing word down the line to halt immediately in front of the Chief's party, they continued their pace the last hundred or so yards, pulling up immediately in front of the Cherokee delegation.

The interpreter spoke first, hailing Edward, "Great Bear, my Chief gives his greetings and asks for your help. We have waited many days for your return and are anxious to return to our village before more snow fills the passes."

Throwing his reins to Aaron, Edward dismounted and walked directly to the Chief. "Please tell the Chief that I am tired from my journey and we have family we need to bury. Perhaps another time would be better. Could we meet in the morning, when the sun rises over the mountains to the east?"

After the interpreter passed Edward's message, the Chief grunted and nodded once, indicating his acceptance, then stepped forward, extending his right hand. Edward extended his, both men gripping the other on the forearm in an Indian handshake. Then, turning to the interpreter, the Chief spoke, the translation of which was he would meet Edward on this spot in the morning.

Edward remounted and the little group resumed their march toward the fort as the Cherokee party moved off to the southeast. The last to enter the fort, Edward was surprised to find it well manned, with the neighbors swelling the population to where a stout defense would have been made against any hostilities.

Having observed their approach through Edward's telescope, Lewis had already passed the word to the rest of the family that they carried Mary's lifeless form across her saddle. Esther, Sarah, and Marie were waiting inside the gate to receive the body of their late relation and took her to Robert's house to prepare her for burial, no words being necessary.

Everyone else gathered around the new arrivals, anxious to hear what had passed between Edward and the Cherokee. In a few words, Edward related their short conversation and suggested to Lewis that all be at their posts before first light, just in case. Lewis then posted a strong watch and released everyone else to get their supper and some rest, it being now sunset, and the group began to disperse to the cabins.

Lewis now had a chance to welcome his father and brothers home, the four then retiring to Edward's cabin to discuss more fully recent events. At the cabin door they found Jenny Thompson, who welcomed them all home, flashing Edward a big grin in the process, before leaving the men to their business.

Betty quickly put supper on the table before excusing herself to help Esther and the men then found themselves alone.

"Best be careful, Edward. Jenny is even better looking now than when we left. Widowhood seems to agree with her," said Robert, grinning broadly at his eldest son's discomfort, the brothers joining in on the fun.

"Now, father, we have serious business to discuss before tomorrow morning and instead you're making eyes at the young women hanging around the fort, and at your age!" That sent them all into fits of laughter as they settled down to eat.

Lewis was unable to shed any light on what the Cherokee Chief wanted to talk to Edward about. He did tell them the Cherokee had been hanging around for weeks, watching the fort closely but not approaching until the previous morning, when Charles' slow alarm permitted them to walk right into the fort.

"I think he wanted to gauge the strength here and maybe to satisfy himself that I wasn't here. Had you moved everyone from the neighborhood into the fort by that time?"

"No, they moved in this morning. I'm sure the Cherokee observed the move, only they didn't interfere in any way. Something is up only I can't figure out what. I'm really glad you're back."

"Why, you seem to have everything here well under control. What do you need me here for? Maybe I should spend more time in Williamsburg so you have free rein here."

Although Lewis failed to see the humor in it, the others did. Edward then explained the main issue in Williamsburg was the French incursion into the western portions of the colony and how Governor Dinwiddie thought this would cause an increase in Indian problems all along the frontier, especially further to the north and west near the Ohio Country.

"Before we left, the Governor told me he intended to send young Major Washington to the French commander with a strongly worded letter of protest. I can't see what that will do, no one being very interested in reading letters of protest. I suspect, if this continues on course, there will likely be another war between England and France, only we'll be on the front line against the Indians."

"Isn't that why Lord Halifax wanted you here, and arranged this land grant and your introduction to Governor Dinwiddie as his 'Military Advisor'?" asked Lewis.

"Yes, I suspect it is. And aren't you all glad I offered to share my misfortune with you? Now, if you gentlemen of dubious property will permit me, I think I'll get some sleep before meeting with the Chief tomorrow."

The four men parted, still chuckling over the familial teasing they all so much enjoyed.

Chapter 43

*B*etty had Edward's breakfast ready early, knowing he had an appointment to keep with the Cherokee. He ate in silence, thoughtful, and she cleared the dishes when he got up to leave.

Opening the door he found Philip, bundled up in his blanket coat, his gun across his lap, waiting.

"I'm going with you, Uncle Edward."

"No, you're not. I need you here, in the blockhouse, looking out for treachery, not out in the middle of the meadow where you can't do me much good if there's trouble. Understand?"

"But Uncle Edward, you've been gone a long time and when you came back you, grandfather, father, and Uncle Henry locked yourselves in your cabin until after mother sent me to bed. It's not fair."

"No, Philip, it's not fair. It's also not fair that Joseph died not listening to me and your Aunt Mary died not listening to your father. See what happens to those who don't listen? Now, what I want you to do is to ask Aaron to unpack the wall guns, then you cover me with one."

"Wall guns, what do you mean?"

"In Williamsburg I purchased two large guns in .150 caliber that mount to the wall because they're too big to hold. Not having cannon, they're the next best thing. Your grandfather carried them home on the back of the riding chair."

It was not the same as going out with his uncle, but it was something so Philip ran off to find where Aaron was already unpacking the wall guns.

"That was a pretty good job of bribing my son, brother," Lewis' said as he approached Edward from behind. "But that part about going out alone isn't going to happen. I'm going with you just like the last time when we dealt with the Shawnee."

"And who's going to be in charge in here if we're both out there?"

"Don't forget, father is an experienced Indian fighter and he runs the blockhouse quite well without either of us. Now, we'd better get going if we're going to be on time."

As they approached the gate, Robert was there to see them off, assuring Edward all the shooting loops were manned in case anything went wrong. He then gave both his sons a hug before they started off through the gate, which he closed behind them.

The Cherokee were already waiting on them as the sun made its appearance over the Blue Ridge to the east. There were four of them, the interpreter, the man they knew as the Chief, and two others. As Edward and Lewis approached, they stood and gave them a friendly greeting. The pipe then came out and after all had smoked, they sat facing each other.

"Governor Dinwiddie sent us this talking paper and we want you to tell us what it says," the interpreter stated after the preliminary niceties were out of the way.

"Who brought this paper to you?" asked Edward.

"An English trader, George Croghan, brought it to us."

"Didn't he tell you what it said when he gave it to you?"

"He did. We want you to tell us, so we know Croghan spoke the truth."

Edward took the paper from the Chief and read the familiar hand of Governor Dinwiddie's secretary. He explained to the Chief the paper warned of an impending war between the French and the English. It went on to ask the Cherokee to help the English in this war, to counter their enemies, the Shawnee and the other tribes aligned with the French. Edward did not mention the veiled threats included should the Cherokee decide to side with the French instead.

"Is this what Mister Croghan told you the paper said?"

The interpreter nodded while the other three Cherokee carried on an animated discussion. When they had finished, the principal Chief again spoke to Edward through the interpreter.

"Great Bear and Wise Owl have treated us fairly and we trust them. We would like for them to send a talking paper to Governor Dinwiddie telling him the Cherokee will not fight the English. Also tell him we will not fight the French. But of our enemies, the Shawnee, we will always fight them, only on our terms, not those of the English. Will you send such a talking paper?"

Edward assured them he would and, after the closing formalities, all turned toward their respective camps and walked slowly away.

"Wise Owl, is that what he called you? I could think of other things to call you, all amplified by the word 'wise,' but 'owl' isn't one of them."

Both were laughing hard when they came back through the gate, much to the surprise of the occupants of the little fort who were not in on the joke between the brothers. When they explained what was on the minds of the Cherokee, there was a collective sigh of relief. They then agreed, to be cautious, all would remain at the fort until the Cherokee left the area. Regular patrols would begin again at noon and continue as long as needed.

Philip came up to Edward as the crowd began to disperse. "The wall gun is something. I had it aimed on the Cherokee the whole time, but I'm really glad I didn't have to shoot it. I saw how much powder Aaron loaded it with and saw the size of that ball. I think it would have hurt!"

Edward patted him on the back as he chuckled and they walked toward Edward's cabin. Jenny Thompson was near his door and asked for a moment of Edward's time.

"I'm glad things went as well as they did. I was so worried for your safety while you were out there, alone and unprotected."

"I wasn't alone. Lewis was there to watch my back, Jenny."

"You know what I mean," she replied, now playfully.

"Jenny, remember what we talked about before? I haven't changed my mind. You're a fine figure of a woman. I'm just not ready to remarry. I'm sorry."

Looking down, she nodded, "I know." Then, looking back up and smiling, "You won't fault a woman for dreaming, will you?"

Returning the smile, "No, I won't fault you for that. I just don't want to get your hopes up."

Lewis, Henry, and Robert approached from one side while Sam and Jubal came from the other. Edward looked from one group to another.

"I feel surrounded."

"If it's alright with you, Edward, we'll bury Mary this afternoon, just before dinner," said Henry sadly. "I thought we'd put her next to Joseph, Lewis thought that would be alright." Edward nodded his assent.

"Colonel, I know this isn't the right time, but we are all wondering about your discussions with Master."

Robert broke in at this point. "I see where Sally has had your child. What is it, a boy or girl?"

Sam broke into a big, toothy grin. "It's a little boy, Sir Robert, a fine little boy."

"What did you name him?"

With that Sam looked uncomfortable, dropping his glance to the ground, looking sideways at Jubal who had also dropped his gaze, before he responded. "Only Master can name a slave child, Sir Robert, so my little boy doesn't have a name yet."

Now it was Edward who broke in, his set jaw and tight lips showing his displeasure, causing Sam and Jubal to become even more nervous than Robert's question had left them. "I'm sick of all this and it's time I put a stop to it. Jubal, go get the others, all of them, the two women included, and bring them here, now, and be quick about it."

Sam stood nervously, not daring to look up at Edward's stern gaze, while Jubal ran to gather the others. Neither knew what they had done to cause this change and both wished they could take back whatever it was, for Edward was not a man they wanted to anger. His fury scared them more than any punishment Mister Gladstone ever threatened.

The laborers came running, Jubal having relayed that something he or Sam had said had angered the Colonel and caused him to call for all of them to gather. There was dread in many of their eyes as they stood quietly in front of the four Jewett men. As Jubal had told them, the Colonel did not look at all pleased.

Once assured he had their undivided attention, Edward started. "We have told you all over and over that slave rules do not apply while you're here with us. I've just been informed that Sam and Rachaels's boy lacks a name because only the master may name a slave child. Well, I'm sick of all of it. Hear this and heed it well, Mister Gladstone has given me your papers, for all ten, now eleven, of you." He paused at this point to let the shock of this development sink in. Once all was quiet again, he continued, "I hate all the slave rules, I don't know them and don't care to learn. Here's what I do know: Sam, Rachael, your son is free born, belonging to no one, and needs a name. So, name him, it's up to the two of you and no others." Again he had to pause for this to sink in.

"Now, you all know my father hates slavery and is against any of his sons owning slaves. Yet here he finds his eldest son a slave holder. I've laid out a considerable amount of money to secure your purchase and expect some return on my investment. Therefore, if you are willing to sign an indenture, remaining here in my employ for the next seven years of your own free will, I will give you all your freedom, today, after the funeral."

Having feared what was about to happen and only to have this news, the best they had dared hope for, was more than most could bear. There were tears of joy and several dropped to their knees, none were untouched by the news. It took a little longer for them to settle down this time, but Edward waited patiently for quiet to return.

"At the end of your indenture, you will be free to remain as hired labor, receiving fair pay, or relocate. It will be entirely up to you what you do at that point. Do any of you have a problem with that?" It was quite obvious none had a problem with this arrangement. They thanked Edward and Robert over and over again before finally disbursing, the grins and tears still much in evidence as they headed back toward their communal cabin at the end of the street.

Turning to his father and brothers, Edward said, "Not exactly how I had planned to tell them, but it seems to have had the desired impact."

The entire fort emptied for Mary's funeral on the little knoll where Joseph had been buried. Without a regular minister, Robert presided and laid his daughter-in-law to rest in a dignified, loving, Christian manner. Charles and Sarah wept openly while Henry strived to be stoic, though the tears running down his cheeks gave away the emotion he felt. Nothing of the fear that drove her from the fort entered into the ceremony and all strived to remember her for her good qualities.

On returning to the fort, Sam stepped forward and invited all to attend a naming ceremony for his son that evening after supper. Edward and Robert took dinner together in Edward's cabin, spending the rest of the afternoon working together to produce all 11 freedom papers and ten indentures.

After supper, everyone gathered in the small street to help Sam and Rachael celebrate naming their child. As Marie and Lewis joined Edward and Robert, they had a peculiar look on their faces.

"What's this, Lewis, Marie, do you know something we should know?" asked Robert with a lighthearted lilt in his voice.

"You'll see soon enough," Marie responded, smiling brightly.

All quieted down as Sam and Sally emerged from

their cabin dressed in their finest. Sam had a catamount hide, carefully tanned, draped across his shoulders. After thanking the Jewett's for allowing them this opportunity, Sam removed the catamount hide, wrapped the squirming child in it, took the child from Rachael and held him up to the now star filled sky and announced, "Behold, I give you my son, named Joseph, son of Sam and Rachael. Watch over and protect him so he may grow strong and live long."

Robert and Edward now understood. Sam had asked Lewis and Marie if he could honor the memory of their slain son by using his name for their new boy. As the laborers began singing and dancing around the happy new parents, Robert smiled his approval, content that they had started something good.

ᏦᎧ Chapter 44 ᏦᎧ

*T*he early patrols reported finding clear signs the Cherokee were making their departure from the upper Valley. A short meeting decided the neighbors would remain that day and, assuming the noon and evening patrols confirmed this report, would return to their farmsteads the next morning. All of them again thanked Robert and Edward for allowing them the safety of their little fort.

Robert and Lewis joined Edward after breakfast to look over the letter Edward had prepared to convey the Cherokee response on fighting for the English. It was a carefully worded letter designed to convey the Cherokee's lack of hostility toward the English as well as their reluctance to join into any fight between the two European powers. After a few minor edits, both Robert and Lewis pronounced the letter to be ready for copying into final form. While Edward did this, Robert and Lewis sat chatting about everything that had been going on the past three months.

"There, finished. I need to take the manumission and indenture papers to Beverly's Mill Place to be properly recorded by the county clerk, so I thought I could take advantage of the regular post rider to send this to Williamsburg. Lewis, do you suppose your son would like to take a ride with his old uncle? I thought I would ask Charles to join us as well."

"I know he'd love it, provided father can spare him from his military duties here at the fort."

"I'm all for it. I think it will be good for Charles and Philip to spend some time together. It might get Charles' mind off his loss."

"Good. I'll go and ask Henry if it'll be alright with him. I hope to start before noon and we should be gone only a couple of days at most."

When Edward was invited into Henry's cabin, he looked around in disbelief. Clearly, Henry was no housekeeper and what was on the table passing for breakfast was nothing Edward would have eaten. After gaining Henry's assent and sending Charles off to prepare himself and his horse, Edward walked next door to his father's cabin.

"Jenny, can I talk to you for a moment?" After a very curious Jenny sat down opposite him at the table, and an equally curious Esther occupied herself near enough to hear without being intrusive, Edward continued. "I've just been to see Henry and I'm afraid he is struggling to keep his household in order without Mary. I hate to ask, but could you see your way clear to helping him out with the domestic chores, cleaning and cooking? It would be a way for you to earn some extra spending money as well. I was thinking perhaps a shilling a week?"

"Make it a shilling six pence and I'll do it."

Sitting all the way back in his chair, something he rarely did, Edward paused before saying, "Why Jenny Thompson, you've become quite the shrewd businesswoman since I left for Williamsburg. A shilling six pence per week it is."

Rising and moving to the door, Jenny quickly came to his side and stopped him with a hand on his arm. "If you had asked me to clean and cook for you, Edward, I'd have done that for free," she said with one of her flirtatious smiles.

Patting her hand, Edward responded, "I'll have to keep that in mind, young lady," smiling back at her and enjoying the confused look it caused to creep over her face as he left the cabin.

By now the boys were ready and mounted and Aaron stood with Edward's horse, his portmanteau tied behind the saddle and holding Edward's rifle, horn and pouch in his hand. Passing his folio containing the documents to Philip, Edward said his goodbyes to his father, brothers, and sister before mounting. Before turning to leave, Esther came over and placed a hand on his bridle.

"That was very cruel what you said to Jenny, brother. She'll stew the whole time you're gone trying to figure out what you meant by it."

"I know which is why I said it how I did. She's been tormenting me something awful and I thought I'd get even a little," he responded with a big grin on his face.

"It's no small wonder growing up with you three for brothers that I never married! Now go on!" she said, now grinning herself.

They left the fort and splashed across the creek, heading northwest for the Virginia Road. Although it continued cold, the bright sun and dry conditions made for good traveling weather. Edward kept the conversation light and the boys responded in kind until all were laughing outright.

Their route missed the Rice and McCrary farmsteads but took them by the Fisher, McNulty and Stuart's, where they paused to look for any signs the Cherokee, or others, had molested the farms or livestock in the owners' absence. All looked peaceful so the three rode on.

The Virginia Road was well packed from the summer and early fall traffic, and dry, so they made good time. The road was empty now, the summer migration south for cheap lands in North Carolina long over and most of those in this upper, or Southern, end of the county still safely quartered with the Jewetts. It was suppertime when they approached Steele's Tavern where they planned to spend the night. Edward noticed off to the west, on a nearby hilltop, what appeared to be a blockhouse under construction.

"Aye, it's a blockhouse alright. What with the French starting trouble in the Ohio country, it won't be long before the Shawnee start raiding here again. We thought we'd take your example and be ready for the savages when they come," Mister Steele told them as he served what passed for supper.

"What does Mister Bordon think of you building a blockhouse at the northern entrance to his grant?"

"Oh, his lordship is very pleased to have me paying the bill for the blockhouse, knowing just having it will make his tenants feel more secure and more likely to remain, paying him their rents for deeds to the land that they'll never get."

"I take it you don't think much of Mister Bordon, then?"

Spitting into the fireplace before answering, Steele said, "Not more than that I don't. But here now, I've said more than I should have, and you sitting on the county court and all."

"Now, now, Mister Bordon and I have little in common and nothing you say will make it to either him or Mister Lewis."

"That's another one for you. At least he's building his own blockhouse to keep his tenants happy, up on the Cowpasture River he is."

As they retired for the night, Philip asked Edward why everyone was suddenly building blockhouses.

"For the same reason we did, for protection. We showed how effective they can be and now all of the people buying land from Misters Bordon and Lewis are asking for arrangements similar to what we've made for our neighbors, who happen to be Mister Bordon's tenants, by the way."

The next morning, they arrived at Beverly's Mill Place and went straight to the County Clerk's office, where Edward presented his papers of manumission and indenture for recording.

"You know you can't manumit your slaves without prior authorization."

"Here is a letter authorizing me to manumit any slave in my possession as I see fit, signed by the Governor and the President of the Governor's Council. As any charges against me would be taken before the Colony's High Court, chaired by one of these two individuals. Who are you to question my authority?"

Philip always enjoyed it when Edward assumed the official air of a Colonel in His Majesty's Army and put some underpaid official in his place. He knew it was wrong, but he could not help it. He was proud of his uncle and the good things he had seen him do.

After entrusting his letter to the Governor to the regular post rider, Edward signaled it was time to start back for home. Before they departed, Thomas Lewis came looking for Edward.

"Have you heard Governor Dinwiddie has sent Major Washington to order the French out of the Ohio Country? I would suggest if you haven't already, that you invest in Ohio Company stock. A man could make a lot of money once that country is opened up to speculation."

"I am aware of Major Washington's mission and I even advised the Governor that I doubted it would have any effect other than to warn the French we are aware of their incursion into the Ohio Country before we're ready to do anything about it. As for investing in the Ohio Company, I have sufficient funds to meet my needs for the rest of my life and provide for my nephews. I need to do no speculating to increase my fortune."

Losing his temper at the ease of which Edward looked down on him, Thomas replied heatedly, "You are a cold fish, Colonel. Don't you see we're on the same side? My God, I don't understand what I've done to cause you to hold such contempt against me and my interests."

Mister Lewis' outburst surprised Edward and he paused before replying. "I hold you no ill will, Mister Lewis. I don't care for some of your business practices, it is true, but as long as everything is done according to the law, I have no complaints. I am just not a speculator, in land or stocks, and rely on my own fortunes to see to my needs and those of my family. I understand not everyone is blessed with such resources at their disposal and must do what they can to provide for their families. I hope that we can get past our different positions and become more amicable."

Thomas Lewis knew instantly his position as a gentleman had just been brought into question. To this he had no response or recourse. Edward had powerful friends at Court and had been presented to, and some said rewarded by, the King himself. No, if Edward brought his position as a gentleman into question, no amount of protesting on his part would do him any good. He decided instead to change the subject and try to win Edward's favor using another tact.

"What do you hear of the bill creating a Virginia Regiment?"

"I helped the Governor draft the bill and made the presentation to the Council, which endorsed it unanimously. All that is left is for the Burgesses to approve and fund the measure. It is a good bill and I'm afraid the Regiment will be called into service sooner rather than later now that the King's Cabinet has authorized our Governors to prevent, by force, any attempts at encroachment on the Dominions of His Majesty."

"I was unaware of that. Will you be the Regiment's Commander, or will you assume command of our county militia?"

"Neither, Colonel Lewis. Lord Halifax has suggested and His Royal Highness the Duke of Cumberland, Captain-General of the Army, has agreed to return me to the active list assigned as an advisor to Governor Dinwiddie. My Royal Commission will prevent me from taking either position though gives me some oversight of both."

Thomas Lewis was suitably awestruck at the ease with which Edward seemed to move at the very highest levels of the English governmental structure and the familiarity he just used when referring to the King's favorite son. No, he thought, I must find a way to garner his favor as to be his enemy would have very dire consequences to my own aspirations. Edward's use of Thomas' militia rank seemed to indicate a softening in his stiff attitude toward Thomas and Thomas chose to take advantage of this.

"I would love to hear more, Colonel. Would you and your nephews care to join me for an early dinner before you start for home?" he asked with the utmost civility.

Looking first to his nephews, whose faces gave

away their desire for a hot meal before their ride, agreed and the foursome retired to the tavern where they enjoyed their meal in a private dining room. The talk was of the latest news from London, including an accounting of the circular Lord Holdernesse, the Secretary of State for the Southern Department, had sent all of the Colonial Governors and the new naval base in Nova Scotia, named Halifax. Edward's relationship with Lord Halifax, a man an expensive new naval base was being named after, further reinforced Thomas' resolve to gain Edward's friendship.

Eating heartily while listening, both Philip and Charles were amazed at how little they really knew of their uncle. The ease with which he tossed out the names of the most important people in the Kingdom, obviously knowing them all, left them more than a little awed. They watched closely how he handled himself in this social situation, just as they had in the fights with the Shawnee, looking to learn and emulate his ways just as both looked to their grandfather for how to handle matters within the family.

Departing later than they expected, they again spent the night in Mister Steele's Tavern. As they sat down to supper in the small tavern's public, and only, dining room, Edward looked to both of his nephews and observed, "It seems you two are most interested in just three things: breakfast, dinner, and supper." Only the arrival of plates of food tempered their laughter.

☙ Chapter 45 ❧

*L*ife at the Jewett's fort settled down to its winter routine readily enough. Robert, Lewis, Henry, and Edward took to riding out each morning, looking over not too distant lands with an eye toward expanding their agricultural interests. The mild Virginia weather and having eight laborers they needed to keep occupied meant a lot of work could be done in advance of the spring planting season. Instructions were passed then to Sam, Jubal, and Miles each evening for the next day's work to be done.

Late in January, Esther and Jenny walked down to the mill. Having not seen much of Mister Agner over the past couple of weeks, they thought to check up on him and found him busy tending a fire under a large copper pot.

"Why, Mister Agner, I do believe you're drunk!" exclaimed Esther when they saw him stagger between wood pile and fire.

"Ah, Mistress Jewett and Missus Thompson, welcome. Drunk I am and drunk I'll stay until there's work to be done and I make no apologies for it. But it's just a little drunk I am."

"So, I assume you're making more whiskey in that kettle?"

"Aye, lassie, and it's getting so I can't make enough to keep myself pleasantly drunk, what with Tom McCrary and Jim Rice buying it up almost as fast as I can make it." Pausing to think, "You don't suppose they're reselling it, now do you? I mean, they always look so sober that they can't be drinking it themselves."

"Does the Colonel know what you're doing down here?"

"No, no, no, no, I don't suppose he does," was the thoughtful reply. "Now, your brother Henry, he knows. Odd thing, he didn't mind, but he also didn't ask for any to whet his whistle. Usually there are those who mind and those who drink. Those who drink don't mind, yet Henry, he don't mind and he don't drink. I'll need another drink to figure that one out."

"No you don't. We're expecting you to join us for dinner and you'd best be sober when you do. And a bath wouldn't hurt you any, either."

"A bath, in this weather? Why, I'd catch my death."

"Have it your way," Esther said as she and Jenny turned to leave. Stepping a little wide, she managed to bump Mister Agner right off his feet and into the mill pond. "Oh, I am so sorry Mister Agner, are you all right?"

After splashing around in the cold water, Mister Agner stood up, the pond only being waist deep, now fully sober. "I'm fine, Mistress Jewett, I'm fine."

"Well then, you might try a little soap with the water," tossing a bar of strong soap to him. "Remember, we expect you to join us for supper, today."

Suppressing their giggles until they were out of hearing, they did steal a glance back to see Mister Agner actually using the soap as he squatted in the cold water, cursing. "That really wasn't very nice, Esther, necessary, just not very nice," Jenny giggled as they continued their walk back to the little fort.

Discussing the development that evening after supper, it was Robert who objected most strongly to Mark Agner's whiskey operation. Even so, he had to admit that whiskey brought a good profit and was one of the few ways for the local farmers to turn their surplus corn crop into a cash crop. Still, he did not like it.

Edward went to see Mark Agner the next day and found Tom McCrary and Jim Rice visiting. These two were more than accommodating, permitting the still to be moved to Tom's farm where they would see to it, providing Mark all the whiskey he wanted, free of charge, and a share of any profits generated. Crisis averted, life on the Jewett Grant returned to peaceful harmony.

A post rider from Williamsburg arrived bringing news of Major Washington's failure in convincing the French to quit the Ohio Country. Relaying the Governor's intention of sending a force of several hundred to the Forks of the Ohio to protect Virginia's interests, it asked Edward's opinion on promoting the young Major to Lieutenant Colonel and second in command of the proposed Virginia Regiment.

The post rider waited, enjoying a hot meal and short rest, while Edward composed his reply. In it he told the Governor he liked Major Washington and that the Major probably had more experience in the west than any of the other candidates. That said, he was too young and inexperienced to be placed in command of a military expedition of such import. Edward saw little good would come of such an assignment. Instead, there was a Royal Army Captain, James MacKay, currently in South Carolina in command of a Royal Army Independent Company, who would be a better choice to lead the expedition the Governor intended.

Two days passed when Nelson Beverly and James Bordon showed up at the Jewett fort enroute to Williamsburg. They informed Edward that a special session of the House of Burgesses had been called over the problems with the French. Edward shared what he knew of the situation and encouraged them to support the bill establishing a Virginia Regiment.

"I think you can see where the creation of a Virginia Regiment is in our best interests here on the frontier. It will do little for the counties around the Bay while it could mean the difference between success and financial ruin for many here in the Valley," Edward said, as he cast a knowing look to each of his guests. His meaning was not lost on them.

Should the French prevail and send their allied Indians into the Valley, their tenants and freeholders would move back east of the Blue Ridge. The loss of the rents and business at, for instance, the mills they owned would cause them to default on their obligations and could spell their ruin. When the two men left to continue their journey, they were completely convinced to vote and lobby in favor of the bill.

"That went well, Edward. You seem to now have won over all three of the area's leading men to your cause. Don't look so surprised. Didn't you expect Philip and Charles to give me a nearly verbatim account of your meeting with Tomas Lewis?" Robert was grinning at his son's surprise. Edward was not the only one who knew how to gather information in this family.

By the time Edward received a letter from Governor Dinwiddie announcing the creation of the Virginia

Regiment, Edward was already aware of the Burgess vote. Nelson Beverly and James Bordon had stopped on their return from Williamsburg to bring him all the news of the special session. They had also told him what the Governor's letter confirmed, the Regiment's Lieutenant Colonel would be George Washington, who had been ordered to Alexandria to recruit and train 200 men for an expedition to the Forks of the Ohio.

The Governor's letter included his reasons for making this choice, the primary one being Washington's status as a Virginian and thus under the Governor's authority while Captain MacKay was in the Royal Army and not subject to the Governor's orders. The letter was warm and enjoined Edward not to mistake the Governor's decision against Edward's advice as in any way being interpreted as his not valuing Edward or his experience in military matters. This was clearly a political decision.

"So, Sarah, I suppose father has told you that young George Washington is to lead an expedition to the Forks of the Ohio soon. I suppose that is of some concern to you," Edward teased his niece.

"It concerns me not in the least. It has been a year and a half and more and not so much as a letter has come my way. In any case, he's so shy I doubt he'll amount to much anyway."

"Oh, I wouldn't be too sure of that. For one so young, he appears on course to start a major war. Whether he will be able to survive it once he sets it in motion, that is another issue all together," concluded Edward, thoughtfully this time.

Letters between Williamsburg and the Jewett fort on the North River continued through the late winter and spring. Edward also wrote, on behalf of the Governor, to Lord Halifax and the Duke of Cumberland outlining the situation and the critical need for their support. Letters to the adjoining colonies yielded no support and, thus far, letters to England had gone unanswered.

Travel down the Virginia Road slowed to a trickle as families stopped moving into territory that might soon come under Indian attack. This was likely good, even if Tom McCrary and Jim Rice did not think so. They saw their opportunity to make a fortune trading whiskey to the travelers turn to a trickle as well, making it hardly worth the trouble to distill it. Robert was secretly glad of the development, even if he would not come right out and tell them so.

Late April brought word that Lieutenant Colonel Washington had left Alexandria at the head of a column of 160 volunteers. Edward noted this was shy of the 200 the Governor had anticipated. It was encouraging that, in early May, the Governor's letter included the release of Captain MacKay's independent company from South Carolina to reinforce Washington. That was something at least. Edward wondered what a force of less than 300 would be able to accomplish if the French sent a large force to stake their claim to the Ohio Country.

Things were developing around their fort as well. The laborers were diligently clearing and planting more fields. They were a happy lot now, no one holding back and most evenings found them singing softly around the little fort they all called home. Edward did worry how long this would last, with six healthy young men being here without women while two of them had wives. He shared this concern with Robert, who also lacked answers or ideas.

Henry's cabin was always neat and clean, good food on the table, and Henry actually started to gain a little weight, unusual for a man who had spent his entire life rail thin. Each and every Friday, without fail, Jenny came to see Edward for her shilling six pence. As the weeks passed, he noticed she no longer flirted with him when she came by for her payment. He wondered.

"Esther, is anything going on between Jenny and Henry?" Edward finally asked.

"Not that either would admit to, but I think they are becoming very comfortable with each other. I wouldn't be surprised to find you are no longer her intended victim. Then again, I'm sure if you wanted, you could win her back." Esther could hardly finish her sentence without laughing and both brother and sister enjoyed the joke knowing Edward would do nothing to interfere, possibly even encouraging the match.

Then came news that caused dread throughout the Valley of Virginia. First it was of the French having evicted the English fortified trading post at the Forks of the Ohio with a large force. Next it was of Lieutenant Colonel Washington's assault on a small French force and his falling back on a hastily built stockade at Great Meadows. Questions swirled around this episode and Edward only shook his head at what he saw as mistakes one would expect in an inexperienced youth, only these could have much larger consequences.

Edward at once began holding regular drill to train his laborers in handling muskets. If trouble came, they would need all the able bodied men they could arm. Sam and Jubal were very helpful but it was Miles who did an outstanding job as Drill Sergeant. He had warmed to the idea of these former slaves being freed, had even come to like them, though he would not admit it openly to anyone but Mattie. They learned fast and readily understood the trust the Jewetts were placing in them. Robert told Edward how one could never have gotten slaves to perform as well as these newly freed men, either in their labors or their drill.

The worst news came with the arrival of Colonel Thomas Lewis and a squad of militia.

"Colonel, we've just received word the French have attacked and defeated Lieutenant Colonel Washington's force at Great Meadow. The militia has been called out and we've been reinforced from Albemarle County. If it is alright with you, I'd like to detail six men and a Sergeant to man your blockhouse. I'm placing similar details in all the blockhouses in the County. They would, naturally, be under your command."

"Just so there is no misunderstanding and in your presence, Sergeant, Sir Robert commands here. You will take your instructions directly from him or, in his absence, Lewis Jewett. They hold ranks equivalent to Lieutenant Colonel and Major, respectively, here. Do you understand?" When the Sergeant acknowledged, Edward turned back to Colonel Lewis, "Any objections to what I've just said, Colonel?"

"None. Sergeant, you heard the Colonel, now see to the quartering of your troops."

Thomas Lewis remained overnight at the Jewett's, enjoying the hospitality. Edward, Robert, Lewis, and Henry gathered with him after supper to more fully discuss what he knew of the events at Great Meadows. Robert saw how troubled Edward was once he fully understood what had transpired. The discussions went on late into the night and, though all were up at their normal pre-dawn hour, it was obvious Edward had not slept.

After Colonel Lewis and the rest of his squad departed, Robert joined Edward in his cabin.

"Edward, it sounds really bad to me. Is it as bad as it seems?

"Worse, I'm afraid. I've asked Aaron to have my

things ready for a trip to Williamsburg, or wherever else the Governor requests me. I'm sure I'll be gone a long time. Do you think you can manage things here? If things get too bad, you can always move everyone east of the Blue Ridge for safety."

"We'll manage, and we'll be here when you get back."

It happened within two weeks, only not quite as Edward had expected. A post rider on a lathered horse arrived at their little fort one afternoon before dinner with a letter for Edward sealed with the Governor's seal. Robert, Edward, Lewis, and Henry all went to Edward's cabin to open it. What they found was a five word note:

'Come quick. I need you. Robert Dinwiddie'

"This is it, father, what we've expected, only from the nature of the note, it must be worse than we thought." And then calling to Aaron, "Make ready. We leave for Williamsburg within the hour."

Chapter 46

hilip and Charles were laughing as they walked back toward the little fort. They had slipped off from doing their chores to watch the militia drill. The Sergeant had his six men and Miles joined him with the eight laborers. What the boys found so funny was how much better at drill the laborers were than the militia men. The boys failed to understand that these were the sons of farmers hit hard by the depressed price of tobacco. They were not soldiers, really, only men whose fathers needed the little cash the Colony paid while their sons were away on militia duty.

The laughter stopped quite suddenly when the boys saw Marie leading a heavily lathered horse from the fort toward the barn. They knew in an instant something was going on and both took off running toward the closest gate. Coming through the gate, Philip saw his father and grandfather standing at the gate opposite, looking out toward the hill that blocked their view of the ford across the North River. Both looked sad.

"Father, what is it? We saw mother with the lathered horse, has something bad happened?" Philip gasped out, breathing heavily from the run he had just completed.

"I'm afraid it has. The Governor has sent for your uncle, rather urgently, and he has just left for what may be a very long time."

Turning to Charles, Philip continued excitedly, "Williamsburg, I'll bet if we hurry we could catch him at the ford and go along."

"Not this time, Philip," said Robert in an unusually stern voice. "Your uncle is going once again off to war, and that is no place for you or Charles." Then, in a quieter tone more for Lewis than the boys, "If it's fighting they want I think they may get their fill staying right here." This caused Charles and Philip to nervously look at each other.

Lewis looked anxiously back toward the spot on the hill where his brother had so recently disappeared. "Boys, there is something you can do. Saddle your horses, mine, and Uncle Henry's and ask Uncle Henry to join us for a little ride. I think you'll find him in the barn, building furniture." Then, back to Robert, "We'd best be passing the news to our neighbors that we may be getting some unwelcome company from the west and north. I'll have Henry and Charles take the closer farmsteads, the Mc-Crary's, Rice's, and Fisher's, while Philip and I ride to the Bennett's, Stuart's and McNulty's. We can then meet at the Gordon's and ride back together. Will you be alright here alone?"

"Alone? Even with you four gone I've got the makings of a good sized company here," Robert said, smiling even though the smile did not extend to his eyes. "You go ahead. And you'd better set up for three patrols a day instead of the two we're now doing. If the Shawnee do come, we want to know it as soon as possible to give those poor families a chance."

As the boys rushed around to get the horses ready,

Robert asked Esther and Betty to wrap up some dinner for the four so they could eat on the trail. Once they were out the gate and on their way, the rest of the little company sat down to a quiet, subdued meal under the awning, as was their habit in good weather, all breaking bread together. All, that is, except for Mister Agner, who only rarely made his appearance at the table. He was sober now as he prepared the mill for this year's corn harvest.

"Sarah," Robert began, "would you and your Aunt Esther please go and see Mister Agner after you're done with dinner and invite him up for supper tonight? In fact, you should probably tell him to plan on sleeping in the fort from now on, just for his own safety. Oh," giving an amused glance in Esther's direction, "please see your aunt doesn't go helping Mister Agner take a bath again, will you? She can suggest it, even demand it, but it is most improper for her, an unmarried woman, to actually help an unrelated widower with his bath."

Esther had to appear indignant while the laughter went around the table, especially from Sarah, Jenny, and Rebecca, the whole while, admitting only to herself, it was pretty funny. "And if I hadn't, who'd have been laughing then?" she quipped before giving into the laughter herself.

Henry and Charles were the first to reach the Gordon farmstead and found them much alarmed. One of the Gordon children thought she spied an Indian watching her as she fetched water from their spring. They were very happy to see help arrive. All remained at the cabin until Lewis and Philip arrived, when the four Jewetts scouted around the cabin for any Indian sign. And sign they found.

"What do you make of it, Lewis?"

"Looks to me to be a small party, maybe just a few scouts looking us over to determine how best to attack."

"There were four of them, father," Philip piped in. "See here, where each hid behind the laurels, probably when Janie came for water. They moved off to the west, see?"

Lewis and Henry scratched their heads. It looked like the boy was right. They had both seen the signs but had not interpreted them until Philip pointed the details out to them. After a brief consultation, they decided to reverse their routes and pass this information on to the farmsteads they had just visited and meet back at the fort. When they told the Gordons what they had seen, the Gordons decided that with only one gun for protection, they would move to the fort now.

Before splitting up again, the Jewetts followed the trail left by the Indians for nearly a mile. As it joined no other groups of Indians, as best as they could tell, they split up to spread the latest news. The Rices, also with only one gun for protection, decided to move to the fort while the other families chose to remain on their farmsteads, ready to move on short notice.

Over the next couple of weeks, signs of small Indian scouting parties continued to appear. All, like the one found near the Gordon's, were small groups of four or five, the largest being six, each apparently moving in to scout a single farmstead before moving back a considerable distance. No one knew if these were multiple groups or if it was the same small band making multiple scouts over several days. Also they found it odd that no sign was found in a place where the Jewett's fort could be observed, only the farmsteads lying nearer the Virginia Road.

Colonel Lewis rode in one day with a mounted militia escort. His news was grim.

"One of my tenants had his place raided up along the Cowpasture two days ago. A boy was taken for sure, two women wounded, and there are others who've gone missing. The Indians were moving west pretty fast and it looks like this was just some mischief they did on their way home. I can't be sure, though, and it's good you're on your guard here. I wish all the settlers were as well prepared as those in this section of the county."

The Indian sign diminished after that and the Gordons and Rices returned to their farmstead to bring in their harvests. Patrols continued at three per day, always on the watch and each patrol visiting each of the seven farmsteads and the fort on their rounds. Lewis managed the patrols while Robert oversaw the watch maintained at the little fort. Robert also had two of the militia men go with Mister Agner each day to guard him as he worked grinding the harvest at the mill. With the laborers now well drilled, everyone went about their business well-armed.

Esther was doing laundry one day when Jenny joined her with Henry's laundry. At first working side by side in silence, Jenny finally spoke.

"What kind of man is Henry?"

"He's a good man, quiet, gentle, prefers to sit back and let others do the deciding. Why do you ask? I'd have thought by now you'd know him as well as any of us." Jenny's blush and her shocked look caused Esther to immediately add, "Oh, no, I don't mean it that way! No one has suggested anything improper is going on."

"Good, because it isn't! No, but I have grown fond of him and Charles without letting Henry know it. I've sort of been waiting for him to say he'd grown fond of me, but he hasn't. I thought I'd talk to you and see if you think it'd be alright if I would bring it up to him. I have been keeping house for him for many months now, you'd think he'd have noticed."

"Henry, notice? Lewis or Edward would have taken

note right away and you'd know one way or the other with them, in short order, like I think you did with Edward." Jenny nodded sadly. "Henry, on the other hand, just accepts things as they are. He does best when he's married and there's someone to kind of goad him on. Don't get me wrong, he's a hard worker, as you've seen, only..."

"So, what you're saying is that if it is to go beyond me just cleaning up after him and cooking for him, I'll have to be the one to bring it up."

"That's the way Mary got him, she had to push him into it."

"Then what do you think the reaction would be from you father and brothers? Am I shameless for bringing this up? Will they argue against me or evict me from the fort? Or do you think they'd welcome me into the family, assuming Henry agrees?"

Putting her arm around Jenny, Esther said, "I would have thought you'd know the rest of us better than that as well, Jenny Thompson. In case you hadn't noticed, you've already been welcomed into the family. Edward and father saw to that. No one here would think the worse of you, a widow, for taking up with a widower, both of you in need of the other. Some of us have been kind of expecting it," giving Jenny a knowing, reassuring grin.

Jenny remained thoughtful for a moment and then nodded as if she had made up her mind, and the two continued their washing in silence.

After supper that evening, Esther noticed Jenny approach Henry and the two walked out of the little fort together, side by side but with clear distance between them. No, she thought, Jenny was attractive and prone to flirting, but she was a good woman and would be good for Henry and Charles. Sarah might even find herself back under her father's roof.

When they returned, it was Henry who was blushing as he went to call on his father. As he and Robert discussed the situation, Esther was in her usual chair, out of the way but able to hear all that was said, sewing. Listening to Henry, more than once she had to stifle a laugh at how little he understood women in general and Jenny in particular. It was also apparent he has grown fond of Jenny as she had of him.

Robert came over to Esther's side after Henry left, "So, I suppose you know something about this?"

"Why father, whatever do you mean?"

"Now, don't play coy with me. Not only did you hear what we were discussing, I have a feeling Jenny talked with you before taking the matter up with Henry. Ah, I can see it in your face that I'm right! Never have you been able to tell a falsehood without giving yourself away! All I have to do now is sit back and wait to see who tells Jenny of my approval first, Henry or you!

They were still laughing when Jenny came into the cabin with Rebecca and Sarah. To their inquiries, Robert waved it off with a simple, "She was just picking on her old, feeble father again. I do hope you young ladies have come to give solace to an old man so abused by his only daughter."

Jenny's "humph" set them all to laughing as the household then prepared to turn in for the night.

◇ Chapter 47 ◇

*I*t had been a long, tiring ride. Without stopping to even brush the trail dust off his clothes, Edward rode directly to the Governor's Palace upon reaching Williamsburg and was shown immediately in to see Governor Dinwiddie. The Governor's appearance was also less than inspiring, dressed haphazardly in a dressing gown, unshaven, and obviously in great mental turmoil.

"Ah, Edward, you arrive at last. Things are bad, very bad, and I need your sage advice to help me with this," he said, handing Edward a single piece of paper.

Reading the paper, Edward could not believe what it said. "Governor, no, you can not resign, not now. Things may well be as bad as you claim, I won't dispute you. Your resignation would only make a bad situation worse."

"Don't you see? I must do something to get London's attention, to get them moving, and if my letters don't have the desired effect, maybe my resigning will."

"What does London say? Nothing? Not because nothing is happening, but because it is too soon for a response to have made it to us. I have written to both Lord Halifax and the Duke of Cumberland on your behalf as well, yet I know it is too soon for London to have received, reacted, and responded. We must be patient. Now, what of young Washington? I assume he has fallen back to Wills Creek? What is the state of his troops?"

All the news was, indeed, bad. With the Burgess refusing to appropriate additional funding in their August session, there was little that could be done. No additional troops could be raised to reinforce those with Washington and there was even little to help supply his dwindling number of troops as desertions escalated.

The two men talked through dinner and supper and well into the night trying to find ways to supply Washington. Something had to be done to counter the French, who had now completely taken over the Forks of the Ohio, or the entire Ohio Country would be lost to England and Virginia. By time they concluded their session, it was clear to both men that this would require help from England. It was not something Virginia could take on alone or even with the help of a couple of adjacent Colonies.

"Edward, you are tired, trail worn, and I haven't even given you time to arrange your lodgings. I took the liberty of renting the Lightfoot house, where you and your family stayed when you first came to Williamsburg. I do hope you don't mind."

"Thank you very much, Governor. By the looks of things, we both need some rest. Shall we meet again tomorrow?"

"Quite right. With your help I finally feel like I can rest. Shall we meet for dinner, then, giving us both time to recover?"

Over the next weeks, the two men wrestled with creditors and suppliers to forward as much in the way of supplies to Washington as possible. Every Royal Navy vessel that made port in Virginia was relieved of some of its ship stores to add to what was otherwise acquired.

Finally a note to Edward from the Duke of Cumberland gave both hope. The King had approved a plan to send two regiments of Irish infantry under the command of a Major General to help Virginia beat back the French, first from the Forks of the Ohio, then northward to New York, and finally on to destroy the forts the French had recently built encroaching on Nova Scotia. When Edward brought the news, the Governor was delighted.

Lord Halifax sent Governor Dinwiddie a copy of the official notification from the Secretary of War, Sir Henry Fox, complete with the name of the Major General to command the expedition, Edward Braddock. He also ordered the two regiments "to repair forthwith to their posts." Lord Halifax's letter showed he was quite pleased with this development and promised more as soon as General Braddock's orders were published.

"Edward, you don't seem pleased with General Braddock. May I ask why?"

Edward hesitated for what he was asked would take him beyond the bounds of propriety. He continued anyway, "He's a good man, good administrator and disciplinarian, though he can be a bit blunt and profane. My concern is that he is not the most experienced at either tactics or battlefield command. European tactics simply won't work here and my opinion is General Braddock will hear none of this. Nor is he at all flexible in interpreting his orders, regardless of conditions he finds on the battlefield."

The Duke of Cumberland forwarded a copy of Major General Braddock's orders to Governor Dinwiddie, and indeed all of America's colonial governors, for they gave the General far reaching powers. Not only was he bringing with him two regiments, the two regiments deactivated in the colonies at the end of the War of Austrian Succession, the three regiments in Nova Scotia, and the seven independent companies stationed in New York and South Carolina were all to be under his direct command. Plus all the colonies were directed to contribute to a common defense fund with the Major General the sole administrator.

Governor Dinwiddie gave Edward the task of preparing for the arrival of the Major General and the troops they thought would arrive shortly thereafter. The most direct route to Wills Creek, where Washington remained, hanging on by his teeth, would be from Alexandria, not Williamsburg, so Edward left word at Norfolk for the troop ships to be sent there directly. Billeting and provisions arranged, Edward returned to Williamsburg just in advance of the General's arrival.

"Colonel Jewett, I wondered if you would show up. I had heard you'd retired to the Colonies but couldn't remember exactly where, or why for that matter."

"General, it is good to see you again. As for the why, you may recall that I was born in the colonies and have simply returned home."

"Ah, yes. Well, perhaps you can help me strap a backbone onto these Colonials so we might get about the King's business."

"General, Colonel Jewett is my military advisor, assigned that duty by the Duke of Cumberland himself, with Lord Halifax's concurrence, to be sure. Rest assured we will be of whatever help we can be."

Edward found himself in the middle between the Governor and the General. The General did little to make friends or allies out of any of the Colonial officials from any of the Colonies and Edward was frequently called upon to try to exert some influence over the General to moderate his responses. That was an impossible task.

At a conference in April between the Major General and five of the most affected Colonial Governors in Alexandria, Virginia, Edward accompanied Governor Dinwiddie. The way General Braddock ordered these governors about caused a lot of discontent that was, in private, visited upon Edward with the usual request to get the General to moderate his stance on one topic or another.

One evening, Governor Dinwiddie asked Edward what he thought of Governor Shirley's suggestion that Fort Niagara be taken before General Braddock proceeded against the Forks of the Ohio.

"It is a good suggestion, as was Governor Morris' that the expedition use the Pennsylvania route, which is 100 miles shorter than Colonel Washington's track. But you heard General Braddock's response, 'It would be against the orders given me by the Duke of Cumberland.' As I think I told you, he rigidly holds to his orders, even those generated thousands of miles away. We've a hard fight ahead of us."

"Go with him, then, and try to make him see things better. Or at least try to make the best of any situation he gets us into. I'll tell him you'll accompany as my personal representative."

Edward left with the General and his full staff to join the Army in Frederick, Maryland. Most of the way there Edward rode beside the General, listening to his ravings about how these Colonials had not been forthcoming in providing his quartermaster sufficient wagons for the expedition or the horses needed to pull them, Pennsylvania in particular receiving his approbation.

Arriving in Frederick, Edward introduced Lieutenant Colonel Washington to the General and, while the two sat discussing the situation, he took the Pennsylvania representative aside for a private conversation.

"Doctor Franklin, I'm afraid the General is most disagreeable toward your Colony right now. Might I suggest it in your best interests if you could provide for the Army's logistical needs, horses and wagons? That shouldn't offend their Quaker sensibilities, should it?"

'Thank you, Colonel Jewett, thank you very much. That is most helpful and I shall act on it. But, see, the General is signaling for one of us, maybe both, shall we adjourn until later?"

It was really Edward the General was signaling for, wondering if he knew anything of the Pennsylvania representative who was to meet them. The General went on about the miserable bunch of Quakers not supporting his efforts before Edward could interrupt him and introduce Doctor Benjamin Franklin, representative of Governor Morris and the Pennsylvania Assembly as well as deputy postmaster general for the colonies.

General Braddock found Doctor Franklin not only charming, but most helpful, seemingly willing to do anything possible to provide for the Army's logistic needs. "If the other Colonies were just this forthcoming, our ranks would be filled and our quartermaster stores overflowing. Now if only he can produce on his promises," the General confided to Edward after Doctor Franklin departed.

Edward took the opportunity to broach a subject considered somewhat delicate. "General, would you consider bringing young Washington along as one of your Aides, a volunteer perhaps? He knows the country well and I think would be most valuable to you on the march. He is willing to forego command of the Virginia provincials to serve on your staff."

The General took the night to consider the suggestion and Edward was able to give George Washington the news he had hoped for, that the General would permit him to serve as a volunteer aide working directly on General Braddock's staff. He also took the opportunity to mentor the younger man in military matters.

"George, you allowed yourself to be surrounded and defeated, not considering that at the time it was more important that you preserve your command than hold your ground. You were so intent on advancing into overwhelming odds that you discounted the strategic value of retreat, if properly executed. I hope the next time you have the opportunity to command, you'll consider that."

Three weeks later, Benjamin Franklin returned with not only 150 wagons and teams, but with 500 packhorses as well as a pack train of 20 additional horses loaded with delicacies, a gift from the Pennsylvania Assembly for the junior officers of the King's Irish Regiments.

"Ah, Doctor Franklin, you have done yourself, and your Colony, well."

"Yes, yes, Colonel Jewett, and it is with thanks to your advice that I was able to avert a crisis and now General Braddock has only kind words to say about Pennsylvania. I can not thank you enough and I have made those who matter in Pennsylvania aware of your assistance in this matter. Rest assured, it won't be forgotten."

"You are too kind, sir. But I also came into possession of one of your handbills that could be read to threaten an invasion from this Army to seize the wagons if they could not be hired. You are a shrewd man, Doctor. I admire that."

Edward left with Doctor Franklin a letter he asked be posted, in Doctor Franklin's position as the deputy postmaster general of the colonies. He wanted his father to know that, despite his best efforts, he would not be able to visit home before the expedition began. He had been gone now eight months, a short time compared to his previous absences, but he had grown quite fond of living in and among his extended family and longed to be back there.

⊘ *Chapter 48* ⊘

*T*his time it was the entire Jewett family, save Edward, who were making the ride to Beverly's Mill Place for Robert to attend the April County Court session. With the addition of the detail of militia at their little fort, the training of the laborers to help defend the place, and putting Miles in charge while they were gone, Robert decided they could all go to town for Henry and Jenny's wedding. It was too bad they could not convince the minister to come to them, but with the uncertainty of the things with the Indians, they understood the man's reluctance to travel alone.

As the little cavalcade approached Steele's Tavern they were met by a post rider out of Williamsburg with a dispatch case for Robert. The dinner pause at the tavern gave Robert, Lewis, and Henry the opportunity to open the case while the others retired into the tavern. Inside was a letter from Edward, written, according to the outside, while with the Army in Frederick, Maryland.

As Robert read the letter to his other two sons he sensed a sadness in Edward's writing that he had not noticed in the letters he was used to receiving, while he was off serving the King in England or Europe somewhere. And there was also the implication that he was at odds with the Major General, a man he knew from before but did not especially think was the right man for this assignment.

For Sarah, he included news of young George Washington, who would be going with him and the Army to the Forks of the Ohio as a volunteer aide to the General. At this point, Robert stopped and lowered the letter.

"My God, Edward is to go with the Army to the Forks. I was sure he'd stay behind in Williamsburg, or perhaps Alexandria."

"Why does that upset you so, father?" Henry asked. "He's traveled with armies and fought in battles before this. Why should this time be different?"

"It's more what he doesn't say, what he implies. He's not happy with how this expedition is going, can't you see? That means he isn't as confident of success as a soldier should be going into battle. A soldier must either be confident or resolved, not resigned as this letter indicates. No, I have a bad feeling about this one, boys. Not a word of this to the women, mind you, but if General Braddock is not successful, we're in for a hard fight here."

Finishing the letter and returning it to its pouch, the three men joined the rest for dinner in Mister Steele's tavern before proceeding on. Robert put on a good show, answering the questions about the letter in a lighthearted manner, painting everything as going splendidly.

Watching her father closely, Esther had her doubts about his honesty, though she did not raise them. She was not the only one in the family who had trouble telling falsehoods.

They arrived at Beverly's Mill Place that evening, just in time for supper, and took up their lodgings in two cabins Nelson Beverly had arranged for them. The following day was set for the wedding. Although well attended, it was a simple wedding in the small building that passed for a Presbyterian Church. The Wedding Feast was at Beverly Manor where the happy couple spent their first night while the rest of the family returned to their lodgings.

The following day was the beginning of the Court Session. Lewis and Henry took the rest of the family and started back for home while Charles and Philip remained with their grandfather. Much like for his son, the crowd that gathered in the courthouse always made way and showed the respect they felt for Robert, resplendent in the suits Edward insisted he have made on their last trip to Williamsburg. As usual, Robert took his place as the presiding Justice and the three days of hearings went on as usual.

There were just three Justices now, Thomas Lewis being occupied with his militia duties. The two younger men always gave way to Robert in the decisions. Robert lacked the hard edge that Edward could show, but his grandfatherly ways, humorous anecdotes, and sometimes feigned forgetfulness were used to great effect to impart justice to each of the cases that came before them. The people filling the courtroom loved him for this. They also liked it when Edward would sit on the bench for he would usually give the large landowners their comeuppance to the great joy of the crowd.

They left Beverly's Mill Place the morning after Court adjourned for the ride home. Robert had a dinner packed so they could eat on the way and would lose no time returning home. He had been anxious ever since reading Edward's letter, a feeling he could not shake, that something was going terribly wrong.

It was well after dinner time when they saw smoke above the treetops. Coming to the Fisher farmstead, they found it completely burned, house, barns, sheds, every-thing. Thankfully, they found no bodies among the wreck-age, only a lot of Indian sign. Now on their guard they started for their fort, cautiously but with due haste. They had not gone far when they met the patrol, led by Lewis, heading for the smoke they too had seen.

"Lewis, it's the Fisher place, completely destroyed. All the sign is very fresh. Where are the Fishers?"

"The noon patrol picked up Indian sign not far west of their farmstead. When advised of this, Abel moved his family immediately to the blockhouse. It sounds like they got out just in time. Could you tell how many Indians there were?"

"Father, it looked to Charles and me like there were five. Are you going after them?"

"Yes. Now, you two get your grandfather home safe, you hear?"

Disappointed at not being asked to join the chase, both boys still answered in the affirmative, then watched as Lewis, Tom McCrary, Jim Rice, and Ben Gordon rode out after the fleeing Indians. Last year's lesson of Joseph still fresh in their minds, they then turned toward home, keeping a sharp watch so they did not fall into an Indian ambush themselves.

Lewis' mind was racing. It had been just a year since Marie was taken prisoner and it was Edward leading that pursuit. How he wished Edward was here now. Instead it fell to him not to make the same mistakes Tommy Thomp-son had made that got Joseph killed. The Indian trail was easy to follow, too easy, and Lewis immediately suspected an ambush. They had the advantage of speed afforded by the horses so, after a brief consultation on what trail the Indians would take and how best to get ahead of them, the little band moved quickly to try to head them off.

The trail the Indians had taken up closely followed the one taken a year ago with their three prisoners, so Lewis cut cross country heading for the clearing where they had rescued Marie. Not finding any sign the Indians had passed there recently, they tied their horses and started cautiously moving back down the trail.

It was Ben Gordon who signaled the halt, not for anything he saw but for something he smelled. He smelled sweaty bodies mixed with Indian paint on the light breeze they had been walking into. The four men looked hard into the undergrowth, trying to discern any movement or sign. They did not have long to wait. An Indian stood up to look down the trail, opposite the patrol but in the direction they would have been coming had they stuck to the trail. Now they had a fix on at least one of the Indians. Using this as a reference point, they slowly were able to make out the figures of the other four in the early evening light.

Using hand signals, each patrol member picked his target and, on Lewis' signal, they all fired at once. Two Indians dropped face first into the bushes they had been hiding behind and another was spun around by a bullet to the shoulder. The suddenness of the attack had the effect Lewis hoped for, giving them time to reload before the remaining Indians recovered. The two uninjured Indians, seeing their disadvantage, slipped into the undergrowth and were gone. Jim Rice managed to get off a second shot at the Indian he had only wounded with his first and brought him down.

"Well, Ben, I see you're shooting hasn't improved since our scrape with the Indians at the ford, what, a year and a half ago was it?" Lewis chided.

"Yes, I missed clean. But Jim only wounded his." And then to Jim, "Took you two!" bringing grins from all but Jim, who looked disgustedly at his sights as if that was the problem.

Returning to the business at hand, Lewis continued their whispered dialogue, "We're losing the light and we know there are at least two more still out there. I suggest we retire to your cabin, Ben, it's the closest, and rest while keeping a good watch. We can then take off after these two in the morning. We don't know but what there are others about as well."

As they began to move cautiously back toward where they had left the horses, Lewis had to stop Jim from taking the scalp of the Indian he shot. "Jim, by leaving them with their hair, we reduce the animosity the Indians show toward us. Leave it."

Shots rang out as they neared the horses and Ben Gordon went down while the others took cover. It seems the hunters had become the hunted. The white smoke left no doubt where the four Indians who had fired were and three shots rang out in response. No sooner did the patrol see one Indian drop than three more came rushing from cover wielding knives, tomahawks, and war clubs.

Three more shots rang out, dropping two more Indians, as the patrol now emptied the guns they had recovered from the three Indians they had just killed in the last engagement. This surprise sent the final Indian running into the dense cover. Jim Rice moved quickly to take up Ben's unfired gun to cover Lewis and Tom as they reloaded. Only when the little party had all seven guns loaded did they take stock of their situation.

"How are you, Ben?" inquired Lewis in a hushed tone.

"Filthy savages hit me in the same leg they got me in the last time. Hurts bad but I've got it wrapped tight to stop the blood."

"Tom, Jim, either of you hurt?" With a negative response from both, Lewis continued. "Obviously there's more here than we thought. We know for sure there are three presumably unhurt Indians in our immediate vicinity. We don't know how many other parties are out here. I think we need to get Ben back to the fort tonight. We can come out again tomorrow, with a larger party than we have now."

All being in agreement, they moved cautiously to the horses. Ben was the only one to mount, the rest leading their horses to make it easier to slip into the underbrush should they come upon another ambush in the growing dusk. It took them a long time to reach Ben Gordon's cabin this way, but they made it unmolested. There they mounted and made quick time back to the now worried inhabitants of the little fort.

Betty once again patched up Ben's leg, with Jenny's help and while Ben's worried wife looked on. He had been lucky, both times shot in the same leg and both bullets had passed through flesh, not breaking the bone.

"It sounds to me like you broke up two raiding parties working together," observed Robert. "My guess is the second group you ran into had been watching the Fisher farmstead and followed you from there."

"That makes the most sense as to how they got between us and our horses so quickly and without detection," responded Tom McCrary.

"I plan to go back after them with a larger patrol in the morning, father. What do you think?" asked Lewis.

After a few moments in thought, Robert responded, "I'd stay put in the morning. We can send out a larger patrol at noon. My suspicion is they'll expect a quick response like that and may just be waiting for you, if there are more than the three we know about out there. No sense giving them what they want."

The Fishers had taken the news of their loss hard. As the men discussed what to do next, Abel announced his family would not rebuild. As soon as it was safe, they were going east. His friends tried to talk him out of it, pointing out the depressed tobacco prices meant he was unlikely to find farm work to the east, but he was not persuaded. Robert closed this discussion by observing no decisions needed to be made tonight. Once the Indian threat was past, then they could revisit who wanted to leave and who would stay and make arrangements accordingly.

"As for me and mine, we're here and here we'll stay. Any who are of the same mind are welcome to stay here with us for as long as necessary. Any who wish to leave for the east when this crisis has passed can do so knowing should they decide to return they'll be welcomed home."

Chapter 49

Edward could not believe his ears. General Braddock had just told Doctor Franklin how the savages would make no impression at all against his disciplined regulars. Both the good doctor and George Washington were looking at Edward now, with shocked looks on their faces. The General was oblivious to all of this.

To compound his error of attitude, he summarily dismissed the women who had come with the Mingos, resulting in most of their men going with them, and then told the leading war chief of the Ohio Delaware's that, once the English were successful, Ohio lands would not be inherited by the Indians who assisted the English. Edward, Doctor Franklin, and George all tried to convince General Braddock how much he needed the Indians allied to his army as scouts and rangers, all to no avail. As a result, there were only seven Mingos with the Army when it left Fort Cumberland for its roughly 110 mile trek through the wilderness.

Each evening, Edward and George tried to convince the General over supper that the army was moving too slowly, that it was too weighed down with heavy artillery and siege guns for the terrain it had to cross. Finally, at the end of the first week, the General seemed to understand their point. Seven days and they had only made 35 miles from Fort Cumberland with nearly double that distance yet to travel.

"I'll divide the army into two columns. The flying column to make all haste for the Forks of the Ohio, cutting a road only wide enough for our purposes. The support column will follow with most of the heavy guns and siege artillery, widening and improving the road as necessary to get the heavier equipment through."

Much gratified by this development, the "flying column" still moved at just three to eight miles a day. Edward became very concerned when he noted the distance growing between the flying and the support columns. By the morning of July 8th, he estimated it had exceeded 50 miles and could be as much as 60 from the reports of orderlies running messages between the two. He was also concerned about young Washington, who was seriously ill yet insisted on remaining with the General and his staff instead of retiring to the support column for medical attention.

The morning of July 9th, they set out to cover the final ten miles to the French works at the Forks. With the seven Mingos in front, followed by an advanced guard of 300 light infantry, then the pioneers to widen the trace into a road with a company to guard them, the main body followed. On each flank, the General had a flanking company broken into small parties. It was the flankers who had detected and broken up an Indian raid on July 6th, so they were especially watchful now that the French were known to be so close.

"Colonel Jewett, I see you dispensed with your regimentals on the eve of the battle and take up the dress of these back country Colonials you're so fond of," the General observed as they sat down to breakfast together. Edward was wearing a brown hunting frock over a brown weskit, laced white shirt with leather neck stock, buff breeches, and boots.

"I thought the General would prefer if I did not wear my regimentals today when it may confuse the troops into thinking I have more than an advisory authority with this Army. You will note that I retain the gorget so my rank, upon closer inspection, will not be questioned."

"Ah, you're quite right. I should have thought of that myself. I thank you for the courtesy you've shown my officers, especially as your commission outranks all of them by a considerable amount."

The column was moving along in high spirits in spite of being on short rations. In the early afternoon, shots rang out with the advance and then three volleys were heard. A messenger from Lieutenant Colonel Thomas Gage, commanding the advance guard, indicated they had met and dispersed a force of French regulars and militia of unknown size. General Braddock was elated.

"See how they run from disciplined troops? Didn't I tell you we would make short work of this..." His voice trailed off as sporadic firing broke out along the flanks of the advance, spreading back with each passing moment. Ordering the main column forward, the General then rode to the sound of the guns.

He had not gone far when he encountered the pioneers, all civilians, streaming to the rear, followed closely by the light infantry. Firing was all around him now as he struggled to regain some control of the situation. With the main column moving forward and running into the retreating pioneers, their formations were broken up, mixing units together. Company and platoon sized units now formed facing the firing and delivered their volleys at unseen enemies in the woods.

Edward and George tried to convince the General, who maintained his composure very well and stayed in the thick of the fighting, to disperse his tight formations and have the troops take cover, as the Virginia Company acting as a rear guard was doing. He would have none of it. The General was thoroughly convinced it would only be a matter of time before the savages would have to give way to his regulars.

"George, the casualties among the officers are very high, have you noticed?" Already mounted on his second horse, he had. "Help me try to get them to dismount and command from foot. You take the left and I'll take the right."

By time they made their way down the road, most of the officers were already down and the few that remained were quick to dismount at their urging. The couple who resisted found themselves dismounted soon enough as their horses were shot out from under them.

Edward was shocked to see British units firing upon other British units, mistaking anything beyond their narrow road boundary as French units. The worst was when he recognized Captain Mercer leading his company to take some high ground the enemy had been using to rain fire down on the troops in the road. Before Edward could stop the firing from the platoons still along the road, he saw a full ten of Captain Mercer's men drop after being shot by their friends. Once he got the troops to realize their mistake, the Indians were swarming in on the survivors and Captain Mercer had to beat a hasty retreat.

At the General's urging, Edward then rode back among the wagons to try to turn them or clear them from the road. Coming up to one, he found the driver mounted on the lead horse of his team.

"Ah, young Boone, good to see you're still with us. I need your help clearing the road of all these wagons. Do you suppose you can help me? It appears you have the last full team on the road."

"I don't think I can help you, Colonel," was the reply.

Edward looked into the young man's scared eyes and realized he had come up to him just as he was cutting his lead horse out of the team. Daniel Boone completed this work and started for the rear, stopping once to turn and look back at Edward, almost sadly, before continuing on his way in the wake of the other teamsters. Edward returned to the General to report the road was choked with abandoned wagons and no way to remove them.

"I believe, General, we can adopt open formation tactics and still make an orderly withdrawal to the river, in spite of loss of the road."

"Hmm, that might just work. Orderly, Orderly! Where is that confounded orderly?" With that, the General's horse went down, his third that day.

"Here, General, take my horse," Edward offered, dismounting and helping the General from his stricken mount. The General quickly remounted and continued to pass directions on, now mainly to those within earshot as all of his orderlies appeared to be down themselves.

"Colonel, are you alright?" It was George, unhorsed himself for the countless time that day. Assured that Edward was not wounded, he continued, "Just look at the fools, they are a disgrace."

"On the contrary, George, they are performing magnificently. The bravery, the discipline, what other units in the world could have stood up to this fire today and maintained their formations? None could have absorbed this amount of punishment and remained in the field. No,

George, the bad tactics are the fault of the officers, but the bravery and discipline of the troops are to their great credit."

Seeing the battle through Edward's eyes, George paused, thought, and realized he had just been given another valuable lesson. An aide brought George another horse, which he immediately offered to Edward.

"No, George, you're still unwell. You go and be available to the General. I'll try to do what I can from the ground." With that, he pulled his short rifle from his shoulder and moved into the fray, giving encouragement and direction while also pausing to take careful aim and fire.

Moments later George was again at Edward's side. "The General is down, seriously wounded. Before being shot, he mentioned a withdrawal. Shall I order the retreat?"

"Yes, George, only make it an orderly withdrawal to the ford in open formation. Go, quickly, while there are still troops to withdraw."

Moving back to the rear guard, he found Captain Adam Stephen's company in open formation, making good use of the cover, and giving a good account of themselves.

"Captain, a withdrawal in open formation has been ordered. Your men are doing quite well. I ask that you allow the Regulars to fall back through you to reform at the river. Then you can fall back on them. Can you do it?"

"We'll try. I've drilled my men pretty hard, but this has been more than any of us bargained for. How well they'll hold while the Regulars pass through is anybody's guess."

The withdrawal went fairly smoothly under the circumstances. The Virginians faltered somewhat, not from the Regulars passing through their open ranks, but when

Captain Stephen went down with a serious wound. In the end, they held the French Indians at bay long enough for the Regulars to reform in their rear. They then retreated, their job done.

Edward was somewhat encouraged by the success of their withdrawal. None of the wounded, other than the General, could be removed from the field, that's how close the Indians pressed them. Yet here they were, reformed now as a rear guard, only it was just a shell of their former strength. Tired and with ammunition running dangerously low, Edward called George over to him.

"George, you are about the only one still mounted. I need you to ride back to the support column and bring up aid to our relief. I'll try to hold the ford as best we can. Take the General with you, there's nothing we can do for him here."

So George Washington set out on what seemed to him to be an impossible task, leading the General, still mounted but now tied onto Edward's horse, toward the support column far to the rear.

Edward knew he had no real authority here and yet all of the Sergeants and men were looking to him for orders. The few officers that remained seemed unable to take command, so shocked were they by the devastating losses they had just endured and lacking some of the hardened discipline of the men. As he started to organize his much reduced force for a defensive stand, there was a chorus of Indian yells very close in followed by a rush from Indians now wielding tomahawks, war clubs, and knives. It was more than the tired, discouraged troops could take and they broke.

At first Edward tried to stem the tide and form a fighting withdrawal, but to no avail. Men who had lived through the past three and a half hours only to find themselves faced by a howling mob while they had scarcely a cartridge left per squad was too much. Edward had no choice but to join them, turning at regular intervals to down one of their pursuers with a well-aimed rifle shot.

After his sixth such shot and covering a distance of maybe 100 yards or so, Edward turned to continue as he started reloading only to find a familiar Indian blocking his path. In the final instant before a blow struck that knocked his hat off and toppled him to the ground, he realized it was the Shawnee war chief Black Fish.

∽ *Chapter 50* ∽

he news hit the Valley of Virginia like a lightening bolt. General Braddock defeated. Over 900 casualties out of the 1300 or so with his flying column. General Braddock dead of his wounds. Most of the officers dead, wounded, or missing. The remaining force totaling nearly 2000 in retreat after burning or destroying their trains.

Few of the little blockhouses and forts that had sprung up across the Valley took the news harder than the Jewett fort. Both Edward and Aaron were known to have departed Wills Creek with General Braddock and nothing had been heard from either of them since. Robert gathered the family together under the awning, the rest of the extended community filling in to hear what the patriarch of the family had to say.

"Edward will return to us, I know it, I feel it, and I will not permit it to be otherwise. And I am sure that if Edward returns so will Aaron. Do you all understand?"

In spite of Robert's proclamation, there were a lot of people in the little fort that felt he was surely lost. Knowing Robert, all of them knew not to utter such sentiments where he may overhear or learn of it. He was determined his eldest son would return.

Henry and Jenny made the best of the lack of privacy the crowded little fort caused. The couple was very happy with each other and it showed. Sarah warmed up to her stepmother quickly, it helping that she and Rebecca, Jenny's daughter, were the same age and best of friends. It was not long before she quit her grandfather's cabin and moved in with her father and his new wife.

Colonel Lewis came by to check on the militia detail at the fort and to pass along the latest news. "We've been told Colonel Thomas Dunbar was the only one of General Braddock's Colonels to survive and he has assumed command of the force. The best information we have is that Colonel Dunbar was commanding the supply column and wasn't actually involved in the battle, though I'm not sure how good that information is. I'm sorry, Sir Robert, but it appears your son won't be coming home."

"That's where you're mistaken, Colonel. Edward is alive and will be coming home, I know it. What other news have you?"

"Most of the families along the Cowpasture have either moved to Fort Lewis or have abandoned their farms for the east. The same thing is happening all across the Valley. Many of the blockhouses don't have enough men left to man the loops and I'm consolidating several of them to make the ones left stronger and better able to resist attack."

"We're seeing a lot of Indian sign in the area, more than we've ever seen. What of the others?"

"I'm ashamed to admit it but you're the one post conducting comprehensive patrolling efforts, most of the others relying on just what information I bring in. Naturally I have patrols out, but Augusta County covers a lot of territory and I can't patrol it all. Stay on your guard because, now that General Braddock has been defeated so decisively, it is only a matter of time before the Shawnee make a concerted attack here."

It was about ten days after Colonel Lewis brought the latest news when Aaron arrived home leading Edward's horse. The whole community gathered around to hear his tale, giving way for Robert, Lewis, and Henry to do the questioning.

"When General Braddock split his force into two columns, the Colonel bid me to stay with the supply column, which I did. The first we learned of the disaster was when Mister Washington came back to us after riding all night to request we forward a supporting force to relieve the survivors. He was leading a badly wounded Major General Braddock riding on the Colonel's horse. Naturally, I claimed the horse as the Colonel's personal property when the General was finished with it."

"What did Mister Washington say of Edward? Was he injured?" asked Lewis, not sure he wanted to hear the answer.

"Well, sir, I asked him what he knew and he told me the last time he saw the Colonel, he was alive and trying to maintain a rear guard action against the Indians, to hold the ford open until all that could escape had a chance to make it out. I inquired of the survivors who made it into camp and the best information I could gather was he became the rear guard of the rear guard. A few saw him, the last man in the retreating column, calming firing and moving back, then firing again."

"So, he made it out!" said Robert, more in hopes Aaron would confirm it.

"No, sir, he never came back. Some thought they saw the Indians cut him off, others weren't sure. What I do know is that I waited until all who were coming back reached the supply column and the Colonel wasn't among them. I then stayed with the Army as it retreated to Fort Cumberland on the off chance he would catch up with us there. When the army began to retreat further toward Philadelphia, that's when I decided to head here. Sir Robert, I hope I did right in your eyes."

Distractedly, Robert replied, "Yes, yes, lad, you did fine. Now, you look very tired and I'm sure Betty wants to get you off to herself. You rest and we'll talk more later."

Robert, Lewis, and Henry adjourned to Robert's cabin to discuss this latest event. Esther, of course, was in her usual place, sewing.

"Well, boys, this isn't good. What do you make of it?"

"Father, there is still nothing that says Edward was killed or wounded. There is still reason to hope and pray he will be delivered to us," said Esther, breaking her long held custom of listening quietly from the sidelines.

The three men turned and looked her way, somewhat surprised by the outburst.

"Well, there you have it. If your sister says there's still hope, then who are we mere men to question her? I assume, dear daughter, that you will also be telling us we need to hold on here for when he returns?"

A little red faced, having surprised even herself by speaking her mind that way, she stammered, "Of course. Wasn't it you, father, who said we were staying just a few weeks ago?"

"We did plant sufficient crops this year to see us through the winter, even with our expanded numbers. I doubt we'll be able to harvest much from the other farmsteads, considering the need for men both harvesting and guarding the harvesters," the ever practical Lewis added. "At least cutting our fields we're within supporting distance of the fort."

"Might I suggest we gather up the livestock from the farmsteads and herd it up here where it might help sustain us through the winter? There's no point leaving it to the Shawnee and it sounds like we'll be forted up for some time to come," added Henry.

"Yes, and when the cold weather comes, it'll be better to have everyone housed in cabins, so let's start emptying our stores from the blockhouse into the tents and move those families into the blockhouse. They'll have less privacy but will be better able to endure the winter," Robert concluded.

Although still early August, the three men planned how they would make it through the winter. That done they left Robert's cabin to pass their plans on to the rest of the residents of the little fort. Even Abel Fisher decided to stay with his family, much to the surprise of all.

As the crowd dispersed to their various chores, Philip confronted his father and grandfather. With tears streaming down his face, he demanded, "When do we ride out and find Uncle Edward? He may be hurt and he's without his horse. He would come for us, nothing would stop him. We need to go for him!"

Robert, Henry, and Lewis looked at each other before Lewis responded, "Philip, it is impractical to go hunt for your uncle, though I would like nothing better. Your grandfather has announced to all that he will be coming home, you just have to believe that."

Philip was unsatisfied and ran off to be alone. He was working hard to believe his uncle would come home, even as the doubt crept into his thoughts. He was not alone long before Charles joined him. Agreeing with the sentiments he had heard Philip express, the two cousins sat silently together, each comforted somehow by the presence of the other.

Henry led a patrol out to bring in the livestock from the various farmsteads, planning on taking two days to accomplish the task. They spent a tense night at Ben Gordon's farmstead, roughly located in the middle of the cluster of farms, after seeing Indian signs all around as they moved through the area. Not able to make it all the way back before dark the second night, what with the slower paced forced on them by the livestock, they stayed out an additional night at the McNulty farmstead.

The next morning, as they rode toward the little fort, they met a relief party led by Lewis coming to find them, just in case they had run afoul of the Shawnee. The reinforced party returned to the fort in time for dinner, much to Robert's relief.

The patrols continued to find a lot of sign, though none approached the Jewett fort as if there was a wall around the entire Grant. Talk in the fort attributed it to the agreement between Black Fish and Edward, the Shawnee marking the extent of the Jewett holdings.

On his next visit, Colonel Lewis reported several of the other blockhouses had been attacked. Nothing serious, more harassing than damaging, but it was keeping everyone on edge. As the furthest settlement out, he half anticipated finding the Jewett fort to have been attacked. He was both surprised and relieved to see it had not happened.

The only news he had from the Army was it had gone into winter quarters in Philadelphia, in mid-summer! A force of 2000 and with over 1300, by all reports, fit for duty! All they could do was shake their collective heads at the disgraceful end of an expedition that started with such fanfare and bombast.

"Grandfather," Sarah asked one night as she sat

with him after supper, "you seem very sad. Are you worried about Uncle Edward?"

Sighing deeply, Robert patted her arm before confessing, "More than you know, child, more than you know."

"If he doesn't come back, do we have to leave here?"

"Why, child, do you want to leave?"

"Oh, no, I want to stay!"

Putting his arm around her and pulling her head to his shoulder, he spoke softly, "Then stay we will, no matter what happens." He was still sad, but having her close like this he did find comforting.

The days took on their normal routine. Each morning before first light, the little company manned the loops in case of a surprise attack. Marie took the horses out of the fort to allow them to graze after breakfast and brought them in again before joining everyone for a communal supper. Everyone then returned to the loops before sunset. Watches were kept from the vantage point of the blockhouse and patrols were mounted each day at noon. The morning and evening patrols had been suspended as being too dangerous with so much Indian sign in the area.

As Marie was leaving the gate one morning, she heard a yelp from Philip, on watch in the blockhouse. The next thing she knew, he came through the blockhouse door and took off running through the gate, past her, and off toward the hill to the north just as fast as he could.

"Philip, get back here!" she shouted, and then, "Lewis, come quick!"

Hearing her shout, Mattie, who was following close behind Marie as she helped with the horses, stepped to the shovel blade hanging by the blockhouse door and began beating out the alarm with the hammer hanging there with it.

Marie had barely gotten the words out of her mouth when Robert came bounding out of the blockhouse. As he got to her, he grabbed the lead line of one of the horses and mounted it bareback before taking off after Philip. Marie then saw they were all heading toward figures that had appeared at the top of the hill. She saw what she thought to be two men and a large horse, possibly a draft animal. Lewis reached the gate and took aim at the figures on the ridgeline before lowering his gun and running hard right behind Robert and Philip.

Philip was running just as fast as he could, his heart thumping hard in his chest and tears streaming down his face. He threw down his gun so it would not slow him down. He heard the sound of horse hooves coming up behind him.

Robert was gaining on Philip, though he was having trouble riding with neither saddle nor bridle. Lewis, still trailing the other two, slowed only long enough to pick up Philip's gun.

Philip reached the figures first and leaped into the taller man's arms, crying openly now as the man grabbed and hugged him closely. Robert was next to reach the group, leaping from his horse and throwing his arms around both the tall man and Philip.

When Lewis arrived, slightly out of breath, he first greeted Daniel Boone with a nod of his head before turning and saying, "Welcome home, dear brother, welcome home."

The End

∞ About the Author ∞

Kenneth Jewett is a Colonel, recently retired from the US Air Force, and a lifelong student of history. He lives in rural Virginia.